The
GOLDEN
HAIRPIN

The GOLDEN HAIRPIN

QINGHAN CECE
TRANSLATED BY ALEX WOODEND

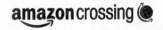

Text copyright © 2015 by Qinghan CeCe
Translation copyright © 2018 by Alex Woodend
All rights reserved.

Previously published as 《簪中录1》 by Jiangsu Phoenix Literature and Art Publishing House in China in 2015. Translated from Mandarin by Alex Woodend. First published in English by AmazonCrossing in 2018.

Published by AmazonCrossing, Seattle

www.apub.com

Amazon, the Amazon logo, and AmazonCrossing are trademarks of Amazon.com, Inc., or its affiliates.

ISBN-13: 9781503952188
ISBN-10: 1503952185

Cover design by Shasti O'Leary Soudant

Printed in the United States of America

The
GOLDEN
HAIRPIN

One

NOTORIETY

Through the dark of night, a heavy rain poured down. The mountains and canyons, both near and far, lost their shapes and faded away. On the mountain road outside Changan City, blooming lilac flowers fell under the force of the pelting rain and scattered along the muddy road. In the depths of night, no one saw.

Huang Zixia trudged along that dark road, holding a sky-blue oil-paper umbrella. The storm showers broke two of its ribs. She glanced up, tossed the umbrella on the road, and kept walking.

The rain hitting her body was so cold, the night sky so dark. The whole world was dark except for a faint light ahead that flickered through the raindrops. A small pavilion stood by a curve in the road. The dynasty had set them up every five miles, and rest areas every ten. A group of people sat inside for shelter from the storm. Changan had a curfew in effect and would not open the city gates until six in the morning. Everyone was likely waiting for the gates to open.

Huang Zixia walked toward the pavilion in her simple blue short-sleeved men's shirt.

"Hey, youngster, trying to make it into the city early too? Come dry out by the fire," an old man called.

In the firelight, Huang Zixia could make out the old man's kind smile. She thanked him, wrung out her drenched shirt, and then sat a couple of feet away from him and helped feed the fire.

The group watched her for a moment and then returned to their conversations. They gossiped about the strange things that had been happening in the empire, as if they'd seen it all themselves.

"Did you all hear about that case in the capital?"

"The Four Directions Case?" someone jumped in.

"In the last three months, three people had been murdered in the capital. The murders took place in the north, south, and west. The only clues left were the words *peace, bliss*, and *self* written in blood."

"People in the east are panicking now because they think a murder will happen there next. I heard everyone able to leave has already left, and it's almost deserted now."

Huang Zixia held a piece of firewood and gently stoked the flames.

One middle-aged man was apparently a traveling storyteller. He held a wood block and spoke. "The empire's in chaos now; all the provincial capitals are in turmoil. And not just the capitals. There was just a case of a whole family being murdered in Shu; did you hear about it? It was the family of Shu's civil governor, Huang Min!"

Huang Min.

Huang Zixia trembled at hearing her father's name. A spark flew back and hit her hand, causing a flash of pain.

No one noticed.

"Wasn't Huang Min a minister on the capital's Board of Punishments? Didn't he solve several cases these last few years? He had a good reputation with the Chengdu magistrate, yes?"

"They say Huang Min didn't do it all himself. When Huang Min was on the Board of Punishments, a lot of people suspect his daughter broke many cases for him at the age of fourteen. The Emperor personally commended her—said if she were a man, she could be prime minister!"

"Prime minister?" the storyteller said with a sneer. "Did you hear the rumor that when Huang Min's daughter was born, the room filled with red light? People took it as a sign that she'd bring misfortune to her family. Now it's really coming true." The storyteller paused. "She's the one responsible for killing that family!"

Huang Zixia had forgotten about the pain on the back of her hand. She stared at the flames licking the dark.

The old man couldn't believe it. "You mean the Huang daughter destroyed her own house?"

"Exactly!" the storyteller shouted.

"Ridiculous—how could a daughter kill her loved ones?"

"It's certain! The court already issued an order. The Huang girl fled Shu, but if she'd been caught, they'd have hacked her to death without burial!"

"If she did it, how savage. She must have no conscience!"

The old man asked, "Such tragedy. Why?"

"Why would the girl be so shortsighted? It must have been for passion." The storyteller smacked his lips and pressed on. "It's said that her husband had been arranged since childhood, but after she grew up, she found another sweetheart. So when her grandmother and uncle came to discuss her marriage, she personally served them poisoned sheep's-hoof soup. Governor Huang; his wife; Huang Yan, her brother; and even her grandmother and uncle were all poisoned to death. Only she escaped, disappeared. Officers found out she went to the apothecary a few days earlier to buy arsenic—they've got written records—and they found the arsenic in her room. Her heart was taken, but her parents forced her to marry someone else, so she poisoned her family and ran off with her lover!"

The crowd in the pavilion listened to this tragic tale with horror and amazement. Someone else asked, "How did she escape?"

"After she poisoned her family, she arranged to meet her lover and run off. But he hated what she had done and alerted the authorities. We

3

don't know how she sensed something was off and managed to escape! There are wanted posters at all the provincial capital city gates. Justice has a long reach. I'd sure like to see the vicious woman arrested and cut into a thousand pieces!"

He was full of indignation. The crowd listening seemed to feel the same.

Hang Zixia held her knees as she listened to the crowd's condemnation and suddenly felt exhausted. She put her head on her knees and stared in a daze at the beating flames. The clothes on her body were damp. The cold air was like an invisible needle piercing her skin, which kept her awake.

The people around her kept gossiping about the capital. The Emperor built another new palace; Lady Zhao, concubine of the late Emperor, was personally sewing the curtain for the temple; and so many ladies wanted to marry the Prince of Kui Prefecture.

"Speaking of which, isn't the Prince of Kui going back to the capital today?"

"Absolutely. He's going for a feast to celebrate the new palace."

"Emperor Xian really favors him. No wonder Princess Qi Le wants to marry him so much. She's tried several times, and now people just laugh at her."

"Prince Yi had just that one daughter; if he knew how pathetic she has acted, he'd turn in his grave."

Huang Zixia closed her eyes and pretended to sleep. She knew of the Prince of Kui and his legendary defeat of Pang Xun. In fact, his arrival was just what she was waiting for.

The rain had stopped, and the sky began to slowly grow lighter. The soft sound of horse hooves came, almost inaudibly.

Huang Zixia opened her eyes and quickly left the pavilion.

The light of the dawn sun began to surface in the sky. A line of guards approached on the winding mountain road. Though their

4

clothes showed signs of being rained on, they were alert, obviously well trained.

In the middle were two flawless black horses slowly pulling a carriage. The carriage had a gold lacquer carving of a dragon and phoenix decorated with large clamshells and turquoise. Two small gold bells hung in the carriage's eaves. As the carriage moved, they gently shook, letting out a crisp sound.

Huang Zixia followed from a distance.

Behind the team was a young soldier who looked uncomfortably from left to right. When he saw Huang Zixia tailing them, he turned and said, "Brother Lu, I don't know if I ate something wrong, but I need to use the bathroom."

"What's going on with you? We're almost to the city; can't you hold it?" The man next to him glared. "We're under strict orders from the Prince. If you get caught, you know what the consequences are!"

"Don't worry. I'll catch right up." He clutched his stomach, turned his horse, and rushed into the dense forest.

Huang Zixia took a few steps into the grass and waited for him there. He was already pulling off his palace guard uniform. He gave his helmet to her and said, "Ms. Huang, you know how to ride a horse, right?"

Huang Zixia took his helmet and whispered, "Big Zhang, you're taking such a risk to help me. I'm so grateful!"

"What are you talking about? If it weren't for you, my parents would be dead! If I didn't help you, they'd kill me." He patted his chest with pride. "And today's just an accompaniment to the capital, not a military operation. If I get in trouble, it's no big deal. Last time Liu said hi to someone on the job, he just got a beating. Say you're my cousin, that you saw I was ill and had to come with me."

Huang Zixia nodded and quickly took off her coat and gave it to him, then put on his clothes. Even though they were a little too big, she looked all right.

After quickly bidding goodbye to Big Zhang, Huang Zixia threw herself on the horse and rode out of the forest.

There was a red glow on the horizon that was spreading brightly across the sky. Huang Zixia urged the horse on and finally got the city within her sights as she caught up to the palace guards.

Changan's Clear Virtue Gate had five tall entranceways. The middle three were closed. Only the outer two were open, but when the royal guard approached, one of the closed doors opened to let them in more discreetly.

Huang Zixia took up the rear and followed the team into the city. As she entered the gates, she looked up and saw her arrest order poster.

The poster showed a seventeen-year-old girl with eyes bright as a morning star and a face with the elegant shape of a peach petal. Her rosy lips turned in a playful arc, and there was humor in her gaze.

Lines of text written next to the image read: *Huang Zixia of Shu has been charged in a heinous multiple-murder case. The provincial capitals are hereby notified to capture her, dead or alive.* Huang Zixia lowered her eyes, but only for a second.

Half her face was covered by her helmet, so Brother Lu, who was next to her, couldn't see her face as he rode his horse along Zhuque Street. "Good thing no one noticed your bathroom break," he said.

Huang Zixia nodded without saying anything.

They passed the royal mansions in Yongjia Square and then went through the East City and north of Xingqing Palace. The Prince of Kui's palace appeared in the distance.

She'd made an agreement with Big Zhang to tie up the horse in the palace stables and slip away. When she got there, everyone was in the yard in front of the stables eating breakfast. No one would pay much attention to her. After she tied up the horse, she turned quickly to leave. Someone called, "Zhang Xingying, are you not going to eat?"

Huang Zixia acted as if she hadn't heard, closed the door, and slipped out.

Behind her, Brother Lu called out, "Diarrhea again? Second time this morning."

Everyone laughed a little and forgot about her as they went back to their meal.

Huang Zixia pulled down her helmet and went out the door.

When she was at the last step, someone behind her said, "Hey, where are you going?"

Huang Zixia wasn't sure if he was calling her. She paused; then the man's voice came clearly again. "Yes, you, the honor guard. We just got word that the new palace is shorthanded; you must go there with the Prince."

Huang Zixia's heart stuttered. She couldn't believe her luck.

She heard him laugh as he said, "Don't worry; you'll get an extra three silvers. Hurry back and eat; we'll leave soon."

Huang Zixia had no choice but to slowly turn around, bow her head in salute, and then walk along the wall back to the yard in front of the stables. There was no way she could eat breakfast with the others, but she couldn't wait in the palace either. If anyone saw her face, all would be lost. Furthermore, she had to leave and find someone who could help her.

She stood in the corner, eyes on the now-unloaded carriage. The yard was noisy with people eating, and behind them, others were busy feeding the horses. In the corner by the entrance where she stood, it was only she and the carriage.

She stepped on the carriage's ledge and carefully clung to the unlatched door to look—there was no one inside, only large seats and a fixed coffee table. The seats were covered with pads embellished with elaborate Kui Dragon brocades that matched the crimson peonies on the dark-purple Persian carpet below. It was luxurious, elegant, and obviously new, not something that someone would come and replace.

Huang Zixia quickly took off her uniform and helmet behind the car and stuffed them in the corner with the stone lantern. Then she climbed into the carriage.

There wasn't much room inside, but there would be space underneath the seat where a storage cupboard usually lay. She opened the curtain under the seat and saw one.

It had a sliding door carved with auspicious clouds. She opened it. To her surprise, there was nothing inside but some spices.

She curled up in the cabinet and pulled the door closed. Nervous, she began to sweat. The door had many holes and gaps carved out, but, thanks to the curtain, she could make out the shapes outside while remaining hidden.

Huang Zixia lay there quietly, not daring to breathe deeply. She could hear her own rapid heartbeat. What if she was brought inside the palace? Were the horses closely guarded? Would she be able to flee when the moment came?

Before she could finish thinking, a sound came from outside. Saddling horses, adjusting uniforms, getting in formation. Then there was only the sense of the carriage moving slightly, the light sound of the door—someone had entered the carriage.

Through the cracks in the cupboard door, she could only see the person's feet. His or her black leather boots with a gold pattern didn't make a sound on the thick carpet.

Once the person was settled, the carriage quickly began moving.

Trapped in the cabinet for a long time, shaking and shaking, she felt like a chick being stuffed back into its eggshell. Huang Zixia fought against the feeling of vertigo and desperately forced herself to slow her breathing to keep from being discovered.

Luckily, the horses rumbled over the sound of her heartbeat and breath.

It was a long journey, but they finally left the city and headed toward the western suburbs. After traveling along a bumpy road, they reached a small bridge, and the Prince of Kui finally said, "Halt."

The carriage came to a gentle stop. Huang Zixia couldn't see the Prince of Kui's face from the cabinet, but she saw him pick up a wide glass bottle from the table, hold it out the window, and say, "Add some water."

There was a bright-red fish in the bottle, dragging its long, gossamer tail as it slowly swam. Against the light blue of the glass, the red fish became a wonderful lavender. Huang Zixia wondered why the powerful king would carry a bottle with a small red fish in it.

She heard the water gurgle and the footsteps of the rushing guards. Soon the bottle was filled. The Prince of Kui took the bottle and gently placed it back on the table. The fish swam cheerfully.

As Huang Zixia contemplated it, the carriage suddenly began moving again. Caught off guard, her forehead hit the door. She bit her lip, not allowing herself to cry out. Though she was sure she was quiet and that the sound of the wheels would shroud any noise, she was still nervous as she peeked out of the seams of the cabinet.

Through the hanging tassels of the cracks in the door, she saw the passenger slowly reach for the green porcelain saucer on the table, lift the teapot, and pour himself some water.

She observed his hand. Its joints were symmetrical and beautifully curved. They were pampered but strong. Huang Zixia had heard about the Prince of Kui. How he was strong and stern. He held the saucer with three fingers. The turquoise dish in his white hands looked like spring water next to pear flesh.

Then he quickly kicked open the cabinet door and poured the saucer of water inside.

Huang Zixia's eyes were suddenly filled with it, and she let out a scream.

He dropped the saucer, grabbed Huang Zixia's shoulder, and pulled her out. He held her by the throat with his right hand and pinned her chest with his left foot.

In a moment, Huang Zixia was as still as a dead fish.

Huang Zixia looked up at him. She was dazed.

He had deep, dark eyes, a long, straight nose, and thin lips that implied a sense of coldness toward the world. He was dressed in azure silk embroidered with a cloud pattern. The gentle colors and pattern made his skin seem paler. His slight sense of detachment only accentuated his magnificence.

The Prince of Kui, Li Zi, Li Shubai, one of the most outstanding figures in the dynasty, still admired by the Emperor—"He makes the world a different place." Rumor had it he was dignified, but Huang Zixia never heard of his demeanor being so cold.

Li Shubai blinked, sensed she didn't know martial arts, and took some weight off the foot on her chest. He put his right hand on her throat and felt around a little to confirm she didn't have an Adam's apple.

Huang Zixia quickly pushed his palm away, stood up warily, and stared at him with two bright eyes like a fearless cub facing its hunter.

Li Shubai's eyes fell on her face. He looked at her awhile, then took a step back. Next, he took out a white handkerchief. After wiping his hands, he dropped it and said with some disgust, "As a woman, you should at least clean yourself up a little."

The handkerchief fell on her like a slow, silent cloud.

She clenched her fists. Her disguise had been uncovered, and the shame made grief well up inside her. She looked at the man and opened her mouth, but no words came out.

She'd been wearing men's clothing since childhood and would go about with her father and brother like that. When she escaped to

Changan this time, she dressed very well, and no one suspected she was a woman. Somehow, he'd been able to tell right away.

Someone tapped on the carriage door. "Your Highness?"

"Yes," he said. "It's okay."

After the carriage smoothly traveled forward again, he said calmly, "When did you get in? What are you doing hiding in my carriage?"

A string of responses ran through her mind. She chose the shortest, most convincing one. She blinked shyly and gently bit her lower lip, acting as if nothing was the matter. Her cheeks grew slightly flushed, and she said, "I'm your guardsman Zhang Xingying's cousin. He had some stomach problems outside the city today and was afraid if he held things up, he'd be punished. I live there, and when I saw him passing, he asked me to put on his uniform and do his duties for a while."

"So why are you in my carriage?"

"I was trying to slip away at the palace, but I got stopped. They said I had to go to the retreat palace. Afraid I'd get found out, I had no choice but to hide in your carriage. I was hoping to wait for a chance to get out." She looked embarrassed and shy.

"Sounds reasonable." He leaned aloofly on the cushion. "What's your name?"

Her heart sank slightly, but she showed no hesitation. "Yang."

"Yang?" He laughed coldly without looking at her. "Zhang Xingying of the second rank is six-feet-one-inch tall, left-handed, was born during the second year of Emperor Xuanzhong's reign in the capital's Puning Square. Father, Zhang Weiyi, from Luoyang, moved to the capital and began serving in Duanrui clinic during the second year of Huichang; Mother, Feng Shi, the only daughter of the former capital's Feng family of Xinchang Square. Last year, Zhang Xingying's elder brother married the daughter of the Cheng family of the capital's Fengyi Square, no children. So where did you, Cousin Yang, come from?"

She never imagined this man would know all the details of an insignificant guard's life. All she could say was, "Actually, Zhang Xingying and I aren't blood relatives . . . We . . ." She had trouble deciding what to say. He pretended not to notice and waited for her to go on.

She didn't know whether he'd already figured it all out. But since she had already started, she had to keep going, shift the emphasis of her lie and change from biological cousins to something more ambiguous. With a look of bashfulness, she said, "Zhang Xingying and I get along well. I like playing polo and dressing up like a man, so I wanted to help since I was worried he'd be punished. His stomach was upset, so I took his horse, and he couldn't catch up. That's what happened."

"Then why didn't you clearly explain this to the officer when you left the palace and instead chose to put yourself and Zhang Xingying in a more precarious position by hiding in my carriage?" He tapped his slender fingers a few times. Their rise and fall seemed to hit her in the heart, and she began to have a sense of dread.

Sure enough, he sneered and mercilessly continued, "You're hiding something, worse than posing as one of my guards, worse than being killed on the spot for."

She was silent, out of her depth. She had taken a risk and been caught. Now she was helpless.

"A woman, early in the morning in the countryside, puts on a man's clothing, which still show the traces of being rained on—if you claim you and Zhang Xingying didn't plan it out in advance, I don't think anyone would believe it."

She bowed silently, her thick, black eyelashes trembling. Her look was one of stubborn resistance, and it made him sneer. "Put out your left hand," he said.

She bit her lip and slowly extended it, palm up.

"Everyone's hand has a record of everything they've done. You can try to hide them other ways, but your hand cannot." He looked down at her palm and finally allowed a slight smile. "Your hand says you come from a good background and have been clever since you were little. At thirteen, there was a change. You left Changan and went to Shu, am I right?"

She looked up at him, trying to keep her voice steady. "Yes."

"There you met your sweetheart. And your palm says you acted deceptively in order to be with him, something like killing your whole family. As for how . . ." He coldly curled his lips. "Poison."

Her lashes suddenly jumped as if poked by a needle. He'd uncovered her true identity. She unconsciously clenched her fist as if trying to fend off the nightmare. She pressed her hand to her chest and looked at him.

He stared back with the look of someone with their prey in the net. "So your name must be Huang Zixia."

She looked at her own palm, and the initial shock began to subside. Letting her hand slip back into its sleeve, she whispered, "Not true."

"Which part isn't true?" he gently asked. "Your background, the murder, or your identity?"

"I am Huang Zixia, but I didn't kill anyone," she whispered, "let alone my family!"

He leaned back on his cushion and smiled coldly. "You mean you've been falsely accused?"

She knelt on the carriage floor and looked up at him. The soft carpet with bright peony flowers woven in reminded her she was as insignificant as a bug, small and thin. The man across from her could squash her with one finger at any time. Kneeling there, she kept her back straight and looked up at him calmly and said even more stubbornly, "Prince of Kui, we all have parents; how could I do that as someone's child? I came all the way to the capital because of this terrible injustice. Being falsely accused is one thing, but I can't let my parents' enemies get away with it. So I made the hard journey to Changan in order to find a way to avenge my family. Zhang Xingying was kind and didn't hesitate to put himself at risk in order to help me. Please forgive him, Prince. Don't blame him."

"Kind? Who's to say his kindness wasn't helping a criminal?"

"If I were the killer, I could find a place to hide. But I won't, because if I do, my family won't be able to rest in peace!"

"No need to explain to me. You can do that to the Central Court and Board of Punishments." He looked down indifferently toward the curtain. "You can go now. I hate to be around disheveled people, especially in such close quarters."

Huang Zixia puckered her lips slightly and saluted him. When she raised her head, her eyes landed on the glass bottle.

The small red fish was still swaying its long, chiffon-like tail in the water.

"This fish is called agashennie, from India. According to Buddhism, they're close to the Dragon Princess and represent uncertainty, often appearing before people who will die a violent death."

The Prince of Kui calmly looked at it. "Really?"

"That is what I've heard people say. In my opinion, they claim that for different reasons. One is to shirk responsibility when someone can't break a case. Another is when a murderer says it so that rumors spread and people get confused."

The Prince of Kui's lips spread slightly. "And?"

She continued to go on her instincts and guess. "The things that appear at murder scenes are jinxed, but the Prince took this with him. This means he and the deceased had a strange relationship. I'd guess the murder is still unsolved."

"So?"

She pondered a moment, then slowly said, "If the Prince is willing to help me, I can find the truth about the murder. It doesn't matter how long ago it was or if the clues are still intact; I'll be able to give the Prince an answer."

The Prince of Kui picked up the bottle and brought it in front of his face, wistfully watching the fish's scarlet light.

The little fish kept swimming, not frightened by the disturbance.

The Prince of Kui touched the fish's head with his right hand and watched it dive under in fright. Then he slowly took his fingers out and looked at the person kneeling in front of him. "Huang Zixia, you've got some gall."

She kept kneeling, her eyes bright like morning dew.

"The Emperor has said he won't get involved, but you want to take it on and think you can break the case?" As he looked at her coldly, she noticed the depth of his eyes, which made him look even more daunting. "That's a court secret, but somehow it got out. How did you hear about the old case and come to want to make a deal with me to take it on?" Her guess turned out to be true.

Huang Zixia hadn't expected there to be so much evil behind this little fish. She bowed slightly, still appearing calm. "Please forgive me, Your Highness; I had not heard. I just saw the fish and thought about that silly saying. The rest I just guessed. I knew nothing in advance."

He put the bottle back on the table and studied her expression. "Do you dare?"

"Uncovering the truth isn't a matter of daring; it's a matter of capability," Huang Zixia said softly. "Hearing the Prince speak like this makes me think the case is disturbing and has wide implications, perhaps beyond the death of my parents. But I think, if someone looks, they'll one day find the truth."

The Prince of Kui didn't answer. He just asked, "Since you came to the capital to find justice, does that mean you have evidence that would reveal the real murderer?"

"I . . ." She was silent and frowned a little. "After the incident, I was named a suspect and could only flee. But if the Prince helps me and gives me some time, I'm sure I can find it!"

He raised an eyebrow slightly. "That reminds me; the year you were in Changan, you broke several cases. And you helped your father solve more in Shu, is that right?"

She hesitated. "Yes."

"So you were a prodigy, but that doesn't mean you still have it. Helping your father break cases at thirteen and fourteen, you must have a lot of people who want to get revenge on you, huh?" He smiled slightly in mockery. "You can't even handle your own problems, and you dare to come bargain with a Prince?"

Huang Zixia was speechless. Li Shubai watched her bite her lower lip and grow even redder. The seventeen-year-old girl, though embarrassed, haggard, and disheveled, still had a bright face. It reminded him of something vaguely similar.

He lowered his voice. "Huang Zixia, everyone thinks you're a murderer. If I speak on your behalf, won't people suspect I'm having an affair with you? And if the Central Court or Board of Punishments intervenes on your behalf because of my petition, does that mean I've wrongly influenced the legal process?"

Huang Zixia, still kneeling, listened and bit her lip without saying anything.

Li Shubai looked past her. "Go. I'm not interested in your business or in disclosing your location to the authorities. Godspeed."

She paused silently and prepared to get out. It was no surprise that the man across from her, though powerful, was not bound to her, and would neither help her nor turn her in.

So all she could do was bow deeply. When she was about to get up, the carriage slowly stopped. A guard outside said, "We've arrived at Jianbi Palace, my lord."

Jianbi was the newest palace to be built on the outskirts of the capital. It was only about ten miles from Daming Palace.

Li Shubai pushed the carriage's curtain aside and looked out. Since the Prince had arrived, there was quite a commotion outside. He frowned slightly and said, "Looks like it'll be hard not to be seen sharing a ride with the murderess."

Huang Zixia whispered firmly, "I didn't kill anyone!"

He didn't pay her any mind as he opened the door and said, "Get out."

She hesitated a moment and followed him out of the carriage. A low stool had been placed outside, and she stepped down upon it. Then someone kicked her lightly in the back of the knee and she fell.

Her whole body splashed into the water. Before her was a pond with freshly planted lotus. The leaves hung listlessly, and the water was cloudy. She choked and coughed as she lay embarrassed in the mud, unable to get up.

Li Shubai turned toward the female attendants who had come and said, "This clumsy person. Clean them up and let them walk back themselves."

As for whether she was male or female, he didn't bother to say.

Two

Omnipresent Bodhi

By the time they pulled Huang Zixia out of the water, Li Shubai had already entered Jianbi Palace.

Huang Zixia blushed as she got out of the mud. Li Shubai didn't look back at her. She clenched her teeth and couldn't help but kick the mud. It splashed, and a couple of cold drops sprinkled her cheek, but she didn't care. Her whole body was already covered in mud.

The eunuchs quickly helped her out, and the ladies took her to bathe. Since she was wearing men's clothing, one of the older attendants said, "Come, sir, we'll get you cleaned up."

"No need." She didn't want anyone to see her naked. If they found out she was a woman, she'd be easily linked to the wanted Huang Zixia. So she pulled her hand away and went straight to the well. There she pulled up a bucket of water and let it fall over her.

Though spring had come, it was still cold. When she poured the bucket of water on her head, the cold made her shiver hard. She poured another bucket over her head, numb from the cold.

The ladies watched her, stunned, unsure if she was crazy or not.

After two buckets of water, Huang Zixia's head felt clear. She dropped the bucket and stood dripping next to the well, shivering and breathing hard. Because of the cold, her ears buzzed, and she couldn't see clearly. Only the phantom of the cold look on Li Shubai's face shone through.

He had said, "I'm not interested in your business or in disclosing your location to the authorities."

Not interested . . .

Her parents' deaths, her family's murder, her false accusation, none of it affected him, so of course he wasn't interested.

In his eyes, she was just a speck of dust.

Still, she dropped the bucket in the well and clenched her fist. Her nail pushed deep into her palm, but she didn't notice.

Prince Li Shubai was more reliable than anyone else she knew. Her father's old friends and relatives lived far from the capital, were low rankings, and lacked direct access to the Emperor.

Still, Huang Zixia, he's your best hope. She said this clearly to herself in her mind and clenched her teeth. The man who had kicked her out, pushed her, and had no interest in her—Li Shubai was her best hope.

Despite her hatred and contempt, she made the decision then and there to stay with him. In the early-spring sunlight with its chilly wind, she shivered and walked slowly down the steps.

She took the steps one by one. She faced the attendants and smiled stiffly. "Could you please bring me some eunuch clothing? I'd like to go wait on the Prince of Kui."

Huang Zixia stood before the two-foot-tall mirror with a bronze frame and looked at herself. In eunuch clothing, with her wet hair hanging down over her shoulders and chest, she looked like a handsome, slender boy. Her features were bright, though her face was still a little worn, and her eyes were still like deep pools.

She took a deep breath and casually tucked her damp hair inside the eunuch cap. Then she turned, opened the door latch, and strode out of the room. Following the ladies' directions, she found Jianbi Palace's main path. The newly completed palace naturally had a distinct atmosphere. In front, the vast lake sparkled, and countless rosewood ferryboats shuttled.

She faced the main hall. A large wall in front had the words *Adviser Mi Zhang* written on it. She stood and looked up at the words, feeling each stroke had a sense of dignity. Then she heard someone behind her say, "This is the Emperor's handwriting. Does it look good to this little eunuch?"

She turned and looked. The man was dressed in purple, looked to be twentysomething, had white skin, and seemed purer than his age. There was a cinnabar mole on his forehead, set against his light skin and dark hair, that gave him a mysterious air.

Huang Zixia realized who he was. She hurried to smile and bow. "Prince of E."

Prince Li Run was the best-tempered of the Princes, an amicable and gentle person. He nodded and smiled, resting his gaze on her face as he asked, "Are you of this palace? In which Prince's care are you? Why'd they send you here?"

Palace eunuchs all knew the tasks at Jianbi were endless, and they rarely saw the Emperor. Like the female attendants, they usually waited until they were old to be sent there.

She looked at herself and said, "Your servant came with the Prince of Kui. When I got off, I stumbled into the water, and the ladies changed my clothes."

Li Run smiled. "Oh. Then your Prince will take you inside."

A lady led the way, and Huang Zixia followed Li Run around the wall. They passed a veranda where a group of people sat listening to a woman play the pipa. Its sound was clear as gems pouring. Coupled with the bright sun, it gave an incredible feeling of coziness.

"Such wonderful pipa, a shame to interrupt," Li Run said as he stopped outside to listen. Huang Zixia waited quietly behind him, and when the song ended, they went in together.

Inside was the Prince of Kui, Li Shubai; the ninth-ranked Prince of Chao, Li Rui; and the youngest, the Prince of Kang, Li Wen. There was also a pretty woman in yellow. She had brilliant begonia flowers tucked beside her temple and held the pipa as she sat opposite.

Prince Li Rui saw the Prince of E and said, "Brother, come quick. I found an incredible pipa player in the conservatory!" Prince Li Rui was a rich idler. He was eighteen or nineteen but still liked to play like a boy. "I just listened to part of a song, really heavenly," Li Run said. He sat to Li Shubai's left. "Brother, where's the Emperor?" Li Run asked.

"The Emperor had a headache this morning. He's seeing the doctor and should be here soon." As Li Shubai spoke, he glanced at Huang Zixia and said nothing. Huang Zixia bit her lip and quickly walked behind him and stood bowing like a loyal eunuch.

The Prince of Kang, Li Wen, was young. He watched her curiously as he listened.

Li Rui chuckled. "Speaking of which, isn't the Emperor worried about Shubai?"

Li Wen immediately turned his head and asked Li Rui, "What's going on?"

Li Shubai heard him but only smiled faintly.

"Heh, look at Shubai, acting like he doesn't know!" Li Rui laughed again. "What else but our Prince's wedding? You've been twenty years without a wife, which is so rare. You can't go on being an ascetic; it's terrible!"

Huang Zixia stood motionless with her eyes on Shubai's back. She couldn't imagine him with a wife.

"Shubai, I heard the Emperor intends to appoint Minister Zhou Xiang to Chengdu Prefecture. What do you think?" someone asked.

Li Shubai said casually, "Minister Zhou sounds like a good choice, but I don't have any relationship with him outside official duties. I do like his son Zhou Ziqin a lot, though."

Li Rui laughed. "Right. Minister Zhou has a good temper. If he gets angry, Zhou Ziqin is surely responsible. I also like him a lot!"

"I've seen Zhou Ziqin. He didn't look like a rebellious son!" Li Run said.

"He's not rebellious; he's just brought a lot of shame to his family's house! Minister Zhou knows how to raise children. His first three or four sons are quite capable. Who would've thought the next would be a good-for-nothing? He doesn't study or read, fight cocks or race dogs; he just runs off to the mortuary. It's become a running joke in the capital."

"Mortuary?" Li Wen said with a smile.

Zhou Ziqin had always wanted to be a medical examiner. He enjoyed studying bodies and doing detective work. His family didn't approve.

Li Rui laughed. "Exactly. Minister Zhou knocked some sense into him; he had to change paths."

Li Wen laughed and said to Li Shubai, "Brother, it'd be good for you to speak with the Emperor and give some advice. When Minister Zhou takes office in Chengdu, the Emperor should personally direct his son to follow him and become constable there and fulfill his silly wish!"

"Right, right!" Li Rui laughed. "The Emperor's so wise. When Zhou Ziqin's appointed constable, what'll Minister Zhou do?"

"I wonder how former Chengdu Civil Governor Huang Min's case is coming along," Li Run said, referencing the murder of Huang Zixia's family.

"I'm afraid Huang Zixia ran off in disguise. It's a big world. If someone takes up in the backcountry, it's not easy to catch them," said Li Rui.

Huang Zixia listened to them talk about her family's murder. She looked calm, almost cold, but a suffocating pain rose in her chest like a strap slowly tightening around her heart.

Li Shubai didn't look behind him and see her. He just said, "Maybe she's audacious enough to have gone to the capital."

"That'd be suicide," Li Rui said.

"I remember when Huang Zixia was known as a child prodigy. I really didn't expect things to turn out the way they did. What a tragedy!" Li Run sighed.

Among those present, Li Wen was the youngest and didn't know the stories from back then. "What did Huang Min's daughter do that made everyone take notice?"

Li Rui laughed. "She helped her father break several cases. Traveling storytellers still relish it!"

"I've never heard of it. Tell me about it, Rui. Let's see if you can do better than the storyteller," said Li Wen.

Amid everyone's laughter, Li Rui sat back. He cleared his throat and said, "Okay, then I'll start from the beginning. Five or six years ago, I received a message late one evening from the Board of Punishments saying a woman in Xingde Square had hanged herself. The examiner rushed to the scene. Turns out, she was a young woman who'd been married less than a month. People said she had a disagreement with her husband the day before. He spent half the day outside sulking, and when he went back at night, he found the suicide."

Jin Nu covered her mouth and her eyes widened. "Women always take things so hard. What a shame!"

"Yes. The examination showed she really died from hanging, so the Board of Punishments closed the case. When Minister Huang reviewed the case, Huang Zixia, who was twelve at the time, was outside, waiting with her brother to go home. People in Changan love a scene, so lots of people were coming and going because of the death. There was a cloth merchant who said when the woman married, she didn't buy wedding dress material from him. This tragedy wouldn't have happened if her dress had been proper. There was a jeweler who said the woman bought a pair of silver hairpins that afternoon and was wondering if her husband still wanted them. A fortune-teller said he'd long known disaster would strike the family this year; shame they hadn't consulted him earlier. Anyway, it was a commotion. Just when Huang Min was finishing up, Huang Zixia suddenly called, "Daddy!"

When Li Rui got to this point, he paused and looked at everyone like a true storyteller. "So, gentlemen, who can guess what Huang Zixia wanted to tell her daddy?"

Li Run laughed. "You just said the beginning. We have no clues. How would we know?"

Li Rui said, "It's just the beginning, but Huang Zixia already knew the cause of death and the bride's murderer, and I already gave you the clues."

Huang Zixia remembered that day. It had seemed so obvious to her.

Everyone looked at one another. Li Wen spoke first. "In my opinion, the fortune-teller is suspicious. Could he have caused harm to get the reputation of a prophet?"

Li Rui laughed hard and asked Li Run, "What do you think?"

Li Run thought it over for a moment. "I don't know. Maybe the cloth merchant hated her because of the wedding dress dispute? Or the jeweler had some disagreement with her when she bought jewelry and took action?"

Li Rui smiled, revealing nothing. "What do you think, Shubai?"

"The husband did it," Li Shubai said casually.

Li Rui had a look of shocked admiration. "How'd you guess, brother?"

"I saw the files at the Board of Punishments, so I know the basic details of the case," he said plainly.

Li Rui sighed. "Right. Huang Min was about to sign off when he heard Huang Zixia call to him. Huang Zixia was pointing at the jeweler.

'Daddy, did you hear what he said? So the lady didn't commit suicide; it was just made up like one—she was murdered!' That's what Huang Zixia said to her father."

Li Wen wore a look of disbelief. "Brother, you said she was twelve. Who would believe her?"

"Exactly. Huang Min also felt it was ridiculous for a girl to say such a thing. He dismissed her. But, sure enough, she was right."

After Li Rui spoke, the hall went silent.

On that day, Huang Zixia had put her hand on her father's file and said, "Daddy, talking at home with colleagues, you said people on the brink of death were often empty inside. Why would she go to the jeweler's and buy custom-made hairpins if she was about to commit suicide?" Huang Zixia would never forget the look on her father's face when she said that. She wished he were here now, still alive.

Li Shubai tapped the table as a signal to Huang Zixia behind him. She slowly knelt down, lifted the jug, and filled his wineglass. He turned slightly and looked at her profile—long eyelashes, thick and curled, covered her eyes deep as lakes. Sunlight coming through the window made them faintly glow.

Li Rui continued his story. "Huang Min was shocked to realize his daughter was right and immediately called for the examiner to take another look at the corpse. After careful examination, he found the rope marks showed a subtle shift that could have only been formed if the rope was moved after the original injury. So they deduced that she was first strangled and then hanged to cover it up. And, naturally, the one who had done it was the first to discover her body and report the suicide—her husband."

Li Wen's eyes widened. "Did he confess?"

Li Rui nodded. "When he saw the examiner had detected those flaws, he was scared out of his wits and kneeled for mercy, confessed his guilt."

The murderer suspected his wife had had relations with someone on their street before their marriage. When she left after fighting with him, he thought she was going to her lover. His anger burned, and when she got home, he grabbed a rope and strangled her. When he calmed down, he quickly hung her on the beam to make it look like a suicide.

"He almost got away with it. Maybe God put the words in the little girl's mouth not to let him," Li Run said.

"Exactly. From then on, everyone in the capital praised her genius. Sometimes, if the Board of Punishments had trouble solving a case, Huang Zixia would help Huang Min figure it out. He never thought his daughter would betray him and become a murderer herself."

Li Shubai saw Huang Zixia's sun-dappled eyelashes twitch. She lowered her head and quivered like a flowering branch in the wind. Li Shubai couldn't believe such a slender and beautiful girl could stay so calm while they talked about her family.

"If Huang Zixia is in the capital, I wonder if she could solve the case," Li Run questioned.

Li Rui asked, "Are you talking about the awful Four Directions Case?"

Li Run nodded. Li Wen asked, "What Four Directions Case? Why don't I know about it?"

"It's a new one in the capital—bloody, strange, and cruel. No one wanted to mention it in front of you because of your age." Li Rui laughed. "Don't worry about it. Listen to your Imperial Academy lectures instead."

"Come on, brother, you speak much better than them. Tell me what it is, please!" Li Wen stood and ran to Li Rui's side and sat next to him. The boy looked at him like a hungry chick would its mother.

Li Run smiled. "Go ahead, brother. I heard about this thing but don't know much. I know you like to go to restaurants and tearooms to hear stories. What's the word?"

Li Rui looked at Li Shubai. "Brother, you are close with the Central Court and Board of Punishments. Have you heard about any new clues?"

Li Shubai slowly shook his head. "No. They're looking but haven't made any progress."

"Then I'll just tell you what I've heard." Li Rui motioned for Jin Nu to refill his wine, then asked Li Wen, "You know eastern Changan is in a panic?"

"Really? No wonder there hasn't been much activity in the east. When I last went shopping, many businesses were closed." Li Wen looked more curious. "What's going on? What happened in the East City?"

"Well, we'd have to start three months ago," Li Rui began. He told the details of the Four Directions Case.

On the seventeenth day of the first month, a guard at the North City's Taiji Palace out on early patrol found a sixty-year-old man had been killed at the base of the wall. The word *peace* was written on it. A month later, the twenty-first day of the second month, a thirty-something blacksmith was killed outside the clinic in South City's Anyi Square. The word *bliss* was written on the wall. On the ninth day of the third month, the body of a four-year-old boy was found in the West City's Nanchang Square, along with the word *self*. The Central Court confirmed the handwriting was the same, so the crimes were likely committed by the same person.

"It says in the *Mahaparninirvana Sutra* that the Bodhi tree's four sides represent *peace, bliss, self,* and *eternal.* North is *peace*, south is *bliss*, west is *self*, and east is *eternal*. Panic in the capital gave way to a rumor that the people were killed by evil spirits, because during the puja ceremony at the beginning of the year, Master Zhuang Zhen read from the Mahaparninirvana Sutra; but he said *release* instead of *reign*, causing evil spirits to stay in the mortal world. They won't leave until they've killed in the four quadrants of the capital," Li Rui finished.

"I remember Master Zhuang Zhen! He's a monk at the Jianfu temple, right?" Li Wen asked curiously, "I heard he passed away a few days ago. Could it be related?"

Li Rui nodded. "When Master Zhuang Zhen heard the rumors, he blamed himself. He died of worry after a few days. But more rumors spread in the capital, saying that the Jianfu Temple is in the middle of the city, and Master Zhuang Zhen's death is related to the Bodhi tree. Since the north, south, and west all had murders, all that was left was the east, *eternal*, death."

Li Run let out a gentle sigh and asked Shubai, "Three people are already dead. Is there really nothing the Central Court and Board of Punishments can do?"

"This murderer is ruthless and skilled. Changan's population is almost a million; finding such a person is nearly impossible. The Central Court and Board of Punishments have made their best effort but so far have no leads. Since the murderer seems to strike every month, he's probably ready to do so again. So the Central Court and Board of Punishments are out in full force, but that's all they can do," said Li Shubai.

Li Run sighed. "Peace, bliss, self, eternal. Buddhist verse as a murderous message. This case is truely horrible."

Li Rui laughed. "Zhou Ziqin always said Huang Zixia was a genius, that there was no case that could stump her, but I don't believe that. She wouldn't be able to do anything with this case."

"Shame she is now a wanted murderer and public enemy," Li Shubai said with a touch of scorn.

Behind him, Huang Zixia was silent and still.

There was a collective sigh. Li Run said, "I think there must be more to this Huang family killing. It's not as simple as it seems."

"But the evidence and witnesses all agree that Huang Zixia was the perpetrator. It couldn't be reversed now." Li Rui shook his head. "Does brother know more details?"

"I don't, but Wang Yun is a good friend. I can't believe it."

Li Wen was curious. "What Wang Yun?"

Li Run said, "The Empress's brother's only child, Wang Yun of the Langya Wangs."

"Of course. Wang Yun was engaged to Huang Zixia." Li Rui looked mysterious. "Rumor has it, Huang Zixia didn't want to marry Wang Yun, had another lover, so she poisoned the whole family to elope."

Huang Zixia still stood silently. For some reason, Li Shubai chuckled.

Li Rui looked at him. "What do you think, brother?"

Li Shubai laughed. "Nothing. I was curious if Run saw Huang Zixia when he was with Wang Yun."

"I've seen her," Li Run said with a nod. "Three years ago, after Huang Zixia helped her father break several cases. The Empress called her in for an award. Wang Yun came that day and told me Huang Zixia was his fiancée. We got to steal a look at Huang Zixia."

"So you're sure you saw her? What does Huang Zixia look like?" Li Wen asked.

"I did. We just saw her from a distance, in the veranda. She was in a silver-and-red robe. She had black hair and white skin. She was thin and had a light step like a blossoming flower."

"Beautiful?" Li Rui asked.

Li Run nodded. "The wanted poster captured her features but not her charm. She's truly beautiful."

"Poor Wang Yun," Li Wen said with a laugh.

There was finally news from the palace. The Emperor, suffering from a headache, wasn't coming. Li Shubai got up to get a look at the completed palace. Of course, it wasn't as luxurious as Daming Palace, nor as vast as Jiucheng, but it took about an hour to tour the whole thing.

Huang Zixia naturally stayed close by. Her lithe body looked even more slender in the eunuch garb. Though she did nothing but silently bow, she looked very good.

Li Rui watched her and laughed. "Shubai, did you switch attendants? I don't think I've seen this eunuch."

Li Shubai acted as if it was of no importance. "Jing Yang and Jing Yu, I don't know who got who sick, but they both have colds."

Li Run kept looking at her face. Something about her was familiar.

Li Rui asked again, "What's the eunuch's name? How old?"

Li Shubai smiled. "It seems the Prince has taken a liking to you. I can't stand your clumsiness. Why don't you go with him?" Li Shubai said to Huang Zixia.

Huang Zixia froze a moment. Seeing all eyes on her body, she slowly knelt and softly said, "Your servant heard that it's hard for a bird to perch on two branches and to serve two masters. It's hard to move a tea tree after it blooms. Your servant is clumsy and afraid it will be hard to adapt after leaving the Prince of Kui and will make a mistake."

Li Rui laughed. "Shubai really is a good master. If I insist, I'm afraid I'll dash your eunuch's hopes."

Li Shubai smiled faintly. "Eloquent."

Luckily, Li Wen said he was tired, and everyone turned his or her attention away from Huang Zixia.

In the garden surrounded by thick walls, Li Shubai eased his pace. Before a fern, it was now only him and Huang Zixia. He turned to her coldly. "Why are you following me, Huang Zixia?"

"Good birds nest in good forests. I want to stay with the Prince and do what little I can to help."

"With what?" he asked.

"The little red fish and the Four Directions Case."

He looked contemptuously at her long face as if she were a speck of dust. "You can't help with the first, and the other has nothing to do with me. Why should you bother?"

She stood under the fern whose thin stalks surrounded her and lent her slender, pale face a touch of turquoise. She looked up at him and spoke in a soft but determined voice, "But the Central Court and Board of Punishments need help. The Emperor is sick. I think you're the only one who can help."

"Are you sure you're not just looking for a patron to wipe your slate clean?" He'd mercilessly exposed her intentions. "Li Rui just asked for you; isn't that a chance too?"

"There's no chance going with him." Huang Zixia's face grew paler. "I don't need a place to hide. I need to stand in the sun and wash away my family's shame!"

Li Shubai fixed his cold eyes on her. As she looked at him pleadingly, she withheld a certain stubbornness like a late-night mist that is difficult to detect but tightly wound. He snorted and turned to walk back toward the Water Palace. Huang Zixia followed behind.

When they reached the entrance, several Princes were waiting to say goodbye to the Prince of Kui. The eunuchs said the Emperor would summon the ministers in a few days to write an inscription on a landscape painting, which caused everyone to exchange amused glances.

Once everyone had left, Li Run and Li Shubai remained. Li Run sighed. "The Emperor is really at ease. Military governors are vying for autonomy, eunuchs are power hungry, and the Emperor still feasts and celebrates every day."

"The Emperor was born to rule over peaceful times," Shubai said. "This is a blessing to him and all the world."

Li Run smiled. "You're right, brother." His eyes fell on Huang Zixia. His warm, soft face was full of doubt.

"Something the matter?" Li Shubai asked.

31

"That eunuch, I seem to have seen him somewhere." He pointed at Huang Zixia.

"It's the first time I've seen him. Why don't you let him attend to you?"

"You're kidding, brother. Rui was just refused. How could I bother?" The cinnabar between his eyebrows gently increased as he smiled.

Huang Zixia silently bowed her head. Going with one of them would mean security, but she would rather choose the difficult path. She wasn't going to live just to live.

Li Shubai only got in his coach after everyone had left. Huang Zixia stood by the door, hesitating. "Get in," he said.

She hurried in and leaned against the door. The carriage gently started moving.

When they were well beyond the palace, with mountains all around, Li Shubai looked outside and said, "Ten days."

She looked at him and waited for him to go on.

"That case we were talking about in the palace. I give you ten days. Got it?"

"Maybe," Huang Zixia responded.

"Just maybe?" He leaned against the carriage wall in a leisurely manner. "Now you have a chance. You can clear your name and avenge your parents, find the truth."

Huang Zixia thought a moment. "The Prince means, if I help him solve this case, he'll lend me a hand in avenging my family?"

"Of course not." He raised his chin slightly, indicating that she sit on the small stool in front of him. "I have something I need help with. But you've only just suddenly appeared. I have no reason to trust your abilities."

"I understand," Huang Zixia said with a slight nod. "If I break the case in ten days, I may earn the Prince's trust."

"At least you would let me know you deserve to be helped. I don't have enough free time to help someone who can't do anything but talk."

Huang Zixia sat on the low stool, her head down, thinking. "The Central Court and Board of Punishments must have a large staff working on the case. In what capacity will the Prince allow me to participate?"

"I will personally go to the Board of Punishments and get the case file for you."

"Okay." Huang Zixia reached toward her temple and pulled the wooden hairpin from her hair. As soon as the hairpin was out, her dark hair poured down over her shoulders. It was still damp like black algae tangling over her pale cheeks. She paused, then brushed it back. "Sorry, I used to have several hairpins in my hair. I got used to taking one out to keep a record. I forgot that now I'm a little eunuch with only one."

Li Shubai frowned slightly, not speaking. She bowed her head and raised her hand to put her hair in a bun in front of him. This girl who had trekked a thousand miles, not once hesitating with fear, now felt shy.

Li Shubai seemed to realize something deeper than when he had his hand around her throat. The person in front of him was not as mature and calm as she seemed on the surface.

She was beautiful.

He thought of Li Run's impression of her when she was fourteen. The girl who reached worldwide fame at twelve was now a slender and delicate seventeen-year-old woman. She'd suffered greatly but had not been defeated. She was struggling to find the truth and relying on her own strength to make it known.

Huang Zixia stared at him and touched her own face, nervous and afraid.

"Kind of similar to the wanted poster." Li Shubai turned and looked at the intertwined branches on the curtain. "Don't show up looking like this in the future."

"Okay," she responded as she tightened her hair. "Does Your Highness remember when they said the crimes occurred?"

"The seventeenth of the first month, the twenty-first of the second month, the nineteenth of the third month," he said without hesitation.

"Today's the sixteenth day of the fourth month. Which means if the timing's about the same, the murderer should strike soon." She slowly wrote on the carriage wall with her finger, thinking. "Within ten days."

"With only those words to help, can you find the killer among a million people in the capital?"

"No." She stopped writing. "Without knowing the killer's traits and motivations, it's impossible to pick them out of the crowd."

Li Shubai looked at her casually. "So you don't have a handle on it?"

Huang Zixia's finger began writing on the wall again. She mouthed to herself, "First month, seventeenth, old watchman dies, killer writes *peace*. Second month, twenty-first, middle-aged blacksmith, killer writes *bliss*. Third month, nineteenth, four-year-old child, killer writes *self*. . ."

"Four Directions Case. First in the north, second in the south, third in the west, southwest to be precise," Li Shubai said.

Huang Zixia thought a moment. "If it really were four directions, they would try to do them clearly in the north, south, west, and east, but the third was in the southwest. It's a bit strange."

"Or maybe he wasn't trying to strike clearly in the west. Maybe he's changing quadrants to avoid being seen?"

"Yes, anything's possible now. It's hard to know the true reason." Huang Zixia squeezed her fingers together to jog her memory. "The first victim was old, the second a strong blacksmith, the third a child."

Li Shubai leaned on his cushion, finding a comfortable position before he spoke. "I asked the Central Court about this. The two men make sense. Maybe the killer was looking for easy targets, but the child surprises me, because it was a four-year-old dying of hunger, abandoned by his parents on the roadside. A passerby already determined he was too far gone. So whether the killer acted or not, the kid probably wasn't going to make it through the night. Still, he sneaked into the shelter to kill him, unnecessarily."

"I see; that really is strange. Why would the killer risk being found out by sneaking into a shelter and killing a dying child?" Huang Zixia frowned, and her fingers started writing *peace, bliss, self, eternal* on the wall again.

Li Shubai watched her. Then he turned outside to look at the landscape through the thin curtain. His voice was calm. "With just these clues, what's key for you to be able to break it in ten days?"

"Without evidence from the previous three cases, the best thing would be to predict the time, place, and target of his next crime." Huang Zixia kept looking at her fingers, slowly counting on them.

"I feel the same way. So if you've got a handle on it, I can give you a few days to work with the detectives working on the case, but you'll have to take care of your hair and not let anyone find out you're a woman."

"No need." Huang Zixia touched the hairpin in her hair and looked at him. Still respectful, her lips raised slightly in a show of confidence and calm. "I already know the killer's motive. If I'm not wrong, I can figure out where he'll appear next."

Li Shubai saw she had thought it through. "So you have a handle on it?"

"Yes, I just need the Prince to give me a Tung Shing almanac." Outside, the wind blew gently and came through the curtain. The slowly rotating sun shone inside, enveloping Huang Zixia's body, making it glow. Her eyes, clear as morning dew, were fixed on Li Shubai without hesitation.

Li Shubai was entranced. A while later he said, "All right, then I'll wait and see."

Three

AS A EUNUCH

Li Shubai brought Huang Zixia to Kui Palace, to Jingyu Hall where he lived.

Huang Zixia flipped through the almanac. Li Shubai sat and watched her turn from the twenty-first of the second month, to the nineteenth of the third month, and then to today's date quickly, then put it down.

"Officers on patrol tonight should keep tight watch on the city's southeastern quadrant, especially pregnant women, who are the likely target of the killer," Huang Zixia said.

"You're sure the killer's fourth target will be a pregnant woman?" Shubai said, raising his eyebrows.

"It's quite likely."

Li Shubai turned and shouted out, "Jing Yang."

A cute eunuch with curvy features came in. "My Prince."

"Take a trip and tell Minister Cui Chunzhan to come."

"Understood." Jing Yang didn't look at Huang Zixia as he gave his salute. Before Jing Yang could turn and leave, Li Shubai pointed to Huang Zixia and said, "Take him down and give him proper accommodations; he's a eunuch."

"Yes, I'll take care of it, my Prince."

The wanted criminal Huang Zixia thus became a palace eunuch.

Jing Yang took her to where the eunuchs live in the north and gave her a private room. He got her daily necessities and three pairs of eunuch clothing. "Little man, you've just arrived, so you won't get responsibilities. Just remember to greet the Prince in his hall every day."

Huang Zixia thanked him again and went next door to ask another eunuch about daily life and then to the kitchen to eat. She'd been running around all day battling what life threw at her and was tired.

She fell asleep before her head hit the pillow.

When she woke up, it was already late morning. She went to the well to fetch water. A eunuch sweeping the courtyard said, "Jing Yang asked us to let you know when you woke up to go to Yubing Hall."

She quickly had a bowl of porridge, asked the way, changed clothes, and went to Yubing Hall. It was the Prince's study and was surrounded by flowers and trees. The doors and windows had transparent curtains.

Before Huang Zixia had entered through a latticed window, she saw Li Shubai sitting and looking at a map of the capital.

Hearing her footsteps, he looked up and said plainly, "Come here."

Huang Zixia went over to him. He pointed at the map and said, "Last night the perpetrator did not appear. But according to your theory, will the killer come out in the northwest tonight?"

Huang Zixia was slightly surprised. "The Prince already knows my method?"

"You can read a Tung Shing almanac; so can I," he said. His slender white fingers touched the twelfth district of the northwest quadrant. "This morning, my men reported there are a lot of pregnant women in this district. Quite a few are already showing signs of it. For example, one near Xiude Square is seven months pregnant. Puning Square has one ready to give birth. Jude Square has two pregnant women, one five months, one six."

"Puning Square." She placed her finger on the map.

Li Shubai tilted the map to get a better look at the detail of Puning Square. "The pregnant woman's home is next to the former residence of Mr. Li, Duke of Ying."

Huang Zixia looked too and suddenly remembered something that made her hesitate. She decided to wait until the case was broken to say it.

But Li Shubai seemed to have thought of it. "Zhang Xingying's house is also in Puning Square."

"Right." Since he brought it up, she decided to pursue the topic. "Has the Prince thought about whether or not to let Zhang Xingying return to the honor guard if we break the case?"

"Impossible," he said without hesitation.

Huang Zixia pressed on. "Zhang Xingying let me pretend I was him and enter the city with the Prince's honor guard. Though he broke the rules, he's a truly good man. Gratitude is one of the great virtues. Could I ask the Prince to forgive him and let him help me investigate the case?"

"Don't be silly," he said. "Though I can understand his intentions, I have no need for a sentimental person."

Huang Zixia bit her lower lip and whispered, "Please show mercy—"

He cut her off. "If someone who makes a mistake can just act like nothing happened a few days later, what's the purpose of punishment? How can I manage my men?"

Huang Zixia lowered her head and gave up. "So what should I do next?"

"Go back to sleep. Tonight, you're going to Puning Square with me."

◆ ◆ ◆

Northwest Changan, Puning Square

People were forbidden from entering the square or walking in the streets after nine p.m., so Li Shubai posed as a scholar and Huang Zixia as his assistant. It was evening, and they were dressed in ordinary clothes on their way to the Puning Square Inn. One was handsome and astute, the other a delicate, refined boy. Even the men turned their heads to have another look. Once they were in the inn, the hostess came four times to bring water, and the owner came the fifth time.

"Maybe I should talk to the Board of Punishments people tonight." Huang Zixia was tying her hair to get ready. "As for you, I suspect the owner and hostess will lock you in here."

Li Shubai said, "You think you can leave me here to be tortured by this hostess?"

Huang Zixia was about to speak when, out the window, she saw the hostess coming gracefully with the teapot. She turned and looked at Li Shubai. He looked back at her with that slight smile on his face. "I'll give you fifteen minutes to be off," he said.

That didn't seem like enough time. The hostess was persistent. Huang Zixia had an idea.

She took a step toward Li Shubai and brought his hand to her waist, and just loud enough to be heard outside the window, said, "Oh, master, we're in public. We need to be discreet! Don't, don't touch me there. Oh, that's worse, stop it, we're both men, imagine what people will think."

The hostess's graceful posture suddenly stiffened.

Li Shubai froze too but only for a moment. He quietly released her grasp and turned to drink tea. "This hostess is always staring. Maybe she knows I like men."

The hostess outside the window trotted away with her teapot, and Huang Zixia thought she could hear the pieces of the hostess's broken heart falling along the way.

Huang Zixia shut the door latch, opened the window, looked back, and jumped out. She waved him along. "Let's go!"

Down the second alley after Li's former residence to number six—the Wei family. Their yard had pomegranate flowers.

Given the high cost of real estate in the capital, their home wasn't very large. The so-called yard wasn't more than ten square feet. Beyond it were two bungalows. The walls were no higher than Huang Zixia's chest.

They quietly hid in the bridge archway behind a few clusters of peony flowers.

It was already nine p.m., and the streets grew quiet. Lights went out.

It was a cloudy night, and the moon shone dimly. She and Li Shubai hid awhile under the peony flowers, admiring the moon's reflection in the water.

Huang Zixia spoke quietly. "Why did the Prince want to come? Where are the court and board people?"

"Didn't tell them," he said casually. He pulled down a peony bud and examined it. "This year, the air's been warm, so some species of peony haven't bloomed, while others are already budding."

Huang Zixia suddenly understood that her only help in catching the terrible killer would be him.

She had to ask, "Why not contact the court and board?"

"The court minister, Cui Chunzhan, said it was critical to concentrate on the east, the fourth direction. He's stubborn, so I let him stick with his position. He's waiting in the east with his men."

"What about the board?"

"The board person on this case is Minister Wang Lin. You didn't marry his son, Wang Yun. Do you want to face him?"

40

The moonlight reflected off the ripples in the water onto her face. Li Shubai saw some tension there, but it disappeared immediately, like a mirage.

"Forget it; let them go to the east side," she said.

It was already midnight when a sound came from the Wei house. A candle was lit in the eastern room, and water began boiling in the kitchen. The family was urgently attending to tasks. A man threw on a coat and opened the door. As he walked out of the yard, someone behind called, "Liu Wenoi lives in the fourth house on Chouhua Alley; don't forget!"

"Don't worry, Mother!" Though the man walked anxiously, there was a bounce in his step.

Huang Zixia fixed her gaze upstairs. Li Shubai let go of the peony branch and said, "Seems ready to bloom."

"Yes." Now she looked at the wall and saw the line of a figure on top beside the pomegranate tree. "Hoo, hoo," it called.

In the darkness, the shrill, ominous voice mingling with the groans of the pregnant woman gave her the creeps.

"Owl," Li Shubai said thoughtfully. "Really ominous."

It was a night owl, which the ancients thought counted people's eyebrows with its hoots and took a number of lives when it got the number right. Since women could easily die during childbirth, the people in the house panicked. An old woman ran out from the kitchen and shouted, "I'm going to cover Daughter's face. Go boil water, Papa!"

The grandpa hurried to the kitchen, and the old woman wrapped cloth around the woman's face to make sure her eyebrows weren't exposed as the owl outside hooted twice. She quickly picked up a clothes-hanging rod and ran to the yard, toward the pomegranate tree, to drive away the owl.

The moment she left, the man was already around the back of the house.

Huang Zixia jumped up, but Li Shubai was faster. He leaped over the peonies. Huang Zixia heard the wind rush past her ear. In a few steps, they were behind the house in time to see the shadow disappear through the back door.

Li Shubai kicked the door open, pushed Huang Zixia in, and hid a few steps behind her.

Huang Zixia saw the murderer raising his dagger high, the pregnant woman's stomach his target. Li Shubai pushed her again. She staggered forward a few steps, then fell down hard. Her shoulder struck the killer's side, knocking him away.

The killer knew he'd been caught in the act and, gripping his dagger, tried to flee. Huang Zixia lay on the floor and pushed a nearby shelf over at his feet.

The flowerpots hit the floor with a bang and caused the killer to stumble. When he fell to the ground, his face hit the dirt.

Before he could stand up, Huang Zixia was already on her feet. She stomped on his wrist, forcing him to let go of his dagger. Huang Zixia grabbed it, then pounced on his lower back and shouted, "Don't move!"

Li Shubai stood in the doorway watching. "Nice," he said. "Quick movements, lacking technique, though."

Huang Zixia couldn't believe it. "Mind coming to help me a second?" She was fighting for her life, and he was standing idly by, his whole body still covered in moonlight.

"A woman's about to give birth inside; how could I, being a man, enter?" He looked up at the moon, turning his back to her. "How is she?"

Before Huang Zixia could answer, the child's cries filled the room.

The mother-in-law heard the commotion and came in from the yard. In the room where her daughter-in-law had been alone was an apprentice holding a dagger at the back of a man dressed in black. There was a squirming baby on the bed, and a man outside looking at the moon. In surprise and fright she shouted, "Good God! Wh-what happened?"

Neighbors who had heard the baby crying came over, and the father-in-law was back with hot water. Amid the chaos, Huang Zixia could only offer a reluctant smile. "I apologize; we came to catch the intruder."

The father returned and called for help.

A patrolman soon came. After he saw Li Shubai, he hurried to tie up the killer.

The midwife came in, amazed. "The mother was afraid and so got the child out in one big push. Luckily, she's okay, and I washed the child."

The child's father held his wife's hand and said sweetly, "Poor woman, how about we call him Surprise?"

She leaned weakly against the bed. "Why not Shock?"

"Good idea. It's decided. Wei Shock. Very good."

Huang Zixia saw that even Li Shubai couldn't help but smile a little.

When Cui Chunzhan and Wang Lin rushed to the Prince of Kui's palace, it was already dawn. Li Shubai offered them tea. "The Four Directions Case's perpetrator has been arrested," he said. "He can be on trial tomorrow."

Wang Lin nodded. Cui Chunzhan hesitated. "My Prince," he said, "We still don't have any motive or evidence for the Four Directions Case. Are you sure the man you caught is the killer?"

"Whether he is or not, you can find out during the trial tomorrow, right?" Li Shubai said as the tea came. "No one has been out because of the curfew, and he was certainly staying in the Puning Square Inn beforehand. You can look for evidence there."

The next day, the Board of Punishments and Central Court determined the weapon the man had was used in the previous murders, and documents at the inn showed handwriting consistent with that left behind at the crime scenes. The murderer had no choice but to confess and tell them his reason for the killings.

And, like that, three months of hysteria over the Four Directions Case ended.

Emperor Li Cui, who had been ill in Daming Palace's Purple Hall, felt better after hearing the news and invited guests, including Cui Chunzhan and Wang Lin from the Board of Punishments.

Huang Zixia had just woken up and gone to Yubing Hall to see Li Shubai.

"Change your clothes and come with me to the palace."

Huang Zixia was surprised. "Go to the palace?"

"As I said, if you solve the case within ten days, you'll have proven yourself worthy of serving me. So from now on, I have something I want you to help me with. And this thing requires you to have a fixed identity." He stood elegantly, not like someone conducting business at all. "In sum, today is an important day for this little palace eunuch. If I don't take you, wouldn't you miss out on a lot of fun?"

She lowered her head and said, "Yes."

Li Shubai walked to the doorway again and ordered the man standing there to summon Jing Yi.

A moment later, Jing Yi came. He glanced at Huang Zixia before asking, "What is it, my Prince?"

Li Shubai asked casually, "You're in charge of the residence personnel. How many eunuchs do we have?"

"Three hundred sixty-seven in total."

"And what if three hundred sixty-seven suddenly became three hundred sixty-eight?"

Jing Yi understood. After thinking a moment, he said, "Your servant remembers that last year, Jiucheng Palace lost quite a few eunuchs in that storm. Most of them were orphans who had been sent to the palace. Some of their bodies were never found."

Li Shubai nodded. "So he could be one of the Jiucheng eunuchs who came back?"

Jing Yi said sincerely, "That would be my guess, but exactly who, your servant can't remember; please allow him to check the file."

Li Shubai motioned for him to go check. He was soon back with a thick file. "Your servant found it. Jiucheng Palace had a eunuch called Yang Chonggu. He was in charge of sweeping the Hazy Hall. Seventeen years old, five feet five, thin. He came to the palace as an orphan and had no friends at Jiucheng. He was in the Hazy Hall alone, so everyone thought he died in the disaster last year, and his name has been removed from the palace roster."

"I see. We will say Yang Chonggu didn't die and returned to my palace." He looked at Huang Zixia. "What do you think about this identity Jing Yi found?"

Huang Zixia stood there, full of emotion. She'd been on the run for months, covering thousands of miles to hide her identity. Who knew that in such a short time she could take on another?

She bowed to him and said, "Your servant Yang Chonggu thanks you, my Prince."

After entering the Daming Palace gates, through the archways and high walls, they saw the towering Hanyuan Hall. There was a line of watchtowers on either side like phoenix wings enveloping those who entered. Behind Hanyuan was the gorgeous Zichen Hall with magnificent, intricate eaves.

Zichen Hall was a sanctuary. In recent years, the Emperor hadn't summoned many ministers there. It was mostly for the Princes. Huang Zixia waited for a short time. Then the Emperor, wearing black and surrounded by eunuchs, entered. He was plump but not fat with a rounded chin and elongated features that gave him an amiable look.

Emperor Li Cui was thirty-nine years old, but since he took charge ten years ago, he'd been indulging himself instead of looking after the affairs of state. His reign was said to be peaceful, with some reluctance, though people's lives were pretty stable.

Huang Zixia thought he looked much gentler than his brother Shubai. Actually, all of his brothers looked less serious than he.

The Emperor sat and smiled. "Shubai, brother, there's nothing you can't do! I was thinking of asking you to help on this Four Directions Case, but before I had a chance, you already solved it."

Li Shubai said, "I can't take credit. It belongs to someone else."

The Emperor's eyes fell on Cui Chunzhan. Cui Chunzhan hurried to bow and said, "This case was broken single-handedly by the Prince of Kui. I'm at fault for not heeding him and focusing on the east. He went alone to the scene and captured the killer."

Then the Emperor looked at Huang Zixia. "Brother, that eunuch behind you, have I seen him before?"

"This is the person who broke the case, my Emperor. I couldn't take credit, so I brought him here."

Everyone looked at Huang Zixia. Her handsome face with its hanging lashes was calm when she looked at the Emperor, which impressed everyone.

The Emperor smiled. "This sanctuary is usually just for my brothers. And now we've added another. Minister Cui is the Empress's nephew; Minister Wang is Lady Cui's uncle. You're among friends, my little eunuch. What's your name?"

"Your servant is called Yang Chonggu, my Emperor." She bowed, holding her hands together in front of her.

46

Li Wen was young, and when he saw she was about his age, he asked, "You broke the case? I'm confused; should it not have been called the Four Directions Case? Why didn't the last murder happen in the east?"

Huang Zixia looked up at the Emperor, and he nodded in approval. "That's just what people came to believe because of the Bodhi 'peace, bliss, self' and the cases happening in the north, south, and west. But the killer had only borrowed the language, not the pattern. Actually, the third victim was in the southwest, not due west. After I realized that, I knew expecting him in the eastern quadrant was a mistake."

Li Rui continued. "So I heard you first thought he'd strike in the southeast and then decided it would be in the northwest's Puning Square. Why?"

"This case is quite complicated, starting from when Master Zhuang misread that sentence," Huang Zixia said. "At Jianbi Palace, I heard the Princes discuss the details. At the puja ceremony, Master Zhuang eloquently read a thousand words. For the killer to know he misspoke, he had to either be Buddhist or very familiar with Buddhist scripture. With the curfew, you have to get lodging ahead of time. The first few murders occurred in places where there weren't Buddhist temples. A monk would attract attention, so the killer was more than likely a layman. Furthermore, if he'd killed several people, he couldn't be a true believer but was corrupted by superstition. All this led me to deduce that he wasn't acting with the four directions in mind but was probably consulting a Tung Shing almanac or divination guide."

She explained that when she looked at the almanac, she found that the locations and dates fit those the almanac said were auspicious. What the almanac depicted fit the killer's movements. So she guessed that the murderer was moving based on the almanac rather than the four directions as everyone supposed.

She added that Li Shubai also figured this out when he saw her consulting the almanac. So in order to stop the attack on the pregnant woman in the northwest near Puning Square, all they had to do was sit and wait.

"I see!" Li Wen said. "So how did you know the killer would target that house? How did you know he was after a pregnant woman?"

"Because the first three victims were an old watchman, a blacksmith in his prime, and a child in the shelter who was weak and on the verge of death. Why would the killer want him?" She paused then went on. "Then I noticed that the blacksmith was killed near a drugstore—in other words, he was getting medical attention."

Li Wen was thinking. Li Run, holding his glass, sighed. "The Buddhist teachings of life's four sufferings: birth, age, sickness, and death."

"Exactly. One old, one sick, one dying. The only one left was birth—and that pregnant woman the only one in northwest about to give birth. If the murderer wanted to strike that day, she was the only possible target."

Cui Chunzhan sighed. "The Central Court and Board of Punishments questioned the killer, and he confessed. His family came upon disaster; in less than a month, he was left as the only survivor. Full of sorrow, he got involved with the beliefs of a sect from the Western Regions. It's causing quite a stir there and somehow spread to the Central Plains. They have a teaching that disaster can be passed on to others. He fervently believed that killing those people would keep him safe from the four sufferings. Even though he's imprisoned now, he says he's following the Buddhist practice of delivering himself—totally unrepentant!"

The inner palace went silent. The Emperor waved and said, "No need to wait till the fall. He already confessed, and we have evidence, what else is there? Get the case sorted out before he makes more of a fuss."

"It's certainly a capital offense; what is Your Highness's will?"

"Cut him in half."

Thus, the murder case that captivated the capital for months came to an end. People thought of the horrible murders and saw the little sixteen- or seventeen-year-old eunuch who looked like a spring twig.

Li Rui smiled. "This little eunuch sure is clever. No wonder last time I asked Shubai, he nodded reluctantly."

Li Shubai smiled. "Don't be silly. I never said no."

"Right, I can vouch for him," Li Wen joined in.

The Emperor smiled at their banter. "Shubai, good things come in twos. Let's celebrate with a feast. And on your special day, the Empress and I will visit your palace to congratulate you." Li Shubai was supposed to soon pick a wife.

Everyone suddenly looked surprised. Li Wen asked first, "Shubai picked his mate? Who's the lucky girl?"

The Emperor smiled. "She hasn't been chosen yet, but soon we'll make an announcement. You boys will be able to withstand the anticipation, right? Of course, Shubai's Princess will be one of the greatest ladies in the world."

◆ ◆ ◆

They feasted until sundown.

Huang Zixia left the palace gates with the carriage. She heaved a sigh of relief when Li Shubai pulled the curtain and said, "Come up."

She climbed into the car. His eyes scanned over her before looking out the window. She watched the ordinary street scene slowly passing outside the lattice window.

"So tell me about your family's case," he said.

Huang Zixia was startled. "My Prince really wants to know?"

"Do you think I would go back on my word?" he said aloofly.

Huang Zixia bit her lower lip. She hesitated and finally said, "I should start from the day before the murder. The weather was good.

Our garden's plum trees were blooming. Yu Xuan and I were picking the blossoms in the snow. It was an exceptionally beautiful winter."

Li Shubai was still watching the street outside. "Who's Yu Xuan?"

"He's an orphan my father adopted after moving to Chengdu. He became a scholar at eighteen, and the government gave him a small house, but he often came to visit my parents."

He turned and saw her face take on a look of longing.

He looked back out the window and calmly said, "Oh."

She took a deep breath and continued to talk about the night, which was now several months in the past but still left a deep impression on her heart.

That morning, a light snow had fallen. Then the sun came out, and the red plum blossoms shone against the background of white, and the world was pure and bright as glass.

Huang Zixia clutched an armful of plum blossom to her breast and smiled at Yu Xuan. He said, "The day before yesterday, I saw some beautiful blue vases and thought they would fit well in your room, so I bought them, but today I forget to bring them with me. In the afternoon, I'll have someone send them."

She smiled and nodded. They held hands and looked at the beautiful scenery. But the beautiful winter day was ruined by two visitors.

The servant let Grandma and Uncle in. Huang Zixia handed her plum blossoms to Yu Xuan, then ran to hug Grandma. Her grandmother had always cared for her and spoiled her, so she loved her very much. Yu Xuan didn't want to be a bother, so he said goodbye. Grandma smiled at him, but after he left, Huang Zixia heard her sigh.

She held her grandmother's hand and was guided into Huang Zixia's mother's room. Her mother laughed and said, "Your grandmother and uncle came to discuss your marriage."

Marriage. Huang Zixia let go of her grandmother's hand and sat silently. Grandma patted her knee and smiled. "The Wang family is an aristocratic family. Wang Yun is their only child, and your father has met him. He believes Wang Yun is a handsome man with a strong character. It will certainly be a successful marriage for you."

Mother looked sadly at Huang Zixia and whispered to Grandma, "Ma, you don't understand; this girl thinks she is in love with someone else. Whenever I mention the Wang family, she gets upset."

"She's still a shy girl," Grandma said with a laugh.

Huang Zixia sighed and was about to make an excuse when the ladies came and told them it was time for dinner. Everyone got up to go to the next room to eat. Her uncle Huang Jun laughed and said, "Zixia, soon you'll be a family's daughter-in-law, and you won't be able to start dinner so late. You'll have to get the rice ready for your mother-in-law."

Father laughed. "The Wangs are an illustrious family. How could they make their daughter-in-law do housework? When Zixia's married in the spring, she'll feel right at home."

Huang Zixia was stunned. She put down her bowl. "Spring?"

"Yes, Grandma and Uncle came to discuss marrying you off next spring. It so happens the Wangs were thinking the same thing," Father said.

"So you've got it all decided, is that it?" Huang Zixia was trembling with anger. She stood. "Dad, Mom, I asked you a long time ago to withdraw the proposal from the Wang family, but you are still forcing me to marry him!"

"Please, child, don't be foolish." Huang Jun had already negotiated with the Wangs. Seeing her this way, his face dropped. He put down his chopsticks and said, "The Wangs of Langya are an old, illustrious family. The last two Empresses came from this family. You think we can just withdraw the proposal? Marrying into the Wang family would be a blessing from the ancestors. You should be preparing the dowry!"

Father was angry too. "Zixia, this wedding, your grandfather arranged this marriage for you with Wang Yun when he was prime minister. Our family has been on a long decline. The Wangs have never wronged us, and it seems they really like you. Marrying Wang Jun would be a good thing. I've met him. He's a good-looking guy."

"But I like someone else; I don't like him!"

Her older brother, Huang Yan, who had been eating, finally looked up and said, "Okay, you don't think much of the royal family. Once you kill us all, you can withdraw the engagement."

Huang Zixia felt her forehead burn. She slammed her bowl on the table. Her hands were shaking as she dropped her chopsticks, and the bowl fell and rolled off the table, shattering with a crash.

The soup splashed on Grandma's dress. Grandma stood up and told her to clean it. "Your temper's getting worse, child. Tell me, how could you break a bowl?"

She felt tears in her eyes. She covered her face, turned away, and went into the other room to cry. She didn't know how long she had been crying when she felt hands softly patting her shoulder. Her mother said, "Zixia, don't be sad. Your dad and I are discussing the matter. If you object this much, we have no choice. Even if we have to offend the Wang family, we can't make you suffer."

She looked at her mother and smiled tearfully and helplessly.

"Go apologize to your grandma and uncle. Is there anything a family can't sort out?"

"But I . . . I'll go . . . so embarrassing," she said, sobbing.

"Go to the kitchen and bring more soup. It's your grandma's favorite. Go. Bring everyone a bowl and apologize. Family will help you find a way."

She nodded and wiped her tears on her way to the kitchen. Then she brought a bowl of sheep's-hoof soup to the table and served everyone. The soup had a fishy smell she didn't like, so she just drank half a bowl of almond milk.

That was the night her whole family was poisoned to death. Poisoned by arsenic in the soup she brought and served to each of them.

Night had fallen. Changan's lanterns were beginning to light.

Li Shubai listened quietly. When she was finished, he said, "This means you didn't poison your family. Is there someone else who had access to that bowl of sheep's-hoof soup?"

"No," Huang Zixia said softly yet clearly. "The sheep was sent by Councillor Cang Cao the day before. That afternoon, since my grandma and uncle were coming, they slaughtered the sheep and made mutton stew, mutton soup, and sheep's-hoof soup."

And there was no problem with the rest of the meal. Even the left-over hoof soup. The servants ate the rest and were fine. Only the bowl Huang Zixia personally served had some poison left. When the maids came later, they were lazy and locked it in the cupboard. The next morning, after the tragedy was discovered, the authorities watched the head maid, Ms. Lu, open the cupboard and take out the bowl. They tested it and found arsenic.

"Did someone put poison in the bowl?"

"No, I was worried my hands weren't clean, so I washed the bowl before I served the soup. And also, there's something else . . . ," Huang Zixia said with difficulty. "They found an empty bag of arsenic in my room."

"Did you buy arsenic?"

"Yes, I bought it from the famous Guiren Temple. Officers checked the sale records and found a clear signature of mine."

"Why did you buy arsenic?" Li Shubai asked.

"I . . ." She hesitated. "Because Yu Xuan and I read a folk recipe in *Holistic Health Daily* that said hemlock juice could be made with half arsenic. I didn't believe it, so we decided to test it ourselves. Made a bet on if it would work. Since I helped the government with a lot of poisoning cases, I tasked myself with buying the poison, while Yu Xuan went to the mountains to collect hemlock, and prepared to take it next door to some vicious dogs to try."

"You two often bet like that?"

"More than once or twice."

"Did you explain it?"

"Yu Xuan vouched for me, but it was dismissed."

Li Shubai raised his eyebrows slightly. "And where was Yu Xuan?"

Huang Zixia was silent for a long time before she slowly said, "He didn't have the chance to do it. When he left my house that day, he went to campus to talk with friends. He went home at night and didn't go out again until he heard about my parents' deaths."

"So you clearly committed the murder," Li Shubai said casually.

"Right, the only opportunity for poisoning the soup was while I was carrying it from the kitchen. And I bought arsenic and have a so-called motive."

Li Shubai nodded. "So the only person who could have killed your parents is you. This case won't be easy to overturn."

As she sat across from him, she looked at the intricate brocade. Gold lines outlined a qilin, the auspicious, mythical chimera, and colorful clouds. There was the wakeful smell of styrax balsam. Reliving her trauma amid the soft fragrance made her feel cold and short of breath.

Her lips were like withered white flowers in the wind. Even the crimson yarn of her uniform couldn't warm her. She looked at him, her voice slightly hoarse. "My Prince, are you like them? Do you think someone in this world could kill their family—for that reason?"

Li Shubai looked at her awhile, then looked back out the window. "Who knows? The human heart is unpredictable, especially in young women like you."

"If the Prince will really help me like he said, I believe the sun will come out from behind the clouds and my parents' enemy will be revealed."

"After summer, I'll go to Shu. I'll take you to look at your parents' files. I believe someone as good at solving mysteries as you, who earned the admiration of law enforcement, will have no problem clearing your name."

She bit her lower lip. "You really believe me and will help me?" Her pale face and clear eyes were striking, more than the sun itself. Such a girl, saddled with the most awful accusations, didn't hesitate to take the hard road. The one that would toughen her up and require persistence.

Li Shubai's long-steady heart was suddenly moved, like the first ripples on a lake in a spring breeze.

But it was only for a moment. He turned and looked outside the carriage again. He suppressed the feeling in his voice and it came out low and a little quiet. "Yes, I believe you and will help you. And in return, you have to give me your future."

Huang Zixia looked up at him and examined his face. In the sunset, his profile was like the beautiful contour of a river along a mountain range, one that after a thousand years of frost stood firm against erosion.

"From now on, as long as you're by my side, you don't have to be afraid."

Now things had changed. Her life had crumbled. Fortunately, her determination had finally brought her an opportunity in the form of Li Shubai.

The carriage stopped. They were already at Kui Palace. Li Shubai opened the door and got out. He turned and saw her coming down as if in a trance. He lifted his hand to help her.

The sun was a gold sliver over the western mountains. She put her hand in his and saw his face and hands in that light shine with vigor.

Four

EXQUISITE GLASS

It was in the season when the world melts that the twelve-year-old Huang Zixia heard her father call her. She turned, and the sun shining directly in her eyes made the world red.

In the strange light, she saw the boy standing next to her father in baggy, old clothes that made him look dim but couldn't cover his pale skin and dark hair. He looked at her with eyes as dark as the quietest night. They seemed gloomy and relaxed, but they cut her heart like a knife, leaving a permanent mark.

She stood barefoot in the pond, her armful of lotus flowers falling in the water.

She saw a touch of amusement in the boy's eyes as he slowly came and helped her pick up the flowers one by one. He must have seen the splash of mud on her legs and the grass stuck to the bottom of her gauze dress, but he just smiled and handed her the flowers.

He looked at her with a gentleness unlike any boy before.

Sometimes it just takes a look for a girl to grow up.

"Yu Xuan . . ."

Huang Zixia sat up in bed and reached out, trying to grasp the remnants of the scene in front of her, but it was only the exquisite glass of a dream.

The whistling wind in the dark, spring night outside the window chilled her to her bones. Huang Zixia clutched the brocade quilt and quietly watched the dream slip through her fingertips. She forced herself to slow her breathing and lie down deep in the silk. After breaking the Four Directions Case, she became a celebrity in the capital, so Kui Palace was quite good to its little eunuch. All her daily costs were covered, even better than when she was the daughter of a prominent family in Shu.

But as she lay in the soft, warm bedding, she felt it was harder to sleep than when she was trekking through the wilderness and weather.

She opened her eyes and listened to the wind blowing in the darkness outside. Sometime later, she pulled off the blanket, got up, put on clothes, and went out.

Enveloped in shadow, she walked through Kui Palace courtyard. The guards on patrol ignored her. Though she was a new arrival, she was already well known and could come and go freely.

She walked to Jingyu Hall and saw moonlight flow over the flowers and trees. It was quiet. It being late, Li Shubai was naturally still asleep.

The dream had given her a sense of urgency, and she wondered how she could wake up Prince Li Shubai. She found a rock by the plants and sat down. She put her face on her bent knees, planning to sit awhile and go back to wait for his call.

Later, the moonlight dimmed, and a faint ink-blue appeared on the horizon. The spring dew was thick and penetrated her clothing. She stared at the grass buds on the ground as if in a stupor; then a pair of black boots stepped on them.

She raised her gaze and saw the dark-blue embroidered dragon on the purple robe, which was tailored to make him look tall. On his waist was the purple jade of the celestial castle, the blue silk sash tied in a knot. His cuffs were trim, his collar square in the capital fashion.

As the Prince of Kui, Li Shubai's cap blew in the wind, she thought about his role as a fashion trendsetter. From his appearance, he was a sheltered royal who liked to indulge in such sensual pleasures.

Huang Zixia rested her head on her knees and gazed at him.

Li Shubai stood and looked down on her. Since she didn't say anything, he turned and looked at the lanterns in the trees. "What flowers did the little eunuch come to admire in this windy starlight?"

She answered quietly. "Last night I had a dream. I want to ask about the thing you want me to help you with. Can I complete it as quickly as possible and return to Shu?"

Li Shubai glanced at her but didn't speak. Then he walked past her to the cloister.

Huang Zixia followed him. He sat down, and she waited for him to speak.

The lanterns painted with Mount Penglai hanging on the portico flickered and rotated in the night breeze. Li Shubai's face seemed to dissolve into the night.

Li Shubai looked at the lanterns hanging from the upturned cornices awhile. Huang Zixia felt uneasy as she waited. She turned and gazed at one, an ordinary octagonal construction carved with openings the shape of clouds over which was stretched white silk painted with the nine pavilions where the immortals come and go.

She couldn't figure out what was special about it. When she turned, she saw Li Shubai was looking at her. In the subtle light, his eyes were as dark as the sky.

She touched her face, but before she could ask a question, Li Shubai spoke slowly. "It's quite the coincidence. I just had a dream too. In the dream, I stood atop Xuzhou overlooking thousands of houses. When I woke up, I couldn't fall asleep again."

Huang Zixia leaned on the railing next to the water and looked at him. She saw his gaze was as bright as the moon and stars and as trancelike as the waves.

"For years, I've had something that's difficult to explain. I've been in a sort of pickle and looking for someone to help me out." He looked at the misty mountains on the lamp. "Do you know why I only gave you ten days?"

Huang Zixia shook her head and looked at him in the lamplight with question in her gaze.

"Because, like you heard at the feast, in ten days I had to choose my Princess. And I was hoping you could help me with it." He took a deep breath and leaned back against the railing. "That year in Xuzhou, I heard a proverb that made me concerned."

Xuzhou. Huang Zixia suddenly remembered hearing about an event there.

"My fate turned at Xuzhou. Everyone says it's my paradise. But no one knows that after I pacified Xuzhou, the night before I went to the capital, I looked down over the city and saw something that left a deep impression on me."

Now he finally looked at her and took a piece of paper from his sleeve.

The paper was thick and yellowed, about eight inches long and two inches wide. It had a strange vermilion snake pattern. Written in bold lettering were the words *widowed, lonely, diseased*. The *widowed* and *lonely* had two gripping, blood-red circles over them.

Li Shubai's fingers ran along the paper's pattern. "This worm-snake pattern spells out the eight characters of my birth date."

Huang Zixia felt a sense of dread as she looked at the three words written over his birthday and the two blood-red circles.

Li Shubai pressed the paper with his hand. "On the night this paper appeared, I was standing on top of the Xuzhou wall, looking down on the city. It appeared on the pile of arrows next to me. When I picked it up, there were only the three words, not the two red circles. Only *lonely* had the faint outline of a circle around it."

Huang Zixia looked at the red circle, pondering.

His fingertip was on *lonely* as if he were touching his own life. "I was lonely after losing my father at a young age. At that time, my mother was still around, so it wasn't so bad. I felt this paper was an ordinary curse. I was going to look around and see who dared to bring it to me. Who knew . . ." He looked toward the lanterns. They flickered in the darkness and made everything blurry for a moment.

"That night I had many nightmares—all about *widowed*, *lonely*, and *diseased*. When I woke up, I wanted to burn the cursed thing, but when I looked at it, I found that *lonely*, which before only had the faintest red circle around it, had a much darker one like it does now." Under the stars, his fingertip touched the word. The red circle was like a strange red flower blooming, or a wound opening—terrible. "That same day, that same time, an urgent message came from the capital eight hundred miles away. When I opened it, I discovered that my mother had died."

On the day the circle around *lonely* turned red, he became an orphan.

She felt compelled to comfort him. "Maybe it's just a coincidence; the Prince shouldn't think so much of it."

He looked at her, not disagreeing or agreeing. He took a long breath.

"When I got the news of my mother's death and began traveling from Xuzhou back to the capital, there was an assassination attempt on me. I was stabbed in the left arm, and though the wound was not deep, the weapon was poisoned. The military doctor with me said my arm was lost. If I wanted to live, they would have to amputate it." He gently stroked his left arm as if the pain still lingered. "At that time, I took that paper out, and the red circle got darker around *diseased*."

The wind suddenly began to blow in the silent night and turn the lanterns on their axes. The light around them flickered, and the corner of the cursed paper lifted. It seemed as though the paper wasn't shifting, but fate was.

Li Shubai looked at her, his expression so calm as to be almost stony. "Do you know what I did then?"

Huang Zixia stretched her hand out to hold the paper down. "I guess the Prince arrested the military doctor for treason."

Li Shubai relaxed and even smiled a little. His cold face now seemed soft and bright as a spring breeze. "Huang Zixia, you're just like me, untrusting."

"I was in Shu for several years and worked on twenty-six murder cases. Eight of them were rumored to be done by spirits, but in the end were just people imitating them. This recent Four Directions Case could be one too." Huang Zixia pointed at the paper. "For example, what the Prince has said so far is enough to reveal people's intentions."

Li Shubai looked at her cheerfully. "Why don't you tell me?"

She touched her temple, about to loosen the hairpin, but then stopped, remembering what happened last time. On the railing, she drew the number one with her finger. "First, this paper could only have appeared if someone close to you put it where you would be expected to go—the tower at Xuzhou."

She then drew the number two. "Second, the red circle changed, so the person not only went up the tower with you but also stayed near you. It must have been someone close to you, like one of your guards."

"Third, the medical diagnosis and treatment coincide with its appearance, which means there wasn't just one person behind it. There were at least two, the military doctor and a bodyguard." Saying this, she took her hand back and blew on her fingertips. "Pursue the military doctor and you'll find the other traitor."

Li Shubai shook his head. "The military doctor killed himself at the first opportunity, and I gradually sent away all the guards I'd trained for years and never called them back."

Huang Zixia looked at the paper. "But there . . ."

The circle around *diseased* had faded and was only faint again.

"My arm survived after six months of treatment, and the circle around *diseased* has gradually been disappearing. But my left arm is weak. I can do daily stuff like write and draw, but can no longer use a sword or bow." He pulled his left hand out and moved the fingers in front of her eyes. "I used to be left-handed."

She thought of how he skillfully got down from the carriage and felt a sense of admiration. She certainly couldn't start over and make her nondominant hand dominant after hardly using it for twenty years.

"Originally, I thought that after I dismissed those people, the thing was over, so I put this paper in a secret place, still hoping to make the circle fade. But when the Emperor mentioned my marriage a few days ago, I thought of its *widowed* and took it out to have a look. I saw there was now a red circle around *widowed*." He took the paper out and put his finger on it with a mocking smile. "It seems me getting married may have unanticipated results."

Huang Zixia took the paper from him and looked at it carefully. The scarlet circle around *widowed* looked newer than the one around *lonely*. The scarlet seemed fiercer.

"Incredible. It seems like some spirit mischief, determined by fate. Three or four years later, another red circle flourishes on the paper," Li Shubai said slowly. "I've changed the people around me several times, and I've hidden this paper as carefully as our military plans. I can't believe something like this, which no one could have had contact with, would send another omen."

Huang Zixia put it down. "It seems this paper might be more complicated than we thought."

"Yes," he agreed. He paused, then said, "I think someone will try to disrupt my marriage." He looked at her, a faint smile on his face. "I just remembered you are Wang Yun's betrothed. You'd poison your whole family to avoid it, which is the biggest disgrace imaginable for him."

"I didn't kill my family," she said, clenching her teeth. "If you want to help me, don't say that again."

He looked at her curiously. "Just relaying common sense. Wouldn't it be foolish of me to collaborate with a murderess?"

She bit her lip, then whispered, "Do you really believe I didn't kill my family?"

He didn't answer as he began to walk along the winding bridge.

They walked along the dimly lit path toward the pavilion. The horizon was turning blue as dawn came in earnest.

"Yes, because I read your palm. It didn't look like you killed anyone," he finally said.

"The last time you looked at my hand, you said it was obvious I'd poisoned my family, which was how you knew who I was!"

"I lied."

"Then how did you know who I was last time?"

"Don't worry about that," he said definitively. "You just need to help me unravel the mystery behind this paper."

"So you can't just read everyone's palm and figure it all out?" she pressed.

"Nah," he said without looking at her, "I prefer watching you playing a eunuch."

◆ ◆ ◆

So the Prince of Kui's eunuch Huang Zixia, or, rather, Yang Chonggu, followed His Highness to Penglai Palace to attend the selection of his Princess.

Though it was already the fourth month, the royal garden blooming with peaches and plums couldn't dispel the cold.

"The ladies have likely all arrived; why doesn't the Prince go inside to see what they're saying?" Huang Zixia asked.

Li Shubai glanced at her. "What's the rush?"

Huang Zixia had to suppress her eagerness to see the capital beauties and wait for him to speak.

He asked, "Is the gift suitable?"

"Yes." She opened the box and looked inside. The whole palace was wondering what jade or treasure the Prince would give his Princess, but none knew that Huang Zixia held it. It was a lucky and rare peony.

Huang Zixia gazed at the incomparable crimson flower. "This morning, I followed the Prince's instructions and cut it down as soon as it bloomed. Gardener Liu didn't know about it and yelled at me! He said it took two months of tunneling and charcoal burning to get it to bloom like that. With this flower cut, there won't be any others like it this year."

"I'll console him a bit later," Li Shubai said indifferently.

"The peony is a really elegant choice for a gift," Huang Zixia said, closing the box.

Li Shubai's expression was blank; he seemed to take no pleasure in pleasing the Princess. Huang Zixia thought that good flowers don't bloom often, and when they do, they wither quickly. Being a smart person, how could he not have thought of that?

She held the peony in her arms, thinking about that cursed paper she learned about a few days ago, unable to feel deep sympathy for whomever was to be Li Shubai's wife.

Soon the Empress's attendant came to say that everyone had arrived and the Prince should come at his leisure.

Li Shubai signaled for Huang Zixia to follow him into the hall.

Traditionally, Princes chose their Princesses from among ministers' daughters or aristocratic women. They naturally didn't line up for the picking. Even though everyone knew what was happening, they just had them eat at a banquet, with the Prince looking on from behind a screen. If he found one suitable, she would be asked to come to him and receive the gift, be asked her name but nothing else, because it was all set ahead of time.

Huang Zixia went into the hall's side entrance with Li Shubai. She saw an elaborately embroidered silk screen separating the front and back. She could clearly see everyone in the front of the hall, but they could likely make out only a vague outline of her.

They probably felt him standing there watching, because the ladies' movements were all a little unnatural. Only one, to the Empress's right, seemed at ease. Huang Zixia looked at the Empress. She had a beautiful face and wore red clothing decorated with clouds. Her eyes were smart and clear, as if glowing with an inner radiance.

She was the second royal Empress from the Langya Wang family. When her older sister died, she entered Yun Palace and became the Prince of Yun's wife. After he ascended the throne, she was named Empress. She was about twenty-seven or twenty-eight but looked like she was only in her early twenties.

The crowd of women in their silk outfits arranged like flowers around the table couldn't detract from her beauty at all. Huang Zixia admired her, thinking that when she entered the palace and saw the Empress three years ago, she didn't understand what it meant for someone to be beautiful enough to topple cities. Now, a little older, she understood how beautiful someone could be.

The girl next to the Empress must have been her younger cousin, another girl from the Langya Wang family named Wang Ruo. Huang Zixia could see that, though they were related, they didn't look alike at all. In fact, their names suited them. The Empress's given name was Shao, a kind of peony, and she looked incredibly beautiful in her red clothing. Wang Ruo, who was wearing a purple jacket, was more charming and delicate like a peach or a plum. Though she couldn't match the queen, she had a naive charm.

Though the other women weren't bad, they were eclipsed by those two. Huang Zixia focused on a girl wearing a wide, light-pink skirt. Her cheeks were plump, and she had beautiful, almond-shaped eyes, but her chin was always slightly raised, which made her seem a little arrogant. Huang Zixia thought it must be Princess Qi Le, who everyone in the capital knew wanted to marry Li Shubai more than anything.

Princess Qi Le was from Shu. She had little royal blood, but her father's success at court granted him the title Prince of Yi. This made her a Princess. Lady Zhao was then in charge of palace affairs, and it was said that Princess Qi Le bribed palace officials to let her copy scripture for her in order to try to get a good word put in on her behalf to be chosen as Li Shubai's wife. Unfortunately, it didn't work, and she became the butt of jokes.

Li Shubai waved the attendant Zhang Ling over and, pointing at Wang Ruo, said, "Her."

Huang Zixia was surprised. How could he choose his wife at a glance?

But she could only ask, "The Prince wouldn't like to think a little longer?"

"What consideration would go into choosing to spend your life with someone from a group of people you don't know?"

"But the woman the Prince chooses must have unique characteristics."

He looked at her sideways, his lips curving slightly into a smile, but there was no joy in his eyes. "Yes," he said, "out of all the candidates, she's the most beautiful."

Huang Zixia was stunned at his brazenness. After a while she said, "Perhaps the Prince should be a little cautious?"

"This is the most cautious choice. Their moral character and family backgrounds have already gone through the selection process. All I have to do is choose the one most pleasing to the eye, don't you think?"

All she could say was, "Congratulations on finding your sweetheart."

He reached toward her face.

She didn't know what he wanted. Then she turned and saw Wang Ruo coming with the attendant.

From the front of the hall came a burst of noise. Princess Qi Le realized that Li Shubai had chosen someone else, and she spilled her soup on the woman next to her.

Qi Le quickly used her veil to wipe it off. "Goodness, how careless . . ." Before she could finish her sentence, her eyes welled up. She bit her lip and turned to the maid behind her and pretended to rinse her mouth in a bowl as she cried.

Huang Zixia had no time to pay attention to her. She hurried and opened the box and put the flower in Li Shubai's hand.

Wang Ruo lowered her head with slightly flushed cheeks as she walked up to Li Shubai.

She couldn't have been more than sixteen or seventeen years old, slender, and more than half a head taller than the other women. Her dress was embroidered with plump begonias and an intricate gold silk pattern. She had six hairpins in her hair and a wonderful jade-pearl necklace that rocked as she walked. In contrast with this magnificent outfit, she seemed innocent and cautious. She kept her head bowed as she walked, too shy to look directly at people.

Li Shubai waited until she was before him and handed her the flower before speaking gently, "You're Wang Ruo?"

She started as if struck by lightning.

She made a fist, then looked excitedly at Li Shubai. Her eyes suddenly became moist, and she seemed to fall into a trance, as if remembering a distant memory. She trembled and clutched her collar, unable to speak.

Huang Zixia watched her.

Li Shubai noticed Wang Ruo's strange response too but didn't say anything.

Wang Ruo finally calmed herself and lifted her hands to her lips. "The Prince of Kui . . . it's really . . . really you," she said.

Li Shubai raised his eyebrows slightly but didn't speak.

"I . . . I never thought I would be so lucky, so, so, I'm acting foolish. Please forgive me." She was helpless. He didn't respond, and she was on the brink of tears.

Li Shubai's expression became gentler. He gave her the peony and said, "You must be used to being at home, not in a setting like this. I startled you."

Wang Ruo nodded tearfully and smiled with a deep curtsy in thanks for the gift. Then she reached out and took the flower tightly into her arms, her face as flush as the begonias on her blouse.

Only Huang Zixia saw the tear fall on the peony flower, gently shaking its petal in a splash before it disappeared into a fine mist.

"What do you think of that Wang Ruo?" Li Shubai asked Huang Zixia on the carriage ride home.

Huang Zixia hesitated and said, "I'm just a palace eunuch; I wouldn't dare comment on the Princess-to-be."

Li Shubai ignored her and picked up the glass bottle, gazing at the red fish swimming inside.

"There seems to be a problem," Huang Zixia finally said.

"Seems?" he said flatly as he flicked the bottle. "Before she saw me, she was calm and serene because she didn't care if I chose her or not."

"But when the attendant brought her to you and she saw your face, her look completely changed. Her shock and joy were too strong, almost suspicious. Like she was experiencing déjà vu."

"Yes," Li Shubai said with a nod, his eyes going from the fish to her. "And, when it was time to leave the hall, we exchanged notes. I found something interesting on hers."

He opened a drawer and took out a small red note and put it on the table, then pushed it toward Huang Zixia.

She picked it up and looked at the writing on it.

The Langya Wang Family's fourth daughter, Wang Ruo, born in the second hour of the thirtieth day of the tenth month during the sixth leap year of our Emperor's reign.

She looked, counted to herself, and gave the red paper back to him. "This note is false."

He nodded slightly. "You can tell too?"

"Yes, the tenth month of the sixth year didn't have a thirtieth, only a twenty-ninth."

"Right." Li Shubai finally gave a slight smile. "Do you have the calendar of every year memorized like me?"

"I certainly don't have as good a memory as the Prince, but I have the ability to count leap years. It's a crude attempt at deception." She looked at the note again. "And the 'leap year' was obviously added later. Usually there's more space between the words on this kind of note. I don't get it."

"Must be because the thirtieth of the tenth month is the anniversary of my mother's death," he said.

She nodded. "So to avoid this, they modified it a bit and tried to get away with it."

"That could be, but there's more." He put a finger on the note. "Their birthdays had to be given to the lady ahead of time so they can make projections. If they saw the thirtieth, they certainly would have noted it was the anniversary of my mother's death, and she wouldn't have been chosen. If someone helped her forge this, it wouldn't have been done so hastily and look this bad. If the lady saw this date, she'd know it didn't exist, and this paper would have never reached me."

"So this Wang Ruo may not have been an original candidate who went through the process before you saw her," Huang Zixia guessed. "Maybe it's because she's the Empress's cousin, and she made a special request to get her through."

"Maybe. But I don't have any worries about Wang Ruo herself; she's just a pawn. What I am worried about is who sent her to me and what they're hiding." He thought it over. "Maybe there's some correlation with that cursed paper."

Huang Zixia nodded and thought of the shocked look on Wang Ruo's face when she saw Li Shubai. As a woman, she felt that emotion was not one a pawn would have. But the specifics were still lost on her.

"It seems picking my Princess has caused you to confront a situation much more complex than we thought."

"The more complex the core of the matter is, the harder it is to keep clues from leaking out, so complexity isn't bad."

Li Shubai examined her. Her face wasn't hesitant but quiet, calm, and confident. He felt something stir in his heart, which made him turn away from her to the world outside the carriage window.

The process of selecting his wife was over. The ladies were all on their way home in carriages from Daming Palace to Changan City. The weeds from last year still lined the road. This year's grass was still only two or three inches long, yellow with patches of green. When the wind blew, the yellow and green shifted slowly. Behind them was the Langya Wangs' family carriage; an old servant unhurriedly drove two robust, mottled horses.

Li Shubai closed the curtain and said, "The Wang family carriage is right behind us."

Huang Zixia thought it over, then stood and opened the door. "When we get to the next intersection, I'll get out."

"What's the rush? There's no time limit for figuring this out."

"Of course I'm in a rush; the sooner I can get back to Shu, the better." The carriage soon reached the intersection. She jumped out.

Li Shubai watched her stumble to a halt, then looked down at the little red fish in his hands.

◆　◆　◆

Huang Zixia watched the Prince of Kui's carriage until it reached Yongjia Square, then turned and walked toward Anxing Square. The Wangs' carriage slowed and stopped by her side. A middle-aged woman looked out the window and said, "Aren't you the Prince of Kui's eunuch? Where are you going?"

Huang Zixia smiled. "Thank you for your concern, ma'am. I'm going to the West City to buy some things."

The woman smiled. "We're going to Guangde Square, right in the West City. If my little man doesn't mind, we can take you that way. What do you think?"

"I don't think so; how could I ride with a lady?"

"Come on; we'll be family soon. You're one of the Prince's people. We'll see each other a lot." The woman smiled, causing her eyebrows to rise in a friendly manner. She opened the door to ask Huang Zixia inside.

Once Huang Zixia got in the carriage, she saw Wang Ruo was there too. She thanked the woman, who looked over forty but had a tactful charm, which her wrinkles only added to. When she was young, she must have been a beauty. Huang Zixia sat by the door with her head bowed, glancing at Wang Ruo. Ruo's posture was wonderful, her hands gently folded on her left leg. The wide sleeves of her lotus-colored silk blouse revealed two soft, pale, slender hands with perfectly shaped pink nails. Huang Zixia looked at those hands and remembered her life in Shu, where even though her family was prominent, she still went riding with her brother and Yu Xuan. She even loved polo and soccer more than the men did. How could she have kept her hands like that?

The voice of the woman brought her back to reality. "Has the eunuch always been at the Prince's side?"

"Just a few days. Before it was another eunuch, but unfortunately, several of them got sick, so I've been transferred temporarily."

"That means you're a good worker and earned the Prince's trust," she said. "You must have an intimate understanding of his daily life, no?"

"Daily, not so much," she said honestly. "I'm clumsy, not really a servant. I just go out with him sometimes."

"Well, you're around him a lot, so you must know," she said, still smiling. "Tell me, what color does he like? What food? What kind of personality would he like in a lady?"

Huang Zixia realized she had gotten herself into a difficult situation. "The Prince of Kui doesn't really like people waiting on him all the time. He's alone a lot. As for the ladies, I don't know."

He's very serious, cold, and difficult, she wanted to add.

"Aunt," Wang Ruo said.

Huang Zixia saw her head was buried in her clothes, her cheeks as red as if she'd been drinking, which was somehow moving.

"Come on, you already have the gift, it's only right to get to know the Prince." She hugged Wang Ruo and laughed.

Huang Zixia felt relived. "Don't worry, the Prince of Kui is easy to get along with. And my lady is from the Wangs of Langya family, and so beautiful. The Prince chose you from among so many and will love you more than treasure, always."

Wang Ruo looked at her and softly said, "Thank you, little man. I hope you're right." She smiled slightly, but her face also took on a layer of fear. "I saw him and had no idea what to do. I could barely walk. You saw. I'm afraid he'll look down on me, and I'm getting anxious that he isn't satisfied. But I don't know what to do. It makes me sweat, and . . . and . . ."

Huang Zixia listened to her grow incoherent and hurried to comfort her. "Don't worry; the Prince doesn't mind. He understands you."

The woman agreed. "Marrying the Prince of Kui is the dream of so many girls. My girl has admired him since she was a child. I'm sure our little eunuch understands her concern."

Huang Zixia nodded. "Yes, naturally."

Wang Ruo took a deep breath. "Thank you so much."

After that, she didn't say another word.

The carriage neared Guangde Square. Huang Zixia thanked them again and got out.

The West City was nearby. She felt like going right back to the palace would be wrong, so she walked to a corner noodle soup shop. The shop was very narrow. The table right up against hers had a mother and a seven- or eight-year-old daughter, who sat on a stool so high her feet didn't reach the ground. The mother used chopsticks to chop the noodles into smaller bites for her daughter.

Huang Zixia watched in a trance. The woman noticed and smiled bashfully. "Noodles are too long for this little one."

"Yes, true," Huang Zixia said, her eyes growing hot. She thought of when she was ten or so and her mother did the same for her. Her father shook his head. "She's old enough; don't spoil her."

Her brother laughed at her as he slurped his own. "Shame, so old but still needs Mother's help. When you get married, your husband will have to take Mother's place."

At the time, she was so angry, she had put her chopsticks down and gone back to her room, refusing to eat. After a while her mother went over and coaxed her into having more. She had a few bites and saw her father looking at her from outside the window. He pretended just to be passing by.

It was such a simple thing at the time, but thinking of it now brought it back so vividly. She even saw the pattern of the gravel under her father's feet, the shadows the tree branches cast on her mother's hands, all clearly. The memory filled her with sorrow and resentment. She bit her lips and trembled as she held her breath to force the grief and tears back.

Father, Mother, Brother . . .

She took some mouthfuls of her soup and swallowed tears with each one. All her grief and agony from the false accusations and loss of her family would one day be redeemed by the truth, and she would return to Shu.

Five

Velvet Gold Mine

Wang Ruo of the Langya Wang family would soon become the Prince of Kui's Princess. Huang Zixia, in her disguise as the eunuch Yang Chonggu, followed the procession through half of Changan and listened as the news quickly spread throughout the capital. People said how truly glorious the Wang family was. After all, in recent years, they'd had two Empresses and a Princess.

Huang Zixia touched her face. Before she went out today, she thought her complexion looked good, well rested. She went to the ladies' quarters and put a little yellow powder on her face so she wouldn't look so radiant at the Wangs' residence. There was also a good chance she would meet Wang Yun, her former fiancé, who wasn't even officially former. Even though she had never formally met Wang Yun, according to what Li Run had said, he'd stolen a look at her just three years ago, so she had to be careful. She decided to use the yellow powder every time she went out from now on.

Of the six marriage ceremonies, the reception at the estate, the asking of the bride's name, and gift exchange were all done. Now Huang Zixia accompanied the sending of the dowry.

The Langya Wangs were one of the top aristocratic families in the capital, so their residence was beautiful. Seven courtyards, two gardens, high walls—a wonderful atmosphere.

Their only eligible son, Wang Yun certainly had the look of a rich family's child. Even though everyone thought Huang Zixia killed her whole family to avoid marrying him, she thought he was still graceful in a crimson robe. He had a smile like spring dawn and a gentle demeanor. Only an old family could raise someone of such a temperament.

When one of the most illustrious noblemen marries a wife from an old, aristocratic family, one expects a grand wedding. The row of chests filled with gifts of gold, jade, and silver the ladies brought attracted everyone's attention. Wang Yun accompanied Wang Ruo to the courtyard where she lived and sent someone to distribute the red seals. He managed the festivities quite efficiently.

Huang Zixia and the female palace attendant Su Qi went over to Wang Yun and saluted him. "We were ordered to teach the Princess the palace rules and court manners."

Wang Yun said, "I appreciate it," and looked at Huang Zixia inquisitively.

Huang Zixia and Su Qi turned to go to the courtyard when Wang Yun said, "Your name, sir?"

She tried to stay composed. "Yang Chonggu."

"The Yang Chonggu who broke the Four Directions Case? Amazing to meet you!" He then asked Su Qi's name and walked them to the courtyard door.

Huang Zixia went under the eaves, feeling something pierce her back. She couldn't help but look over her shoulder. He was standing in the yard entrance, staring at her thoughtfully. When he noticed her looking at him, he smiled, saluted, and said, "We'll be eating the five fortune cakes soon. Please don't be late, little eunuch."

She bowed. "Of course. Today I'm greeting the Princess, and tomorrow I'll start teaching." She hadn't read the etiquette book yet, so she couldn't say how she'd start.

When she entered the corridor, four ladies came and welcomed her. The room was full of harmonious laughter and flowers. Plum branches lined the windows, and begonias filled vases that matched the floral tiara of Wang Ruo, who lounged on a shiny wooden couch. Wang Ruo's clothing was different today. She wore a short, purple jacket with a red peony pattern. It was so lively and cheerful. Her hair was tied in buns, and the exquisite peony Li Shubai gave her was tucked inside, along with two jade hairpins. Her aura was at once solemn and altogether hers.

Seeing the dowry arriving, everyone stood up to meet it. Wang Ruo bowed and listened as Xue Shangshu from the Ministry of Rites read out the letter of appointment. As it dragged on, Huang Zixia grew bored and looked out the window and was surprised to see swallows twittering among the beams. The earth was full of life in the beauty of spring.

Wang Ruo took the letter and smiled faintly at Huang Zixia. "I was born humbly and have never seen the prestige of a royal family. I don't know palace etiquette. I would be so grateful for your instruction."

Su Qi quickly said, "Please, not at all, the Princess is truly ladylike and courteous."

Wang Ruo just looked at her and smiled like an innocent child. The other ladies had been called in to help with the ceremony, of which the Wang family had held several. But Wang Ruo wouldn't have known those ladies, which must have been why she was pleased to see Huang Zixia.

The joy on Wang Ruo's face made Huang Zixia feel a little ashamed. She wondered if such a beautiful, innocent woman could really be hiding a secret, as she suspected. When it was time to leave, Huang Zixia headed for the door, but felt someone tug at her sleeve. Wang Ruo had an uneasy look on her face.

Huang Zixia smiled and saluted her. "How may I serve you, Princess?"

"It's good to see you," she whispered. "I don't know anyone."

"What about the woman I saw in the carriage before? Why isn't she with you today?"

"Oh . . . when I was chosen to be Princess, Auntie rushed back to Langya to get my daily things." She seemed slightly uncomfortable as she considered adding more. "She's getting on in years, so she might not come back. She might stay and just enjoy home."

"Won't the Princess miss her? It is the aunt who helped raise you, after all."

"Yes, but there's nothing I can do; I have to adapt. I'm okay. She's getting old." She smiled reluctantly, revealing a pair of little dimples. "And at least I know you. This morning, I was afraid the person who'd teach me would be a serious, old-fashioned eunuch. I was surprised it was you."

Huang Zixia smiled. "That's very kind of you. I was lucky to get a ride in your carriage."

Su Qi called her out, and the two went to the hall for snacks. The Wang family's five fortune cakes were, of course, unlike any found in restaurants and teahouses. They had Fuling, hawthorn, pine nuts, red dates, and sesame and were arranged on a crystal plate. Wang Yun personally came to Huang Zixia and asked, "What flavor does my little man like?"

Huang Zixia looked at him and said nothing. He took a Fuling cake and offered it to her saying, "Our chef makes the best Fuling. They're uncured but still have a wonderful taste. Try it. Of course, you've got to try each of them. It is five fortunes, after all."

Huang Zixia quickly thanked him, took a white Fuling cake, and began to eat it slowly. Wang Yun sat next to her. "Where is the little man from, the capital?"

She nodded. "From the suburbs."

"It seems like you also have a slight Shu accent. Have you lived there too?"

Huang Zixia shook her head. "I haven't. But my mother was from there."

"Oh . . ."

"I was purified when I was young and assigned to Jiucheng Palace. Now I'm in the Prince of Kui's palace. Since I can read a little, the Prince asked me to teach the Princess. It's an incredible honor."

He didn't say anything, but he did seem to be doubtfully examining her face. "I was just curious. Are the Prince's palace rules difficult, little man?"

"Not so much. The Princess is smart. She'll get it in no time."

Li Shubai had twenty or thirty thick books in front of him.

Huang Zixia was stunned. "The palace has this many rules?"

"No," Li Shubai said, opening his mouth slowly.

She was relieved.

"No, this is only a part," Li Shubai said gently. "Only a part of the royal customs."

Huang Zixia almost gagged. "I have to learn all this in a few days and teach the Princess?"

"No, you should have it all memorized by the end of the night."

"Could anyone memorize all this?"

Li Shubai tossed a volume toward her. "Open up to a page."

Huang Zixia picked one and looked at the top. "Number Thirty-Five, New Year, Article Nineteen."

"Number Thirty-Five, New Year, Article Nineteen. On the spring equinox, the kitchen presents spring cakes; wives of officials are awarded ten pieces of silk and five of cotton; ladies, eight silk, three cotton; parents, five silk, three cotton. First-level palace attendants receive twelve pieces of silver; second, five; and third, three. The rest, one," Li Shubai said.

Huang Zixia's mouth twitched. She turned to another. "Number Sixteen, Speaking, Article Four."

"Sixteen, Speaking, Four. The court must appoint an official to teach the Prince from the Four Books, Five Classics, music, and etiquette until he is twenty, after which he can choose his own material and receive lessons every ten days."

No wonder he can randomly recite all the biographical information of a bodyguard. Huang Zixia was impressed. She turned to another page. "Twenty-Four, Pavilion Station System, Article Ninety-Three." Li Shubai paused. She looked at him with glee. "Finally stumped?"

"Of course not, Pavilion Station System only has ninety articles. Where'd number ninety-three come from?"

Huang Zixia couldn't help but be in awe. "To be honest, I've never seen anyone with such a memory in my life."

"With some effort, you can remember everything." He put his hand on the pile of books in front of him and smiled almost imperceptibly. "So tomorrow, I'll test you like this. Better put in some effort."

Huang Zixia was speechless as she watched him leave. Then she put her head on the table and let out a cry.

Though memorizing all the rules in one night would be impossible, Huang Zixia tried to muster her spirits and read it through to get a general sense.

The next day, when she went to the palace thinking she was going to get a tough quizzing from Li Shubai, it turned out he'd gotten up early to inspect the capital guard. He left a message saying that if Yang Chonggu hadn't memorized the rules, he could take the book to the Princess and begin her teaching.

She felt relieved but also annoyed. Did he scare her into not sleeping the night before just for fun?

Wang Ruo was wearing a light-blue dress with brilliant flowers blooming around the hem. Her black hair was tied loosely with a couple of flower-shaped stays tucked by her temples. Her playful appearance carried an unspeakable charm. When she saw Huang Zixia arrive, she suddenly smiled, picked up her skirt, and went over to greet her. Her cheer was contagious, and they felt as familiar as old friends.

"This morning Su Qi told me about all the lords and ladies in the palace. There are so many, I can hardly remember! Then she told me I have to study rules with you. This is hard."

Huang Zixia smiled. "Don't worry. The Princess is very smart. Remembering things is always a process."

"When I was little, I studied music and could only learn the simplest song, and everyone learned faster than me. My teacher said I was stupid and put so much pressure on me!" She stopped, looking a little bashful. "Are the palace rules hard to learn?"

"It should be fine; the Princess is from an old, illustrious family, which may have even more rules." Huang Zixia took out the book and, seeing the confused look on Wang Ruo's face, added, "This is only one part. When the Princess is done reading it, I'll bring another."

Huang Zixia spent the whole afternoon eating snacks and guiltily looking over her shoulder while Wang Ruo carefully studied the palace rules.

If she didn't know them as well as the Princess, it would be embarrassing, but she wasn't as nervous as she had been last night. Soon her thoughts wandered, and she realized Wang Ruo was in a daze too.

Then she closed the book.

"What is the Princess thinking?" Huang Zixia asked.

"I'm thinking . . . about something Su Qi taught me," she said.

Huang Zixia smiled. "What thing would that be?"

"She told me about the *Lessons for Women*. In the devotion section. It says husbands can remarry, but wives absolutely cannot. I know a lot of women who have been dissatisfied with their husbands and gone to the temple for help. It's really contradictory. Women having to be chaste from beginning to end is really important to royalty."

Huang Zixia nodded. "*Lessons for Women* was used to teach literacy in the harem. Why are you thinking about that?"

"I've of course never read it before," Wang Ruo said quickly. "I just thought of something and felt torn."

"What thing? Would the Princess mind telling me?"

"I heard that Empress Wu used to be one of Emperor Tai's ladies, and Emperor Xuanzong's Yang Guifei used to be Princess Shou . . . ," she said.

Huang Zixia didn't expect it to be such an intractable problem that countless historians had been unable to whitewash. What could she say? "This dynasty does have some issues."

"So in the Han Dynasty, Emperor Wu's mother, Wang Zhi, was married and had a daughter outside the palace. Then she abandoned them and got remarried in the palace, claiming it was her first, and finally became the Empress, isn't that right?"

Huang Zixia was caught off guard. "Throughout all of Chinese history, there are some unusual cases, but they're the minority."

Wang Ruo looked down at the book on the table and hesitantly asked, "So what does Chonggu think would happen to an Empress who hid her marital history and got found out back then? What would happen to her?"

Huang Zixia couldn't help but laugh. "Why is the Princess worried about the ancients? The Empress became the Queen Mother and prospered. Her daughter who she abandoned visited her later and called her sister. I think royals have compassion and can work things out reasonably."

"Yes, I think so too." She took the book back.

Huang Zixia repeated the words she just said to herself in her head but was unable to grasp the point. Then she set that aside and looked at Wang Ruo, then the peony on the table.

It was the one Li Shubai gave her, now in a large crystal bowl filled partway with water that kept it alive. Nonetheless, it was showing signs of wear. Its petals were slightly curved and a couple were drifting on the surface.

Wang Ruo saw her looking at the flower and suddenly blushed. She lowered her head deeper into the book, looking shy and uncomfortable.

Her strange behavior made Huang Zixia think she had really fallen for the Prince of Kui. Huang Zixia could sense it was the first time she'd fallen in love and was longing for Li Shubai.

Wang Ruo leaned forward and gently touched the floating peony. "You must think I'm silly, Chonggu," she said softly.

"Why would I think that?" Huang Zixia said, smiling.

She put her hand over her mouth shyly and whispered, "I don't know if you can understand. Before, I used to wonder about my future husband, what my daily life would be like, what kind of person would I be bound to forever, but when I entered the rear of the hall and caught a glimpse of the Prince of Kui, I suddenly understood the life ahead of me, and all my fear of the future vanished. In that moment, I knew he was my soul mate."

Huang Zixia thought about the way Wang Ruo looked when she saw Li Shubai, and how that didn't seem to be the case. Still, she smiled and said, "I could tell."

"Don't tell anyone."

"Okay." Huang Zixia sat beside her, looking at her crimson cheeks and ardent eyes. Her thoughts returned to an early summer evening. Dragonflies flying over the pond, she with an armful of lotus flowers, that boy looking at her from afar.

She began to feel overwhelmed. When she came back to reality, there was a slight pain in her heart. She turned and saw the red light of the sunset and slowly stood. "Your servant must go back. The Princess can keep these books and continue reading."

"Okay." Wang Ruo absentmindedly stroked the peony petals.

Huang Zixia walked to the doorway. Wisteria bloomed in the small courtyard. An enchanting purple wrapped like fog around a shelf. The spring sunset bathed it in dazzling gold. She suddenly felt Wang Ruo's timid joy in her chest.

She turned and looked at Wang Ruo and smiled. "Don't worry, Princess, I won't tell anyone. I'll just let the Prince know you love the flower he gave you."

Wang Ruo smiled.

The carriage sent by the Prince of Kui had already arrived outside the palace. Huang Zixia got in and rode through the streets of Changan. When they neared the East City, the driver suddenly called the horses to a halt. She wanted to see who would dare stop the Prince of Kui's carriage. She lifted the curtains and saw they were outside a restaurant. On the second floor, someone was looking down at them.

The sun shining on his purple body made it as wonderful a sight as the wisteria in Wang Ruo's garden. He looked as nonchalant as usual, his face more profound in the light, which did little to reveal his emotions. The Prince of Kui was looking at her from upstairs. She jumped out of the carriage, entered the restaurant, and knocked on the door of the upstairs dining room. Someone opened it immediately—it was Jing Yang, the other eunuch who always accompanied Li Shubai. His cold still lingered. He told Huang Zixia to be attentive to the Prince, closed the door, and left.

Li Shubai wasn't alone. Also in civilian clothing were his brothers Li Rui and Li Run, as well as a woman playing the guqin. She looked to be in her forties and had beautiful features, despite their color being a little worn. When she saw Huang Zixia enter, she didn't speak, only gave her a slight nod and plucked some clear, moving notes.

"She's Dong Tinglan's protégé, Chen Nian. The day before yesterday, Li Rui said she'd arrived in Changan, so Li Run and I asked her to come play for us," Li Shubai said.

Musical instruments from the western region of Hu were very popular with that dynasty. The guqin was often called tasteless and irrelevant. Few people appreciated it.

Huang Zixia greeted the woman with a nod.

Li Rui smiled and said, "Brother, you're getting a lot of use out of this little eunuch. What's he up to today?"

"He has a great memory. I asked him to teach in the palace."

"Oh, so he can break cases and has an impeccable memory like you?" Li Rui joked.

Huang Zixia saw Chen Nian squint as the setting sun shined in her eyes. Huang Zixia went and pulled down the bamboo curtain.

Li Rui watched. "Chonggu really is attentive."

Chen Nian finished playing "Yu"; its beautiful sound captivated everyone's attention, so no one responded to Li Rui. The sound just echoed on, and Chen Nian calmly touched her instrument and stood to bow to her audience.

"Wonderful, you can feel Dong's great style," Li Run said.

"You really played well. Interested in joining the faculty? We could refer you," Li Rui asked the woman.

Chen Nian slowly shook her head. "I'm getting on in years. I'm a court musician in Jiangnan's Yunshao. I lead an easy life. I don't know if I could adapt to the institute."

"Then why did you come to the capital this time?" Li Rui asked.

"When I was studying with Feng Yi, it felt right. We supported each other for two years and became partners. A few months ago, she suddenly left me, saying she would escort an old friend's daughter to Changan and that it would take up to four months. But she's been gone five months, and I have not heard from her. I asked all over, and no one could say why she went to Changan or whom she escorted, so I came to find out more. I found nothing and ran out of money. Luckily, I met other students who helped me get this incredible opportunity," Chen Nian said.

Li Run smiled. "I think I know what you mean. You want us to help find your partner, right?"

"Right, if you can find her, I would be so grateful!"

"Changan is a big place," Li Run said. "How about I write you a letter, and you can go to the ministry, and they can draw you a portrait to use."

Chen Nian thanked him profusely. "No need to make a special drawing. I have a little picture from a couple of years ago. I always keep it with me, and we look alike. I'll take it and show them."

"That's even better. Give it to us and I'll write a letter."

With a look from Li Shubai, Huang Zixia went obediently to get a pen and ink from the manager. Then Li Run sat across from Chen Nian and wrote the letter. Huang Zixia helped her open the rosin powder box so she could apply it to the strings.

Chen Nian was pleased with Huang Zixia's attentiveness. She looked at her hands and said, "Can the little man play guqin?"

"I tried learning pipa and konghou, but I didn't have the patience for it. I only learned a little before giving up."

"Shame, your hands are perfect for it."

"No one has ever complimented my hands before."

"Your palm looks strong. It's good for it to be a little bigger to stretch and reach more strings."

Huang Zixia smiled. "Must be because I used to like to play polo."

"The little eunuch likes to play polo?" Li Run said. "Next time we play, I'll invite you."

"I've just played a couple of games," she hurried to say.

"You don't look like the polo type. Too thin to play such a dangerous sport." Li Rui squeezed her shoulder. Huang Zixia leaned back slightly and glanced at Li Shubai. He looked away and coughed. Li Rui heard, then got up and sat next to him.

Huang Zixia kept watching Chen Nian apply the rosin powder. Her loose skin, high nose, and small chin reminded her of her mother. "If I really want to learn guqin, which songs should I start with?" Huang Zixia asked.

"For a beginner, 'Memory,' 'Thinking Often,' and 'East Fence Flower' are good places to start. They sound nice but are simple and easy."

"What about 'Flowing Water'?"

"You're kidding. 'Flowing Water' is very difficult. Even when my master played it, he wasn't satisfied."

"Well, is there a beginner's song that starts with the word *flowing*?"

She thought a moment and said, "I've been in Jiangnan for so long and taught a lot of songs, but I can't think of any like that."

"What about one that rhymes with *flowing*?"

Chen Nian thought it over, then let out a small cry. "There is one. It's soft and lingering, popular in Yangzhou. A lot of girls in Yunshao Court start with it. 'Flowing Cotton.' But as you're a capital person living in the Prince's palace, you definitely don't know it."

Huang Zixia thought of Wang Ruo's shyness as she felt embarrassed. "I suppose not."

"Yes. Girls from good families don't bother with folk music."

As the two of them spoke, Li Run finished his letter and sealed it.

Huang Zixia knew Changan well. She went with Chen Nian to get the portrait of her and Feng Yi. She told Chen Nian she would keep it safe. In the little portrait were two women, one sitting, one standing. Chen Nian was sitting and was painted vividly, a good likeness. The one standing had a crescent moon smile and was still charming in her forties.

"This is Feng Yi?" Huang Zixia asked.

"Yes, my partner was blessed with beauty."

"Everyone is special in their own way," Huang Zixia said slowly.

"My partner has an incredibly charming personality. It doesn't show in the portrait, but when you meet her, you'll see," Chen Nian said cheerfully.

True, Huang Zixia thought. Little do you know I saw her a few days ago on the outskirts of Changan with the Prince's future wife, Wang Ruo, when she offered me a ride.

The Wangs of Langya's daughter claimed a Yangzhou musician's partner was family. How could the high-ranking Wang Ruo's parents know and entrust Feng Yi to send her to Changan? Huang Zixia decided not to tell Chen Nian. After all, a lot of people in the world look alike. Maybe the ministry had some record of Feng Yi and she was somehow related to the Wang family. Regardless, the whole situation was strange in more ways than one.

"The portrait is small and you can't see it, but she has a mole above her left eyebrow, which anyone who saw her would probably notice," Chen Nian said. Huang Zixia thought of that woman in

Wang Ruo's carriage but remembered only that she wore a headband that covered her eyebrows.

Huang Zixia put the portrait away and bade farewell to Chen Nian. The carriage started toward the ministry.

The dynasty's main departments were all in the imperial city. She entered the secure gate and walked toward the ministry. The officer, named Hu, was very enthusiastic. He helped her check the files on women recently in the capital. In the end, she found no one that fit the age, description, or name Feng Yi.

After she thanked him and turned to leave, she thought of something else. "Officer Hu, I have a request. A couple of things I'd like your help with, if you can."

"I'm at your service, little man." The Prince of Kui was a powerful man, so the officer naturally respected his people.

"The thing is, our Prince has already chosen the Wang family daughter and will marry her soon. I went to the palace a few days ago, but my memory's so bad I forgot the name of the person with the Princess. I heard this family member entered the capital with the Princess; I don't know if you can do me a little favor and let me look at their log."

"Of course," Officer Hu said as he turned and pulled out a file. "I remember very well—the twenty-sixth of last month. The Langya Wangs asked me to register the residence of the daughter of the fourth concubine. Right, here it is, four people in total."

Huang Zixia looked at it eagerly and saw only: *The Langya Wangs' fourth daughter, Wang Ruo, went to the capital, attended upon by Xian Yun and Ran Yun, fifteen years of age, male servant Lu Yi, year of thirty-five.*

The dynasty's household registration system was quite strict, especially in the capital, so close to the Emperor. People coming from anywhere, even temporarily, had to report their dwellings to the ministry. "Darn, it only has these two girls' names. Seems I'll have to swallow my pride and inquire about the others," Huang Zixia said. Then she thanked Officer Hu, got her things, and left.

As she was putting away the little portrait, another officer caught a glimpse of it and took on a very surprised look. "Officer, have you seen this woman?" she asked.

"Uh . . . I saw someone who looks like her, but I'm not sure if it's her," he said.

"Where did you see her?"

The clerk hesitated again. "West City mortuary."

Mortuary. The word made Huang Zixia fill with dread. Anyone in the mortuary handled by the ministry was probably an unclaimed body.

"In the West City, several drifters from Yu were found dead. This morning, I went to register them. One of the victims and the woman you're asking about look very much alike." He opened the book and read, "Female victim, name unknown, in her forties, five feet three inches tall, petite, white skin, thick black hair, high nose, mole above her left eyebrow.

Mole above her left eyebrow.

Huang Zixia straightened up and said, "Is this body still in the mortuary? Could you allow me to take a look?"

The clerk put the book back and shook his head. "Not possible. They died of disease, so their bodies and possessions have already been incinerated."

"Oh. So there's no way." She carefully wrapped the portrait up and thanked the clerk. "Looks like I'll have to ask after the person who looks like the one in the picture. If I can't find her, I'll have to tell her friend she may have already died."

She turned and left the ministry, rumbling along in her carriage. She kept looking at the portrait of the two women smiling, silent, thinking about what Wang Ruo said. When she was selected as Princess, her aunt went back to Langya to get her things. Her expression had been somewhat unnatural when she said it, and then she hurried to add that she was getting old and might not come back.

Not coming back. She really may not.

Huang Zixia thought of Wang Ruo's little dimples, her extremely cute, shy look, and felt slightly entranced, as if she were gazing at the wisteria in the yard again.

Huang Zixia didn't go to Chen Nian. She went to Kui Palace and handed the portrait to Li Shubai. She went over what happened at the ministry in detail, pointing at her eyebrow and saying, "Feng Yi and that body both have a mole on their left eyebrow, but I couldn't tell whether Wang Ruo's aunt had one."

"Either way, it's a starting point." Li Shubai gave her an unusually pleasant look as he put the glass bottle gently on the table. "Sounds like there's a lot to look into," Li Shubai said with satisfaction, as if feeling that there was an order to things in the world. "Anything else you noticed that was amiss?"

Huang Zixia took her wooden hairpin out and put it on the table. "I thought . . ."

She quickly put her long, messy hair back in its bun.

Li Shubai looked at her silently. She folded her hands on her lap in embarrassment. "Force of habit. I always forget the little eunuch always wears his hair in a bun."

"What's going on with you? You can't even remember two plus two." Li Shubai frowned and handed her a piece of high-quality paper.

Huang Zixia picked up a pen, thought a little, and wrote "one, two, three." "First," she said, "the circumstances of Wang Ruo's birth. Second, the identity of the woman accompanying her and whether or not she's related to the Langya Wangs. Third, Chen Nian said Feng Yi was escorting an old friend's daughter to Changan I think Feng Yi was probably the Princess's music teacher. The first songs she learned would have been from the Yangzhou Court, like 'Flowing Cotton.'"

"The Langya Wangs are an old, illustrious family; for them to have such a woman teach their daughter and send her to the marriage ceremony is too strange. Also," Li Shubai said as his gaze grew colder and his voice quieter, "her death. The Wangs may have decided her life could be an inconvenience to them."

"More importantly, is the victim who looked like Feng Yi actually her?"

Li Shubai tapped his finger on the desk a moment. "From what I know of the ministry, their men do lazy work. They couldn't have burned the body and buried it deep."

Huang Zixia suddenly felt a sense of dread, and a tingle on her scalp.

Sure enough, Li Shubai opened the drawer and gave her a little goldfish. "Zhou Ziqin lives in Chongren Square, near the grave of Dong Zhongshu. Go and find him."

Of course, Huang Zixia remembered the undertaker Zhou Ziqin. Her dread grew more intense. "The Prince wants me to go?"

He looked at her, his lips curving into a slight smile. "Of course. You can dig up the body with Zhou Ziqin and take a look."

"My Prince! I'm a girl! I'm a seventeen-year-old girl! You're asking me to go to the graveyard with a strange man in the middle of the night and dig up a body?"

"Didn't you used to help your dad on cases? I bet you've seen more than a few bodies." He was unmoved by her plea. "Or is your talk about avenging your parents just talk?"

As Huang Zixia looked at his lips and confident brow, her heart filled with resentment. Hearing him mention her parents made her blood run cold.

"Didn't you already determine your sole purpose was to right the injustice done to your family?"

She clenched her teeth, took the goldfish off the table, and turned to leave.

Hearing the sound of the water clock, Li Shubai added, "Hurry, the curfew will start soon."

"Give me a horse!" she said.

"You can have two. You better hurry," he said, waving her away.

Six

CAGED BIRD

With two horses, riding one and leading one, Huang Zixia passed Anxing Square and Shengye Square. The streets were already empty.

Huang Zixia went to the house in Chongren Square next to the tomb of Dong Zhongshu, got off her horse, and knocked. A porter opened it, saw her eunuch clothing, smiled, and asked, "Who is the little man looking for?"

"The undertaker Zhou Ziqin," she said, giving him the goldfish.

As soon as he saw the Prince of Kui's name written on it he said, "Wow, hold on."

She stood in front of the house, watching the moon rise. The drums signaling the start of the curfew made her anxious. It was the practice in Changan for the gates to be closed upon the sound of six hundred drumbeats at dusk and opened with four hundred the same way at dawn.

Luckily, a young man soon came outside. He looked younger than twenty years old, smart and elegant in a thick robe. The gorgeous embroidered purple top with white dragon on the waist, jingling purse, perfumed bag, and white jade pendant were typical but looked extraordinary on him. "Is the Prince of Kui looking for me, little man?" he said.

"Zhou Ziqin?"

"Yes, that's me." He looked from side to side. "Does he need to use my place again? I heard he mentioned my name to the Emperor, said I can finally go with my father to Shu and become a policeman!"

"The Prince of Kui first has a very important job that only you can do," she said anxiously.

"Really? More important than being an officer?"

"Yes, for now. Digging up a body."

"The Prince knows me well." He didn't ask for details, just snapped his fingers and said, "Hold on! I'll get my tools and be right back!"

Huang Zixia and Zhou Ziqin rushed through the streets toward Jinguang Gate. Just as the last drumbeat sounded, their horses passed through the gate and the officer shouted, "Close!" They rode along the canal toward the wilderness west of the city. They traveled through lush forest to the mortuary. Inside, only a single lamp was lit, and the old watchman was asleep.

Zhou Ziqin took off his fancy robe and put on a brown one. He took out a piece of copper, gently unlocked the door, quickly pushed it open, and shut it quietly.

Huang Zixia was impressed. Zhou Ziqin was skilled as a fox.

He took her hand and crept inside. Then he opened a wooden cabinet, took out a book, and turned to the most recent page.

"Fourteen refugees from the State of Yu, twelve male, two female, all buried next to the forest on the west side of Qishan Hill." He ran his finger along the line and then pointed to the hill outside and mouthed the words, "Let's go."

He used the copper to slide the latch back inch by inch and waved her on. Huang Zixia understood why Li Shubai asked her to find Zhou

Ziqin. He was a swift thief. After walking a long way, Huang Zixia asked, "Do you often do this kind of thing? Seems so easy for you."

"Exactly," he said proudly. "In fact, all my skills came from practicing on unclaimed bodies."

"And the lock? Practicing with the most skilled thieves in Changan?"

"Been working on it about six months."

Huang Zixia laughed. "The latch on the window didn't seem to be locked. Why'd you go in through the door?"

"Window?" Zhou Ziqin went quiet. After a while, he cried, "I wasted six months of hard work!"

They reached the hill and brought the horse to a trot. Zhou Ziqin led it to the north side of the hill where an area of dirt had recently been turned. He took the basket off the horse's back and removed the folding hoe and shovel. He threw the shovel to Huang Zixia.

She caught it. "You even have this? So professional."

"The Prince of Kui got that for me from the army. When my dad saw it, he almost killed me!" He then took garlic, ginger, and vinegar from the box.

She was expecting him to take some bread out next, but instead he took out two pieces of cloth, smashed the garlic and ginger into them, and doused them in vinegar. He gave one to her and said, "Keep this over your nose. The smell of the corpses is strong."

"They say these people died of disease."

"All the more reason. Keep it tight," he said proudly. "It doesn't smell good, but it's an ancestors' trick."

Huang Zixia almost fainted from the smell. "Your dad's in the government, right? Still into that ancestors stuff?"

"Not my ancestors. I begged Changan's most famous undertaker, Zhu Dabao, until he told me the recipe."

She picked up the shovel and began digging with him.

"So you're the Prince of Kui's new love?" Zhou Ziqin asked.

Huang Zixia was glad her face was covered so he couldn't read her emotions.

"Yang Chonggu, right?"

"Yes," she said, thinking. "What do you mean by 'new love'?"

"I don't know. Just heard rumors. The Prince of Kui has a pretty eunuch with him. His brother asked to have him, but the Prince wouldn't give him up. I saw what you looked like and figured it was you."

Huang Zixia didn't want to listen to such ridiculousness, so she just kept digging.

He wouldn't stop, though. "I heard you're good at solving cases. Broke the Four Directions Case, right?"

"Got lucky."

The wind whistled through the pines in the misty moonlight, and the two of them spoke in the empty wilderness. Eventually, something other than dirt appeared. "Hold on," Zhou Ziqin said. "Let me see." He jumped out of the shallow pit, put on a pair of thin leather gloves, then picked up a piece of the skeleton. "Good. A cremated corpse. But look, this finger is thick. It definitely belongs to a male. We'll have to look a little more for the female."

Huang Zixia crouched next to the hole. "Yes, we're looking for a woman, around forty years old, five feet three inches tall, medium build, guqin player."

"All right." He rummaged through the earth with his small shovel. It took a lot of work to get fourteen skeletons out, but the women's bones were easy to differentiate. When Huang Zixia studied the heap of half-burned bones and flesh, she knew Li Shubai was right. The workers had done the cremation and burial hastily, not burying the bodies as deep as the law required.

She went to the box and put on gloves so she could pick up the women's hands. It was late and dark, so she couldn't see clearly, but it didn't matter much. The smell was terrible, though, coming right through the vinegar and spices.

She tried to hold her breath, telling herself, *You've seen the bodies of your own family members. This is nothing.* Her nausea slowly subsided as she tried to calm herself down and focus on the body before her.

"Looking at the bones," Zhou Ziqin said, "these two females are a little over five feet tall, but another with slightly weaker bones, a little stooped, seems to be about fifty. That must be the one you're looking for."

She looked carefully at the charred skull. "Is there any way to tell if she had a mole above her left eyebrow?"

"No, that's all on the skin, which has burned away."

"Then are there any other identifying marks here?"

"Hold on; I'll take a look." He went to the box and took out a leather bag. When he opened it, the moonlight showed little iron tools: a knife, hammer, and awl. He turned the bones over, then he cut open some remaining skin. "The jaw is stuck. The fingers are completely burned, and the eyes and ears are gone."

Huang Zixia crouched and listened, looking at the moon.

He kept rummaging. "There's no way to see any identifying marks."

She put her chin on her knees. "They don't examine the bodies before they dispose of them? No record in that book in the mortuary?"

"With a disease victim, no one does an exam. They just want to get it done as soon as possible," Zhou Ziqin said, then pointed at the box. "Hand me that little bag."

Huang Zixia threw it to him. He took out a thin, fingerlike piece of silver and a small bottle. He poured the liquid in the bottle on a piece of cloth and wiped the silver until it was shiny. Then he pinched the deceased's jaw to make its mouth open. He pressed the silver inside, then closed the mouth and sealed it with a piece of paper. "Wait a little bit."

Huang Zixia had been on enough cases to know this was a poison test. The silver is soaked in honey locust. After a half hour, if it comes out black, the victim was poisoned.

"Can you test the male body too?" Huang Zixia asked.

"Sure." He began the test on the male body.

She couldn't help but add, "Don't forget to check the stomach. Last time we tested a mouth, but it turned out to be misleading."

"Wow, really?" Zhou Ziqin's eyes lit up. He climbed out and stood with her below the pines, then took off the cloth around his face. "Hold on," he said. He went to the box and took out a bag. "Here, take half."

She smelled something nice and looked down but felt nauseous. "We're here to dig up bodies, burned bodies! You brought roasted chicken?"

"Come on; I didn't eat dinner! When I was getting the garlic and vinegar, this was the only portable food around, so I wrapped it in a lotus leaf and brought it. My house's cook is great!"

Huang Zixia's mouth twitched. She had no idea what to say.

"Now tell me more about this poisoning." His teeth tore into a hunk of chicken.

Huang Zixia shook her head and continued. "A girl in Longzhu died suddenly in her home, and the undertaker did that test. But I— but since the officer who first arrived on the scene found bruises on her wrists, not like the grapes on her bracelet but another shape, like a pomegranate, it was determined another woman had been grabbing her before she died. So they examined her nose and mouth and found dried blood. After questioning her family, it turned out the girl had discovered her sister-in-law and neighbor having an affair. The sister-in-law grabbed her hand, and the neighbor forced his hand over her mouth, but they were too rough and ended up suffocating her to death. Then they gave her poison and tried to make it look self-inflicted. The poison being found in the throat but not in the stomach allowed them to break the case."

"Really?" Zhou Ziqin asked. "Who was attentive enough to find all that through the impression of a bracelet?"

She hesitated. "Guo Ming, an officer in Chengdu."

"No way! I've met Guo Ming, that big beard. Sloppy. How could he notice the bruises on the girl's wrist?"

Huang Zixia looked up at the moon and rolled her eyes. "No idea."

"I have a guess. Civil Governor Huang Min's daughter, Huang Zixia?" he said. "I heard she's great at using clues like that to break cases."

"I don't know." She rested her head on her knees, gazing at the moon for a while. "I think I've heard of her."

Zhou Ziqin didn't seem to sense her coolness. "I knew you weren't from Changan!" he said gleefully. "And you never lived in Shu either, right? She's famous in both places! I want to be a detective because of her. Because of Huang Zixia!"

"Oh."

"Oh, yes! Civil Governor Huang's daughter, Huang Zixia, she's my sweetheart. She inspires me."

"You wouldn't recognize her if she were standing in front of you, would you?"

"Of course I would! There are wanted posters of her at the entrance of the city. I always stop and look. So pretty! You know you're beautiful when you look good on a wanted poster." Zhou Ziqin sighed longingly.

"What makes you admire her so much?"

"It started five years ago! I was fifteen; she was twelve. When I was fifteen, I hadn't decided what I wanted to do. I couldn't stand the idea of being like my brothers, buried in the ministry, drafting documents. Everyone said they were doing great, but I didn't think so. Life is so beautiful. To spend it all in an office would be a waste, right? In this, my darkest, most indecisive time, Huang Zixia came along!"

Huang Zixia looked at his eyes shining in the moonlight and had the urge to tear a piece off his chicken wing and eat it to calm herself down.

"Huang Zixia wasn't twelve yet, still a little girl, but she'd already started helping solve cases and made a name for herself. And me? What was I doing at twelve? Hearing about her made me realize what I should do."

Huang Zixia couldn't help but stop him. "Huang Zixia killed her family and fled into exile. You've seen the posters."

"Impossible." He waved the chicken leg in his hand with determination.

She had never seen anyone so confident. Though he was a little dim-witted, she was still moved. She looked at him. "Why do you still have faith in her?"

"Because Huang Zixia broke all those cases. If she really wanted to kill someone, she'd do it in a way that was impossible to detect. Why would she kill her family in such a crude way and ruin her reputation? Why would she leave a trail of evidence? She'd be more careful."

By the time Zhou Ziqin was done eating, nearly half an hour had passed. Then he took out a bag of melon seeds and gave half to her. This time she didn't refuse and began nibbling on them. The moonlight was slanting west. It must have been around two in the morning.

Zhou Ziqin took the silver from the three corpses' mouths and found that only the silver from the corpse that looked like Feng Yi had turned black. He carefully wiped it off and looked at the deep green-gray residue. "Poisoned, for sure."

Feng Yi, Yangzhou court musician and the Princess's teacher, was poisoned and died among Yu migrants. According to the Princess, she was supposed to be going back to Yangzhou.

Huang Zixia was still thinking this over when Zhou Ziqin said, "To be careful, let's check the stomach."

Even though it was already pretty much dry, opening the stomach was revolting. Steel-nerved Zhou Ziqin even had trouble tolerating it. He twisted his expression and only looked out of the corner of his eye. As he was sealing in the silver, he suddenly cried out when his fingers touched something cold and hard. "Hey, Chonggu," he said excitedly, "look at this!" A small object in his palm shone coldly in the moonlight. Huang Zixia put on gloves, picked it up, and examined it carefully.

It was a piece of white jade. It was translucent and no bigger than a fingernail. In the moonlight, she wiped the blood and dirt off to reveal a small engraved word: *Nian*. The white of the jade looked both bright and dim, flowing wavelike in the moonlight. She stared and stared at that *Nian*.

When she showed it to Li Shubai, he looked at the engraved word without taking it. "What is it?"

"Take it and see for yourself," Huang Zixia said.

Instead, Li Shubai took the jar off the table and watched the little red fish swim. "Take it? What if it was taken from the mouth of the dead? They need that for safe passage to the next life."

"No," Huang Zixia said earnestly, "it wasn't taken from the mouth of the dead."

Only then did he extend his hand and pinch the jade between his thumb and index finger. He read the word again. "The same *Nian* as Chen Nian," he said. He put it down and thought for a moment. "Are you going to give this to Chen Nian?"

"Then we'd have to tell her Feng Yi is dead. Chen Nian would certainly make a fuss and tip off our suspect."

"Yes, keep it to yourself for now." He gave the jade back to her. Huang Zixia wrapped it back in its cloth and put it in her pocket.

Li Shubai frowned. "I don't understand. Such an important indicator of identity. Why would the killer leave it with Feng Yi?"

"Because Feng Yi swallowed it before she was poisoned."

Li Shubai's eyes actually widened. Huang Zixia was pleased. "Feng Yi's body was half-burned, but the internal organs were basically intact. We scooped it out of her stomach."

Li Shubai looked at his fingers. His typically calm face faltered.

Huang Zixia looked at him. "Fortunately, Zhou Ziqin and I finished and reburied the body before dawn, so any trace of our work has disappeared."

Li Shubai couldn't stand it any longer. He grabbed the porcelain bowl and began washing his hands. "I'll make you disappear, Huang Zixia!"

Though she'd been up all night working with a corpse, seeing Li Shubai flustered made it all worth it. "Yes! As you wish!" She happily left for her room to go to sleep.

The Prince of Kui, Li Shubai's marriage ceremony was scheduled for May 16.

According to custom, the bride-to-be must go to Xianyou Temple on the outskirts of Changan to pray ten days prior to the wedding. Wang Yun came to see Li Shubai beforehand, and by the time the bride-to-be left for the temple, it had been cleared of unauthorized personnel.

Huang Zixia, Su Qi, and ten ladies accompanied Wang Yun.

Xianyou Temple was beautiful, and many ladies and concubines had had good pilgrimages there. So although there were many temples in the city, Xianyou was very popular with the court. The expansive Xianyou Temple was built on a hillside. In front was a smiling Buddha, in the back the venerable Arya. In the main hall were Tathagata, Manjusri, and Samantabhadhi. To the west were Amitabha and other Bodhisatvas. To the east were the Buddhas of medicine, sunshine, and moonlight, eighteen arhats, and five hundred rohans.

They went to the temple to burn incense and bow, then went to the main hall to pray. Su Qi and some of the ladies were already tired. When they saw the apse was still a ways up the hill, Su Qi stopped and said, "I'm exhausted. You go with the Princess, Yang Chonggu."

Huang Zixia agreed. She and Wang Ruo climbed the steps with incense in hand.

There was some moss on the bluestone steps, so they had to keep their eyes down. The temple was deserted. There was only the occasional birdcall and a single white bird flying in the sky. It crossed the sky into the peaks and ridges ahead. Their eyes followed it to the entrance to the temple, where a man was standing.

He appeared so suddenly and silently, it was as if the bird itself had transformed into him.

Wang Ruo hesitated. Huang Zixia gently tugged on her sleeve. "Prince Wang and the palace guards are inside. Don't worry."

Wang Ruo nodded, and the two of them climbed the last ten or so steps until they reached the entrance of the rear hall and bowed. Lanterns illuminated the Buddha within, and incense swirled around it. Wang Ruo kneeled before the Buddha, murmuring. Huang Zixia looked back at the man who was standing outside the door. The faint mountains were behind him, along with the azure sky. He had on a blue shirt that melted vaguely into the background. He seemed to feel her looking at him. He smiled. He had plain facial features, an ordinary, handsome man, but his smile was gentle and peaceful, with a touch of softness that gave her a feeling of familiarity.

Huang Zixia bowed her head slightly as if responding to his greeting, and she noticed he was holding a birdcage. There was a white bird standing in the middle. The bird seemed very humanlike. When it noticed the attention, it chirped and jumped around the cage. Wang Ruo finished praying and looked at the bird. There was no one around but the three of them. The man lifted the birdcage.

He smiled gently. "How do you like the bird?"

"Did you raise it? It looks clever," Wang Ruo said curiously. The bird seemed to understand and jumped even more joyfully in the cage with no sign of stopping.

"Yes, very clever. When I let him out of the cage, he flies to the forest, but as soon as he hears my whistle, he comes right back." He stroked the bird's head with two fingers. The bird affectionately kissed them.

Huang Zixia took Wang Ruo outside to avoid trouble. But when they were passing him, he said, "After all, no matter how we act, everything we've done and experienced is deeply imprinted on our hearts and can't be hidden from others or ourselves."

Huang Zixia sensed Wang Ruo's body stiffen as she stopped walking.

"It's like there's an invisible rope around your neck, and the more you struggle to escape, the tighter it gets," he said, looking at Wang Ruo. He laughed. "No worries, I'm only talking about this bird."

Huang Zixia faced him. "Do you know to whom you're speaking this nonsense?"

"Of course I know," he said calmly. "If all goes according to plan, she'll be the Princess of Kui within ten days."

"That being the case, please don't bother the lady any further."

"Of course I don't want to bother the lady. I just wanted to show Wang Ruo something fun." He walked closer, then leaned forward to bow and held out the birdcage. "This servant only wants the Princess of Kui to smile."

The bird that had been inside the cage was gone. The fine bamboo structure was empty. Wang Ruo looked at Huang Zixia in surprise. Huang Zixia looked silently at the man.

"I beg the Princess to be careful. Otherwise, she may disappear like this bird from its finely woven cage." He turned toward the temple and whispered, "A bird in its cage suddenly disappears; riches are like clouds, a never-ending dream."

The sun was setting. A bell rang, and the monks began heading to their evening classes amid singing. With that, the man was gone. The birdcage was left on the ground. Huang Zixia turned and hurried inside, but there was no one there. Wang Ruo's face had turned as pale as a withering flower.

"Ruo, why are you standing still like that with Yang Chonggu?" someone behind them called. It was Wang Yun, who had been waiting for them at the foot of the mountain. They'd been so long, he came looking for them. He went down the steps. His white satin clothing flowing in the wind made his figure look clean and bright as the sky.

He saw the empty birdcage on the ground and asked, "Where did that come from?" He saw Wang Ruo's expression. "What happened, sister?"

"Bro . . . brother," Wang Ruo said, her voice trembling as she looked at him with tearful eyes.

"What happened?" Wang Yun said with a frown.

"Just now . . . a strange man. He—he said . . ." Wang Ruo's voice trembled and she couldn't get the words out.

"Before the Prince came up," Huang Zixia said, "a man with a birdcage appeared and somehow made the bird disappear. He said that the Princess might also disappear that way."

"A man?" Wang Yun looked around, stunned. "The temple was cleared before you went in, and I've been standing guard with soldiers at the foot of the hill. How could anyone get in?"

"He couldn't have escaped the temple. Go look and you'll find him," Wang Ruo said, trembling.

Wang Yun nodded. "Don't worry. Nothing is going to happen to the Langya Wang daughter soon to be the Princess of Kui."

Her eyes filled with tears. "Maybe I'm thinking too much. With the wedding coming, I've been having trouble sleeping."

Wang Yun smiled. "I know. I've heard all brides-to-be are like that. Maybe it's anxiety."

Wang Ruo nodded slightly and bit her lower lip.

"Oh, sister, the Prince of Kui is such a good person. Are you worried you won't be happy in the future?" Wang Yun said. "Let's go; don't believe that nonsense."

Wang Ruo lowered her head and went down the steps with Wang Yun to the main hall on the mountainside. Huang Zixia was close behind. "Chonggu," Wang Ruo said.

"I'm here," she responded.

"Do you also think I've seemed worried and anxious lately?"

Huang Zixia thought a moment and said, "The Princess is too concerned about the Prince, which has made her nervous."

Wang Ruo pouted her lips and looked at her with teary eyes. "Maybe," she said quietly.

The monks were still in class, and the late bell chanting lingered around them. Hearing the Buddhist verses, Huang Zixia remembered her grandmother's words. *All love fades. It causes worry and terror.* She looked at Wang Ruo's hanging head and thought, *Was she really like this because of Li Shubai?*

Wang Yun and the guard captain, Xu Zhiwei, spoke briefly, then divided the soldiers into two groups: one to search the main hall and monks' quarters and one to search the temple. Since everyone was in evening class, there were no monks absent from the main hall. None could have appeared in the temple where they burned incense.

When darkness fell, the soldiers reported back. They decided to divide the temple into fifty areas and conduct a detailed search with ten men. They combed the area so thoroughly that not even a termite could have gone unnoticed.

The only discovery at all was a rusted arrow in front of the Buddha in the incense temple. It was engraved with the barely discernable words *The Tang Dynasty Prince of Kui*. The same arrow the Prince of Kui used to kill the traitor Pang Xun.

Seven

SCARLET DREAM

When Huang Zixia returned to Kui Palace, Li Shubai was alone in the parlor eating dinner. He indicated for his attendants to leave and for her to sit in an empty chair. Huang Zixia sat. Li Shubai handed her a pair of ivory chopsticks and pushed a small bowl toward her. He looked around and saw only shadows on the partition before picking up some golden cakes and cloves and putting them in her bowl.

"I heard someone pulled off some wonderful magic at the ceremony today," Li Shubai said casually.

"Yes," Huang Zixia said. "Quite wonderful, but I think the Princess's response was more wonderful."

"Princess-to-be," Li Shubai corrected her.

"The Emperor called for the wedding personally, and she's from the Empress's family. Is there really any way around it?"

"It doesn't matter. If she's deceiving me, then she must be exposed," Li Shubai said. "Did she seem worried her identity was revealed?"

"I don't think so. The strange man alluded to a secret about her past, which clearly frightened her."

"Did you notice how he appeared and how he disappeared?"

"Not at all. And how he got through the guards and away from them, I have no idea." Huang Zixia closed her teeth around the chopsticks and frowned. "The temple was searched thoroughly but no trace was found. Seems like he turned into a bird and flew over the wall."

"Have you read Huang Fu's essays?" Li Shubai asked.

Huang Zixia shook her head. "What's that?"

"A book. It tells about a 'Jiaxing rope' stunt. During the middle years of Emperor Xuanzong of Tang's reign, the Jiaxing County supervisor wanted to have some entertainment at a feast, so he looked for a stuntman among the local prisoners. One said he had rope skills, so they brought him to an open space and gave him a hundred feet of rope. He tossed it up, and it stayed as if someone were holding it. He kept tossing more and more up until you couldn't see the end of it. Then he climbed up and disappeared to escape."

"From any imaginable point of view," Huang Zixia said, "this is impossible."

"Why? Aren't there stranger things in the world?" Li Shubai pursed his lips. "For example, it's said my future Princess may disappear like the bird in the birdcage."

"So the Prince is also taking that man's words seriously?"

"I don't think it came from nowhere for no reason." He leaned back and looked at the shadows fluttering across the partition. "Huang Zixia, what was your favorite place in Changan growing up?"

"Huh?" Huang Zixia was caught off guard with a golden cake in her mouth. She stared at him a moment, then said, "Probably the West City."

"Right, West City. I liked it there when I was little too," he said thoughtfully. "Who wouldn't? The liveliest place in the whole capital, even the whole world."

Changan's West City

All the shops were busy and bustling. Persian jewelry, Tianzhu spices, Dawan horses. There was Jiangnan tea, Shu brocades, Saibei fur, and crowds of businessmen at the street food stalls, girls selling flowers, and thin-waisted foreigners in restaurants.

Changan's West City couldn't be stifled by the curfew. From Kaiyuan through Tianbao, it grew more and more prosperous so that even some of the surrounding squares became crowded and noisy at night. But this was daytime, and the late-spring/early-summer light shone on the streets' locusts, elms, and jasper. Li Shubai and Huang Zixia walked one in front of the other in the shade. Since Li Shubai was in disguise, Huang Zixia forwent her eunuch uniform and wore ordinary men's clothing, which made her look like a young teen. They peeked into shops, but Li Shubai had been wealthy since he was a child and found nothing up to his standards. Huang Zixia, meanwhile, was penniless, still unpaid, so neither bought anything.

That is until they reached a shop selling koi, and Li Shubai bought a small bag of fish food and contemplated a uniquely shaped fish tank inside.

Huang Zixia encouraged him. "Pretty nice, and the little fish will have more room."

He picked it up, looked, and put it back. "All the space wouldn't be good for a domesticated fish."

"You can't let him free once a day?" Huang Zixia muttered.

"How long would he be happy in that situation?"

She didn't know what to say to a man who made such a big deal about the little fish.

◆ ◆ ◆

It was still early, so the jugglers hadn't come out yet. Huang Zixia asked someone and discovered that the jugglers appeared a little later to make use of the busiest time. When noon came, Li Shubai finally indulged and took her to Zhuijin, the most luxurious restaurant in the West City. They sat in a room to try some food she hadn't seen at the palace. The restaurant was quite elegant, and it was crowded and noisy. There was a sudden knock on a wood block, which made the restaurant go quiet for a moment.

It was a storyteller who sang along to the sound of a small drum. First he sang the well-known "Butterfly"; then he put his drumstick away, cleared his throat, and said, "Ladies and gentlemen, I am not talented, but I will tell you about the latest news from the kingdom." As soon as he spoke, Huang Zixia recognized him as the man telling stories in the pavilion outside Changan. "In Changan's Daming Palace, the Emperor reigns," he began. "Beyond it are Princes; one is the Prince of Kui, Li Shubai."

Someone shouted, "I love stories about the Prince of Kui. Tell us the one about him battling Pang Xun!"

"Soon! This matter is much more important than his battle with Pang Xun!"

Despite the story being about him, Li Shubai didn't pay any attention. He just kept slowly eating, calmly looking out the window at the people walking by. Huang Zixia listened. "It's said the Prince of Kui has himself a new problem."

That same customer shouted, "The Prince of Kui just broke the Four Directions Case and is preparing to marry. Everything's going so well."

The room filled with chatter.

"Didn't you hear? The Kui Princess-to-be, the Langya Wang girl, went to Xianyou temple to burn incense?"

The person rushed to say, "I heard the Empress's cousin is gorgeous as could be!"

"She must be incredibly beautiful; why else would the Prince of Kui pick her over Princess Qi Le?"

"That Princess Qi Le is really the most pitiful creature in the capital. Women really shouldn't bare their hearts so clearly."

The storyteller listened until they calmed down and then said, "But did you know, even though the Wang girl became the Princess of Kui-to-be and the envy of all the capital women, the marriage process hasn't been without its twists and turns?"

The room went quiet. The storyteller was really exaggerating. He told of the trick at Xianyou Temple and mixed in a lot of speculation and fantasy. He even said the man was ten feet tall and six feet around with green fangs and wings and had the intention of taking the Princess away, but that Wang Yun fought him off during a swordfight that lasted hours. The assassin couldn't win, so he fled and shouted that the Prince of Kui better be careful during the ten days until the wedding because he was going to go deep into the palace and snatch the Princess from under everyone's noses.

The more he spoke, the more excited the storyteller became. He hit his wood block with a captivated look on his face. "Wang Yun was furious at the assassin's claims. He raised his sword and rushed at him. Suddenly, the monster disappeared in a puff of smoke and left an arrow engraved with *The Tang Dynasty Prince of Kui*, the same arrow the Prince of Kui used to kill the traitor Pang Xun!"

The audience burst into thunderous applause.

Huang Zixia was the only one quietly shaking her head. "What? Not well told?" Li Shubai asked.

"It doesn't make sense. If he can fly, why turn into smoke? Why not just fly away?"

"Don't you think it's more exciting that way?"

Huang Zixia took a moment to calm down. "Didn't the mayor, Yin, put some regulations on these storytellers?"

"What's wrong with a little fun?" Li Shubai said, indifferent.

All she could do was listen to the tale spinning outside. The man told the story of Li Shubai and Pang Xun.

In the ninth year of Xiantong, Pang Xun led a mutiny in Guilin. Two hundred thousand men marched on the court to make him military governor. The court refused, so he killed the governor and made himself king. At that time, each military governor raised his own force, so the Central Court was unable to mobilize. Only Li Shubai rose to the task. He brought one hundred thousand troops and negotiated with six other military governors. In September of the next year, they smashed the army and killed Pang Xun.

In the heat of battle, Li Shubai shot Pang Xun through the neck with an arrow. Chaos spread as Pang Xun fell from a tower, smashed into the ground, and was trampled by horses galloping in the mud. Only the bloody arrowhead remained. It was enclosed in a crystal box and placed in the Xuzhou drum tower as a warning to others.

That was when Li Shubai got the cursed paper on his birthday.

Last month, a rumor spread that the crystal box in the Xuzhou drum tower hadn't moved, but the arrowhead was missing. Officials searched long and hard but found no trace of it until it showed up in the temple where Wang Ruo met that strange man.

"Something is amiss here, huh, gentlemen?" The storyteller seemed to magically bring everyone to life. "Could it be that Pang Xun's spirit is seeking revenge on the Prince of Kui by attacking his marriage?"

"Come on, only good people's spirits live on. He was a usurper."

"Maybe an evil spirit, then."

The conversation took a bizarre turn and Huang Zixia looked at Li Shubai.

Without looking up, he said, "What are you doing?"

"I'm thinking about when you were nineteen and shooting Pang Xun. What was going through your mind?" she asked, holding her chin.

He looked as unruffled as usual. "It'll only disappoint you."

"No way. Let's see."

"I was thinking it would be a shame if a gust of wind came and blew the arrow off course."

Huang Zixia had no response.

"Some things aren't worth knowing." He pointed out the window and said, "The performers are out. Let's take a walk."

Huang Zixia, stomach growling, looked down and noticed she'd hardly eaten any of her food. Then she stood up angrily and followed him out.

The performers were finally out and about. But it was only typical hoops and bowls. Only one sword swallower. "Sword swallowing is so common. What's the point?" she asked a man pushing his way to the front of the crowd.

"This isn't the same!" the man said. "The sword's four feet long, and the dwarf swallowing it is only three feet tall!"

Huang Zixia suddenly couldn't help but squeeze closer herself. Li Shubai looked at her disdainfully and turned to leave. Huang Zixia followed him, thinking, *Can such a person with no interest in anything fun ever be happy?* Li Shubai walked ahead of her. He turned slightly and glanced at her. She was two steps behind him, watching a young husband and wife holding the hands of a little girl between them. The girl bounced, sometimes jumping to hang and swing like a little monkey.

Li Shubai stopped and waited for Huang Zixia.

She stood and watched the family walk off. She was silent, and the sun lit up part of her face, leaving the rest in shadow. Then she suddenly thought, *What about me? My parents and family are dead; I've been charged with murder but have no leads on how to prove my innocence. Will I ever be the playful girl I once was?*

After a while, Li Shubai said, "Let's go."

There was another crowd ahead. A slippery-looking husband and wife, who looked to have made a difficult journey from Jianghu, stood in the middle of the crowd and first turned into a monstrous fish. Then the woman held out paper flowers and changed them into real ones. Though it wasn't very original, it was moving when she threw the flowers in the air.

When the performance was over, the onlookers left, and the couple gathered their things to leave. Huang Zixia saw Li Shubai wink at her, so she approached and said, "Wow, that was really amazing!"

The man smiled. "You liked it, little man?"

"Yes, I really liked that paper-flower trick. I know the real flowers must have been up your sleeve, but where did the paper flowers go?"

The man laughed. "I can't tell you. It keeps food on the table."

Huang Zixia turned and looked at Li Shubai. He gave her a piece of silver. She put it in the man's hand. "Sir," she said sincerely, "to tell you the truth, my master has a bet. You must have heard about what happened last night. The bird who disappeared from its cage outside Xianyou Temple?"

The man took the money and smiled. "I hadn't heard, but making a bird disappear from its cage is easy as pie."

"My master has a friend who says it's impossible. They made a bet. He has to demonstrate it within three days. Would you be able to teach my master how?"

"It's basic stuff," he said. "The bird is trained to go to a certain part of the cage when it hears its owner's verbal command. There's a mechanism in place so when the owner presses a rod, a trapdoor opens, and the bird flies into his sleeve pocket."

"Oh! So that's it," Huang Zixia said. Li Shubai passed her another silver ingot. "So since you know this trick, you must have such a birdcage, no?"

"We did," the man said, looking sad as he saw the silver. "We sold it a few days ago."

"I told you," the woman said. "That bird was from our master and worth a lot more than five ingots. Even twelve would have been too little."

"Was it a starling? Could it learn a trick like that in a few days?"

"No," he said. "It was but a white one. Gorgeous."

"Ah, shame you sold it," Huang Zixia said as she gave the man the silver. "Do you know who bought it? Maybe I could find them. We'll try our luck at getting it ourselves."

"That I really don't know. He learned the trick and left. Didn't even get his name."

"Do you remember what he looked like?"

"Yes, a young fellow around twenty years old, medium height, good-looking. He had a red mole on his forehead."

"The mole was right in the middle," the woman added. "He was really good-looking. With that birthmark, he was just like someone in a painting."

Huang Zixia was wondering about the details of the whole thing. The strange clues weren't coming together. She looked up and found that Li Shubai was already far ahead of her. She hurried to catch up. It was dark, and the streetlight had been lit. Two rows of lanterns lined the street, shining like red halos. Li Shubai glanced back at her. His cold face had a touch of warmth from the orange light, and his eyes took on a misty look. She realized she cared for him and felt a little embarrassed.

When she caught up to him, she finally said, "I don't think this was the work of Pang Xun's ghost like the rumors suggest. I don't think it was a street performer either."

"Yes, he couldn't have anything to do with Pang Xun, and couldn't have hidden from everyone at Xianyou."

But he could have let others into Xianyou, they both thought. "Not to mention, he had plenty of followers who could have shown up for him, no need to go learn from a couple of street performers himself."

The street was bright as day. As they stood silently, a carriage began approaching slowly. It was full of a group of eunuchs and guards sitting in neat rows. They stepped aside in order to avoid being seen, but someone looked out the window and saw them.

The carriage stopped, and the door opened. It was Li Run.

He was a handsome, elegant, and gentle man who always had a smile on his face. With a bright-red mole on his forehead, he looked like a man in a painting.

◆ ◆ ◆

Li Run walked over to them. "What are you doing here, brother?" he said with a smile.

Li Shubai nodded slightly. "Brother."

Li Run nodded at Huang Zixia. "Clear weather tonight. The lamps are like stars. Good for a walk. But going out with just a eunuch isn't very safe. You should have guards."

"If I'm with too many people, I wouldn't be able to enjoy the quiet."

Li Run looked around at the empty streets and nodded reluctantly. "That's true. We grew up amid hustle and bustle. This kind of setting is a sight."

Li Shubai didn't want to say too much. "It's almost curfew time. You should be heading back."

He nodded, then seemed to think of something. "If you have time, you could come to my palace for a little gathering. Dong Tinglan's protégé, Chen Nian, is serving as music master."

"She didn't go back to Yangzhou?"

"Li Rui took her to the palace to show her skills to Lady Zhao. The Emperor and Empress were there too. Lady Zhao loves pipa, and the

118

Emperor doesn't love guqin. You know the Empress prefers quiet. Chen Nian wanted to stay in the capital and keep looking for Feng Yi, so we asked her to stay."

Huang Zixia and Li Shubai looked at each other a moment. Li Shubai stayed calm. "I see. I'll be free in a few days and will head over."

"Good. I'm looking forward to it."

It wasn't until after Li Run's carriage had vanished in the distance that Li Shubai looked at the lanterns in front of him and slowly asked, "What do you think of him?"

She thought it over. "If he wanted to disguise himself, it would be difficult. I think that may be why he was picked to distract us."

"Is there another possibility?"

"The other possibility is that Li Run naively went to the West City to learn the trick on his own, then went and taught whoever scared your Princess." She leaned against the willow behind her and said casually, "Regardless, I think the first possibility is more likely."

"I know that wasn't him, because I don't believe he would move against me," Li Shubai said slowly in a tone colder than usual. "I just want to know who wants me to suspect him. Who really wants to deceive me?"

The ninth day of the fifth month. Seven days until the Prince of Kui's marriage.

It drizzled all night, and the capital was enveloped in misty rain. En route to the Wang household, Huang Zixia lifted the carriage's thin bamboo curtain and saw flowers hanging heavily from the rainwater. The peach blossoms had already bloomed, and the scholar trees were in the process, which gave the air a faint aroma. The strings of white flowers in the branches seemed almost colorless. Every now and then, she'd heard something hitting the carriage. Now she realized it wasn't water but flowers.

The Wangs' people were already waiting at the entrance with umbrellas. When they saw her, they hurried to bring her one. "Mr. Yang, so nice of you to come. The Empress has already called Wang Ruo into the palace. She'd like you and Ms. Su to join the audience."

"Yes, of course," Huang Zixia said with a nod. The rumors in the capital were intense and had already spread to the Empress, who'd long lived in the inner palace. Her calling them in meant she'd have a lot to say. The Empress was kind, but stern. The Emperor adored her and would always do what she said. As Huang Zixia thought this over, she took an umbrella, entered the antechamber, and walked through the corridor.

Wang Ruo's courtyard was covered in orchids, and a few long banana leaves stuck out. Her wooden-lattice window lacked warmth, given the weather. Huang Zixia gently opened the umbrella and stood outside the window near a large vase with three or four red-and-white carp swimming in the water. She watched the rain hit the banana leaves and splash into the vase. During a quieter moment, she heard the vague sound of voices inside, as if people were whispering about something.

Huang Zixia looked out the window and saw Wang Ruo sleeping restlessly on the couch. She was frowning and had a panicked look on her face. Her hands clutched the edge, and her forehead was covered in sweat, as if she were being tortured. Huang Zixia wondered if she should wake her up when she heard her murmur, "Scarlet . . . scarlet." She was surprised and leaned closer to listen. Wang Ruo's tone turned to pleading. "Feng Yi, don't blame me. You shouldn't . . ."

The rain suddenly intensified and hit Huang Zixia's upper body. She moved to get shelter and heard Wang Ruo shout and wake up.

Huang Zixia calmly brushed the water off her clothing and knocked on the door. "Princess," she said quietly.

There were two girls sitting inside. One named Xian Yun came over and opened the door. "Mr. Yang, it's you. The Princess was just having a nightmare."

"Oh, I was outside and heard her wake up." Huang Zixia brushed more rain off herself as Wang Ruo slowly sat up. Their eyes met, and Wang Ruo still looked somewhat terrified. Huang Zixia went over to her and said quietly, "What was the Princess dreaming about?"

"Chonggu!" Her young eyes filled with tears. "I—I dreamed that I actually disappeared from this world."

Huang Zixia sat next to her. "Dreams are the mind thinking. Whatever the Princess was thinking about during the day, she'll dream about at night. If you don't think about what that man said, you won't have such a dream."

"Really?" She trembled as she gripped Huang Zixia's sleeve. "Chonggu, the Prince will protect me, right?"

"Right," Huang Zixia said without hesitation. She thought of what Li Shubai said—*It doesn't matter. If she's deceiving me, then she must be exposed.* But Huang Zixia's response put Wang Ruo at ease.

She breathed a gentle sigh of relief and leaned on the cushion quietly for a while. "Right," she murmured, "the Prince of Kui will protect me. I have no reason to be afraid."

Eight

TILTED WORLD

The Penglai Hall of Daming Palace

Three levels above the ground floor was the Empress's living quarters.

Huang Zixia followed the palace attendants, along with Wang Ruo, Su Qi, and some of the Wangs' ladies up the white jade steps to the ninth doorway. The door was a twelve-panel agarwood screen. The top of each was carved with flower gods surrounded by clouds that faced their Queen Mother in the Kunlun Mountains. Wang Ruo stopped and stood with her head bowed. All was silent.

Huang Zixia wondered about what she'd heard Wang Ruo raving about in her dreams. It seemed that the woman who looked like Feng Yi definitely was Feng Yi. But what does "scarlet" mean?

A thick, red piece of Persian silk appeared, and everyone put their hands together in salute, not daring to raise their gazes. The Empress must be coming, so Huang Zixia bowed too and looked at the clouds on her clothing.

The Empress walked behind the screen with her ladies and sat on the exquisite couch surrounded by burning incense. She picked up a light-green teacup and thought awhile before finally saying in a clear, bright tone, "Wang Ruo, you don't look so good. The wedding is in only seven days. Aren't you excited?"

Wang Ruo sat next to her on the couch. "Some silly things happened recently that have me worried," she said quietly. "Nothing worth troubling you with."

The Empress looked at her and held her hand without speaking. The Empress looked indifferent but also gentle.

"There's bound to be something trying to bother you. Why pay it any mind?" The Empress gently held Wang Ruo's right hand as if it were a baby bird. Huang Zixia felt something indescribable, something like fear. "Who was sent here by the Prince of Kui?"

Su Qi and Huang Zixia quickly said, "Your servants."

The Empress looked at them a moment. "The Princess is young and will need a lot of care when she moves to the palace."

"Yes," they responded.

"Chonggu and Su Qi are loyal servants," Wang Ruo said. "They have been so good to me."

"All right. Tell us if there's anything you don't like," the Empress said, standing up with Wang Ruo's hand still in hers. "In seven days, it will be your send-off. We've prepared some things for you. Go to the inner palace and look."

The group waiting outside in the inner palace could be heard, if you listened closely. Soon the Empress and her attendants left and asked everyone to follow them to a small room for a meal. Huang Zixia took a few bites and put her chopsticks down. The girl next to her, Xian Yun, tapped her and said, "Mr. Yang, why don't we go to the hall entrance and look around? You can see the whole lake, and it's incredibly beautiful."

Huang Zixia had been to the Wangs' as a eunuch many times now and knew Xian Yun well. She was chatty and had a reputation for being mischievous, so people who knew her very well didn't like her. Huang

Zixia didn't want to eat anymore, so she left with Xian Yun and stood at the railing of a balcony facing north.

The weather was nice. Small waves rippled on the nearby lake. The island in the middle looked mythical, a light embellishment on the flickering water. "How beautiful, no wonder they say it's the most beautiful place on earth." Xian Yun reached out her hand as if trying to grab the beauty.

"Yes, really beautiful," Huang Zixia said. If anything, it was too beautiful. It seemed unreal, like the jade palace on the moon.

One of Empress Wang's officers, Yan Ling, came and said, "The Empress has asked everyone to the side hall. The Princess would like to rest awhile. If you want to enjoy the palace sights, you can go to the lake, but not too far."

"Really?" Xian Yun said. "Amazing!"

Yan Ling called to an older lady named Yao Yue and asked her to take them for a walk along the lake. Huang Zixia and Xian Yun went with Yao Yue to the lake. They looked up and saw a boat with an old servant shouting from the bow. Someone called, "Lady Zhou has arrived. Make way."

The boat stopped, and several eunuchs and ladies came ashore. A girl with a round face and almond eyes got off. Huang Zixia was surprised to see it was Princess Qi Le. She remembered the rumors about how Princess Qi Le copied scripture for Lady Zhao to get ahead in the competition to marry Li Shubai. It was also said she was sick over losing. Huang Zixia couldn't believe she'd come today.

The servant let Lady Zhao out of the cabin. She entered the palace as a concubine at thirteen and had children at fifteen. At twenty-four, she became concubine of the late Emperor. She even had her own room in Daming Palace. Compared with the others, who were dispatched to Taiji and Xingqing Palaces after the Emperor's death, she was obviously favored.

Huang Zixia and Xian Yun hurried to greet her. Hearing they were the Prince of Kui's people, she asked their names and sized up Huang Zixia. "You're the Yang Chonggu who broke the Four Directions Case?"

"Yes," Huang Zixia said with her head bowed.

"I see, well done. The Prince of Kui has always had good taste," she said. "You're accompanying the Princess to the palace today? This widow will see her too." Lady Zhao laughed heartily and went with her people to Penglai Hall. Huang Zixia waited for them to get ahead, then followed. Suddenly someone pulled on her sleeve. A girl next to her pursed her lips and said quietly, "We meet again, Mr. Yang."

It was that pipa player from the academy who was with Li Rui last time. Huang Zixia nodded. Jin Nu smiled. "Lady Zhao wanted to hear pipa today, so Li Rui sent me."

Huang Zixia remembered that Lady Zhao was Li Rui's mother. The Empress came out to meet Lady Zhao personally. Huang Zixia stood at the foot of the steps and watched the Empress escort Wang Ruo and her attendants.

Empress Wang looked down at Huang Zixia and the others waiting. The water in the lake was suddenly stirred by the wind. The Empress's skirt rolled up, its gauzy layers like peony petals adding to her weightless grace. Her face shone like the moon, and even Wang Ruo's beauty couldn't compare.

Huang Zixia couldn't help but stare. She felt small and ashamed. She heard Jin Nu let out an almost imperceptibly quiet sigh.

Empress Wang's gaze passed easily from them to Lady Zhao. "Welcome, my lady."

"Oh, this widow doesn't care much for decorum. You're in charge now. If it weren't for your generosity, this old lady would be out on the street." Lady Zhao smiled and took the Empress's hand as they walked inside.

Lady Zhao and the Empress laughed quietly as Huang Zixia went with the group to Penglai Hall. Three white marble levels above, the lady and Empress looked closely at Wang Ruo and spoke to her, laughing from time to time. The inner palace bustled. Huang Zixia and those who weren't part of the family stood quietly outside. Beads of sweat ran down Jin Nu's face, nearly washing all her makeup away. "You okay?" Huang Zixia asked.

"I'm . . . pretty hot," she said hoarsely.

Huang Zixia looked at the spring sun and felt the wind blowing over the water. It didn't seem very hot to her. She took out her handkerchief and gave it to Jin Nu.

Jin Nu's hands shook as she took it.

She wiped her face and forced a smile. "I could be getting sick. I'll go back and get some rest and be fine."

Huang Zixia nodded.

Jin Nu hesitated a long time before quietly asking, "That one in red must be the Empress?"

"Yes," Huang Zixia replied with a nod.

"So the one behind her is the Princess of Kui?"

Huang Zixia nodded again and studied Jin Nu's expression. There was something she couldn't put her finger on. A sense of recognition, maybe.

Jin Nu seemed dazed. "Impossible," she muttered. "How could the Princess of Kui be her?"

Huang Zixia knew there had to be a reason Jin Nu had so many questions, but Jin Nu was just a pipa player who was new to the palace. Maybe that was why she was so curious.

She was about to ask another question when the Empress's attendant Yan Ling came and asked, "Which is Jin Nu?"

"Me . . . ," she said, holding the pipa.

"The lady wants you," Yan Ling said, glancing at Huang Zixia. "Why aren't you waiting on the Princess?" she asked.

Huang Zixia hurried ahead. Jin Nu hesitated, then took Huang Zixia's hand. Jin Nu's hand felt weak and cold with sweat. Huang Zixia knew Jin Nu didn't have the strength to carry the pipa, so she helped her carry it inside the hall. Jin Nu bowed as Huang Zixia gave her the pipa and her jade pick back. Then she went to Wang Ruo and stood by Jin Nu.

Wang Ruo's face was as pale as a wilting flower. Her eyes were downcast, as if she didn't dare to face anyone, especially Jin Nu.

Princess Qi Le had her eyes fixed bitterly on Wang Ruo like sharp knives. When she noticed Huang Zixia looking at her, she didn't look away but stared back aggressively. Her gaze was full of righteous indignation that she wanted Huang Zixia to see before she finally looked away.

Lady Zhao smiled at Empress Wang. "This is a new pipa player from the academy. She's amazing. Li Rui loves her and says that in time she'll become a master."

"Really? She's so young; can she really be that good?" the Empress said, smiling as she glanced at Jin Nu.

Jin Nu held the pipa and bowed slightly. "I'm just a student. I'll never surpass my teacher. She's the true master."

This seemed to get the Empress's interest. She looked at her again but didn't speak. Lady Zhao smiled. "Which master is your teacher?"

"She's from the Yunshao Court of Yangzhou. Her name is Mei Wanzhi. Has the lady heard of her? I'm her only protégé."

The Empress looked like she flinched, but just for a moment.

Mei Wanzhi. Huang Zixia had never heard this name, but the Yunshao Court of Yangzhou made her think of Chen Nian and Feng Yi, and now Jin Nu. They all came from the same court. Quite a coincidence. No one else seemed to recognize the names. Only Lady Zhao seemed pleased. "Then you must be very talented to have earned your teacher's respect."

"Yes. When I was five, my hometown was flooded. My family fled to the suburbs of Yangzhou. One died of hunger, and they had no choice but to put me up for sale." She held the pipa tightly and spoke quietly. "My master passed. She ordered the driver to stop. She had one of her people bring money to buy me. She said my hands show that I was born for playing pipa."

Everyone looked at her hands. They were white with shapely joints and palms slightly large for a woman. The pipa was resting on her chest. Jin Nu smiled, her left hand pressing the strings on the neck, her right plucking them with the jade. Her hands were no longer trembling, and her face had a touch of red to it. Her fingers moved faster than the eye could see. The music poured out like pearls dropping in the hall, but each note was distinct. There were round, brisk, transparent, and soft ones. Thousands coming together on the platform and echoing faintly in the hall.

After the song, everyone remained entranced by the music. It even took Wang Ruo a long time to take a deep breath.

Lady Zhao smiled at the Empress. "What do you think?"

Huang Zixia realized then that only the Empress had an indifferent expression. "Not bad," she said. Huang Zixia remembered that it was said that the Emperor loved a good party, while the Empress preferred quiet and wasn't interested in dances and feasts.

Jin Nu put the pipa down, stood, and bowed. "Master said my playing is full of fire but lacks tranquility, which must be the limitation of my talent."

"You're young and beautiful," the Empress said, "and in the prosperity of the capital. It's good that you haven't learned that yet."

"The Empress is right," Lady Zhao said. "You haven't experienced great sadness; how could you know tranquility? I hope it lasts your whole life, my child!" Jin Nu bowed and prepared to retire. "Now," Lady Zhao said, "is your master still in Yangzhou? She must be marvelous. When can she come to the palace to play pipa for me?"

Jin Nu forced herself to smile. "Master already passed away." She glanced at the Empress.

"Shame," Lady Zhao said. "I love pipa. I even asked Master Cao's protégés to enter the palace. Unfortunately, that great talent is lost to us now too. From your tone, I bet your master was incredible, huh?"

"Yes. Unsurpassed in the world. If the lady would like, I can tell you a story about her."

"Are you feeling up to it, Wang Ruo? Maybe you'd like to rest?" the Empress asked.

Wang Ruo shook her head. "I'll lie down soon. I'd like to hear the story."

Princess Qi Le said cynically, "Yes, better for the Princess to be among people, otherwise . . ." She didn't say what, but everyone knew. Lady Zhao gave her a look, and she didn't say more.

Jin Nu sat down, holding her pipa. "Eighteen years ago, in bustling Yangzhou, my master and five of her sisters cofounded Yunshao Court. They called them the Six Women of Yunshao. Then master got married and had a daughter, which coincided with the Emperor's great celebration. Five of the Six Women of Yunshao went to the capital. Only my master stayed behind with her newborn."

She launched into the story of one of her master's most stunning moments.

Every year in Yangzhou during the winter solstice, Jiangdu Palace opens, and men and women join together in song. Then the best musicians come to play for the dance.

Eighteen years ago, there was a rival musical group called Jinli Park. They brought thirty-six Persian girls to upstage Yunshao. As usual, the Yunshao court dancers were dancing in the palace. Before the first dance was finished, music came on from the opposite stage. Amid the thirty-six girls, twenty-four played instruments—harps, flutes, and pipes. The other twelve sang and danced. The girls wore gauzy clothing and didn't cover their feet. They moved their waists sensually. Coupled with their flowing blonde hair, it looked very erotic. The noisy crowd rushed to the other side to watch. The Yunshao dancers were at a loss, and just stood there, panicked.

The foreigners played their flutes furiously. Their flirtatious waists and winks won warm applause from the audience. Those on the other side were calm and focused on getting their things together and going over there. Master Mei Wanzhi walked over to a pipa player and took her instrument, then sat to the side of the hall and began playing along.

The sound resounded throughout all of Jiangdu Palace. The birds were frightened as it echoed through the mountains and valleys. Soon, the foreigners couldn't keep up. They lost the tune and stopped playing. The only sound in the palace was the ring of the pipa like heavy raindrops on flowers. When the song was over, snow began to fall over the winter solstice sunset. That day, the hundreds of people in Jiangdu Palace all silently listened to that pipa as the snow fell, and no one dared to even breathe loudly, lest they interrupt the music.

"I was only seven at the time," Jin Nu said.

Jin Nu's story made everyone gasp. "How amazing!" Lady Zhou said.

As Huang Zixia imagined the scene, she was fascinated.

"Yes. I may never hear pipa playing like that again," Jin Nu said with a smile filled with longing. "When that song ended, master played another, making people dance. The Yunshao Court dancers got their spirit back and lined up to sing and dance. All the attendants were overwhelmed. They danced arm in arm all night as the snow fell. Now there's a legend in Yangzhou about Mei Wanzhi possessing hundreds of dancers with her pipa."

"I don't believe you," Princess Qi Le said. "How could anyone play that well? You're definitely lying."

Jin Nu smiled and lowered her head but didn't respond.

"Or maybe the memory's grown richer over time," the Empress said gently. Then she turned and said to Zhang Ling, "Tell the academy to bring a pipa as a gift for Jin Nu." The Empress smiled slyly at Jin Nu.

"My pipa was given to me by my master. It's called Autumn Dew. I've grown used to it over the years and am afraid I wouldn't be able to change it."

"Then have them bring a jade pick, strings, and rosin powder. They should be useful."

Jin Nu thanked her. Lady Zhao waved her hand and said, "Well, I've seen the Princess of Kui. Think I'd better go get some rest. The Princess should take care of herself too. Soon it'll be your celebration day."

"Thank you, my lady," Wang Ruo said with a deep bow.

Lady Zhou and her entourage left. Zhang Ling motioned for Jin Nu to leave too. Her gifts would be on the way.

Huang Zixia and Wang Ruo got up and went to the side hall to rest.

As they left, Princess Qi Le said, "Beauty is truly rare. I think that pipa player is prettier than a lot of ladies."

Wang Ruo knew she was talking about her, but didn't say anything. After a while, Jin Nu laughed coldly. "The Princess must be joking. I'm not beautiful. My master was a magisterial beauty, though."

"Your master?" Princess Qi Le said, staring at her. "Who other than the Empress is worthy of the word *magisterial*?"

"The Princess is right." Jin Nu didn't seem to mind the rebuke. She smiled and turned to Huang Zixia with eyes squinting with delight. "Mr. Yang, remember what I said to you last time? Lots of girls love the Prince of Kui, even lots of students in the Yangzhou Academy. It'd be nice if you could get him to visit more often."

Huang Zixia smiled and nodded.

When Jin Nu left, Princess Qi Le said, "She's talking about the academy girls liking the Prince of Kui?"

Huang Zixia didn't respond. *You compared her with the Princess of Kui; why should she compare you with the academy girls?* she thought. As she watched Jin Nu's graceful outline disappear, she felt some relief as well as a little concern for her.

Wang Ruo remained in the side hall to rest. Huang Zixia, Su Qi, Xian Qun, Ran Yun, and others sat outside so as not to disturb her.

Su Qi and Zhang Ling looked at the new palace's flowers. Huang Zixia felt drowsy, having not slept well the night before. She drifted off to sleep.

When Huang Zixia suddenly awoke, she jumped up and found Su Qi and Zhang Ling had left the flowers and gone to the hall. She heard commotion. She hurried inside and found Wang Ruo curled up on the couch, shivering with fright. A chunk of her hair had been cut.

Zhang Ling pointed toward the window. "There," she said in a panic. "The assassin escaped through the window."

Huang Zixia ran to the window, but no one was in sight. She looked above and below the window to see if the assassin was hiding but didn't see anyone. There was nowhere to hide. If Zhang Ling saw them go over the wall, there was no way they could escape her gaze.

Where could he have gone in such a short time?

She hesitated before looking back at Wang Ruo. Wang Ruo was holding a blanket as she sat on the bed, the evening light illuminating half her face. Some hair from the part that had been cut hung over her cheek, casting a shadow that made her seem frailer.

Empress Wang came from the main hall and listened to the story of what happened. "In this palace," she said furiously, "attacking the Princess right under our noses! What the hell are the guards doing?"

No one dared to answer.

"We must speak with the Emperor. This is no trivial matter," she said, walking toward the door. Then she turned and looked at everyone. "If this gets out the rumors in the capital will intensify. Make sure no one speaks a word of this outside the palace walls. Yongqing, hurry and inform the Prince of Kui. Ask him to come immediately."

Yongqing, a eunuch from Penglai Hall quickly walked out.

After the Empress left, they comforted Wang Ruo. Xian Yun said, "The Empress is truly concerned about the Princess and will keep her safe." Wang Ruo stared silently, frightened.

Before long, the Emperor's command came down. The Princess of Kui would stay in Daming Palace's Yongchun Hall, and the court would mobilize one hundred guards led by Wang Yun. The Prince of Kui sent another one hundred troops, and the two hundred people took turns guarding the hall just in case. "Daming Palace has three thousand men standing guard day and night. There's nowhere for a troublemaker to hide," an attendant said joyfully.

Wang Ruo smiled with reluctance.

Yongchun Hall of Daming Palace was a small hall in the southeast corner. It was originally the palace treasury, so its walls were extremely thick, making it perhaps the safest in the palace. The hall's south and east sides both had gateless, fifty-feet-high walls nearby. Atop the wall was a tower with a guard always on watch. There was no way someone could have entered from there. The west side was a defensive focal point. The hall was impenetrable.

In accordance with the security plan, there were three lines of defense around Wang Ruo. The innermost consisted of the ladies and eunuchs always by her side. The next was about thirty people, throughout the hall, who could see anyone coming and going. There were six units of thirty soldiers. Half were on duty at any given time and led by eight lieutenants and two captains, making for two hundred people in total.

"The hall has been thoroughly searched. There are no intruders. Please be at ease, Your Highnesses," the two men in charge of the guards said to Wang Ruo and Wang Yun.

Wang Yun nodded and stood to leave. "Please believe that your safety has been ensured. It's getting late. Get some rest. I'll be in the front hall. If you need something, call for me."

Wang Ruo and Huang Zixia walked him to the door and watched him leave.

Standing in the entrance, looking out at the guards on the verandah and in the rock garden as if a battle were imminent, she thought of the mysterious man and his birdcage. Who could have known that the cage had a contraption that with a slight touch would magically make the bird disappear? Wang Ruo was just like that little bird, sitting alone in the hall, watching the ladies light the lamps.

Huang Zixia walked over to her. "What are you looking at?"

Tears like crystals flickered in Wang Ruo's eyes. "Chonggu, I . . ." She choked up and could barely manage to speak. "I feel like I've been floating in a dream this month. I've found myself in an unbelievably good situation but, like the light of spring, it's going out." There was deep sadness, sorrow, even, in her voice.

Wind slowly came through the palace gate and made the lamps rotate and flicker. The wind dimmed the lamps, and the rain fell. Huang Zixia looked at Wang Ruo's face and thought that worry was aging her. Though Wang Ruo probably had something to do with Feng Yi's death and may not be so beautiful on the inside, Huang Zixia still felt some pity and whispered, "Be at ease, Princess. There are many guards closely watching the palace now. Even an insect couldn't come in undetected."

Wang Ruo nodded but still looked heavyhearted.

Huang Zixia didn't know what else to say. She thought the Empress had put too much pressure on Wang Ruo. Then she looked outside and saw Li Shubai appear in the bright light. He came to the entrance of the hall. Xian Yun and Ran Yun bowed quickly, and Su Qi and Wang Ruo stood and did the same. Wang Ruo's eyes glowed brilliantly like pearls when she looked at him. But she couldn't shake the shyness and grief from her face.

Li Shubai glanced at her but didn't speak, just indicated for Huang Zixia to come out. Huang Zixia bowed to Wang Ruo and left. She and Li Shubai went through the rock garden to the front hall's verandah. They were only feet from Wang Ruo and could keep an eye on any movements.

"What's the arrangement tonight?" Li Shubai asked.

"Su Qi, Xian Yun, and Ran Yun will accompany the Princess in the inner palace's east hall. The rest of us will be nearby in the west hall, ready to handle anything at a moment's notice."

"I don't think anything bad will happen in Daming with all these guards," Li Shubai said, "But with so few days to the wedding, the Empress putting on such a big show of force seems problematic." Huang Zixia was wondering what the problem was when Li Shubai said, "I originally thought we'd take care of the paper over the next couple of days. Time is short." He spoke as flatly as if discussing the weather—no hesitation, no rancor—heartless.

Huang Zixia gave him a slightly confused look. "Does the Prince wish to reveal the truth to the Princess? I don't think the Empress or the Wangs will like it."

"I'll take care of it privately. I wouldn't disrespect the Wangs."

Huang Zixia was at a loss when Wang Ruo came out of the hall. The cool night air blew her clothes and hair. She was wearing a thin yellow garment and had her hair in a loose bun, a leafy golden hairpin at her temple. She came toward them through the rock garden with Ran Yun.

She bowed deeply and said, "Hello, my Prince."

Li Shubai nodded, indicating for her to rise.

She did so and whispered, "Thank you so much for coming in person. The palace is heavily guarded and should be safe now." Despite her words, her eyes were wide and helpless like a doe's. If he left, she'd be heartbroken.

"Certainly, no need for worry. You can go rest and have a peaceful day tomorrow," Li Shubai said.

"Yes." Wang Ruo bowed. She blinked, and there seemed to be a glimmer in her eye, which Huang Zixia thought was a tear.

She rose and went back to the hall.

Li Shubai and Huang Zixia watched her pass slowly through the rock garden. In the entrance, she seemed to be in a trance. She tripped on the threshold, and Ran Yun helped her regain her balance and straighten her skirt.

"Since there are so many guards, I'll go back to the palace. You stay extra vigilant."

"Okay," Huang Zixia said, still looking at the hall. Xian Yun carried a container of food to the rear kitchen, and Ran Yun lit the way with a lamp as they spoke in whispers.

"What are you looking for?" Huang Zixia called.

Ran Yun cupped her hands around her mouth. "The Princess's hairpin is missing!"

Huang Zixia waved at Li Shubai and said, "I'll go help them look."

As Huang Zixia crossed the rock garden, she saw a small piece of gold, leafy with two pearls. Wang Ruo's hairpin.

She picked it up and walked quickly to Ran Yun and gave it to her.

Ran Yun took it, and the two went to the hall entrance where Xian Yun was returning with food. She angrily opened the container. "The cook is already out, so I could only find some walnut biscuits. Will you eat them?"

"Eat, eat, eat. All you do is eat. Have you seen your waist lately?" Ran Yun asked.

"Well, Yang Guifei was round as a pearl and was still Empress dowager."

"You're comparing yourself to Yang Guifei? That was a hundred years ago. She's certainly not a plump beauty anymore. Now the Princess, that's a nice figure . . . We retrieved the hairpin by the way."

Huang Zixia stood inside the hall, listening for noise in the east room. She heard nothing. She walked quickly to the door and looked inside. The bed's brocade curtain hung neatly. The ornate couch was in place under the window. There were two cushions on the Persian rug. The engraved sandalwood wardrobe stood in the corner. The lantern light spilled into the night, but there was no sign of anyone. Wang Ruo, who so many people had seen go inside a moment ago, seemed to have disappeared like a wisp of smoke.

Huang Zixia looked everywhere. She leaned over the couch, opened the window, and peered out. Two guards stood facing the window. She saw Li Shubai in the front hall speaking with Wang Yun.

She signaled there was trouble.

They hurried through the courtyard, saw the empty room, and ordered their men to search the palace. Every corner was searched, but there was no trace of Wang Ruo. When the Empress's attendant Zhang Ling heard the commotion, she brought Su Qi inside and asked, "What happened?" When she saw Li Shubai, she immediately bowed, then looked at Ran Yun and Xian Yun, who whispered, "We don't know where the Princess went."

"Su Qi and I were just bringing flowers and clothing. How could this happen in such a short time, with so many people around?"

"Go back to the Empress," Wang Yun said. "I'm going to take my men and search Yongchun Hall. If we find her, we'll send word right away."

"I'll leave a few people to help and get back to Penglai," Zhang Ling said, indicating for the attendants to put the things down.

Wang Yun began giving orders. With all those people, they were able to search every inch of Yongchun Hall several times but found no clues.

Like the prophecy, Wang Ruo disappeared.

Nine

Autumn Dew

Soon the Emperor's eunuch Yong Ji came. Yongchun Hall was packed with eunuchs, ladies, guards, and soldiers. Li Shubai was annoyed by the commotion and ordered everyone out, apart from Wang Yun and about ten of his men, so they could find whatever traces they could.

Li Shubai and Huang Zixia went to the entrance and carefully surveyed the surroundings.

Quiet had returned to Yongchun Hall. In the darkness of night, it looked no different than any other.

"We were standing outside, close to the veranda, when we watched Wang Ruo go inside the hall. She still had some distance to travel when she went through the rock garden, but we could still see her silhouette. We clearly saw her go in and not come out."

Li Shubai nodded.

Huang Zixia continued to go over the details. She recounted how Xian Yun went to the kitchen and Ran Yun came out to search for the hairpin. "This is something we need to look into. In a time like this, why would Xian Yun and Ran Yun come out together leaving Wang Ruo alone?" Huang Zixia sat down at a table and instinctively reached to undo her hair, but she felt her eunuch cap and stopped.

Li Shubai frowned slightly.

Huang Zixia didn't look at him. "I found the hairpin and gave it to them, as Xian Yun had just returned with walnut biscuits." She looked closely at the map and traced a line from the inner hall to the kitchen. "Yongchun Hall has a small dining area in the southwest corner. It's Xian Yun's first time here, but she got there and found food incredibly quickly. Is that good luck, or does she have a great nose?"

Li Shubai watched her unconsciously playing with her hairpin. "Anything else?"

"The inner palace is nearly impenetrable. It consists of three parts, the east hall, main hall, and west hall, respectively. If you want to get into the east hall, the only way is through the main hall. And with Xian Yun, Ran Yun, and I standing at the entrance of the main hall, apart from climbing the wall, her only way out was through the window."

"But there were two guards outside the window," Li Shubai said. "I was outside. If someone opened the window, we would've seen it."

"Another possibility is that the hall has a secret passage."

"A tunnel? Could be," Li Shubai said.

They went back to Wang Ruo's room. Li Shubai sat at the table and poured some tea.

Huang Zixia started looking around herself, knocking on the floors and walls. She even moved the wardrobe and examined the wall behind it. Li Shubai drank his tea and watched her as if it all had nothing to do with him. When Huang Zixia's fingers got sore, Li Shubai tossed her a chunk of silver, thick and square, about one pound. It looked like someone cut an ingot in half.

She lay on the ground and hit the floor with the silver and listened carefully but didn't hear anything unusual. She lifted up the carpet and knocked underneath.

She got to the part of the floor where Li Shubai's feet were. He moved indifferently to the other side of the couch. "Why does the Prince carry an ingot around? Half, at that."

"I don't," Li Shubai said casually, pointing at the teacups on the table. "It was there, under the teacup. I found it when I picked up the cup."

"Strange. Who would have put it there?" She picked the ingot up and looked at it closely. On the back, according to casting conventions, it said, *Deputy Liang Weidong, Deng Yunxi*, and so on.

Li Shubai took it. "In order to make sure no one cuts corners and the makeup of the silver is correct, one minister and two deputy ministers have to examine it and engrave their names."

"I know; so after it was cut in half, it cut off a deputy minister's name and part of the denomination. It was probably twenty silvers," Huang Zixia said, weighing it.

Li Shubai pointed at the names. "These two people aren't responsible for examining currency."

"You even know who the treasury officials are?"

"Actually, there was a bribery case there once, and I had to examine dozens of account logs. I also looked through all the records on gold and silver ingots and remember the names of the ministers."

She was amazed. "Could this be a privately cast ingot?" Then she shook her head. "Then they'd engrave the owner's name, not that of a fake official—so it's a forgery?"

"No. Its purity and weight are accurate." He looked at her thoughtfully, then held up four fingers. "It seems this is the fourth thing to consider—half a silver ingot of unknown origin."

Why is it half? Huang Zixia said to herself. She wasn't expecting any easy answers, so she put it on the table. "And what do you want to do?"

"With regard to that, there are things I have to take care of. Tibetan emissaries are arriving in the capital tomorrow. I have to receive them at the Ministry of Rites." He stood and brushed his clothes. "As I said, you're taking the lead on this. Now the worst has happened. You need to go forward and figure out how she disappeared."

Huang Zixia stood up. "By myself?"

"The court and palace will certainly help. I'll speak with them and make sure you—right, if you need help with a body or something, get Zhou Ziqin."

Huang Zixia's mouth twitched. *His betrothed disappeared before his eyes and he's already thinking about bodies; what kind of man is this?*

Huang Zixia went back to Yongchun Hall and examined every corner. She considered several ways to sneak out of windows and doors but none seemed promising. At the Empress's orders, men searched the rest of the palace but nothing turned up. They remove all the furniture and decorations but still nothing. Soon the Central Court's Cui Chunzhan also came to undertake a review.

Following Li Shubai's orders, Huang Zixia went to see him.

Cui Chunzhan was only thirtysomething years old and full of energy. He reminded her of Wang Yun. He asked her to sit and said, "You're a young little man but quite the sleuth. I'm sure you'll be very helpful in solving this one."

"I'll help in any way I can."

The court questioned Su Qi, Xian Yun, and Ran Yun. But they all said the same thing. Neither Li Shubai nor any of the eunuchs or attendants saw Wang Ruo leave. The guards in the courtyard, faithfully watching the window, saw nothing move until Huang Zixia opened it.

"Of course, Wang Yun took every possible precaution. Still, this happened." Cui Chunzhan sighed. "Does the little eunuch have any leads?"

Huang Zixia shook her head. "Before you came, Li Shubai and I looked thoroughly but found nothing."

After all the searching, the only item found was a chunk of charred wood on the stove in the small dining room. Huang Zixia took it and examined it closely. Its shape was basically intact, vaguely like a water chestnut, narrower on one end and curved on the other.

"It's probably just a piece of wood from the firewood store. Nothing important," Cui Chunzhan said.

Huang Zixia nodded and gave it to a court staffer. "Let's make sure, just in case."

"Yes, Mr. Yang's right. Hold on to it." Cui Chunzhan then ordered his men to get the paperwork in order and finish up for the day.

When Huang Zixia said goodbye to Cui Chunzhan, he smiled. "Good to see you today. We'll be working together a lot in the coming days. Why don't you let me treat you to a meal?"

Huang Zixia was on the case at the Prince's orders, so she had to agree. When she got to the restaurant, there were already some people sitting in the private room.

Jin Nu was there, and so was Zhou Ziqin in his blue silk robe with red trim and yellow belt. He gave a giddy explanation of how to tell how long ago the animal died based on the taste of its meat.

Wang Yun gracefully sprung up to greet them.

"Chonggu!" As soon as Zhou Ziqin saw her, he forgot his lecture and waved. "When I heard one of the Prince of Kui's eunuchs was helping on the case, I knew it was you!"

Huang Zixia ignored the open seat next to Wang Yun and sat next to the terribly dressed Zhou Ziqin. "Didn't expect to see you here," she said.

Cui Chunzhan smiled. "Ziqin has a nuanced understanding of the human body. We often ask him for help. Shame he's going to Shu with Minister Zhou soon. We won't see each other as much. Let's have some drinks."

Zhou Ziqin looked at him angrily. "Every time we drink, you act like an old lady and finish after one or two!"

Cui Chunzhan laughed. Eight hot dishes came, and everyone took some.

"Are there any clues about my sister's disappearance?" Wang Yun asked.

Cui Chunzhan shook his head. "Seems we need more time."

Wang Yun looked worried but didn't seem to want to press Cui Chunzhan.

Zhou Ziqin looked at the fish. "Huh? Ms. Li didn't cook the fish today?"

The server was surprised. "How'd you know? She's home tonight."

"It's clearly the work of a novice. The belly's overdone. The fat and epidermis are destroyed, so the unique flavor is lost! And the black meat of the anus isn't all the way clean. Ms. Li would've gotten it easily!"

Everyone laughed. "You've met Ziqin before, Chonggu?" Wang Yun asked.

Huang Zixia looked a little helpless as she watched Zhou Ziqin put a large piece of fish in his bowl. "Once or twice."

Cui Chunzhan smiled. "Ziqin hits it off with everyone, as we all know."

"Chonggu and I are like blood!" Ziqin said.

Didn't we just dig up a corpse together? Since when are we blood? Huang Zixia thought bitterly as she began to eat some fish herself.

"I'm not kidding. You won't find a better judge of fish anywhere!" Ziqin continued. "When I was little, my dad wouldn't let me go out, so all I did was study the cook preparing meat. Cattle have one hundred and eight bones, chicken one hundred sixty-four, but fish bones vary a lot. Take the carp today—its bones are very evenly distributed. Here, let me teach you a trick. Don't tell anyone. The meat on the back can be taken off in layers. That's very important."

Everyone listened and drank and made jokes.

Huang Zixia noticed that Wang Yun looked a bit at a loss, though he managed to fit in and smile.

"Did you hear the latest rumor?" someone said.

"What rumor?"

"About Princess Qi Le. She's so happy about the Princess of Kui's disappearance, she went to pray at the temple. Of course, no one knows what she was praying for, but people can guess." This didn't surprise anyone.

Jin Nu laughed. "Not a coincidence, then. When I went to play pipa for Lady Zhou, I saw Princess Qi Le."

"When the Princess went missing, Qi Le was in the palace?" Cui Chunzhan asked.

"Yup. She was making copies for the lady—I heard she'd been doing that for a while in order to gain favor and try to become the Princess of Kui herself."

"Yes, when rumors spread that the Princess might go missing before the wedding, I'm sure she was the happiest to hear it." All the men besides Wang Yun laughed. His presence wasn't enough for them to restrain themselves.

Cui Chunzhan maintained some composure. "It's a difficult situation. The court has never questioned a Princess before."

"Ask the court about it tomorrow," Cheng Fu, an official from the court said.

Huang Zixia looked helplessly at the men and thought about Princess Qi Le a moment.

The room was full of noise and activity, but Wang Yun was within himself. His black clothing and serious expression made him stand out among these men.

Soon everyone was full of food and drink. It was late. The server came to light candles, and Jin Nu picked up the pipa and tuned it for the final song.

"Ah, this weather," she said. "It rained all day, which made the strings moist and loose. Doesn't sound good."

"How do you fix it?" Huang Zixia asked.

"Just need to rub some rosin on it." She took out an intricate box and used three fingers to pinch some rosin powder and carefully rubbed it along the strings. "This came from the palace today. Look, even the box is beautiful."

Huang Zixia didn't understand why she was so proud. She looked at the pipa and said, "This 'Autumn Dew' is really beautiful."

She smiled slightly and kept rubbing the rosin. Her smile grew wider as she took the jade pick and began to play a cheerful song.

When the song stopped, Cui Chunzhan said, "Grace is truly a burden. We must do everything we can to break this case and regain the trust of the Emperor, Empress, and Prince of Kui. I hope everyone will pitch in with advice and suggestions. We'll finish soon, by the grace of heaven!"

With that, their feast ended.

The court people paid the check and saw Cui Chunzhan and Wang Yun off. Only Zhou Ziqin, Jin Nu, and Huang Zixia were left. Zhou Ziqin saw a few of the dishes hadn't been touched. He tapped a couple. "So they have lotus leaves, right? Pack this chicken, fish, and pig's feet up for me."

"It's true," Jin Nu said, "Mr. Zhou doesn't waste anything."

"Animals have a certain dignity. Why turn it into swill for nothing?" Zhou Ziqin smiled. "That one in front of you, yes, the cherries—help me pack it."

"Cherries have dignity too?" Jin Nu watched her own white fingers struggle to fold the cherry into the lotus leaf and give it to him. She frowned and said, "These stems are so hard. They poked my hand."

"I knew your hands were tender, but not that tender. Thanks," Zhou Ziqin said as he tied the packages into a bundle.

"When would be convenient for me to visit you?" Huang Zixia asked Jin Nu.

"Oh, Mr. Yang's interested in pipa too?" She batted her eyelashes.

"Just some things I want to ask."

"About my master?"

Huang Zixia had no interest in her, but she smiled and said, "Of course, it's related to your classmates who had their eyes on the Prince of Kui."

"Sure, why not ask the Prince of Kui to come himself? I'll certainly point out all the girls that like him." She laughed.

"Jin Nu," Huang Zixia couldn't help but add, "that day in Penglai Hall, you said something that really concerned me."

"What?" Jin Nu looked at her innocently.

"You said the Princess shouldn't be her." Huang Zixia spoke quietly but clearly.

Jin Nu's face suddenly stiffened. "Don't say it. It upsets me. Really, it's just that Princess Qi Le looks more like a Princess, that's all."

Huang Zixia wanted to ask more, but Jin Nu was already out the door, telling the driver to hurry before the curfew started. Huang Zixia helplessly watched her carriage go, worried that if Li Shubai and the Central Court arrested her, she'd be doomed. She couldn't even take the pain of picking up cherry stems, after all.

The Zhou carriage was waiting outside too. "Where are you going, Chonggu?" Zhou Ziqin asked.

"Back to the Prince of Kui's."

"I'll drop you on the way," he said, motioning her to get in.

Huang Zixia smiled. "On the way? Kui Palace is much farther than your house."

"I'm not going home!" he said, waving her on again. The driver didn't wait for his orders to start driving north toward Xingqing Palace.

Changan's curfew had started. The moon rose as darkness fell, and the streets were quiet. Outside the Xingqin Palace walls, emaciated beggars sat around fires on the rocks by the moat. The carriage stopped, and Zhou Ziqin jumped out. He brought the packages of food and set them on some rocks, untied a package of roast chicken, and got back in.

The driver began heading toward Kui Palace.

Huang Zixia pulled the curtain aside and looked back.

The beggars had gathered around the food and were eating excitedly now. Huang Zixia couldn't help but smile. "I didn't know you did more than study anatomy."

"Oh, it's nothing," he said, waving his hand.

Lanterns hung along the neighborhood walls, illuminating the silent streets. As the carriage passed, some light flickered through the windows. Zhou Ziqin's smile seemed gentler and simpler, even innocent, in that light.

It made Huang Zixia feel a little nostalgic. The smile on the person before her was gentle and pure—effortless.

And she, who had experienced so much evil—did she still have a soft place inside?

When she got back to the Prince of Kui's palace, it was already about ten. By the time she heated water, took a bath, washed and hung her clothes, and went to bed, it was midnight.

At dawn, she was startled awake by a knock on the door. "Yang Chonggu! Get up!"

Huang Zixia sat up with difficulty and said, "Who is it?"

"The Prince sent orders for you to go to the gate of Daming Palace immediately."

She felt miserable. "Isn't the Prince at a meeting?"

"The Emperor isn't feeling well this morning so they canceled, and the Prince would like you to go immediately. What's it matter to you, anyway, little eunuch? Just do as you're told."

"Right, right, right . . ."

She washed quickly and hurried to Daming Palace, but by the time she got there, the sun was already high. Li Shubai was at the palace gate speaking cheerfully with a Uighur person. She didn't understand a word. Huang Zixia stood next to them. Li Shubai apparently said goodbye, and the man left. Then Li Shubai invited Huang Zixia into his carriage.

He closed his eyes and smiled slightly. "What were you talking about?" Huang Zixia asked.

Li Shubai looked at her. "You wouldn't want to know."

Huang Zixia felt this meant "beg me." She decided to humor him. "Really. What were you talking about?"

"This is a good eunuch, cheerful and still manly."

"Guess I shouldn't have asked." Huang Zixia turned to look out the window. "Where are we going?"

"There are no clues in the case, right? I'll help you find some."

Huang Zixia's eyes lit up. "Li Run's palace?"

Li Shubai smiled and nodded. "It'd be hard for you to go alone, so I'm taking you."

"Right. It seems Li Run is housing Chen Nian. If there are any clues, they're with Feng Yi's body or Chen Nian." Then she remembered to tell him about Jin Nu. After, she asked, "Do you think we should tell the court to question her?"

Li Shubai nodded. "Sooner the better."

The carriage suddenly stopped.

A guard tapped the wall and said, "Princess Qi Le has stopped us."

Li Shubai frowned slightly and looked out the curtain. Princess Qi Le's carriage was ahead. She was walking toward them.

The normally haughty Princess Qi Le teared up and bowed at the sight of him. "Hello, Your Highness."

Li Shubai bowed back. "How can I be of service to the Princess?"

"Prince of Kui, sir, I heard the rumors about the Princess of Kui came from me. I hope I haven't worried you, but I just felt so uneasy . . ."

Her sparkling almond eyes suddenly looked at him. The plumpness of her cheeks had lessened greatly. Obviously, she had not been well since Li Shubai chose his Princess.

Li Shubai just looked at her calmly. "No matter. Wang Ruo's disappearance in the palace was strange, but that doesn't mean we won't find her. When we do, you can make amends."

"But I heard that . . ." She swallowed and whispered. "Ghosts may be responsible, and she may already no longer be with us." Huang Zixia studied this attempt at desperation that couldn't conceal her glee. Everyone could see right through her acts.

Li Shubai was unmoved. He comforted Princess Qi Le, but she cried harder. He hesitated, looking helpless, then wiped her tears away.

Huang Zixia saw the desperation on his face. "Princess, Jing Yu already let Li Run know we're coming. I'm afraid he may be waiting, you know."

Li Shubai nodded. "I must be going. Please be calm, Princess. I'll take care of everything."

Princess Qi Le stood watching him get back in his carriage. Only then did she return to her own.

"You think I should have ignored her instead of helped her?" he asked.

Huang Zixia didn't respond, but she knew she was wearing her heart on her sleeve.

"Before, when the Emperor died, she was the only one who held my hand and comforted me."

"So you keep stringing her along and make her the talk throughout the city."

He glanced at her but didn't speak. The clear water in the glass jar hanging on the carriage wall shook slightly with the bumps. The red fish seemed accustomed to the circumstances as he lay placidly on the bottom.

Sometime later, he said, "You know she was born with a defect that won't let her live past twenty?" Huang Zixia stared at him. He looked at the fish. "Even though the Prince of Yi was part of the royal family, the Emperor had no son, so he granted him that title so he could prepare to take the throne. If it weren't for a battle at court, he would have ruled the world. He was heir to the throne, but that birth defect kept him from it. The Prince of Yi died, and Qi Le's brothers died, leaving her all alone. How else could she dare take my hand when my father the Emperor died?"

Huang Zixia didn't answer. She thought about the girl with apple cheeks and almond eyes who had become a citywide laughingstock. After a time, she whispered, "Does Princess Qi Le know?"

"I think she knows her situation's bad but not how good it could have been," he said, slowly closing his eyes. "Let her fantasize for a few days. Later, she won't have the chance."

Ten

THE SIX WOMEN OF YUNSHAO

The carriage rolled through the streets of western Changan and arrived at the gates of Li Run's palace.

Huang Zixia followed Li Shubai out. Li Run was already waiting for them. He still looked handsome and refined, a restrained smile on his face, his clothing and body gently luxurious. The cinnabar mole on his forehead made his thin facial features take on a beautiful brilliance. He smiled and nodded at Huang Zixia, then greeted Li Shubai. "Weren't you supposed to meet with the Uighur Prince at Daming Palace this morning? How do you have time to see me?"

"Nothing important, just routine stuff. But he gave me red sandalwood beads. I thought you might like them, so I brought them to give to you."

"You know me well, brother!" Li Run took them happily and felt them one at a time. "Come sit. I just got a cake of tea from Tianxi. It's very fresh. Come drink some."

The drawing room's windows and doors were all open. Outside, there was a small spring surrounded by some white stones and a large shrub. Huang Zixia sipped her tea. Two poems by Wang Wei hung on the wall. One said, *The pine wind blows through the forest, touching my clothes tenderly. The mountain moon shines on me as I play my instrument.* The other said, *The moonlight shines on the pines; the creek flows over the stones.*

Li Shubai tasted the tea. "This is a really poetic atmosphere."

Huang Zixia immediately understood what he was getting at. "If there was music, that'd be incredible," she said softly.

"Chonggu's right. Luckily, I have a musician right here." Li Run smiled, nodded, and called for Chen Nian.

"Mr. Yang," she said, happy to see Huang Zixia.

Huang Zixia nodded, and her right hand involuntarily twitched in its sleeve. Her pocket held the jade from the skeleton. Huang Zixia was moved at the sight of her. *This jade has your name engraved on it. Feng Yi never let it leave her side!* She stayed calm on the outside. "Chen Nian, I'm sorry, but there's no news from the ministry on the whereabouts of your partner. We'll have to keep waiting."

She nodded a little tiredly. Still, her playing was amazing.

"I don't think anyone in the academy can match Chen Nian!" Li Shubai said.

Li Run smiled. "I don't think so either. She's one of the best in the empire."

"Chonggu," Li Shubai said casually, "last time you heard Chen Nian, you asked about songs and wanted to learn guqin yourself. Now's your chance. Why not ask Master Chen?"

Huang Zixia was amazed at his ability to sound so natural while lying. She helped Chen Nian put the guqin back in its bag and carried it to the music room. Li Run had treated Chen Nian like a guest of honor. Her room was next to a small courtyard in the eastern corner of the palace. It was full of bamboo, sparse and quiet.

"Learning guqin is a lifetime of hard work. It might be hard for you to learn with your busy schedule. If you just want to whet your appetite, then I can teach you a few simple songs. Have you learned the basic positions and finger techniques?"

Huang Zixia asked her to teach her, and Chen Nian did. Soon it was afternoon, and the palace staff brought them lunch. Huang Zixia noticed Chen Nian ate very little. "Master Chen, you look thin these days. Please don't worry too much. I'm sure Feng Yi wouldn't want to see you suffering."

Chen Nian looked up at her and smiled reluctantly. "Thank you, little eunuch, but I can't relax. When I close my eyes at night, I see her face. We were inseparable for ten years. Now it's just me. I don't know how to go on."

Huang Zixia patted her hand and thought of her parents. She clutched the white jade in her sleeve. She gave the portrait back to Chen Nian. "I asked them to make a copy so they could keep helping you look, okay?"

Chen Nian took it. "Of course. Thank you so much."

"You were so close to Feng Yi, but she never told you who asked her for help?"

"No. Feng Yi didn't hide anything from me, but this time all she said was she couldn't pass up the opportunity."

Huang Zixia thought a moment. "She didn't hide anything from you; can you think of an old friend who would excite her like that?"

Chen Nian tuned the strings. "She really didn't hide anything. Though we grew up together, studied together, fate was not good to her. Once, she was sold to a brothel. Luckily, a patron bought her to be his wife. The woman of the house hated her, so she had to save money to buy freedom herself. After, she joined the Yunshao Court musicians. I was always in Luoyang. I only found out she was in Yangzhou when I got a letter from her a few years later. It said, 'Chen Nian, we promised to be by each other's side forever.'" Tears started falling down Chen Nian's face.

So Chen Nian didn't know who her old friend was either?

Chen Nian saw her thinking. "Little eunuch," she said, "are these things related to finding her?"

Huang Zixia hesitated, then nodded. "The ministry didn't find any records, so I sneaked a look myself. Since something happened at the palace recently, I'm working with the board and court and might have another chance to help you find Feng Yi."

"Thank you so much, little eunuch! If you need to ask me anything, I'll tell you whatever I can."

"I think the most important thing is to find out who the old friend who asked her to go to the capital was."

"I guess I must have asked at the time, but I really don't know."

"I think the old friend would most likely be one of her peers, someone who left Yunshao Court."

"Okay, in that case, it must've been someone she met while we were apart," Chen Nian said carefully, holding up her index finger. "When Feng Yi and I were together, we were so close. Everyone she knew at Yunshao, I also knew. Must be someone I wasn't familiar with. Otherwise, she would have told me who asked her to escort their daughter."

"How long ago did you two separate? Is there anyone who would know what was going on back then?"

"Must be fifteen or sixteen years. Yunshao Court is a bustling place. People come and go all the time. The old people who were around are mostly all gone."

"But for someone to ask for this favor more than ten years later means they wouldn't have been a casual acquaintance. At the least, whatever happened back then wouldn't have been easily forgotten." Huang Zixia thought a moment. "Could there be something she didn't tell you about?"

Chen Nian thought a moment, then suddenly said, "Ah, the Six Women of Yunshao."

The Six Women of Yunshao. Huang Zixia remembered Jin Nu mentioning the founders of the Yunshao Court.

"Over ten years ago, the six best female performers in Yangzhou joined to establish Yunshao Court, and named it after China's Wu Zetian, China's first Empress's courtyard. They still use her dagger during rituals!"

How strange, Huang Zixia thought, a musical academy worshipping with a dagger. "How did it end up in Yangzhou?"

"The oldest of the Six Women of Yunshao was a descendent of Gong Sun. At that time, Gong Sun was renowned for her sword dancing, so Emperor Xuanzong gave the dagger to her. After the trouble in Anshi, Gong Sun gave it to one of her disciples' disciples, who ended up being the eldest of the Six Women of Yunshao, Gong Sunyuan."

"Who among the six was closest to Feng Yi?"

"When I went, only Sunyuan remained. They said the others had married or left. Feng Yi said if it weren't for the Six Women of Yunshao, she couldn't have paid the ransom that got her out of that brothel. I think they wanted to sell her again, but because of her talent, they made a deal and bought her themselves. It's a shame they hardly kept in touch. I only met Sunyuan, the oldest, and Lan Dai, who is the third oldest. Even though they were famous in Yangzhou, they still came out of a music academy, so marrying into a good family wasn't easy."

Huang Zixia nodded. Though she couldn't be sure the woman who called on Feng Yi was one of the Six Women, it was a lead. "Do you know Jin Nu?"

"Of course. Last time I played for the Princes was because Jin Nu set it up."

"Please tell me more about her." Huang Zixia took her hand. "Like her background, whom she was friends with."

Chen Nian frowned slightly in recollection. "There were a lot of musicians in Yangzhou, but Jin Nu's playing was amazing. A prodigy, really. She knew a lot of important people and their children, and never seemed to make enemies. We didn't talk much, but she is a good person. She saw me here after I ran out of money. When she found out my situation, she helped me find a place to stay and pay rent. I think she got along well with people at the academy. As for the girls here, I don't know."

"I heard her master was called Mei Wanzhi, one of the Six Women?" Huang Zixia asked.

"That's what I heard. Wanzhi was the best player back then. She adopted Jin Nu when she was five and treated her like her own flesh and blood. Later, when she had her daughter Xuese, people said she still treated Jin Nu better."

"Xuese?" She wasn't sure if she'd said Xuese as in "snow" or Xuese as in "blood red." Huang Zixia's mind suddenly flashed.

Chen Nian didn't notice. "Yes, Xuese." Snow.

"Mei Wanzhi married an artist with the surname Cheng. He was very good-looking and a good painter, but deep down he was different from other people."

Huang Zixia could tell the memories were coming back. She squeezed Chen Nian's hand. "Her daughter Xuese. How is she now?"

Chen Nian looked at her in surprise. "Her daughter didn't have the best fate. Her mother died before her fifth birthday. Her father took her back to his hometown of Liuzhou, but there was no way to make a living. She lived in poverty and ill health during her childhood. Greedy relatives quickly forced them to sell their land, leaving Xuese without a home. Then, some of the remaining Six Women heard and brought her to Yangzhou. Everyone was excited. When she arrived, I went with

Feng Yi and a big group to greet her. The thirteen-year-old girl had traveled thousands of miles. She was disheveled, dirty, and thin. She wasn't nearly as beautiful or elegant as Wanzhi. The people cried, saying they couldn't believe her daughter had suffered like that."

"So where is Xuese now?"

"Lan Dai took her to Puzhou. Feng Yi and I only saw her that once in the crowd. We didn't even get a good enough look at her to remember what she looks like."

"I see. Does she play music?"

"I really don't know. Her mother was a wonderful pipa player, but when Xuese came along, she was already past her prime."

"Mei Wanzhi was very beautiful?" Huang Zixia asked.

"I never saw her, but I heard she was truly beautiful!" Chen Nian said firmly. "Yunshao Court is always full of beautiful women. Jin Nu is one, but Feng Yi always said Xuese was far from matching her mother. As far as beauty goes, Mei Wanzhi was the only truly stunning one."

"I see. Jin Nu did say her master was a world-class beauty."

"When Mei Wanzhi died, Jin Nu wasn't much older than ten, but she was always talking about her. It wasn't just that Mei Wanzhi saved Jin Nu's life. Jin Nu worshipped her. I heard, when she left Yunshao Court for the capital, she went out of her way to go to Puzhou to see Lan Dai and visit Xuese. Holding her pipa in her arms, she kneeled in front of Mei Wanzhi's portrait for half an hour."

"Mei Wanzhi has a portrait?" Huang Zixia asked.

"Mei Wanzhi's husband was a painter. Poor as he was, he was good. He even painted a group portrait of the Six Women of Yunshao. Lan Dai has it."

Huang Zixia nodded. "Would it be possible to borrow that and have a look?"

"Certainly. When Lan Dai left Yangzhou, she left me her address in Puzhou. I'll ask Xuese to send it over. Should take a day or two."

"Really?" Huang Zixia said. "That's great. If Xuese can personally send the portrait, I think that will help."

"Sure. I'll write Lan Dai a letter today."

"Thank you so much."

Back at the palace, Li Shubai frowned as Huang Zixia told him what she'd learned. "How could something so long ago and so far away be relevant?"

"I was surprised too," Huang Zixia said, "but there's good reason to believe it's related." They walked over a bridge toward Jingyu Hall as they discussed the case. Li Shubai didn't like to be surrounded by attendants, so there were a few eunuch guards following far behind. On the bridge, it was just the two of them. Lanterns hanging between the shore and forest had been lit. They looked down. The lanterns were reflected in the water with the moon and stars, twinkling. The two seemed to be suspended in space.

Li Shubai turned to look at Huang Zixia, who was a few feet behind him, and paused to admire the beauty of her eyes in this light.

Suddenly, a clamor of footsteps broke the peace. Someone ran toward the bridge shouting, "Prince! My Prince!"

It was a frightened Zhou Ziqin.

Li Shubai signaled for the guards to let him come over. They walked to the pavilion and motioned for Zhou Ziqin to sit. "What happened?"

Zhou Ziqin looked confused and hesitant, his fists clenched.

Li Shubai frowned. "*What* happened?"

"I . . . I may have . . ." Zhou Ziqin was pale and trembling. He looked at Li Shubai and Huang Zixia before finally forcing out some words: "May have killed someone."

"May have?" Li Shubai said.

"I just can't say it right. Chonggu knows. I never wanted to kill them!"

Huang Zixia was shocked. "What does it have to do with me?"

"Because the people who died were the beggars I gave food to last night!"

Huang Zixia gasped.

Li Shubai glanced at her. "Ziqin, tell me exactly what happened."

"Right," Zhou Ziqin said nervously. Zhou Ziqin told Li Shubai about that night and giving the food to the beggars. "I do it a lot and never had any problems."

Huang Zixia nodded encouragingly.

"Then, this morning after I got up, I heard the board people are examining corpses found next to Xingqing Palace, so I went and found out that it was the beggars from last night!"

"So the food we gave them was poisoned?" Huang Zixia asked. "But we didn't notice anything unusual while we were eating."

Zhou Ziqin anxiously grabbed her hand. "Really! They died from poison. I secretly took the lotus leaves I used to wrap the food home for testing and found traces of poison, and it's a poison we rarely see."

Li Shubai looked at their hands. Huang Zixia brought hers quietly back. "What poison?"

"The sap of a poisonous tree. The Nanman call it antiaris. Anyone who ingests it dies before they can take ten steps. It's one of the most poisonous substances in the world." Zhou Ziqin frowned. "It's rare in the capital. I'd only heard of it in books. It causes black ulcerations all over the skin. Pus and swelling make people unrecognizable. It's horrible!"

"The beggars were like that?"

"Yes, and the board is determined to find the killer." Zhou Ziqin's lips were pale, and his shoulder was still trembling. "But, Chonggu, you know I had no intention of harming anyone!"

Huang Zixia frowned. "How did our food suddenly get poisoned on the way? We're all fine."

"We ate the food, and it was we who wrapped it up and gave it to them."

"I think the most important thing," Li Shubai said, "is who it was you were eating with that poisoned the food."

Huang Zixia nodded. "Minister Cui, Wang Yun, us, some court officials, and Jin Nu."

Zhou Ziqin seemed to count them on his fingers and decide they couldn't be murderers. "Chonggu, do you think we'll be blamed?"

"What do you think?" Huang Zixia said.

"When we were walking there, it was almost curfew, so no one saw us, so I think maybe as long as we don't say anything, we'll be fine."

"I don't know about anyone else, but I'd check the stomach contents. Beggars don't get to eat food that good very often, so the range of suspects will narrow. And the lotus leaves were fresh. Usually, the kitchen uses spare dry ones for that. Why would they use fresh ones just to pack food? The capital is at a low altitude, wet and cold. The ponds just filled up, so restaurants have to get lotus leaves from fisherman outside the city. They send them with fish and shrimp in the morning. They're not easy to come by."

"Then maybe they used lotus leaves for takeout to be misleading."

"Maybe, but before considering that possibility, detectives will have visited the major restaurants and found out that Zhou Ziqin, who never wastes food, wrapped up those specific dishes—unambiguous evidence. You could be under investigation immediately."

Zhou Ziqin collapsed in his chair. His face went white and his eyes wide.

"Don't you always work with bodies?" Huang Zixia asked reluctantly. "Why are you so afraid of death?"

"I like to study bodies," he said weakly, "not turn people into dead bodies."

As Huang Zixia and Li Shubai exchanged a look, Jing Yu arrived. "Prince, Minister Cui has come to see you."

"What does the court want with me?"

"He said it has to do with the case."

Zhou Ziqin jumped up. "No, it can't be. Does he know I'm here?"

"Ziqin," Li Shubai said. Zhou Ziqin snapped out of it. Even if Cui Chunzhan knew he was responsible, he wouldn't immediately come to Kui Palace to find him. "Ask him to come in," Li Shubai said.

Cui Chunzhan approached them, bowed to Li Shubai, and nodded at Ziqin and Zixia. He didn't seem to pay much attention to them, which calmed Ziqin down some.

It was surprising when the first thing he said was, "You must know why I've come today, my Prince. Ziqin, Mr. Yang, you also know, right?"

Zhou Ziqin jumped up. "I-I know."

"Yes, so you also heard." He looked at Li Shubai before continuing. "The body's skin was festering with black pus, face bloated and twisted . . ."

Zhou Ziqin turned pale. He trembled as he spoke. "I saw."

"What? You already saw it?" Cui Chunzhan was shocked. "Seems Ziqin has quite the reputation. The palace calls you first, even on such a big case like this."

Huang Zixia and Li Shubai looked at each other, realizing he was talking about a different body.

But Zhou Ziqin was still rattled by guilt.

"You examine a lot of bodies, but it's the first time you've seen this too, right? The killer's cruelty is truly unthinkable!" Cui Chunzhan shook his head and sighed. "It even scared me half to death. This is the most brutal case the capital has seen in over a decade! Ziqin, you know a lot about poison. What type was it?"

He opened his mouth but couldn't make a sound.

Huang Zixia was trying to kick his foot when Li Shubai said, "This is why Ziqin came to me. He thinks the killer used the sap of a poisonous tree."

Cui Chunzhan nodded. "I knew this fellow would figure it out."

Zhou Ziqin looked like a man with a guilty conscience. Huang Zixia stared at him hard. *Why couldn't you play it cool? Now that we're directly involved, how are we going to find the real killer?*

"Where was Wang Ruo's body found?" Li Shubai asked.

Huang Zixia couldn't believe he was able to keep his composure so well. It made her shiver.

Zhou Ziqin jumped up. "Wh-what? The Princess who disappeared from the palace is dead? And you already found the body?"

Cui Chunzhan looked shocked. "Isn't that what we've been talking about?"

"I . . . I thought you were talking about . . ."

"Before you came, we were talking about the vicious murder of a group of beggars. Ziqin thought that's what you were referring to," Huang Zixia said.

Cui Chunzhan waved his hand. "A few beggars! We're talking about the Empress's cousin here. Much more important."

"Beggars are people too," Ziqin said weakly, "especially when there's three or four of them." Huang Zixia kicked him, and he finally shut his mouth.

"If you were discussing the beggars," Cui Chunzhan asked, "how did you know I was talking about the Princess?"

"You rushed over here on just any night needing to speak with me immediately. What else could it be?" Li Shubai said calmly.

"In that case . . . we've all been talking about the same thing?" Zhou Ziqin had finally shaken off the glaze over his eyes.

Cui Chunzhan nodded. "Yes. I think there was a misunderstanding. I was confused as to how you went to see the body of the Princess."

Of the four, only Huang Zixia remained focused. "Minister Cui, where was Princess Wang's body found?"

"If I told you, you wouldn't believe it," Cui Chunzhan said with a frown. "An hour ago, her body suddenly appeared in Yongchun Temple's east hall."

"What?" Zhou Ziqin said, jumping up again. "Didn't she go missing from there?"

"Yes, since the incident happened, the place has been tightly guarded. Today, the eunuchs went inside to have a look, because someone smelled something in the afternoon. Inside, they found the Wang girl's body in the bed. She still had the same clothing and leafy golden hairpin as the day she went missing, but the body was festering and black—poisoned to death!"

Huang Zixia frowned slightly but didn't say anything.

"This is incredible," Zhou Ziqin said. "How can someone mysteriously disappear without a trace and then mysteriously reappear?"

"Exactly. It's like she was never gone, there the whole time, but in two or three days became unrecognizable." Cui Chunzhan shook his head. "This case is a tough one."

Faced with such an important event, Li Shubai didn't bother observing the curfew. He asked Jing Yu to come help him change, so he could go to Yongchun Hall.

Huang Zixia straightened up her own clothes. "How could something be invisible?" she mused.

Cui Chunzhan looked pained. "It must be possible. How else could it have passed under two hundred people's noses?"

"I'm going to run home and get a few things. You chaps have to wait for me and let me go to the hall with you!" Zhou Ziqin joined in.

Li Shubai ignored him and began walking away. "Don't. She's royalty, regardless. You can't put her under the knife."

"Then, can I at least look?" he asked.

Li Shubai titled his chin toward Cui Chunzhan. "Doesn't the Central Court ask you to look at a lot of crime scenes? What's one more?"

Cui Chunzhan waved him on. "Come on, Ziqin. My carriage is this way."

Eleven

UNSEEN AND UNHEARD

Though it was nighttime, Daming Palace was full of light. The lanterns lit pavilions from below, giving them a noble appearance. The two carriages arrived at its eastern gate. They got off and, escorted by eunuchs holding lanterns, walked straight to Yongchun Hall in the corner of the palace grounds. The gate was closed, so they had to walk westward along the wall until they reached the southern side and could turn north where there was an entrance.

"Can't believe such a closed place couldn't keep a rumor in," Cui Chunzhan said.

As the three of them entered, they heard people arguing. They stood in the outer hall and saw several members of the Langya Wang family. Huang Zixia recognized Wang Yun and his father, Wang Lin, from the Board of Punishments.

Wang Yun was saying, "Wang Ruo is family. She was set to marry the Prince of Kui. A maiden is a precious thing. How can we let an examiner cut her open? It's unthinkable!"

Minister Wang sounded miserable. "You know your father here is a minister on the Board of Punishments. The law says the bodies of those who die suddenly should be examined. If we don't do an exam, what do we say to the court, or to the Prince of Kui?"

"Did you ever think doing an autopsy on the Princess-to-be might be a slap in the Prince of Kui's face? I don't care who thinks it's right; I don't think the Empress will allow it."

Wang Yun was ready to walk away when he saw Li Shubai and Huang Zixia standing on the veranda and hesitated.

Li Shubai's face had a rare smile on it as he walked toward Wang Yun. "You know me well. Of course I don't want some examiner touching Wang Ruo. That's why I brought the very best."

Wang Yu quickly greeted him and motioned Zhou Ziqin toward the body. "I think we all know him, the son of Zhou Xiang. He can look at Wang Ruo's body, as long as he doesn't use tools."

"Very thoughtful of you," Wang Lin said with a sigh.

Zhou Ziqin gave them all an apologetic look, then took Huang Zixia into Yongchun's eastern hall.

The east hall was lit with countless lamps. Everything was the same as it was the day of the incident. Since it was the imperial palace, everything had been put back after the search.

And in this bright, familiar environment was a body. It was dressed in a yellow robe, her hair in a loose bun, feet in silk slippers— just as she was when she disappeared. But her skin was festering and black with streams of blood and pus. Her face looked nothing like before. No one would be able to tell now that she was blossoming and young.

Huang Zixia looked at her quietly. Then she thought of the leafy hairpin of gold and pearls she had on the side of her head. A moment later, she pursed her lips and went over to the bed.

Zhou Ziqin brought a chair to the bedside, put on a pair of thin, soft leather gloves, bent over, and took the body's face in his hands.

Though Huang Zixia was used to the sight of dead bodies, this swollen, distorted face was unbearable to look at. She turned away. "I thought you didn't bring tools. When did you get the gloves?"

"When I left this morning. I heard about the poison murders by Xingqing Palace and grabbed them. When examining a body that's been poisoned, especially with something this toxic, the skin can break, causing poisonous fluids to spread onto your hands, so gloves are absolutely necessary. Who knew I wouldn't use them then but use them now?" Zhou Ziqin looked closely at the eyes, nose, and ears, then opened the mouth to see the tongue.

"The body's wearing Wang Ruo's clothing. Is the age and build hers too?"

"The victim is a young, slim woman. About five feet seven inches tall. It's unusual for women to be that tall, so it basically matches. Did Wang Ruo's body have any moles or birthmarks?"

She though back to her time with Wang Ruo. "I don't think she had any marks like that, but there were some freckles on her right wrist. Do you see them?"

Zhou Ziqin rolled up her right sleeve, took a look, and said sadly, "I'm afraid the poison spread from her right hand. The skin there is so black, nothing can be made out, not moles, and certainly not freckles."

"I see." Huang Zixia looked at the disfigured hand and thought back to the first time she met Wang Ruo in the carriage. Her hands were so beautiful then. "How did her hands get like this?" she asked. "They used to be so slender and nice."

"Slender?" Zhou Ziqin took the body's fingers into his. "Impossible. Her hand bones are relatively large. No way they were slim, even before being poisoned."

Huang Zixia gasped. "Give me the gloves."

Zhou Ziqin looked at her doubtfully. "Why?"

She just stuck her chin up and squinted. Zhou Ziqin obediently handed them over.

Though the gloves were made of soft leather, they were men's gloves after all, and a little big on Huang Zixia. Taking that into consideration, she compared her gloved hand with the body's. The swelling was mainly horizontal, but they were still longer than hers, which Chen Nian said was good for playing the guqin.

"Look," Zhou Ziqin said. "You're male but were probably purified at a very young age, so your hands are even smaller than hers."

What does purification have to do with hand size? Huang Zixia wanted to say as she pinched her own fingers through the gloves, then did the same to those of the body. She had to pinch deeper and deeper because of the swollen flesh. What she felt confirmed Zhou Ziqin's conclusion—the hand bones were far from slender.

"Don't press too hard, Chonggu," Zhou Ziqin said nervously. "The skin's already weak."

Huang Zixia stopped and looked to make sure she hadn't broken any. Luckily, only some on the palm was cracked. A thin white layer of skin showed, but there was no blood.

"It's a callus. And all her skin is festering; breaking a little of the callus doesn't matter," Zhou Ziqin said. He looked at the crack below her pinkie finger and smiled. "Strange, in all these years, I've never seen a callus here."

"Yes, logically, people get the most friction between the thumb and index finger. The outside of the palm is more likely." Huang Zixia took another look. There was also hard skin between the middle and third finger and some on the thumb. She thought about writing, embroidery, and clothes washing, but nothing fit.

Zhou Ziqin put his gloves away and said, "Nothing noteworthy besides that. This girl was born well off. Her hair and teeth are in good shape, and her body doesn't seem to show any signs of wear. This person might not be Wang Ruo, but we don't have good reason to say so."

"The safest thing would be to state the cause of death but avoid that issue altogether."

The two opened the door and went into the outer hall where everyone was waiting. Zhou Ziqin bowed to the crowd, then read his conclusion. "The deceased is female, five feet seven inches tall, with distorted facial features and swollen, festering, black skin. Her teeth are complete, her hair long and healthy. The body shows no signs of trauma, and was likely poisoned to death."

"How terrible!" Wang Lin said. "I never thought my niece could be killed in such a heavily guarded place!"

Two of Wang Ruo's brothers who had come from Langya for the wedding turned pale. The older one said, "So what's the cause of death?"

"Poisonous tree sap," Zhou Ziqin said.

Everyone looked at one another. "The one the Nanman call antiaris?" Wang Yun asked.

"Yes, it's very uncommon in the city. But another group of people were killed with it last night," Zhou Ziqin said. Huang Zixia was keeping quiet.

Before long, Empress Wang came. She looked at the woman on the bed and quickly turned and held on to Zhang Ling to keep from falling. She staggered away, hiding her face, without saying a word.

That night, Zhang Qing and a group of court servants worked silently to recover the body. The Wang family carriage left with the body. Li Shubai stood at the palace gate to see them off.

Zhou Ziqin went with Cui Chunzhan into his carriage. Huang Zixia prepared to mount the horse tied to Li Shubai's, but one look from him was enough for her to get down and go into the cab and sit on her usual stool.

The horses took them all the way to Kui Palace.

Li Shubai didn't look at her. He just fingered the glass jar holding the little red fish, which chased his fingers, its gossamer tail flowing behind it.

"I heard the conclusion of the examination. Do you have anything else to add?"

Huang Zixia looked at the little fish. "She did die from poisonous tree sap, last night. But unlike those beggars, whose throats were swollen, she didn't ingest the poison; it entered her externally. If Zhou Ziqin is allowed to do an autopsy, we can confirm this."

"If it came from outside, how?"

"That's one of the strange things. Though the body is swollen and full of ulcers, there's no sign that a weapon was used. Based on the skin discoloration, the poison likely spread throughout the body from the right hand."

"Right hand," Li Shubai mused. "Can poisonous sap kill from skin contact?"

"No, so it's still unclear how the victim was poisoned."

Li Shubai suddenly looked from the fish to her face. "When your parents died, and you started disguising yourself as a man, did anyone suspect it?"

Huang Zixia didn't know why he'd suddenly brought this up. "No. I often dressed as a man growing up to help my father with cases. I've managed to avoid suspicion."

He didn't elaborate. His tight lips turned slightly upward for a moment.

Huang Zixia touched her face hesitantly. He turned, not admonishing her for her girlish gesture. "Apart from that, are there any marks on the body? Is it Wang Ruo or a decoy?"

Huang Zixia was surprised. "What made you think of that?"

"I think everything has a reason. Using a poison to make the body unrecognizable must have been to hide something."

"Good guess. That body isn't Wang Ruo's because the hand bones are much larger than hers." She held out her right hand to look at it. "Another thing I don't understand is the calluses—on the fingertips of the pointer, middle, and ring on the left, and between the thumb and forefinger, on the outside of the palm on the right," she said, pointing at the spots on her own hand for Li Shubai. "There was another below her little finger. Hard to make out but certainly there."

"There aren't a lot of movements that would wear the skin that way." Li Shubai held out his slender, white hand, made a fist, then released it again.

"Any ideas?"

"I thought of something, but I can't remember now." He frowned and put his hand back down. "The most important thing about this case right now is invisibility."

Huang Zixia nodded. "That man's sudden appearance and disappearance in Xianyou Temple, Wang Ruo's disappearing despite being heavily guarded, the body appearing from nowhere, and even its invisible hand wound."

"Really, it's just like a magic trick. But normal people are unable of thinking in that way, so they can't see it. There's another possibility too," Li Shubai said as he held the glass jar up to light. The jar's shape was suddenly obscured by the sunlight, and the fish floated in Li Shubai's palm like a phantom. "The other possibility is that she's right in front of us, but because of our perspective and attitude, we can't see her, so she doesn't exist."

Huang Zixia stared at the red fish, took a deep breath, and murmured, "I've never seen a case with fewer, more confusing clues, and no starting point."

"Don't stop. You'll keep looking and find the terrible thread connecting all this." Li Shubai put the jar back on the table, a faint smile on his lips. "This case must be related to the struggle between the Empress and the concubines, the Langya Wang family's honor, Prince Yi's survival, the last of Pang Xun's rebellion, even . . ." He stopped speaking and looked at the fish. His face was calm as usual, but Huang Zixia felt some force pressing on her chest that made it harder to breathe.

She looked at him, thinking, *Even what? Besides the royal family, its relatives, and rebels? That unspeakable thing?*

He looked at his fingers, which seemed capable of crushing the fish, and thought of the first time they met—what he said to her about the fish.

Huang Zixia stared at the ignorant red fish. *Where did this thing he always kept by his side come from? What secret does it hold?*

The light coming from outside flickered on Li Shubai's face as the carriage bounced. His clear outline wasn't obscured by the sun like the jar's had been. In the light, his normally elegant face seemed more vivid and striking.

She looked quietly as the carriage bumped along, and suddenly she felt at a complete loss.

The weather was good the following day.

"This should be all the clues related to this case," Huang Zixia said. Li Shubai and Huang Zixia sat before a seven-foot-long, eight-foot-wide piece of paper filled with dense, small letters.

Li Shubai stood over it, reading each line.

Wang Ruo's identity: an aristocrat but escorted by a Yunshao Court musician to the capital and studied folk music with academy musicians from a young age.

Feng Yi's death: Who is her old friend? Why did she die among Youzhou migrants? Did Wang Ruo know?

172

The Xianyou Temple prophecy: How did the man get in and out despite tight security? Who is he? What unknown part of Wang Ruo's past was he hinting at? Why did the arrow used to kill Pang Xun appear?

Yongchun Hall: Who came to kidnap Wang Ruo? How did she disappear in plain sight? What is the origin and meaning of the silver ingot that appeared under the teacup?

Jin Nu: Did she know Wang Ruo before? What is the meaning behind what she said?

The death of the beggars: Is it related to this case? Why were they poisoned in the same way as the woman whose body appeared in Yongchun Hall?

The false body: Who is she? How did the poison get through her hand? Why did she appear where Wang Ruo went missing? Who is behind it?

Li Shubai pointed at "Jin Nu" and said, "Jin Nu's gone."

"What? Missing?" Huang Zixia said.

"When you mentioned her yesterday, I asked someone to look into it and found she didn't go back to the academy yesterday and still hasn't been seen as of this morning."

"Do you think it's related to this case?"

"Don't know. The schools aren't as strict as they used to be, and it's not uncommon for women to spend the whole night out. But my people couldn't find out where she was," he said, putting the paper in the fire. "Let's forget about her for the moment. Who could our suspect be?"

Huang Zixia hesitated. "On the surface, it seems like it should be Princess Qi Le. She has a motive. Everyone knows she wanted to be your wife. When Wang Ruo disappeared, she was at the palace, so she had opportunity."

"Who else?" Li Shubai said.

"Second is Li Run. He could have been the person who learned the magic trick in the West City based on the description of the mole.

Though his reasons for keeping Chen Nian make sense, it seems a little far-fetched."

"Who else?"

"Third, what's left of Pang Xun's followers, using this opportunity to get revenge on you."

"Who else?"

Huang Zixia hesitated again. "Someone at court who wants to undermine your power or hurt the Wang family."

"That's a lot of possibilities." His face had that hint of a smile. "No one else?"

"There are some less likely candidates, like an enemy from Langya or one from Yangzhou related to Feng Yi, and so forth."

"But the incidents seem more directed at me, is that right?"

"Yes," Huang Zixia said with a nod. "It's unlikely that their enemies would come to the capital to commit these crimes, and they would be less likely to be able to act from within the palace."

"There's something you haven't mentioned," Li Shubai said, leaning back in his chair.

Huang Zixia ran through the details again in her mind. "What am I missing?"

"What people in the capital think. Ghosts." Li Shubai rested his arm on the chair as his cold smile grew. "Right? Pang Xun's ghost made that cursed paper appear, left the arrowhead in Xianyou Temple as a warning, stole my Princess-to-be, and killed her before sending her back."

"Right, this explanation ties together the motives and methods well," Huang Zixia said.

"If you really can't figure it out, have the Board of Punishments and Central Court close the case on that basis."

Huang Zixia shook her head slowly. "I'll get to the bottom of it. This killer got Wang Ruo, Feng Yi, and several beggars. For Chen Nian and the beggars who will be forgotten, I must bring the murderer to justice. And . . ."

Li Shubai watched her expression fall and fire grow in her eyes. Her voice was weary yet resolute.

"If I can't crack this case, how can I return to Shu and avenge my parents?"

Li Shubai remembered his own commitment, so he didn't respond. He stared at her as she gazed at the sky beyond the window.

"Oh yes," she said suddenly. "What about that cursed paper?"

"Guess." He stood and took a small box from a cabinet. There was no obvious lock, just eighty blocks with characters on them arranged randomly on the lid. It was a combination lock. If the eighty characters weren't arranged in a certain order, there was no way into the box besides breaking it.

She turned, not wanting to see the combination. Once Li Shubai opened it, he took out an egg-shaped object and put it on the table. There were cracks on the top, and on the bottom three ringlike bulges.

"These three rings all have twenty-four small bumps that can be rotated. When they're lined up, it opens. If you force it open, the object inside is destroyed," Li Shubai said as he moved them. It seemed Li Shubai had guarded the cursed paper quite well. Once the three rings had been rotated into their correct positions, Li Shubai put it on the table, then pressed it slightly. It opened like a blooming flower. In the center was the cursed paper. It was thick and yellowed, two inches wide and eight long with a strange pattern. On it the words *widowed, lonely, diseased* were written clearly. The circle around *lonely* was still blood red. And the red circle around *widowed* had faded, as had the one around *diseased*.

Huang Zixia looked up at Li Shubai, stunned.

He lightly ran his hand along the open egg, and it closed again. "It's clear that Wang Ruo's death has nullified this marriage, and I seem to have escaped grave danger." Li Shubai casually put the egg back in the box, scrambled the lock, and put it back in the cabinet.

"That curse," Huang Zixia said quietly, "it's always been guarded properly?"

"I don't know if it's properly, but I've never shown anyone," he said, slowly turning to face her. "Since I left Xuzhou, you're the only other person who's seen it."

Huang Zixia's heart skipped a beat. She looked at his quiet, deep gaze. He seemed to be looking at her and not looking at her at the same time. Maybe he saw something faintly in the distance, or felt the things close at hand were out of reach.

Huang Zixia couldn't help but turn and look out the window.

The sound of their breathing resonated quietly in Yubing Hall. Outside, the sound of birdsong mixed with cicadas. Summer had begun.

Huang Zixia went to the Zhous' house near Chongren Square and knocked. The doorman opened. "Hello, sir, could you please call the young master for me? My last name's Yang."

The doorman hurried away, while others asked Huang Zixia to sit and poured her tea. Huang Zixia sipped and listened to them chat.

"Did you take care of it?"

"Yes, the master leaves in a month. We've got to pack thoroughly."

"But the little master doesn't seem too pleased recently."

"Yes, I mean the Emperor appointed him to be a detective in Chengdu. Isn't that what he always wanted? Why is he suddenly shut up in his room all day?"

Zhou Ziqin suddenly appeared. "Chonggu! You're here!"

"Young master!" The servants stood quickly and greeted him.

"Go do your chores," Zhou Ziqin said with a wave. He took Huang Zixia's hand and said, "You made progress on the case, right? Right?"

Huang Zixia shook her head. "I wanted to come talk things over with you."

"Okay, come in." He pulled her farther inside. "I heard that since the weather's getting hot, that body isn't holding up well; even in an ice cellar, it'd rot, so the Empress decided that as soon as the seven days of mourning are over, it'll be sent back to Langya."

"I see." Huang Zixia waited until they were seated to say, "We must get to the bottom of this before then. Once they move the body, everything will be harder."

"So we still don't have any leads on the beggars I killed either," Zhou Ziqin said sadly. "But how are we going to solve such a complex case in such a short period of time? Not even my hero, Huang Zixia, could do that."

Huang Zixia's lips twitched. "The Prince of Kui said if we can't solve the case, we'll have to tell them the body isn't Wang Ruo. As long as the body hasn't been buried, we can fight for more time."

"But how? Where to begin? There aren't any good clues." Zhou Ziqin put his head on the table. "If only Huang Zixia were here. She'd know where to start."

Huang Zixia felt her mouth twitch again. She tapped the table. "The Prince of Kui and I already went over the facts of the case and figured out the direction we need to go in."

"What direction?" Zhou Ziqin said, looking up.

"Jing Xu has already arrived in Xuzhou to find out more about the arrow that killed Pang Xun. If we can find out how it appeared in Xianyou Temple, it will be a big help." She took out the silver ingot and put it on the table. "And this is the clue I'll look into."

"Half a silver ingot?" Zhou Ziqin turned it over. "You short on money? I can lend you some!" He laughed.

Huang Zixia pointed at the writing. "Look."

"Deputy Liang Weidong, Dengy Yunxi . . ." He seemed puzzled. "Nothing strange, right?"

"No one by those names has ever worked in the treasury."

"Privately cast? Or a forgery?"

"If it were privately cast, they would put the owner's name. Why try to say it's from the treasury? It's not a forgery either—definitely real silver," she said. "Most importantly, the Prince of Kui and I found this in the east hall after Wang Ruo disappeared. It was underneath a teacup."

Zhou Ziqin perked up. "The Prince of Kui is one of us. Even with a rotten body in the room, he can just sit and drink tea."

"At that time, the body still hadn't appeared. Wang Ruo had just disappeared," Huang Zixia said.

Zhou Ziqin ignored these details. "So what do you think we should do next?"

"We have to go to the Ministry of Personnel and find out whether or not there are records of these people."

When Huang Zixia handed the officer on duty at the Ministry of Personnel the piece of paper with the two names on it, his face twisted like he'd gotten a mouthful of medicine. "Well, mister, I don't suggest you wait around here. It'll take ten or fifteen days, if we're lucky."

"Ten or fifteen days?" Zhou Ziqin said. "That long?"

The officer pointed at the two-level, seven-room area in front of them. "Right. Those are the official archives from the founding of the dynasty. Some of the information has been lost, but we have a lot. This is only one section. There are three more just like it."

The two of them stood in quiet defeat.

"What do we do? How can we find who we're looking for among that many records?" Zhou Ziqin asked.

Huang Zixia thought a moment, then suddenly took a step toward the officer. "Could you help me find Xuzhou officials from the last ten years?"

"Xuzhou? I don't think there are many records on them." The officer called an assistant and took them to the second level of the fourth room. "This is where the information on Xuzhou officials is."

Zhou Ziqin stared at the rows and rows of shelves with barely enough space to walk between. "Still seems like a lot," he murmured.

"Thanks so much. I'll take a look now," Huang Zixia said as she walked in.

Zhou Ziqin watched her go right to the files covering the nine years of Emperor Yizong's reign. She removed the early and middle years from the shelf and quickly turned to the pages dealing with the officers appointed by Pang Xun and disposed of by the court. The room was a bit dark. Dust floated in the sunshine coming through the window. Zhou Ziqin looked at her. Her powdered skin was made paler by the light. The dusty room made it a flawless white. Her long eyelashes like butterflies fluttered over her eyes like spring dew.

Zhou Ziqin had seen a lot of feminine eunuchs over the years, but with his experience studying human anatomy, Chonggu stood out: his rounded jaw, slender neck, gently curved shoulders. Based on Chonggu's skeleton alone, he'd say she was a woman.

No wonder everyone said Yang Chonggu was the Prince of Kui's favorite, riding in the same carriage and going into the same rooms. He forced himself to stop thinking about their relationship and picked up records from the middle of the pile.

"Look," Huang Zixia said.

Zhou Ziqin looked. It said, *Pang Xun's treasury appointees: Master Zhang Junyi, Deputies Lu Yuxin, Deng Yunxi, Liang Weidong, Song Kuo, Ni Chufa,* and so on. The silver ingot the Prince of Kui found was from a rebel treasury.

Huang Zixia looked at him. "Seems the silver ingot was cast when Pang Xun had declared himself ruler."

Zhou Ziqin slapped the book, unconcerned about the dust he sent flying, and roared with surprise. "It's been the ghosts of Pang Xun's followers all along!"

"Why would they leave a silver ingot?"

Qinghan CeCe

"Could it be about ransom money?" Zhou Ziqin said, touching his chin thoughtfully. "But how could a Princess be worth twelve silvers?"

Huang Zixia ignored him, picked up pen and paper, and began writing. "Regardless, it's a clue. We'll report back to the Prince."

◆ ◆ ◆

As they walked out of the Ministry of Personnel, it was nearly noon. Zhou Ziqin grabbed his stomach. "Oh my, I'm so hungry. Let me treat you to a meal, Chonggu!"

Huang Zixia hesitated. "I'd like to get back to the palace as soon as possible."

"The Prince is so busy every day. Working hours are still not over. How could he be waiting for you?" Zhou Ziqin grabbed her hand and started heading for the West City. "Come on, come on. I know a great restaurant. They make the best donkey! You know why? Because he meticulously cuts each strip according to the pattern of its muscle fiber. Particularly tasty boiled! I imagine it's the same as if you were to kill a person. You have to be careful with the knife. If you cut against the muscle fiber, the wound opens jaggedly. If you cut along it, it opens smoothly, and the blood doesn't splash everywhere—"

"The key to whether the blood splashes or not is whether or not you cut through to the vessels," Huang Zixia interrupted. Then she added, "If you keep talking about muscles and bones, I won't be able to eat."

"How about organs?" Huang Zixia turned to leave. Zhou Ziqin grabbed her arm. "Okay, okay. I swear I won't bring it up again!"

Twelve

Partition Shadows

After eating, Huang Zixia walked outside into the crowd. She saw a man and hurried toward him. "Zhang Xingying?" she called quietly.

"Who's that?" Zhou Ziqin said. "You know him?"

"Yes, he helped me out before, and now it's costing him." She sighed and unconsciously followed his route. Zhou Ziqin didn't understand, but he didn't ask further and went along through the crowd.

Zhang Xingying was slowly carrying a dirty sack toward Puning Square. Huang Zixia had been very familiar with the capital when she was young. She remembered there was a big locust tree near Puning Square. Zhang Xingying's house must have been near there. Indeed, Zhang Xingying lived next to the flourishing locust. Given the warmer weather, several women were sitting on a bench beneath it, chatting and sewing, watching their children play nearby.

Huang Zixia slowly approached Zhang Xingying's home. Though his courtyard wall was only three feet tall, there was a hedge on top that concealed her from view. She looked through a gap in the branches and saw Zhang Xingying pour out the contents of the bag—herbs set to dry on the bluestone.

Qinghan CeCe

One of the old women nearby saw her and said, "Who are you looking for, sir?" She didn't dare look at Zhou Ziqin, perhaps for fear that his jewelry would blind her.

"I'm a friend of Big Zhang's, come to see how he's doing."

"Oh, their youngest? The Prince of Kui kicked him out, right? Now he and his father work in Duanrui Clinic. They say he's an apprentice, but really, he just does odd jobs. Sometimes they run out of herbs, and he goes to the mountains to find them." The old woman stopped and shook suddenly. "He did something wrong at the palace. Got thrashed three hundred times before he was sent back. Why would you two come for him?"

"Twenty thrashings." Rumors were truly outrageous.

"Oh, in any case he got messed up good. Have you heard?" The old woman looked excited. "It was related to the Princess of Kui's death."

Huang Zixia was shocked. "How could that be? When he left, the Princess of Kui hadn't even been selected."

The old woman shook her head and sighed. "Such a good boy. Only the best get into the Prince of Kui's guard. Everyone was so envious when he was selected. Who knew after a few months he'd get kicked out?"

Huang Zixia stared at her for a moment, then whispered, "It's not so bad. The Prince of Kui might ask him back."

"The Prince of Kui is so strict. How could he let someone who made a mistake go back?" The old woman glanced left and right; then her face took on a mysterious look and she lowered her voice. "Ah, you chaps don't know. There used to be a lot of families here who did matchmaking. They wanted my daughter to marry him. Now no one's saying a word about that. Now he's not even as good as my son, who has been studying with carpenter Liu for a long time. Now he's almost done with his apprenticeship!"

Huang Zixia was silent for a while. Then she turned to leave. "You're not going in?" the old woman said. "He's home today."

182

"No thank you, ma'am."

Huang Zixia heard the old woman talking to herself as she left. "Good kid, just a little feminine, like a eunuch."

Zhou Ziqin couldn't help but laugh out loud. Huang Zixia ignored him. They exited Puning Square and walked through streets and alleys. When they reached Phoenix Boulevard, Huang Zixia came to and said, "Thanks for helping me look through the records today. If any clues turn up, we'll be in touch."

Zhou Ziqin noticed the dip in her mood. "Don't worry about your friend. I'll help you fix it."

Huang Zixia looked up at him in shock.

"A buddy just told me the royal guard is expanding its cavalry division. You know, as far as civil servants go, the cavalry are the most striking. They get to ride around the city on horses in those uniforms with those swords. Lots of girls peek out at them. He'll have no problem getting one. And, the salary isn't bad. A lot of people try to use their connections to get in. If your friend weren't sturdy and handsome, I wouldn't refer him!"

"Really?" Huang Zixia said.

"Of course. The head of the cavalry guard is a good friend. Promise!" Zhou Ziqin said, patting his chest. "When this case is done, I'll take you to see Captain Xu Congyun."

"Thanks so much!" Huang Zixia was moved. "If it really happens, how could I thank you?"

"Ha ha, just let me talk about whatever I want when we go out to eat." Huang Zixia looked uncomfortable. "Just kidding. It's nothing. Actually, I respect you more than anyone besides Huang Zixia. I'll do whatever you wish!"

He patted her so hard she almost threw up. She grimaced and said, "In that case, once this case is done, I'll treat you to a feast at Zhuijin, and you can talk about whatever you want!"

"Then you'll need some money. Unless you're getting rich working for the Prince of Kui?" He laughed. "I have a little money. Come see me sometime, and I'll feed you well."

"Since when do the Prince of Kui's people need you to feed them?" They turned and saw Li Shubai. His carriage was stopped at the intersection. He was looking at them with the curtain pulled aside, a calm expression on his face. Huang Zixia didn't dare look directly at him. She just stood there wondering what he was thinking as she approached him.

Zhou Ziqin wasn't shaken. He smiled and nodded. "What a coincidence. The Prince was coming through here too?"

"I'm back from sending the Turkic envoy to the inn," he said.

Zhou Ziqin nodded. "My Prince, Chonggu is always so straight-faced with you, but he looks great when he's cheerful. You should make him smile more!"

Huang Zixia felt her face about to twitch. Of course, her face went dark after the Prince of Kui showed up.

"Really?" Li Shubai glanced at Huang Zixia. "What good news made Yang Chonggu so cheerful?"

"Nothing. He's just doing me a favor," Huang Zixia hurried to say.

Zhou Ziqin nodded, and Li Shubai didn't inquire further. He looked at Huang Zixia. "Did you get anything useful at the Ministry of Personnel today?"

"We made a big discovery!" Zhou Ziqin said excitedly. He pulled on Li Shubai's sleeve like he wanted to discuss the case in the street. Huang Zixia was speechless. She coughed gently and Zhou Ziqin glanced at her.

Li Shubai pointed at a tavern behind them. "Stop, we can't talk about this in the street!" Li Shubai got out, and the three of them went inside to a nice room on the second floor with a pot of tea and four appetizers.

When they were alone, Zhou Ziqin began speaking quietly. "Chonggu's the smart one. He figured the silver ingot had something to do with Pang Xun, so we looked at the records of officials in his pseudogovernment, and, sure enough, it was cast by his men."

Li Shubai looked thoughtfully at Huang Zixia.

Zhou Ziqin was in awe. "How'd you know it was related to Pang Xun?"

"The silver's blackened, so I figured it couldn't be from recent years. Since it wasn't privately cast or a forgery and had the word *treasury* on it, I figured it was from a rebellion. And the last rebel who could've made silver is Pang Xun."

"Right! Why didn't I think of that!" Zhou Ziqin said.

"But we don't know how many were cast or how many survived," Huang Zixia said. "If it's a lot, it'll be hard to investigate further."

"Not many, and they're all numbered," Li Shubai said. "In the initial chaos of the rebellion, they didn't have an official treasury or seal. Only after I brought the six governors together to lay siege to Xuzhou did he come up with the seal to buy people off, strengthen their ties, and keep morale up. So the treasury was only running for a short time before they had to retreat. After Pang Xun died, I reviewed the accounts and found they made only five thousand six hundred silver ingots. Only eight hundred were twelve-pieces, and the government seized almost all of them. I ordered seven hundred ninety-four to be melted on the spot, leaving only five as evidence. The mold was destroyed too, so no more could have been made."

"So there's one twelve-piece ingot left?" Huang Zixia asked.

"If the Board of Punishments kept five, then that would seem to be the case."

She took the one they found in Yongchun Hall out of her pocket and put it on the table.

"This is the only piece that was lost in the inventory of evidence against Pang Xun," Li Shubai said.

Zhou Ziqin scratched his head. "Why would the only missing silver ingot appear in Daming Palace's Yongchun Hall? And why half?"

"It's mysterious. This case is very complex and seems to be related to Pang Xun. Or someone wants us to think it is," Huang Zixia said.

Li Shubai looked nonplussed. He put the cover over his tea-cup and stood. "Let's leave it at that for now. Ziqin, go to the Board of Punishments and find out where the other five silver ingots are. Chonggu, find out what other clues we can track down."

"All right!" Zhou Ziqin said. Though it was already the afternoon and the various administrators had been dismissed, he was ready to run to the Board of Punishments to have a look. At least he was well connected there.

Huang Zixia went back to Kui Palace in Li Shubai's carriage. On the way, Li Shubai was quiet and didn't look at her. Huang Zixia felt a lot of pressure, but she forced herself to sit on the stool, wondering what was wrong and if she'd done something.

He finally spoke. "Help with what?"

Huang Zixia's heart beat harder. She couldn't say it was about Zhang Xingying. "Just a little favor. Not worth the Prince's time."

"I don't have time to bother with such things, anyway."

Huang Zixia felt relieved, but waited for him to continue.

He didn't speak again. He just sat there reading papers—very fast, about ten lines at a time. He flipped the pages without even glancing at her.

Huang Zixia heaved a sigh of relief. She noticed he was reading some foreign text, maybe Tibetan, and was in awe.

After the uncomfortable ride, they got out at the palace. Jing Yu was awaiting orders at the gate.

"Tell Jing Yi to come." Li Shubai said this one sentence, then went straight to Yubing Hall.

Huang Zixia sighed with relief again and took a few quiet steps backward, hoping to go back to her room. Li Shubai, as if he had eyes in the back of his head, said, "Come" without turning around.

She clenched her sweaty hands and thought, *Oh, Huang Zixia, Huang Zixia, why'd you chose such a difficult master? All he has to do is say the word and you throw yourself into danger.*

Jing Yu had already set everything up: refreshments and incense, the fine bamboo curtains closed. Li Shubai washed his hands in the golden pot a servant girl brought him. Then he wiped his hands slowly on a white towel, emotionless. Huang Zixia stood waiting while he read documents.

Luckily, Jing Yi came. She wasn't sure she could stand the tension alone.

"How long have you been here, Yang Chonggu?" Li Shubai said, getting right to the point.

"Thirty-seven days in total," Jing Yi replied without hesitation. "Over a month."

"He still hasn't been paid?"

"The palace pays monthly salaries on the fifteenth. He had only just arrived when the last payment came, so he only received two silvers."

According to custom, Huang Zixia had treated some of the other staff to meals in order to get to know them, so her money had long been spent. Huang Zixia kept her dissatisfaction to herself. It wasn't easy being a palace eunuch, though they gave her food, shelter, and clothing. When she escaped from Shu, she had traded her gold hairpin for money to make the trip to the capital. The rest was lost when Li Shubai kicked her into the pond.

"How would the Prince like to set Yang Chonggu's pay grade?" Jing Yu said.

Huang Zixia's heart beat faster. She'd never had to worry about money growing up because her parents had always given her an allowance. But she'd always envied her brother and others who worked in law enforcement. She was female, so although she helped them solve a lot of cases, she couldn't become an official employee and earn a salary. And now, she'd finally reached a place of stability, where she didn't have to rely on a husband or family.

Li Shubai glanced up at her from the document, and his gaze seemed to say, "I've been waiting a long time for this chance."

Her heart suddenly filled with foreboding.

"There must be fairness for everyone. Otherwise, what's the point of palace laws?" Li Shubai said.

Jing Yi nodded. "The Prince is right. So for now Yang Chonggu is junior eunuch with the same stipend as the rest and may be eligible for promotion at the end of the year."

"Okay." Li Shubai was acting like he always went along with whatever everyone else said.

The annoyance in Huang Zixia's heart grew stronger. "Excuse me." She couldn't help but ask, "What do junior eunuchs get?"

Li Shubai looked at his document and gently said, "First, junior eunuchs don't speak without being spoken to. When they do, they're fined one month's salary. Second, junior eunuchs must adhere to section four, article thirty-one of palace law. You don't know it, because you were unable to memorize the palace law, so you'll be fined three months' salary. Third, junior eunuchs are not allowed to have private relations with outsiders, at the penalty of twelve months' pay."

Jing Yu looked at her sympathetically, as if there was nothing he could do about her losing sixteen months' salary in one breath.

Huang Zixia was stunned. *The first time she'd tried to stick up for herself against this man, she'd been robbed! A bullying, vindictive, domineering master is definitely not a good master!*

Jing Yi smartly left.

Huang Zixia took the half ingot out of her pocket and tapped it against her forehead.

Li Shubai looked up at her. "Did you find more clues?"

"No," she said stiffly. "I'm broke. I can't even buy a bowl of soup when I'm working a case. If I faint in the street, I don't think I'll be able to serve Your Majesty any longer. My hunger makes it hard to focus on the case. So in the interest of solving the case, I've decided to spend the evidence."

Li Shubai looked at her, lips turning upward slightly. He slowly opened a drawer and put a small plate on the table. "Take this."

Huang Zixia picked it up and realized it was a small golden token, about half the size of her palm. It had been cast with a pattern of lines and said, *The Tang Dynasty Prince of Kui*. The other side said, *Made in Gentian* and had the seal of the imperial treasury. Huang Zixia held it in her fingers and looked at Li Shubai, puzzled.

Li Shubai kept looking at his documents. "There's only one of these in the world. Each prefecture has one. Take care of it. It'll be problematic if you lose it."

"Huh?" Huang Zixia still didn't know what he was getting at.

He raised his voice a little. "You're one of my people. Next time you get in trouble, don't ask someone else for help. Is there anything at all I couldn't take care of for you?"

Huang Zixia saw no sign of emotion on his downcast face. It was obviously the same Prince of Kui she'd known, but for some reason, in the sunlight coming through the curtains with the sound of the cicadas near and far, she felt something shift in her heart, a warmth. She stood motionless for a long time, and he finally looked at her. Before anyone could speak, the gold token slipped from her hand and made a biting ring on the slate floor, breaking the silence. She hurried to pick it up and took a deep breath as she stood, trembling.

"What's wrong, not enough?" Li Shubai asked.

"No, not that. I'm just flattered." She blushed.

He looked at her for a long time, then stood by the window, looking out at the sky. It was boundless and blue. Some thin, yarny clouds smeared the air, so low it seemed as if you could touch them. He suddenly felt the sky and clouds were like his lonely life. A pure, bright girl had shown up and caught him off guard, changing his fate.

He covered his eyes as if the sun was too bright. He turned and looked at Huang Zixia. "I'm not giving it to you; I'm lending it."

Huang Zixia nodded and looked sadly at the token. "Can I ask you something, my Prince?"

He looked at her.

"Will the restaurant owners and street salesmen recognize this Prince of Kui token?"

"Huh?"

"It's . . . I mean . . . ." She hesitated. "Can I go to the taverns, bakeries, butcheries, and stores and use this as credit?"

Li Shubai glared at her. Huang Zixia knew trying to use the token that way was beneath them. She looked down guiltily and hid it in her hand.

Li Shubai sat on the couch and pointed.

Huang Zixia obediently kneeled before him. He'd taken sixteen months' pay from her with a word. Did she have any choice but to obey him?

He poured himself a cup of tea. "What I'm about to say is very important, so don't repeat it to Zhou Ziqin. But I think if you want to break this case, you must be aware—this matter has great bearing on the case."

Huang Zixia nodded and looked at him with bated breath.

He held the teacup with three slender, white fingers, which made the light-green teacup look like jade. "In fact, that silver half ingot—Pang Xun made eight hundred of them. In other words, there was no twelve-piece lost. The one that went missing, I spent."

Huang Zixia was stunned and she froze, holding the teapot. "Impossible. The Prince of Kui was short on money too?"

Li Shubai tilted his head but didn't respond. "I found it while raiding Pang Xun's palace. When I saw the ingot before, I didn't think of it."

Huang Zixia listened and poured herself some tea. Then she took a snack off the table and began eating slowly.

It had happened three years ago, but Li Shubai's memory was so good, he didn't forget anything.

After Li Shubai killed Pang Xun in the tenth year of Xiantong's reign, his supporters scattered or surrendered. Within thirty minutes after Xuzhou was sacked, imperial troops began looking for Pang Xun's followers. Li Shubai ordered them to kill any looters. The soldiers moved quickly, and within two hours, Li Shubai was in Pang Xun's palace.

"Maybe our troops moved too fast. There were several men still in the palace, trying to make last-ditch efforts to defend it. They were soon killed." He spoke so casually that Huang Zixia wondered if his rushing into the enemy camp was incredibly brave or incredibly reckless. Maybe he didn't consider the possibility of dying at all.

But she didn't dare say anything.

During the rush to hunt down the fleeing rebels, Li Shubai found himself alone in a courtyard with thick walls. He heard a woman scream. He saw a man in a window outside the walls grab a delicate, disheveled girl. He began dragging her, saying, "I'm taking you and some money to the carriage. We'll go far away from here and live a long, happy life."

Li Shubai left out some of the vulgar things the man said. "That man was big," Li Shubai continued, "with a meaty face. He held the girl to his chest. She couldn't struggle free, just screamed as he dragged her out the door."

Li Shubai couldn't find the door to reach them, and the wall was too high to climb. He thought he should go back and order his men to intercept the carriage and kill the man. Then he saw a figure stagger in to save the girl. It was another girl, this one taller. She was also disheveled, her face obscured by dirt. She took a skewer from the grill and shoved it in the man's back. Unfortunately, the man was so big and the girl was so weak that the skewer didn't go in far at all. The man didn't even let go of the girl. He turned and roared at the tall girl and kicked her away. His boot landed on her chest. She flew into the wall and coughed blood.

The brute wasn't finished. He took a few steps forward to hit the tall girl again. The one he was holding tried desperately to pull him back, but she couldn't budge him. He lifted his big right fist and smashed it into her belly. Li Shubai drew an arrow and regretted his hesitation. He may have missed his chance to save the girls.

Huang Zixia straightened up. "And then?" she asked urgently.

Li Shubai took a sip of tea and said, "Then I heard the man scream."

He saw the girl holding a bloody silver ingot. She was collapsed in the corner, shaking. She'd snatched it from the man's bag and smashed it into his head. The man clutched the back of his head and slapped her in the face. She hit the wall but still clutched the ingot to her chest.

The man grabbed her by her collar and raised his hand to slap her again. Then the tall girl rushed back with the skewer. The bastard heard and turned around, but before he knew it, the iron rammed right into his right eye. At the same time, Li Shubai's arrow pierced his left eye.

As the man screamed, the small girl with the ingot went into a frenzy and smashed his head again and again. The man kicked and kicked but soon fell to the ground. The tall girl rushed with the skewer and stabbed him all over. His body twitched and finally went still.

The two bloody girls dropped their weapons and huddled together, shivering, looking at the body. Only then did they realize there was an arrow in the man's left eye. They looked around in terror, then saw

Li Shubai outside the window. "Don't worry," Li Shubai said. "We're here to put down the rebellion. Wait there and we'll come in and sort things out." The girl with the skewer pointed to Li Shubai's right. He used his sword to pry open the lock and kicked the door in. When he approached them, they were still so frightened, clutching each other and shivering.

Li Shubai glanced at his clothing. There were only a couple of bloodstains. He didn't think he could have looked too terrifying, but they looked at him with pure fear. Li Shubai stepped forward gently and asked, "Who are you? How did this bastard catch you?" His gaze was gentle. He squatted down and whispered to soothe them.

After being taken captive, they endured the daily chaos of war, endless bullying, and the sight of the radiant Li Shubai was like stepping into another world. They let their guard down a little. "You came to save us?" The voice of the girl holding the ingot wavered like the wind. Her face was pale.

Li Shubai took an arrow from his quiver; its feather was the same as the one stuck in the body. Li Shubai's personally engraved arrows had been used up, so these were standard issue. When the girls saw it was the same, they kneeled in thanks and cried. The tall girl was shyer, but the small one was bolder. "Thank you so much for saving us," she said. "She's my sister, Little Shi. My parents died, so I came to Xuzhou from Liuzhou to be with my aunt."

"How did you fall into the hands of the rebels?"

The bold girl, whose surname was Cheng, had trouble speaking her answer. "Pang Xun's rebellion caused such chaos, my aunt had already fled when I arrived. We were taken captive with a group of women. The day before yesterday, when the imperial siege began, no one was paying attention to us. Today they scrambled to take all the money they could. They said if they ran out of food, they'd eat us!"

Li Shubai put his teacup down with a thoughtful expression.

"And then?" Huang Zixia asked. "What about the other captive women?"

"When I heard that, I was shocked too. I immediately rushed out to save more."

Li Shubai hurried in the direction the Cheng girl pointed and saw a parked carriage. He jumped on the horse and looked back. Tears ran down the Cheng girl's face, revealing the crystal white of her skin. Though her tears made her fearful eyes swell, he could make out their beautiful contours. And that Little Shi clinging to her had a wonderful silhouette. Li Shubai thought they must have been captured because they were beautiful. He was determined to help them but was also worried about the other captive women. He hesitated, but luckily, some of his men came in and saluted him. "General!"

"Huh?" Huang Zixia said. "Why did they call you general?"

"Because the court charged to lead the force to put down the rebellion. We weren't at court, so the soldiers naturally used my military title."

Li Shubai asked the soldiers to take the money from the carriage and keep a record of it. As they prepared to leave, Li Shubai asked the girls what their plan was.

"We want to go to Yangzhou. My aunt left a message saying she went there," the Cheng girl said.

Li Shubai asked them whether they needed soldiers to escort them back. They looked afraid, shook their heads desperately, said they didn't want to travel with soldiers. Li Shubai thought they must be afraid of soldiers, so he didn't coerce them, just suggested they pick up the ingot and skewer. "These are murder weapons. You don't want to leave them at the scene. The ingot will be useful as money. Take it." The silver ingot was covered in blood and brains. Little Shi looked at it and began retching. The Cheng girl ripped a piece of fabric off the body, wrapped it around the ingot, and held it loosely in her hands.

Li Shubai flicked the reins, and the carriage began to move. The girls held on to each other tightly during the bumpy ride. There were a lot of people walking along the road to the outskirts of Xuzhou. They had fled the city during the turmoil. Now that they'd heard Pang Xun was dead, they were happily going back.

Li Shubai helped them out and told them to stay on the main road to avoid trouble.

"You made it from Liuzhou to Xuzhou, so I'm sure you'll have no trouble making it to Yangzhou."

They just looked at him and nodded silently.

Li Shubai turned to leave.

As he was about to get in his carriage, someone clutched the bridle and shouted. It was the Cheng girl. She looked up at him with her dusty face and shyness in her bright eyes.

"What is it?" he asked.

She removed a silver hairpin from her hair and held it out. "Sir, my father gave this to my mother for their engagement. After I was captured, I lost everything. Bring it to Yangzhou when you visit me. My aunt's name is Lan Dai."

Lan Dai, Xuese's adoptive mother.

The name made Huang Zixia sit up straight in surprise.

Li Shubai looked at her. "What's wrong?"

"That name! That name is . . ." Huang Zixia was too frantic to be coherent.

"Lan Dai," Li Shubai said. "This sort of dazzling but old-fashioned name surely belongs to a tramp."

"But that's the name of the third woman of the Yunshao Six!"

Li Shubai frowned slightly. "What? That Yunshao Court again?"

"Yes. Go on. What happened next?"

"Of course, I didn't go visit her, nor did I go to Yangzhou to visit a tramp. So I looked at her and said that saving her was just luck. I told her to keep the hairpin. She kept holding it out to me. The sharp end toward her and the decorative end toward me. It was a leafy hairpin."

Huang Zixia gasped. "Leafy? How?"

"About four inches long, silver, fine, lifelike lines. The leafy part had two pearls inlaid like drops of dew."

"It was silver?"

"Yes. I wouldn't misremember that," Li Shubai said. "I don't know women's jewelry that well, but I think it was similar to the one Wang Ruo was wearing when she went missing. Is it a popular style?"

"No. Hairpins like that typically have the shape of a whole leaf, not thin lines with gaps between them. It was the first time I'd seen such a sophisticated design. If it's as similar as you think, there must be some connection."

"It seems the girl I met back then has a lot of connections with what's going on now."

"Yes, I think so too," she said. "Did you take it?"

"The hairpin?" Li Shubai asked. "No. I wasn't going to take it, so she put it on the carriage shaft and ran off. I picked it up and threw it on the side of the road."

Huang Zixia looked at him and blinked.

"What?" he said indifferently.

"Why couldn't you have taken it back to the city and gotten rid of it?"

"Get rid of it then or later, what's the difference?" Li Shubai said. "Then I saw Little Shi looking at me, so she should have been able to get it and give it back to the Cheng girl."

"If it were me, I wouldn't have told my friend. Someone throwing away something you just gave them . . . ," Huang Zixia said. "It would just make the friend sad."

"I'm not interested in learning how women get along," Li Shubai said.

196

Huang Zixia didn't want to discuss matters of the heart with such a cold-blooded person either. She pulled the wooden hairpin out of her hair and dipped it in the tea, then drew the leafy hairpin on the table with it.

Li Shubai looked at her. "Not afraid of it falling down?"

She casually held up her hair for a second. "Not really."

"Luckily, you're disguised as a little eunuch. If you were trying to look like a Buddhist monk, how would you take out a hairpin to draw?"

"They have wooden fish." She kept drawing. Before she knew it, she'd drawn that silver half ingot too. "Maybe the girls broke the ingot in half so they could both have part," she murmured.

"With a murder weapon like that, they probably had it changed into coins pretty quickly."

"Possibly." Huang Zixia looked at him. "Do you still remember what they looked like?"

"They were disheveled, covered in mud and blood, and I only met them briefly, so I didn't get much of an impression. They were only thirteen or fourteen at the time. I'm sure they've changed a lot. If they stood before me now, I wouldn't recognize them."

"Right." She nodded and her hair fell down.

Li Shubai instinctively caught it and frowned. "Maybe it'd be better to pretend to be a monk."

She didn't answer as she pulled her hair up. A strand hung over her face, and she spun it up with frustration, then put her hat back on.

"Never seen anyone draw while they're thinking about serious things," he said disdainfully.

"Old habits die hard," she said quietly.

He scoffed. "How'd you get such habits?"

"When I used to go out on cases with my father, it was always hard to find pen and paper. I was in girls' clothing then, so I always had a few hairpins. I'd take one out and draw on the ground to get a sense of the case. Now it helps me arrange my ideas."

"And then?"

"Then what?"

"The hairpins you drew on the ground with. I care about details."

Huang Zixia looked at him, puzzled. "I wiped them off and put them back in, of course."

"Oh," he said. She was still staring at him. "The first time I met Zhou Ziqin, he had a bag of pine nuts as the mortician did an autopsy, even handing him tools."

"He was eating during the autopsy?"

"What do you think?" Li Shubai said.

"I got it."

"So when I heard Zhou Ziqin worshipped Huang Min's sleuth of a daughter, my first thought was of a girl eating pine nuts at a crime scene."

Huang Zixia's eyebrows jumped a little. "And now?"

"Now I'm pleased to know you just scribble, and even wash the hairpins afterward."

"I'm not Zhou Ziqin."

"But you're his idol," Li Shubai said.

"That's just his fantasy. In fact, if he knew I was Huang Zixia, his long-held dream might collapse."

Li Shubai smiled faintly and nodded. "Maybe. So you keep being a eunuch in front of him."

"Of course. I don't want to spoil his dream." Huang Zixia nodded.

They'd talked so long, it was nearly dusk. She left Yubing Hall and retired to her room. She let her sleeves hang, and her hand unconsciously gripped the Prince of Kui's token. The sight of the sunset stirred a sentimental feeling in her.

It had already been six months since her parents died, and she still hadn't found the killer. The current case was so confusing. There were so many leads and details, she wasn't sure she'd ever get to the bottom of the case. It was the first time she'd doubted herself. She asked herself,

If things keep going like this, will you ever be able to take off the eunuch's clothes and proudly tell the world, "I am a woman. My name is Huang Zixia"?

She tossed and turned the whole night but could not figure out where Wang Ruo had disappeared to or where that girl's body had come from.

When she got up the next morning, she felt unsteady, with a headache and backache. She sat at the table and looked at herself in the mirror—pale as a ghost. It didn't matter. No one would notice if an insignificant eunuch looked like a ghost. Tiredly, she began getting cleaned up. She went to the kitchen and the cook immediately smiled and gave her a plate of spring rolls. "Congratulations, Mr. Yang. I heard the Prince finally granted you status."

"*Puh.*" Huang Zixia suddenly spit out the food in her mouth. "What status?"

"In the morning discussion, they said you're officially part of the government staff, a registered eunuch."

"Oh . . ." She put another spring roll in her mouth. "A junior eunuch?"

"You've got quite a bright future!" she said. "A few years ago, during the Suizhou famine, a lot of people cut off their lifeblood to become a eunuch and still couldn't! I've been cooking here for twenty years, and I'm still not an official servant of the royal family. You're already there after a month or two, along with all the other famous palace eunuchs!"

Huang Zixia was speechless. She didn't realize how enviable her position was. It was a shame someone else couldn't have the spot.

There was a shout from outside. "Yang Chonggu! Where's Yang Chonggu?"

She hurried to take a gulp of milk. "I'm here!"

"The Prince has ordered you to go to Chunyu Hall. Someone is waiting for you there."

Who would call for her so early?

Huang Zixia walked to Chunyu Hall and was surprised to find Chen Nian with her guqin.

"Chen Nian, why'd you come to see me?"

Chen Nian smiled. "You've got to keep up with your studies. It's been a few days, so I had to come to you."

"So sorry, Chen Nian," Huang Zixia said, knowing she was joking. "I've been busy recently, and completely forgot about elegant sounds."

"I heard about the unfortunate Wang girl. Everyone in the capital envied her. Heard her body was in bad shape, such a pity," Chen Nian said as she adjusted her strings.

Your friend Feng Yi's body was the same, Huang Zixia thought. She saw the gloom in Chen Nian's eyes and wanted to take the piece of white jade she found on Feng Yi's body and tell her she was dead. But seeing the white hairs Chen Nian had recently begun to grow, she couldn't.

Chen Nian gracefully began playing "Ode to the New Moon," but only half of the piece. The sound rang out through the room.

"No one can match you, Chen Nian!" Huang Zixia said.

"Not true," Chen Nian said, looking up, her hands still on the strings. "I can't hold a candle to Jin Nu."

Huang Zixia remembered Li Shubai said she was missing. "Have you seen Jin Nu lately?"

"No, that's why I came to find you," she said. "Yesterday, I went to Guangfang Square to find her, but heard she hasn't been at the academy in several days."

Huang Zixia frowned slightly. "She didn't speak with anyone before she went missing?"

"No. The teaching staff had someone open her room. Turns out, some of her favorite clothing and jewelry were gone, along with that pipa her teacher gave her. The staff was angry, saying she must have fallen for a man and eloped. I heard the staff's been relatively lax since Xuanzong took power. Things like this have happened more than once or twice."

Huang Zixia nodded.

"I don't think she would do that. She and Li Rui had some chemistry, and I gave her advice several times, but she wouldn't listen," Chen Nian said.

"Tell me more about her recent movements," Huang Zixia said, pulling a chair over for herself and sitting.

"The school staff said the last time they saw her was three nights ago. She came back a little drunk after curfew, said she had a few at Zhuijin."

Huang Zixia nodded. "I was there too that night. It was after the incident at the palace. A group of us went there to eat and discuss the case. Jin Nu was cheerful and helped us pack up the cherries—but her hands were so delicate, she even complained the stems hurt her."

"She's like that, sharp-tongued and softhearted. Good person, just too chatty."

"Chen Nian, did you get a response from your letter to Lan Dai?"

"No, even if Lan Dai received the letter and sent Xuese to come to the capital, it was only a few days ago. She wouldn't have had time to get here yet."

"Xuese would call Lan Dai 'aunt,' right?"

"Yes. Lan Dai and Mei Wanzhi were sisters, so she's Xuese's aunt," Chen Nian said with a nod. "Lan Dai was the third oldest of the six, the best dancer."

"Do you remember if Xuese arrived in Yangzhou alone that year? Was there another girl with her?"

Chen Nian gasped. "Actually, I think she arrived with a girl named Little Shi. They saw Little Shi's parents die during the war. She and Xuese became sisters when they had no one else left."

Huang Zixia nodded. Her suspicion had been verified, but she didn't know what bearing it had on the case. She only sensed that it must be the glimpse of a vital thread.

A case is a lot like a tree; the part that people can see above ground is only ever a small part. Underground are enormous and deep roots that you'll never know unless you dig them out.

Tears began rolling down Chen Nian's cheeks.

Huang Zixia hurried to pat her shoulder. "Chen Nian," she whispered, "don't be sad."

"How can I not? I know Feng Yi isn't coming back." Her eyes swelled, and the tears came harder. "I saw her in my dream last night, transparent as glass. She said, 'Chen Nian, the years of youth quickly wither away. Now only you are suffering in the world.' When I woke up, I just knew. I know she's already gone."

Huang Zixia filled with grief. She took out a handkerchief and helped Chen Nian wipe her tears, but she forgot about the paper wrapped in the handkerchief, and it fell out. It rolled toward Chen Nian.

Chen Nian didn't notice. She was too disoriented to feel it.

Huang Zixia hesitated, then picked up the little paper bag and held it out. "Chen Nian," she said, "look at this."

Chen Nian rubbed her eyes. Her voice was hoarse. "What is it?"

Huang Zixia just looked at her.

Chen Nian hesitated, then slowly took it and lifted the white paper off. Inside was the flawless white jade. It was no larger than a fingernail but incredibly exquisite. Chen Nian's hand suddenly began shaking as she clutched it and read the *Nian* written there.

Chen Nian shut her eyes. She shut them so tightly and desperately that it was as if the word had blinded her and she would never see again.

She was like that for a long time. She trembled as she asked, "Where is it from?"

"The body of a forty-year-old woman among a group of sick migrants from Youzhou. Her body was burned, so this is all I found." She didn't say what they found in Feng Yi's stomach, fearing it would hurt Chen Nian too much.

"Twenty years ago, Feng Yi and I were still young. We weren't well known, not terribly talented. We saved money for a long time, then bought two pieces of white jade with our names engraved on them. We gave them to each other and swore we'd always do our best to support each other." Chen Nian pulled a red string from her breast pocket and showed hers. She tightly held the two pieces of jade together and burst into tears.

Huang Zixia sat quietly next to her, watching the light wander on Chen Nian's face.

"Who was it? Who killed Feng Yi?" Chen Nian asked.

Huang Zixia took a deep breath and shook her head. "We don't know yet. But I think it may be related to the Princess's disappearance."

"The Wang girl?"

"You heard about the catastrophe surrounding the Princess of Kui, right?"

Chen Nian held the jade and numbly nodded.

"I've already determined that the old friend's daughter Feng Yi escorted was Wang Ruo. I actually met her once in that context, but I was afraid if I told you, word might get out."

Chen Nian was at a loss. "But now, I heard Wang Ruo is dead . . ."

"Yes. I think Feng Yi's death is closely related, but how, I have no idea."

"Will you be able to get to the bottom of it?" Chen Nian whispered.

"I will do my best."

◆ ◆ ◆

When Chen Nian left dizzily, it was going on noon. Huang Zixia thought about the case as she turned and walked inside. She was so lost in thought that she tripped on the stairs and almost fell. Luckily, she was able to catch herself on a tree.

The porter got a stool for her to sit on and poured a cup of tea. Some idle eunuchs were chatting nearby. She sat beside them, gulping down her cup of tea and then another.

The eunuch named Lu Yun who was responsible for sweeping Yanxi Hall was barely twenty. He loved gossip above all. When he saw her sit down, he quickly elbowed her and raised his eyebrows. "Hey, tell me, Chonggu, you spend the most time with the Prince. Do you think the Wang girl's death is the worst thing that's happened to him in years?"

Huang Zixia stared at him without understanding. "What?"

"Must be, right? After the Hou Jing chaos, the Langya Wang family was falling. No great people have emerged in the last few generations. Not very important at the upper levels. They relied on the last two Empresses to maintain influence. It could even be said they didn't produce any good girls either. They finally got one to be Kui Princess, and she suddenly died. So without the Kui line of advancement, there's only Wang Lin on the Board of Punishments."

Someone nearby interrupted. "The Wangs have an Empress and a high minister, but people still say they're declining."

"That's right. The Cuis of Boling had about a dozen high ministers. How about the Langya Wangs? Even if you added the Tayuan Wangs, would they compare?"

Huang Zixia silently sipped her tea, thinking that Cui Chunzhan's uncle Cui Yanzhao was also well regarded and acted like a minister. "It wouldn't be surprising if the Cuis produced a high minister soon."

"Not bad. What about the Xies of Chen? I heard after the Hou Jing chaos, they were almost finished," someone else said.

"No, if the Wangs were really in such decline, why would the Lis marry them? You have to remember they still have their son, Wang Yun.

He might not match our Prince of Kui but still has great character. And the Prince has a good relationship with him. They often ride together. They're like the sun and moon, pulling girls out of their homes to watch their first and second choices for husbands pass," yet another person said.

"That's true. A lot of people say Wang Yun isn't as well rounded in the arts and sword, but two months ago, he led an imperial unit to pursue bandits on the outskirts and got them all—beheaded!"

"Gee, I don't know," Lu Yunzhong said. He gestured for everyone to lean toward him and spoke more quietly for dramatic effect. "I heard this mess is related to Pang Xun! Some of his former soldiers have come to the capital to assassinate the Prince of Kui!"

Everyone was shocked. "Why did we hear it was just bandits?"

"Of course, the court is trying to keep it hidden! When Wang Yun heard, he immediately ambushed them in the middle of the night. Got a clean kill. They buried the bodies right there, said it was just bandits, and left no evidence!"

"Huh? Then how do you know?"

"Hey, I have a military connection!" Lu Yunzhong said proudly. "And my uncle's brother-in-law works for the War Ministry. They're the ones that buried the bodies!"

"Wow!" everyone said.

"That being said, if Wang Yun was so great, why wouldn't the Huang girl marry him?"

"Oh, that. Yes, I heard she even poisoned her whole family to avoid marrying him! Could marrying him be that bad?"

"That's 'cause the Huang girl went crazy!"

Huang Zixia joined in with everyone's laughter.

When the laughter died down, the conversation ended. Huang Zixia continued holding her teacup, staring at the enamel pattern for a long time. The things she had kept inside were the subject of laughter now. It was like a rush of water stirring up sediment in a stagnant lake.

Her parents had been dead for nearly six months. The case was getting harder and harder, her hopes of solving it slimmer and slimmer. But all she could do was try her best to solve the case and earn Li Shubai's support so she could seek justice.

"Chonggu, when the Princess went missing, you were there too, right?" Lu Yunzhong said.

Huang Zixia nodded.

"I heard the Wang girl suddenly burst into smoke in front of thousands of people and flew away in the wind."

Huang Zixia began to sweat. Rumors. "Complete nonsense," she said.

"Yes, I knew it wasn't possible," someone else joined in. "I heard they already found the body. It was all covered in black boils, and anyone who got within thirty feet of it died! How could she turn into ash?"

Huang Zixia was shocked. All she could say was, "The Board of Punishments and Central Court are conducting an investigation. Before they close it, all conjecture is irrelevant. Please don't repeat baseless rumors."

They ignored her and kept talking. "I heard that since the Wang girl died, Lady Zhao is going to give Princess Qi Le to the Prince of Kui. Is that true?"

Huang Zixia was now fed up. She turned her hands upward and said, "I'm sorry, but the case is still underway, and we can't share any information with the public until it's solved."

Everyone had been there longer than she and held higher positions, but she was close to the Prince and was even participating in the investigation, so none of them dared to challenge her.

She hurried to thank them for the tea and praise its lovely taste. Then she excused herself, saying she had something to do. She walked through the palace gates and looked up at the sky. Her mind wandered to the details of the case. Then she heard the faint sound of bells. A carriage slowly approached and stopped before her. She turned and saw someone get out of the car.

Speak of the devil. It was Wang Yun.

Since he was mourning his sister, he was dressed plainly. He wore a white silk robe. Only the collar and sleeves were decorated with a Buddhist pattern. His green sash was knotted with a white jade pendant. In his hand was a fan with a jade spine and ink painting of bamboo on the surface, showing off the luxury of his illustrious family. Often dazzled by Zhou Ziqin's ostentatious purple clothes, Huang Zixia couldn't help but sigh at how different young men could be.

Seeing the sweat beads on her nose, Wang Yun handed her his fan. "I've come to talk to the Prince about my sister's funeral arrangements. Could you take me to him?"

Huang Zixia looked at the fan he was holding out, took it, and fanned herself as she nodded. "Come," she said.

They entered the gate, and the porter and group who had been gossiping stood up, looking guilty and bowed. Unaware, Wang Yun just glanced at them and smiled as he followed Huang Zixia into Jingyu Hall.

Jing Yu and Jing Yang were waiting in the front hall, drinking tea and chatting. Seeing Wang Yun arrive, Jing Yang stood quickly and asked him to sit. Jing Yu went through the small courtyard to notify the Prince of Kui.

Soon, Li Shubai came out to greet him and asked him to come in.

Huang Zixia was wondering whether or not she should go in. Li Shubai turned and gave her a look, so she hurried to keep up. The two of them sat in front of the western window. Jing Yang prepared hot water for tea over a stove. Huang Zixia self-consciously helped them clean the cups and went out with Jing Yang for pine branches.

Their voices came through the window. Wang Yun said, "It's started getting hot, as you know. My sister's body is becoming unbearable, so we discussed it as a family, and in four days it will have been seven. We'll seal the coffin and send it home to be buried straightaway. It's a little rushed, but it's the only way."

Li Shubai pondered a moment. "You've found a cemetery plot."

"She was so young," Wang Yun lamented. "Who would have a plot? At present, we're thinking of using the one that was set aside for her aunt. As for the tombstone, people have already been sent to carve it."

"Your sister was to be my wife. I'll certainly attend the ceremony."

"Thank you, Prince," Wang Yun said.

Wang Yun said he was burdened with mourning, so he didn't stay long after tea.

Huang Zixia saw Wang Yun's white figure brush past the front hall's cluster of hosta flowers. She hurried up to him. "Prince, your fan."

He turned and smiled at her. "You're not keeping it?"

"No, no," she hurried to say. "I just wanted to keep it safe in my sleeve pocket."

"Drinking tea now, no wonder you're sweaty." He didn't take the fan, just looked down at her. "Keep it."

She hesitated, wanting to hand it back to him, but he turned with a wave, saying, "Use it. You can give it back next time."

Huang Zixia stood, unconsciously fanning herself, feeling irritated.

Thirteen

LONG, LONELY STREET

Sometime later, she turned and saw Li Shubai looking at her through the front window. She didn't know how long he'd been standing there. He lowered his chin slightly, indicating for her to come in.

She hurried to fold up the fan and went in. The room was quiet, the tea cleared. Jing Yang lit ice incense, which made it feel like there was a breeze in the room.

Li Shubai motioned toward the seat across from him, and Huang Zixia sat.

Huang Zixia waited until Jing Yang had left and got right to the point. "It looks like we need to solve this case within four days or we'll lose the body."

Li Shubai nodded slightly. "You just keep at it. If we can't, I'll make sure the body doesn't go."

Huang Zixia agreed. "Chen Nian visited me this morning. I think as long as nothing else comes up, we shouldn't have a problem solving it."

"Oh, really?" Li Shubai said, squinting at her. "What did Chen Nian say that was so helpful?"

"First of all, I think that body . . ." She reached and touched her hairpin, as was her habit. Li Shubai looked away helplessly. He smiled ever so slightly, took a slim box out of the table drawer, and slid it to her.

"What is it?" she said.

"Take a look."

"Does it have something to do with the case?" she asked as she took it.

Li Shubai tilted his head and looked at the fish in the jar swimming quietly. "Basically," he said coldly. "To help you break it."

Huang Zixia opened the box and saw a hairpin on a layer of silk. She picked it up, puzzled. It was about five inches long with a silver body and jade top caved in a beautiful, meticulous pattern. There was nothing unusual about it, suitable for a little eunuch like her, but the weight was off. She took a closer look and found an orifice. She held the bottom of the leaf and heard a soft click. The silver part came off. Inside was a thinner, white jade hairpin. It was cool to the touch and shone from within. "It's a gift?"

"You're always touching your hairpin, but not being able to take it out makes me uneasy. And if you do take it out, people will be able to tell you're a woman, which would be trouble. So yes, it's a gift."

Huang Zixia put the box away. "Thank you, Prince. It's what I needed most."

"I'm not sure if the craftsman understood my instructions, or if it'll meet your needs."

"Thanks for your effort. The craftsman did well. It'll be very useful."

"How can you know if you haven't tried it?"

"Oh . . ." She realized that she hadn't been wearing her hat lately and her hair was just up in a bun. She put in the pin from Li Shubai and pulled the old one out. Then she pinched the new hairpin and pulled out the smaller hairpin. The silver body that had surrounded it was still in place.

"It works great." She put the jade pin back into the silver part. It locked in with a soft click. Huang Zixia liked it a lot. She kept touching it, her sleeves falling and exposing her wrists as she smiled. "Thank you so much, Prince! Now I can sort my thoughts out anytime."

"You'd be better off stopping the bad habit," he said.

Huang Zixia ignored him and pulled the inner hairpin out again. "Back to Chen Nian. Based on what she said, I think there are two key things about the body."

"Really?" Li Shubai poured a cup of tea and put it before her.

Huang Zixia was so focused on the case, she didn't notice. Then she quickly took a sip, put the hairpin on the table, and looked at him. "The body that appeared in Yongchun Hall isn't Wang Ruo."

"Yes, you mentioned your doubts before."

"But this time, I'm sure. The body belongs to Jin Nu—you probably realized it too—the pipa player close to Li Rui."

"You're sure?"

"Basically sure. The calluses on her hand were probably caused by years of friction on that spot from using a pipa pick."

"That makes sense, but there are a lot of pipa players in the world. How can you be sure it's Jin Nu?"

"Jin Nu disappeared when that body appeared in Yongchun Hall."

Li Shubai nodded slightly. "Do you have anything more concrete than that?"

"Yes." Huang Zixia drew an arrow on the paper with her hairpin. Then wrote *Chongren Square*. "The night Jin Nu disappeared, Zhou Ziqin took leftovers from Jinlou and poisoned the beggars."

Li Shubai nodded again. "I remember you said Jin Nu was there too."

"Yes. The food Zhou Ziqin sent them was what we had all been eating, but no one was affected. We gave it directly to the beggars and watched them eat it. So there are only two possibilities. First, there was something wrong with the lotus leaves we used. But Zhou Ziqin

211

said that antiaris poison is extremely toxic, and the leaves would have quickly turned black. However, the leaves we used were freshly washed, pliant and green, so they couldn't have been laced with poison."

Li Shubai nodded. "The other possibility is that there was poison on your hands."

"Right. There were three of us. I didn't have any issues, Zhou Ziqin was safe and sound, so the only possibility was that there was poison on Jin Nu's hands," Huang Zixia said with a sigh. "She complained that the cherry stem pricked her. Actually, the poison would have already been penetrating her skin and causing her hands to feel irritated. No one's hands are that delicate."

"Would antiaris poison have such an effect through surface contact?"

"It shouldn't, so there's still something I'm unclear about: when Jin Nu was poisoned. There was no wound on her hand, and it didn't enter orally. And she was always with us that night, but when we were about to leave, the poison . . . Given antiaris's toxicity, no one could have done it in front of us. So how and when she was poisoned, I really can't say."

"But at least the body's build, markings, and manner and time of death are consistent. Should be conclusive." Li Shubai nodded. "What about your second point?"

Huang Zixia used the hairpin to draw a second arrow and the word *Xuzhou*. "As you suspected, the girls you saved in Xuzhou are important."

"Oh?" Li Shubai actually looked a little surprised.

"Chen Nian is expecting someone to arrive in the capital. When she comes, we should be able to solve the case."

"Who?"

"Cheng Xuese, one of the girls you rescued in Xuzhou. She's bringing a painting. I think it will be the most compelling evidence in the case." Her expression was dignified, her tone confident.

Li Shubai, sitting in Jingyu Hall, looked up slightly at Huang Zixia. Sunlight flashed through the curtains, making her seem transparent and bright, enough to banish all the darkness in the world. He took a deep breath. "Very good. I hope your bet pays off."

"I won't let you down." Huang Zixia felt loyal to him. He was the only one that could overturn her false conviction and avenge her family.

Unfortunately, Li Shubai was unmoved. "So what are you going to do next?"

"Going to pursue the Jin Nu angle. Before too much time passes, I'll look at her room at the music academy and see if there are any clues." Huang Zixia thought a moment, then added, "I'll say my Prince sent Jin Nu an important gift, and I'm here to look for it."

"Don't use the Prince of Kui's token," he said coldly.

Huang Zixia stood and bowed. "Rest assured. If I say a Prince sent me, everyone will assume it's Li Rui."

"Mm," he said. "You don't need dinner?"

"No need. If I wait any longer, curfew will pass," she said. "Oh, and in order to avoid using the token, I requested funding of ten silvers and twenty coppers."

Li Shubai was surprised. "What's the twenty for?"

"To hire a carriage for the ride back."

Li Shubai looked at her. "How are you that broke?"

"Because Junior Eunuch Yang Chonggu has been penniless ever since she started working for you," she said with no shame.

"Why not find Jing Yi and have him get the bookkeeper to give you an advance?"

"Once it's approved, it'll probably take a month. By that time, I'll have received my salary, and it won't be of much use."

Li Shubai raised his eyebrows slightly. His ever-fearless face finally showed some compassion. He opened the drawer, took out a purse, and tossed it to her.

"Thank you, my Prince!" Huang Zixia caught it, turned, and left.

◆ ◆ ◆

The Changan of the Tang Dynasty had two academies. The pipa, guqin, and arts academy was on Guangzhou Square, not far from Kui Palace.

Huang Zixia hurried over. She found an old woman sitting in the entrance, nibbling on seeds, who raised her hand to stop her.

Huang Zixia quickly bowed. "I'm sorry, ma'am. I'm here for Jin Nu."

"Huh, what a coincidence. Everyone's looking for Jin Nu." She brushed some seed debris off herself as she stood. "Are you also coming to find something you gave her 'cause you heard she ran off with someone?"

Huang Zixia gasped. "Someone else already came?"

"Sure. Such a woman I've never seen before," she said. "That face, that figure, prettier than a lady in a painting."

"Did you get her name?" Huang Zixia asked.

"No. Quite different from this eunuch coming with nothing but words. She had a letter Jin Nu had written her. But I can't read!"

Seeing the old woman's resistance, Huang Zixia smiled and took some money from the purse. "Ma'am, look. I was ordered here. When my Prince heard the girl ran off, he was very angry. If I don't get his gift back, how will I return home?"

"Oh, no, I can't stand to see people suffer." She took the little silver and grinned. "Come, come. I'll show you Jin Nu's room. It's at the east end of the second corridor, room three. Hurry, we're closing up in less than an hour."

Huang Zixia thanked her and went. When she got there, Jin Nu's door was open, for some reason. Two girls were in the doorway talking.

"Excuse me," Huang Zixia said, "the beautiful lady?"

The two girls sized her up, undoubtedly noting her eunuch uniform. "Whoa, where are you from? The academy, or a Prince's palace?"

"My Prince left something with Jin Nu. Since she's gone now, he asked me to come find it. Though it's not valuable, it's precious to the Prince," Huang Zixia said. "I heard a beautiful woman was just here?"

"Of course. Jin Nu was pretty good-looking, but who knew there was someone like that?" the girl on the left said, looking inside. "Didn't she say she was coming back? Where is she?"

"Yes, I'm eager to see her picture," the other girl said, frowning.

Huang Zixia was shocked. "What picture?"

"One of those famous six women, amazing performers from Yangzhou."

"The Six Women of Yunshao?" Huang Zixia said, dumbfounded.

"You're just a eunuch. You don't study music; why would you want to see the picture?"

Huang Zixia was speechless, confused about where she got that from. She thought the beautiful woman with the picture must be Cheng Xuese. Why hadn't Chen Nian brought her to her first?

The two girls waited awhile. Seeing she wasn't coming back, they stomped off. "Can I go in Jin Nu's room?" Huang Zixia asked.

"Sure. When she left, she took her money and important things. People here divided up what was left. They said they were helping Jin Nu get rid of it, but of course they just wanted it for themselves. Look for yourself. There's basically nothing there."

"Even so, it's worth a try," Huang Zixia said. She said goodbye and went into the room and looked around.

Jin Nu's room was quite stylish. The patterned window frame had purple chiffon curtains, and there was a beaded curtain dividing the room.

There were a couple of chairs by the window with some things on them—a white porcelain pot with two withered tea plants.

There was no one inside. The woman who came must have gotten what she wanted and left.

She sat in a small chair, thinking about the case, and waited for Cheng Xuese to come back.

The sky grew dimmer, making the lamplight outside seem brighter. Cheng Xuese never came back. Huang Zixia couldn't wait any longer and decided to take a look. She stood up and went to the wardrobe and looked inside with the help of the light coming in through the window.

Sure enough, everything of value had been taken away. There were only a few pieces of wrinkled clothing and the furniture. Nothing useful.

She paced throughout the room, eyes sweeping over every inch. Finally, a glint of reflected light through the window made her stop. She lay down on the ground and reached toward the corner of the flower rack. Taking the shiny thing in her hand, her eyes suddenly widened with surprise.

A silver half ingot.

It was about the same size as the one they found in Yongchun Hall. The engraving and quality seemed the same. It was probably the other half. She held it in her arms as she carefully searched the room once more to make sure she hadn't missed anything. Then she left.

She hurried to leave the school before the gates were locked. She stood alone in Guangzhai Square. The curfew was starting soon, and Changan was silent. She couldn't find a carriage to hire.

She sighed reluctantly and began walking toward Kui Palace. The drums signaling curfew pounded in the distance, so she walked faster. Guangzhai Square was in the north, near Daming Palace and Taiji Palace, but no one was out. She seemed to hear her footsteps echoing loudly through the streets.

A voice called from behind her. "Who's that? What are you doing out this late?"

Huang Zixia turned and faced two mounted patrolmen. "I'm a eunuch from Kui Palace. I was delayed on an errand and am hurrying back."

They softened noticeably. "Do you have an errand letter or something?"

"No need. I know him. He's Yang Chonggu," the other one said.

Huang Zixia recognized the voice and felt relieved. She bowed. "Commander Wang."

The commander of the right guard was on patrol that night.

Wang Yun looked down at her from his horse, but he didn't seem arrogant, rather gentle and modest. "Mr. Yang, I saw you passing the time by watching the clouds this afternoon. What could you be so occupied with now?"

"I misjudged the time, thought I could get back before curfew."

Wang Yun nodded, indicating for the other man to continue on the route. Then he patted the back of his horse. "Come on. I'll send you back to the palace."

"Oh, no need. The commander is busy. I'm just a servant." She smiled stiffly and started to walk.

The clap of Wang Yun's horse followed behind.

She turned and looked at him. "It hasn't been very safe lately. I'll go with you," he said gently.

"Thank you so much, Commander Wang." It was hard for her to get these words out. She wouldn't speak again.

The long street was silent. The lamps in the corners of the squares shone peacefully. There was an occasional breeze that made their flames undulate light and dark like waves washing over Changan.

They went like that to Kui Palace: Huang Zixia on foot and Wang Yun on horseback. His horse was well trained and gentle, keeping a steady gait the same speed as Huang Zixia's.

They trod on the watery light through Changan's straight, wide streets. It was the world's most prosperous city, with thousands of buildings lit as bright as stars.

Many aristocrats lived in Yongjia Square. The music was carried along the wind to their ears—bits of strings and voices.

The parasol shadow outside the pearl curtain is the first to know the autumn frost.

Huang Zixia, walking in a daze, heard Wang Yun chuckle. "It's not even summer yet. How could there be autumn frost?"

It took a second for Huang Zixia to realize he was talking about the song lyrics. "It's about the feeling, not the actual things."

He tilted his head. "Yes, I'm too focused on actual things."

"Wang Ruo's coffin will soon return to Langya. The commander must be very busy. How did he find time to go on patrol tonight?"

"There are so many people at home. As long as they know what to do, it'll get done. No need to always keep an eye on it." He looked out into the night. "And I like the look of the city at this time. It's quieter and deeper than during the day. The silhouettes of the buildings are magnificent. There seems to be something hidden inside them; it's spellbinding."

"If you could see everything, of course, the spell would be broken."

He smiled. "Mr. Yang is correct. Things are always clearer to a bystander."

The lights near and far created a kind of haze, making her unsure if there was another layer of meaning to his smile.

Huang Zixia cringed. Wang Yun acting like this with a eunuch was completely improper.

Did he already figure out who she really was, or just have suspicions? How could she start protecting herself? She lowered her gaze to avoid his. "Almost there. Commander Wang can go back now."

"Sure. Try not to lose track of time and stay out so late again."

He stopped his horse in the street and watched her leave.

Huang Zixia walked quickly to the northwestern gate of Kui Palace and knocked. She went inside and looked back at Wang Yun as it closed.

He was still watching her, his dimly lit face looking as soft as a spring breeze.

◆ ◆ ◆

Soon, another rider came up beside him. "When will you return, son? There are many things to attend to at home."

"Straightaway," Wang Yun said, turning his horse and starting off. "Father, why did you come out alone?"

Wang Lin sighed. "The Empress called. How could I not?"

Wang Yun nodded, and the two rode slowly off.

"Did you take care of the thing I asked?"

"Yes," he said calmly. "Used some herbs to get rid of some of the blood, so no one can tell."

"You acted alone?"

"Of course. Got a scapegoat too."

"Reliable?" Wang Lin said coldly. "You know only the dead can be relied on."

"Yes. I'll keep my eyes peeled for an opportunity."

Neither spoke as the Wangs' palace came in sight. They went inside, and the porter helped them take the horse. Father and son walked through the corridor to the inner courtyard.

A lantern painted with the word *Wang* on the ground gave the deserted mansion some warmth.

Wang Lin suddenly stopped in the darkness and faced Wang Yun.

Wang Yun waited.

Wang Lin looked pleased at his boy, who was half a head taller than him. "Son, I really didn't want there to be blood on your hands."

Wang Yun pursed his lips. "I'm a Wang. I'll do anything for the family, even sacrifice my life."

Wang Lin patted his shoulder hard. "Good kid," he said. "Shame this generation just has you."

"Though sister's a woman, she's resolute and courageous. Now she's Empress. I'm sure she's sacrificed a lot for our family."

Wang Lin's expression slowly changed to a frown. He nodded. "Yes. She's a Wang too."

"And if nothing had happened to Ruo, she'd certainly be the Princess of Kui."

"Right. The other Wang girls of this generation are weak. No one else would have tempted him so," Wang Lin said with a sigh. "Back when the Emperor was the Prince of Yun, he came to one of our banquets and took a liking to your sister as well. Clearly attractive people are always striking."

Wang Yun listened to his father complain, looking at the red lanterns hanging under the eaves, and thought of Huang Zixia. Three years ago, when she was fourteen, he secretly followed her slim, red figure, fresh and charming.

He went on to remember Huang Zixia slowly turning around and then—her face melded with that of Yang Chonggu, and they became the same person.

Huang Zixia and Yang Chonggu, a thirteen- or fourteen-year-old girl; a seventeen- or eighteen-year-old eunuch; one delicate, one fine; one light-skinned and confident in the old court, one weak and thin, serving cautiously by the Prince of Kui's side.

He was clearly a little palace eunuch; why did he keep associating him with Huang Zixia? There was something strange when they first met, though. Is it because they're both good at solving cases, and he looks like the picture on the wanted poster?

He'd even quietly looked into Yang Chonggu's identity and found a clear trail from Jiucheng Palace to Kui Palace. Even the pledge he'd signed when he joined Jiucheng was still there—but Yang Chonggu was illiterate and just signed with a circle.

Then there was Li Shubai himself.

Doubting Yang Chonggu was the same as doubting him. He thought of how Huang Zixia humiliated him.

"Son, the Wang family has fallen in the world. I'm afraid the ancestors must be ashamed now all our hope is with you. I hope you can bring us back to our old glory, or at least resist the forces bringing us down!"

Wang Yun nodded solemnly. "Our family has the Empress, and you as minister. We're not weak."

"You're wrong. The most influential person we have in the empire isn't the Empress or me." Wang Lin smiled slightly, with a touch of pride. "You forgot there's someone else who can bring about a new order. It's just that no one pays attention to that Wang."

Wang Yun lowered his head and was silent for a time. "Yes."

"After Wang Ruo's coffin is sent off, go visit him," Wang Lin said. He thought a moment, then added, "He likes fish. Remember to bring him a few—red would be best."

"I don't know if they already served dinner." Huang Zixia's stomach was aching.

Apart from a few spring rolls in the morning and some tea in the afternoon, she hadn't even had a single grain of rice while she ran around all day. She clutched her stomach on the way to the dining room, but the stove was cold and no one was there.

"I can't handle this." Huang Zixia was angry at herself for not asking Ms. Lu where she kept things. Now, without her there, she couldn't find food. There were a couple of stale buns in the cupboard. Huang Zixia took one in each hand and gnawed on one on her way to her room.

When she reached the courtyard entrance, she saw the light in her room was on. She was surprised and went to the doorway to have a look. The buns almost fell from her hands.

Li Shubai looked up and waved her in.

She hesitated before going forward. "My Prince, what are you doing up so late?"

He just raised his chin a little to point out a box of food next to him.

She opened it slowly and removed its contents: a cup of porridge, a plate of fried sweet buns, a bowl of pork tenderloin, roast quail, and her favorite grilled shrimp and frogs with bean sprouts. It was somehow still hot. She glanced at Li Shubai and saw he was still ignoring her. She immediately threw away the buns in her hands and took the ivory chopsticks out of the box and gave Li Shubai a pair. Using her own, she plucked up one of the roast quail.

Li Shubai put down his reading. "Any developments?"

She put the half ingot on the table.

Li Shubai took it and turned it over in his hands, looking closely.

On its back were two lines of writing. The first said, *Deng Yunxi, Song Kuo.* The other, *twenty silvers.*

Huang Zixia took the other half ingot from the drawer and handed it to him.

The two pieces were indeed part of a whole. The words on the back were now complete. *Deputy Liang Weidong, Deng Yunxi, Song Kuo, and Master Zhang Junyi, cast twenty silvers.*

Li Shubai put it down and looked at her. "Where'd you find it?"

"In the room, below the flower stand."

"Couldn't be," Li Shubai said confidently.

"Really. Lots of people had already been through the room, so that ingot shouldn't have still been sitting in such an obvious place." She drank some porridge. "So it must have been put there by Cheng Xuese, who had just left."

"Cheng Xuese?" Li Shubai was finally a little excited. "She's in the capital?"

"Yes, but I didn't see her, just heard some of the students say a gorgeous woman with a portrait came to Jin Nu's room, but she was already gone when I got there."

"Well, you missed her," he said with a frown. "Why didn't Chen Nian tell you?"

"Or, Xuese and Jin Nu were so close, she went to Jin Nu's first?" Huang Zixia said thoughtfully. "But Chen Nian and Feng Yi's thing should be most important. Either way, she should have brought her to me right away."

Li Shubai nodded. "Chen Nian's at Li Rui's palace. We can go there to see her tomorrow."

"Right. Also, I looked at the area outside the academy today and found a place. It was too late, but if we go and look tomorrow, we might find something."

"Looks like you'll be busy all day again tomorrow." The candle was going dim. He closed his book, picked up a pair of scissors, trimmed the wick, and it got brighter.

The flickering candlelight made the room feel calm. As Huang Zixia ate, she noticed Li Shubai was looking at her and couldn't help but pause.

Li Shubai looked away and casually picked up a pair of chopsticks, lifted a few bean sprouts, and put them in his bowl.

It took Huang Zixia a while to get the words out. "Thank you, Prince, for getting me this—"

"No need," he interrupted her. Then he looked at her for a long time. "A full horse runs fastest."

Her mouth twitched a little. "The Prince is wise."

"So run faster tomorrow. Don't forget the Wangs are going to send the body off soon."

"Yes . . ." This reminded her that she saw Wang Yun that night. She held her chopsticks in the candlelight and thought it'd be best not to mention it.

It was just a chance encounter unrelated to the case.

The weather was good the next day with a lofty, blue summer sky, bright and piercing. As per their agreement, she met Li Shubai in the stables.

He was already atop a strong, dark horse, trotting to warm it up. He wore a gray-purple robe. When the light hit it from the right angle, you could make out blue and purple beads woven into it—sublime and bright. He pulled on the reins when he saw her and pointed to the back of the stables with his whip. "Pick one."

Huang Zixia untied a white horse and got on. Last time she went to see Zhou Ziqin, she rode a different horse and brought this one. It won her over on that trip.

Li Shubai liked her taste. "That's a good one," he said. "I used to ride it a lot. Called Nafusha."

"Interesting name," Huang Zixia said.

"In Dayuan, it means a noble and gentle temperament. It's obedient and easy to approach, tame, so it can forget who its master was," Li Shubai said with a frown, as if remembering something in the distant past. He patted the proud, dark horse below him and added, "This one, Di'e, by comparison, is much better."

"Di'e?"

"In Dawan, it means daylight." They rode to the gates and out of the palace. She trailed about half a horse-length behind.

"Di'e's temper is much worse. It took me three days and four nights to break him. Only in the morning after the fourth night was he finally unable to stand, and bowed down to me," Li Shubai said. "No one else has ever been able to control him."

Huang Zixia looked at Di'e, wondering whether or not she could ride him. He had long, flat eyelashes. His eyes crossed, and he kicked his right hind leg, sending sand into Nafusha's belly. Nafusha let out a cry and leaped forward, nearly causing Huang Zixia to fall off. Angry, she kicked Di'e. She hit him in the neck and he became furious, but Li Shubai pulled on his reins and he obediently calmed down, nostrils flaring. He looked disappointed.

Huang Zixia couldn't help but point her whip at him and laugh.

This was one of the only times Li Shubai had heard her laugh. He found himself looking at her for a long time. She had a smile as gorgeous as the early summer sun, as if all the world's light shone in her clear, young face.

As if afraid of being burned by the sun, he turned away.

Huang Zixia looked at him, puzzled. He coughed and said, "Let's go. Li Run's palace."

Fourteen

Bright Sky, Dark Clouds

They met Li Run in that carefully decorated tearoom again. When Li Shubai said they had come to see Chen Nian, Li Run was shocked. "Why would you want to speak with her today, brother?"

"Just a little something I want to ask her about."

"How unlucky," Li Run said helplessly. "Chen Nian already left."

"What? Chen Nian left?" Li Shubai said. "When?"

"Yesterday. She got her things and left the palace, didn't say good-bye. All I got was a letter. I'll show you."

A servant quickly brought it over, but it wasn't really a letter, just a note:

Your Royal Highness Li Run:

I will never forget the prince's incredible kindness in receiving me. Now this old woman's only wish is to leave the capital and never return. May Your Highness live a long and fruitful life.

Your servant, Chen Nian

The handwriting was beautiful, but it looked rushed. Huang Zixia looked at the word *wish* and thought awhile, then handed it back to Li Run. "That being the case, it's unlikely we'll see her again. Unfortunately, my guqin playing is so poor. I really wanted to have another lesson!"

Li Run smiled. "There are a lot of good teachers around, some of them masters. Oh, right, yesterday was the twelfth. Before I paid my respects to the lady, Chen Nian said that since the lady loves pipa the most, she could show her the portrait of the Six Women of Yangzhou in a few days. When I mentioned it, she just laughed."

"So when you came back from the palace, Chen Nian was already gone?" Li Shubai asked.

"Yes, so even if the lady wanted to, I wouldn't have been able to show her the painting," Li Run said with a smile. He seemed to be in a very good mood. Clearly, Chen Nian's leaving hadn't upset him at all.

Li Shubai nodded. "She's gone, so it won't be easy to find her. Thank you so much for making tea, anyway."

"Don't mention it. It's great to have you here."

Li Shubai and Huang Zixia left on horseback.

It wasn't until Li Run's palace was far behind that Li Shubai pulled on his reins, and the two of them stopped on the street.

They both looked thoughtful.

"Where did you say you wanted to take a look yesterday?" Li Shubai asked.

"The channel outside Guangzhai Square. It's still morning. There might be people collecting water there. Afternoon would be better."

Li Shubai nodded, then turned his horse. "Let's go to the West City."

Huang Zixia gently swung her whip over Nafusha's rear. "Oh? To watch more magic tricks?"

He didn't answer. "What do you think the key to this case is?"

Huang Zixia took a moment to think about it. "This case has so many difficult components, but in my opinion, the biggest is how Wang

Ruo disappeared from Yongchun Hall while it was closely guarded by two hundred people. By what means could someone vanish like that?"

"Yes. Wang Ruo's disappearance is crucial to solving this mystery. Maybe we should focus on that." Li Shubai slowed down, allowing them to ride alongside each other. "I was thinking about this earlier. The thing about that birdcage trick is that there is a trapdoor that lets the bird out, so maybe there is something like that in Yongchun Hall."

"But then how many ways out could there be in a room with almost no furniture?" They thought about the lanterns hanging from the caisson ceiling—no skylight, not even a beam. The four walls were all solid, no gaps.

"She disappeared just like that from a sealed room like a birdcage," he concluded.

"Right, and a few days later a completely different body appeared, but not of the person who disappeared."

They lowered their voices to a whisper. They'd already arrived in the West City. They tied their horses in the borough stables and joined the bustling crowd. There were lines of people shopping for exotic animals and fine alcohol, blue-eyed foreigners. The extravagance of the current Emperor had spread throughout Changan. The fish shop owner was still there teasing the fish, ignoring the customers who came in. Li Shubai bought the same fish as last time, looked back, and saw Huang Zixia giving him a complicated look. He didn't feel like explaining but eventually said, "That fish likes this food, seems to be fattening up."

Huang Zixia was speechless. "How 'bout we go see that magician couple."

The couple was early that day, already performing on the street. They were doing a trick where an egg turned into a chicken. Though Huang Zixia knew it was just sleight of hand, she still felt moved by the sight of the chick running along the ground and even helped them catch it and put it back in its cage.

After the crowd dispersed, the woman noticed them and smiled. "What trick do you want to learn today?" she asked.

"We still haven't gotten that birdcage one to work," Huang Zixia said. "Can't find a trained bird! Do you know any simpler ones?"

"Bring the birdcage over," the woman called to her husband. "And that cloth. Yes, the black one."

The woman shook the black cloth to show it held nothing. Then she put it over the empty birdcage and looked at Huang Zixia. She didn't move or speak, just smiled.

Huang Zixia knew that it was top secret and the woman wouldn't reveal it easily. She reached a hand out to Li Shubai for payment.

He understood and took a small ingot from the purse and handed it to her.

The female performer took the money, and her eyes gained a certain brilliance as she removed a bird from another cage and gently put it inside the one with the black cloth over it. Then she brought her hands away slightly and flicked them open to show they were empty.

Then she put both her hands behind her back. It seemed the little bird really was in the cloth-covered cage.

She smiled at them and took the black cloth off. The cage was empty.

Huang Zixia instinctively lifted it up and looked carefully inside. It really was empty, and it was crudely made, apparently without hidden doors.

The female performer smiled. "This time, I didn't touch the cage, and the bird was freshly hatched—no training. It also takes no special skill. As long as you know how it works, you can do it."

Huang Zixia's and Li Shubai's eyes fell on the piece of black cloth. There was something wiggling inside.

The woman smiled and opened the black cloth. Inside was a small pocket. The chick's head peeked out.

Seeing it was so simple, Huang Zixia couldn't help but laugh. "So that's how you did it . . ."

Images raced through her mind.

The prediction of the man who suddenly appeared at Xianyou Temple; the invisible assassin in Penglai Hall; the leafy hairpin that fell in the rock garden; the tight protection of Yongchun Hall . . . They all had an invisible thread connecting them. Her sudden realization made her sigh as if she couldn't bear it as she stared ahead in a trance.

Li Shubai patted her on the shoulder. She didn't respond, so he took her by the sleeve and led her away.

Her hand was slim and soft, like a little pigeon in his palm.

Huang Zixia followed him, looking drained, under an elm. She sighed and said, "I need to talk to Zhou Ziqin."

Li Shubai slowly let go of her hand and frowned. "What'd you realize?"

"I want to see if I'm right, and I'll need Zhou Ziqin's help," she said. "Are you going back to the palace?"

Li Shubai grunted. "No."

"Do you want to go see Zhou Ziqin with me?"

He turned toward their horses. "Might as well."

The Zhou family porter immediately smiled when he saw them. "Back again, Mr. Yang? And who's this?"

Li Shubai didn't get off the horse. "You go in. I'll wait," he told Huang Zixia.

Huang Zixia dismounted and tied up the horse. The porter smiled and said, "The master said to take you right to his quarters. Come. I'll show you the way."

Huang Zixia thanked him and followed inside. They walked to a courtyard covered in creeping fig by a corner of the flower garden. The door was open, and inside were two servants playing cat's cradle under the grapevine. Zhou Ziqin's voice came faintly: "I said I need help; how about it?"

"Master, it's not that we don't want to help it. That thing's just scary. How can we touch it!" one of the servants said without looking away from their string.

Huang Zixia could hear his exasperation. "You two dolts would rather play girly games than help your master. I've had it up to here."

The porter was unfazed. He calmly smiled and left. Huang Zixia walked inside. "Come on out, Zhou Ziqin. We've got important business to take care of!"

His voice was rapturous. "Chonggu! Come help! It's an emergency!"

Huang Zixia went inside and found him lying on the ground with two bronze human figures pinning him down as he clutched a white skull in his hand. She didn't know what was going on, but she dragged the bronze figures aside. They were nearly solid and very heavy, so she had to sit and recover for a while.

Zhou Ziqin was wearing a green robe embroidered with purple peonies and a big red belt, still bright and garish despite getting dusty from the ground. He got up and affectionately touched the skull. "Lucky it didn't break, or I'd feel terrible. I paid fifty for it. Used to belong to a young man. Look at this beautiful arc, nice white teeth, deep eye sockets—"

"How'd you end up like that?" Huang Zixia interrupted.

"I slipped when I was getting the skull off the shelf, and the statues fell down. I had to dive to save my precious skull and—good thing no one makes solid bronze figures, or I'd be in serious trouble!"

Huang Zixia looked at the handsome, healthy, good-natured guy holding the perfect white skull and realized why he hadn't found a wife yet. No woman wants to compete with bones for her husband's affection. It also must have been why he stayed in that remote corner of the complex.

"Right, so what's the important business, Chonggu?"

"You remember those beggars who were poisoned to death?"

Zhou Ziqin jumped. "Of course! How could I forget? I have to figure out how they died!"

"I have some ideas. If you want to get to the bottom of it, I need you to help me do something." Huang Zixia motioned for him to put the skull down, then headed out. "You should change into some light-weight, coarse clothing. The worse, the better."

They got ready and joined Li Shubai. The three of them rode northeast.

Zhou Ziqin quickly approached Huang Zixia. "So you know how the beggars died?"

"Yes, I have a good idea. I just need someone to appear."

"Someone? Who?" Zhou Ziqin asked. "Someone really important?"

Huang Zixia nodded slightly. "If my guess is right, as soon as she comes, this awful case will finally be solved."

"Who could that be?" he said, amazed.

She smiled. "It's just an idea. I haven't even seen them yet!" Zhou Ziqin looked at her doubtfully. She didn't say more; he could guess himself. Tough-tempered Di'e rushed ahead with Nafusha close behind, and Zhou Ziqin's horse in the rear.

They went like that through the streets of Changan. Zhou Ziqin slapped his forehead. "I got it! I know who you're waiting for."

Huang Zixia looked back at him, shocked. He had one hand on the bridle and one waving excitedly in the air. "Is it a girl?"

"Yes."

"Sixteen or seventeen years old?"

"Yes."

"A beautiful girl?"

"Well . . . probably."

"I know!" Zhou Ziqin pulled her sleeve. "Is it Huang Zixia?"

"Huh?" She was stunned.

"A sixteen- or seventeen-year-old, beautiful girl who will quickly solve this case!"

Li Shubai ignored them, but Huang Zixia noticed a twitch of his shoulders like he was trying to keep from laughing.

She kept riding, silently looking at the sky.

She couldn't imagine how many tears would stream down his face if he found out Huang Zixia was right next to him. When they neared Taiji Palace, they dismounted and walked to a secluded alley.

Zhou Ziqin glanced back at their horses. "They'll be okay?"

"Don't worry about it," Huang Zixia said as she walked ahead with Li Shubai. "Di'e's there. Anyone who tried to steal him would lose a leg."

Zhou Ziqin looked envious. "Wow, the Prince of Kui's horse is theft-proof."

Huang Zixia led them to Guangzhai Square, to the right of the academy.

Zhou Ziqin tugged on the clothing he borrowed from the gardener as they walked along the channel. "Chonggu . . . this seems a bit far from the place where the beggars died."

"Don't call attention to us. Let me see." From outside Taiji Palace in Guangzhai Square, Huang Zixia saw the wall of Yuanwang Palace and the entrance of the academy. She estimated the shortest route and turned to some shrubs next to them, found signs of upturned stones, then pointed at the channel. "Jump in."

Zhou Ziqin was stunned. "Chonggu, first, it's not swimming weather yet. Second, I'm not very good in water . . ."

"You don't have to be. It's not deep here. You just need to go down and pick something up," she said.

Li Shubai didn't seem to hear them as he admired the scenery all around.

"What thing, Chonggu? I'll call someone to help you."

"I want to find evidence related to the deaths of the beggars."

Zhou Ziqin began to undress.

Huang Zixia looked up at the sky. Li Shubai said, "Why do you have to take off *those* clothes?"

"Oh, right . . ." Zhou Ziqin put his clothes back on. "Prince, Chonggu, tell me earlier next time you want me to go in water. I'll borrow a suit."

"Come on, this has to be a secret. No one can know." Huang Zixia held her hands out and apart to about the length of a pipa. "It should be about this big, wrapped. Find what you can."

"Okay." Zhou Ziqin jumped in the water with a crash.

Li Shubai stood on the ground, looking at the blue sky, white clouds, and lush elms. "Bright sun, a few clouds. The fog's cleared. Very nice."

Huang Zixia found a relatively flat blue stone and sat down. She'd become more like Li Shubai by being demanding with Zhou Ziqin and felt sad.

Before long, Zhou Ziqin stuck his head out of the water and took a deep breath. "This ditch is really deep, and the water's really dirty. It's all mud and weeds on the bottom. Hard to find anything. Why not call some people to come do a thorough search?"

"Can't," Huang Zixia said seriously, squatting on the bank. "I already told you, we have to do it ourselves or we might arouse suspicion."

Zhou Ziqin grimaced and pulled himself ashore. "But me searching this big channel for I don't even know what is hopeless!"

"Don't worry. Based on the distance, direction, marks, and other factors, I think this would be the killer's first choice of location."

"But this is so far from the Xingqing Palace where the beggars died, there's no way," Zhou Ziqin muttered. Huang Zixia pushed his head back down underwater.

Zhou Ziqin struggled out angrily. "Chonggu, you bastard. Give me some warning. My foot got caught on a plant."

"Huh? No way! Sorry. Come on; I'll help you out."

"It's tangled pretty tight, pulling me down . . ." He shook his leg as Huang Zixia pulled his hand as hard as she could. Eventually, Li Shubai couldn't even bear it anymore and lent a hand.

They pulled and pulled for a long time before he finally got his foot free.

Huang Zixia and Zhou Ziqin sat down to catch their breath.

"What weed would be tough enough to grip a person so tight?"

"Forget it. I'm so tired. It wrapped around my foot like a bandage. When I was under, it looked like a black mass." He held out his hands to show how big. "It wrapped around my foot, and I couldn't get it off."

In return, Huang Zixia unconsciously gestured the size of the thing she wanted to find.

Zhou Ziqin was stunned.

They looked at each other for a long time. Then, Zhou Ziqin finally stood up and dove in the canal.

When Huang Zixia started getting impatient, he suddenly burst out of the water. "Hurry! Hurry up! Found something!"

"What?" Huang Zixia glanced at Li Shubai, wondering what the chances were he'd go in to help.

"The water was so cloudy, it just looked like a shadow, but now I can tell. There's not just a parcel. Also a body!"

Even Li Shubai was surprised. "A body?"

"Yes! And it's headless. I'm sure!"

The thing that caught Zhou Ziqin's foot was a package. Inside was a pipa, two outfits, a jewelry box, and a large stone.

And the body of a headless woman. She'd been weighed down by a stone too. Zhou Ziqin cut the rope attaching the stone and dragged it ashore.

"I'm so tired." Zhou Ziqin climbed out and collapsed on the shore, panting.

"The stone isn't very heavy. How did it make it sink?" The other two began examining the body.

The headless woman had obviously not been in the water for long. The skin had become paler but not too swollen. She wore a thin, soft robe and had a thin waist and slender limbs.

"Ziqin, you know bodies best. Tell us about this one," Li Shubai said.

"You should have told me there'd be a body," he said regretfully from the ground. "I didn't bring tools."

"I didn't know there was going to be a body either. Just thought there was a package."

Zhou Ziqin got up and gave it a look. "The deceased was about five foot three, body type . . . very good, about the best I've examined. Good shape. Inch taller, too tall; inch shorter, too short."

"Get serious," Li Shubai said.

"Okay. She was thrown in the channel after the killer cut her head off. The scene shouldn't be far from here, and the killer was experienced. The wound across the neck is very clean, which took a lot of skill. It won't be easy to find evidence, since they probably cleaned it up, especially with all this grass and weeds around."

"Yes, a headless body will certainly be harder to identify," Huang Zixia said as she took the pipa from the parcel and looked at it. The strings were broken, but its inlaid peony mosaic was intact and shone brightly in the sun.

"Makes sense . . ."

"So the killer just took some clothes, trying to make it seem like Jin Nu eloped."

"And this body?"

"Jin Nu was five foot five. You said this body is five three. Can't be Jin Nu."

Zhou Ziqin was still confused. "Then how could it show up here so coincidentally?"

Huang Zixia looked at him. "You tell me."

Zhou Ziqin looked at her, then at Li Shubai. "Ah," he said, "the killer wanted it to look like Jin Nu."

"Right. The real Jin Nu," Huang Zixia said, "is lying in Wang Ruo's coffin."

Zhou Ziqin jumped. "Wh-what? You mean—"

"Yes. Someone disguised Jin Nu's body as Wang Ruo's and used this body to cover up the Princess's disappearance."

"How awful!" Zhou Ziqin's eyes widened. "Why would the killer want to hurt Jin Nu?"

"'Cause their bodies have similarities, I guess. Wang Ruo's pretty tall, about a head above average. This body doesn't have a head, but we can still estimate its height. And the body of a pipa player isn't as important as a Princess's. The authorities won't examine it too closely. And after a few days in the water, it would have bloated more, making figuring out its height much more difficult." She put the pipa back and signaled for Zhou Ziqin to take it away. "Keep the evidence at your place. Too inconvenient to have it at ours."

"Oh, okay," Zhou Ziqin said, ignoring the muddy water dripping off as he picked up the package. "What about this body?"

Huang Zixia sighed. "Can you take it to your house?"

"You think it's possible?" Zhou Ziqin asked.

"Tell Cui Chunzhan straightaway," Li Shubai said. "Say you found a parcel and a headless, female body here. Don't interfere with the

Central Court's identification process. Also, keep all of the evidence safe. When we call for it, you bring it."

"All right," he said with a bitter face, waiting for Huang Zixia to go tell Cui Chunzhan while he stayed with the package and body.

◆ ◆ ◆

Huang Zixia and Li Shubai walked through the bushes next to the channel to a path that led to a neighborhood where a few people sat, chatting in the shade.

"We found a body in the water there!" Huang Zixia shouted.

Suddenly, some of them got up quickly. Others rushed over to see what the commotion was about. Still others went to inform the local authorities. All bases were covered.

Li Shubai and Huang Zixia walked to the empty alley. Di'e and Nafusha were gingerly eating grass. The bridle made it very hard for them to eat much, but they scrounged a little out of boredom.

They mounted their horses and realized Li Shubai, despite having stood off to the side almost the whole time, had gotten his clothes dirty. They didn't worry about it, though, just rode off slowly.

"Did Jing Xu send news from Xuzhou yet?" Huang Zixia asked.

"Yes. The arrowhead disappeared when Pang Xun's defeated followers were fleeing Xuzhou."

"It's said that when the arrowhead went missing, the lock of the crystal box that contained it was untouched. Is that true?"

"Yes. Jing Xu looked into it thoroughly and asked all the soldiers who were guarding the tower at that time and found out Pang Xun had bribed them to steal it and blame spirits."

"And news of what happened in Xuzhou instantly spread to the capital," Huang Zixia said thoughtfully. "Spirits. Seems someone is deliberately using Pang Xun as cover."

"But they may be trying too hard and wind up fooling only themselves."

"Yes, it seems like we're close."

They continued talking as they rode through the squares of Changan.

Under the blue sky, the seventy-two squares of Changan stood firmly amid the wind and dust. The early summer sun was warm, making some sweat appear on Huang Zixia's neck in spite of her thin clothing. She used her sleeve to wipe it as she slowly rode under the shade of the Sophora trees lining the streets, pondering the case's mysteries.

Li Shubai gave her a white handkerchief. She took it and used it before she turned to look at him.

The May sun flowed through the trees and onto his face like strands of gold. His body took on a faint glow. In the hazy light, his usual look of indifference seemed to carry something else, flowing through the air between them.

Huang Zixia bowed and silently rode on with him. When they neared Yongjia Square, she suddenly turned to lead Nafusha to the north.

"Are we going to Daming Palace's Yongchun Hall?"

"Yes. Need to check one last thing. We'll get to the bottom of this mess."

"You already have it?" He looked at her with some surprise. The shade of the locusts thinned, and the golden sun sprinkled down on them. The light in Huang Zixia's eyes seemed to come from within.

He looked slightly hurt. She went straight through the gate and along the brick road to the rock garden, then dismounted and squatted down at a point near the hall. "This is where I found Wang Ruo's hairpin."

Li Shubai nodded and watched her take the inner pin out of her own hair and touch it to the ground.

"The rock garden between the front and rear halls. Here . . ." She used the hairpin to draw a circle and tapped its uppermost point. "Right where Wang Ruo lost her hairpin."

Li Shubai pointed at the ground. "Where we're standing."

"Right. The guards in the corridor were looking at the hall door, and the guards in the rock garden were watching the window." She picked up her hairpin, wiped it off, and put it back in. Smiling, she said, "This case is closed."

Li Shubai stood and looked around. Twilight had begun to fall.

They left Yongchun Hall through a side door. When they were approaching Kui Palace, Li Shubai suddenly spoke. "So you're sure the body in Yongchun Hall was Jin Nu's?"

"Yes," she said. "I'm sure."

"What about this new body?"

"I have a pretty good idea." She looked at him. "This is all because you saved those girls three years ago in Xuzhou."

Li Shubai stopped Di'e and thought awhile.

Sometime later, he raised his eyebrows and looked at her. "Could it really be?"

Huang Zixia nodded. "No one else had the chance."

Li Shubai frowned. "If that's the case, it will cause a storm in the Tang court."

"Oh well, the dynasty has been pretty lenient, no?" Huang Zixia sighed.

Li Shubai thought it over. "What if I ask you to give up?"

Huang Zixia bit her lower lip. "This started from you. If you want to give up, I have nothing to say."

"But . . . could it really be that simple?" He sat on Di'e's back, looked at the sky, and exhaled deeply. His gaze was deep and distant, as if looking far, far away. "You wouldn't be content for such a secret to stay hidden, would you?"

"It's not about secrecy," Huang Zixia said, following his gaze to the sky. "I just want to speak the truth for Feng Yi, Jin Nu, and the beggars who died in Chongren Square."

Li Shubai looked up without speaking. He noticed the light between the leaves changing. It would soon be dusk.

"In fact," he said slowly, "if the person behind all this is whom you think, it could be a great opportunity for you."

Huang Zixia looked at him in shock. He turned to look at her, gentle and forlorn. "I can help you bring this about, but I need you to tell me everything you know. At least I can guarantee your life."

She looked up at him slightly. It was sunset. Di'e and Nafusha, arriving back at their familiar Kui Palace, rubbed their necks together. Meanwhile, the two riders seemed closer than ever, close enough to feel the other's breath.

Huang Zixia unconsciously turned Nafusha, now a foot away from him. Quietly she said, "Thank you, my Prince."

The sun began to set, and their shadows stretched out long—near to each other but with a distance that was hard to close.

Fifteen

FALSE TRUTH

When Li Shubai and Huang Zixia arrived, the ceremony had already begun. The white mourning banner hung in the rain. Paper money fell in the courtyard like snowflakes. Daoists chanted. Xian Yun and others cried. Wang Ruo's spirit tablet had been placed in the center of the mourning hall with incense.

Li Shubai brought Huang Zixia to the center, and the Wang family saluted him in thanks.

"It was so sudden; you've had to do a lot," he said to Wang Yun. Though Wang Ruo's death was sudden, Wang Yun organized the services efficiently.

Wang Yun was wearing a simple silk robe with a layer of linen on top. He seemed concerned but not sad. "It's my duty."

Li Shubai walked with him outside under the veranda. "Her parents haven't arrived yet?"

"It was so sudden. We just had someone go to Langya to tell them she's on her way."

Li Shubai turned and looked back at the coffin in the hall. It was closed; clearly no one was prepared to look at the body.

Huang Zixia could tell he was wondering how to broach the subject of keeping the remains in the capital. As he opened his mouth to speak, a porter ran out and interrupted his thought. "My Prince, the Emperor and Empress have come to pay their respects."

Huang Zixia and Li Shubai were shocked. The Empress was part of the Wang family, so that made sense, but not the Emperor. Wang Yun was unfazed. Apparently, he already knew they'd be coming.

The Emperor was known to have a gentle demeanor. The Empress was more dignified in comparison. He always agreed to what she wanted. So the Empress getting the Emperor to come to her Wang family funeral probably didn't take more than asking.

They entered the hall, and the Empress lit incense for Wang Ruo. They came with a small entourage of about a dozen people. They both had on plain white clothing. The Emperor had on a white cap too, while the Empress wore a hairpin with pink beads. Her plain dress made her dark eyes and red lips stand out. She was so beautiful that it was hard to see anything else.

The Emperor found Wang Lin and asked about progress on the case, though he would have known there were no major leads. When Wang Lin confirmed that no progress had been made, the Emperor nodded and turned to leave. Li Shubai asked him to walk outside with him. Huang Zixia followed them to the front hall and felt relieved to be away from all the smoke.

"Brother, what do you think about this Wang girl business?" the Emperor said.

"Fate often surprises," Li Shubai said.

The Emperor sighed. "Even from the palace, I've heard rumors this is related to Pang Xun. What do you think?"

Li Shubai shook his head. "I'm afraid not."

"Oh? You already have a handle on the case?"

"I'm so busy and mourning that I haven't been able to really think it through. Yang Chonggu here has some thoughts, though." Li Shubai turned toward her, and she quickly bowed to the Emperor.

"Yang Chonggu must be the eunuch who solved the Four Directions Case. Just using some stray words to solve such a mystery takes true talent! What has he found now?"

"He believes it started sixteen years ago in Yangzhou. Not something I could sum up in a few words."

The Emperor looked surprised. "I heard it had something to do with Pang Xun's former followers taking revenge, but this sounds deeper than that."

"It is. And the person behind it may affect the court and royal family, even implicate an old, aristocratic family."

The Emperor looked back at the mourners. "A girl died. You think there's a conspiracy behind it? That's not an accusation to make lightly."

"I wouldn't," Li Shubai said.

The Emperor turned to Huang Zixia.

The funeral hall was filled with smoke. Twenty-four Taoists were chanting with wooden swords in their right hands and bells in their left. Their voices boomed. "The earth is dark and heaven gray; the five Emperors' edicts move the spirits like rain and thunder. They depart to their ancestral villages; all ill will is released. Blood is indiscriminate. The new lotus shines like the spirit of eternity. Go forth." Eight sturdy servants gripped the ropes and heaved the coffin, carrying it out the door.

"Wait." The sound wasn't loud, but everyone could hear where it came from. The room went quiet out of fear, and all eyes fell on Li Shubai. He walked into the hall, touched the coffin, and took a white jade bracelet from his pocket. "I intended to give this to her when we married. I want to give this to her for her journey to the afterlife, for though we couldn't marry in this world, I still belong to her."

Everyone was stunned. The Prince of Kui was known for not displaying much emotion, but he had clearly been moved so deeply by the Princess's death.

"Thank you so much for your tenderness, Prince of Kui. The Langya Wang family will be eternally grateful," Wang Lin said.

"The Prince of Kui's gesture is much appreciated," Wang Yun said in a mellow voice. He bowed to Li Shubai. "I'm afraid, however, that Ruo's body is too disfigured to wear your bracelet."

"It's adjustable, so it should fit." Li Shubai took it apart and gave it to Huang Zixia. "In my memory, Wang Ruo is as beautiful as a peach blossom. I don't dare disturb that image. You put it on for me."

Huang Zixia took it, knowing the task of touching the corpse had fallen on her. Wang Yun couldn't protest. The hall went quiet. Everyone looked at the bracelet, feeling moved by the Prince of Kui.

Some servants lifted the coffin lid about a foot.

Huang Zixia took a deep breath and held it, then quickly lifted the rotten hand. She paused for a moment so that everyone could see her holding the corpse hand. She clenched her teeth and turned to Li Shubai. "Prince. I have something to say."

"Speak," he said.

Huang Zixia let go and kneeled. "My Prince, when I was putting on the bracelet, I noticed something unusual. It's very important, even for the Emperor, so maybe all uninvolved parties should leave."

The Emperor thought a moment, remembering that Huang Zixia had some theories about Wang Ruo's murder. The Emperor nodded.

Wang Lin frowned slightly and waved the attendants away.

"Actually." Huang Zixia cleared her throat. "Xian Yun and Ran Yun should stay." The two attendants froze. They looked at the ground as they walked back over to those who would remain.

Soon it was only them, the Emperor and Empress, Wang Lin, Wang Yun, Li Shubai, and Huang Zixia left in the room with the corpse.

Huang Zixia put her hand on the coffin. "Emperor, Empress, I don't think this body is Wang Ruo!"

Everyone gasped. Empress Wang stood up in shock.

Li Shubai even acted surprised. "The body has been guarded in the palace. How could it have been switched?"

"Yes," Wang Lin agreed. "The hall has been under constant watch. And who could make a replica of such a deformed corpse?"

"Let me clarify, Minister Wang. What I mean is that the corpse has never been her."

Wang Yun frowned and touched his father's elbow. Wang Lin looked at the Emperor in horror. The Emperor looked confusedly at the coffin.

Empress Wang was calm. She pursed her lips. "You're Yang Chonggu?"

"Yes, a servant of Kui Palace."

"I've heard you're a savvy investigator. So tell us why you think this body isn't Wang Ruo."

"My Empress, I was tasked with teaching the palace law to Wang Ruo. We were together many times, and I know her hands were small and slim. But this body's palms are very large in comparison."

"But you know her body swelled after being poisoned, right?"

"The swelling only occurred in the muscles and skin, not the bones. This woman's hand bones are certainly larger than Wang Ruo's." Huang Zixia straightened up. "Minister Zhou's son Zhou Ziqin examined the body before. He knows all about this. Maybe Your Majesties would like to call him here to explain his findings."

Wang Lin jumped in. "Mr. Yang, the coffin is about to leave. Are you trying to embarrass our family? Your speculation is keeping her from resting in peace."

Empress Wang nodded. "Mr. Yang. This death has been awful for our family. Why make it worse?"

"I wouldn't dare," Huang Zixia said, lowering her head. "I just know there are significant differences and would like to take a closer look so we don't get it wrong. It would be a shame to lay the wrong body to rest in her name."

"Chonggu's right," Li Shubai finally said. "He's right. How could the illustrious Langya Wang family insult their ancestors by burying a strange corpse among them? Why don't we have Zhou Ziqin come and take another look? What does the Empress think?"

Empress Wang frowned and turned toward the Emperor. "It would indeed be a shame to the family. We must know. Go call Zhou Ziqin."

Zhou Ziqin had already packed up everything pertinent to the investigation according to Huang Zixia's orders. He had the records from last time; Ah Bi and Ah Yan followed behind him with a heavy box. They put it down, bowed, and quickly left.

Zhou Ziqin greeted the Emperor and Empress and then looked at his records. "After Yang Chonggu and I examined the body closely, I wrote: 'The deceased is female, five feet seven inches tall, with distorted facial features and swollen, festering, black skin. Her teeth are complete, her hair long and healthy. The body shows no signs of trauma, and was likely poisoned to death.' I also noted discrepancies with the hand bones and other issues, but because I couldn't undertake a closer examination, I kept that in the file." He closed the record and continued. "Combining this with Pao Ding's articles on bovine anatomy, I learned that muscles, joints, and bones are related according to certain laws. If you would allow me, I should be able to make a replica that restores the skin and muscle features to their original shapes."

The Emperor raised a hand. "Do it. Quickly."

Wang Lin cleared the hall so that Zhou Ziqin and Huang Zixia could work.

Zhou Ziqin took a mask coated with garlic and vinegar, and a pair of thin leather gloves from his bag. He handed them to Huang Zixia. She took the gloves and put them on even though she had already touched the corpse with her bare hands. She helped him hold the body's hand, which he felt and squeezed. Then he drew a complex network of lines and points in his notebook.

Zhou Ziqin opened his box and took a firm hunk of yellow clay from one of its compartments. He kneaded it into the bones of a hand to match the drawing and then connected them with pieces of fine wire. Next, he took out a softer piece of clay and sculpted it around the bones. He let it dry, then used fish gelatin glue to paste a layer of thin white cloth to the outside.

"What do you think?"

Huang Zixia took it. It had a slender palm with thick, strong fingers. It looked nearly real. The strangest thing was that it was just as she remembered Jin Nu's hand. "Amazing!" Huang Zixia said.

"All right! I wonder if it would impress my sweetheart, Huang Zixia?"

Huang Zixia looked away.

Word came that the Emperor wanted Zhou Ziqin to take his things to Yanji Hall. Ah Bi and Ah Yan didn't dare complain. They took the heavy box to where they were called. Huang Zixia asked Xian Yun to go with her to Wang Ruo's room to get a bracelet.

The Emperor and Empress were seated at the head of two rows of twelve chairs. Li Shubai and Wang Lin sat in the next two, and Wang Yun stood behind his father. Huang Zixia asked Wang Yun for a tray and put Zhou Ziqin's model hand on top and held it for the Emperor and Empress. Zhou Ziqin then put his own next to it and said, "Look, the length of the palm isn't much smaller than a man's, but the finger bones are thick and strong. The hand clearly belongs to that of a relatively robust woman. Also, there is a callus between the thumb and forefinger on the left hand."

Huang Zixia looked at Xian Yun and Ran Yun. "How does this compare to Wang Ruo's hand?"

They looked at each other. "Um . . . it's about the same. I don't know," Xian Yun said.

"Say it!" Wang Yun snapped.

"Her hand was very slim and delicate. Su Qi bragged about it after she started teaching her the palace rules," Xian Yun said.

"That's what I thought. There is more evidence." Huang Zixia took Wang Ruo's bracelet. Then she started to put it on. It squeezed the clay but wouldn't fit. "This is Wang Ruo's bracelet. We've all seen her wear it. It clearly doesn't fit."

Everyone looked at one another. Wang Yun spoke first. "If this body isn't my little sister, then where is she? And whose body is it?"

Huang Zixia instructed Zhou Ziqin to hold up his drawing. She pointed to the calluses on all three fingers. "Only a pipa player would have such markings." Huang Zixia mimed holding a pipa's neck with her left hand and plucking with her right.

Wang Lin frowned. "But there are so many pipa players. How can we tell which this is?"

"I think I know," Huang Zixia said. "A pipa player recently disappeared from the academy. Her things were found outside the academy. There were only a few pieces of clothing and jewelry, which were obviously not packed by her. Most importantly, she was also poisoned to death."

Zhou Ziqin gasped.

"This is Jin Nu!" Huang Zixia said. "Do you all remember when Jin Nu told the Empress and Lady Zhao about her past? We all saw how large her hands were."

"What about the beheaded body that was found outside the academy?" Zhou Ziqin asked.

"The headless corpse isn't Jin Nu. The corpse made to look like the Princess is Jin Nu." Huang Zixia told everyone about the night Jin Nu helped pack the leftover food for Zhou Ziqin. She explained how just a simple cherry stem was too rough for her fragile hands. It was with that prick of the cherry stem that Jin Nu was poisoned.

Zhou Ziqin was even more shocked. "But Jin Nu was at the table with us. She didn't leave. She ate the same food. Why are we okay and she got poisoned?"

"Because the poison was mixed into the rosin she used on her pipa," Huang Zixia said with a sigh. "She played some songs at first, but the pipa didn't sound right because of the humidity, so she rubbed rosin on her strings. Remember?"

Zhou Ziqin nodded. "Yes."

"The antiaris poison would have slowly spread through her system. She would have fallen into a coma, and the swelling would have made her face unrecognizable. It would have made her body perfect to take the place of the Princess's," Huang Zixia said.

"Why would the killer go to such pains to find a substitute for Wang Ruo's body? And how did they get Wang Ruo out of the palace? What's the motivation for all this?" the Emperor asked.

"Ziqin," Li Shubai said. "You worked hard on that hand. Why don't you go take a rest?"

Zhou Ziqin looked puzzled. "But Yang Chonggu hasn't finished."

Li Shubai just glared at him. Even Zhou Ziqin understood that it wasn't a request. "I'll be going!"

Zhou Ziqin left, and Huang Zixia closed the door. She bowed slightly to the Emperor.

"I believe the killer is in this hall." Her words resounded clearly throughout the room, causing her listeners to straighten up like they'd been pricked by a thorn.

Empress Wang sneered. "Nonsense. You mean they're part of our family?"

"I would only say such a thing if it were the result of a careful investigation. I only want to tell the truth."

The room filled with gasps and whispers.

The Emperor raised his hand. "Let's let Chonggu finish."

"Thank you, my Emperor!" Huang Zixia bowed to the Emperor. "Remember when that aristocrat took a risky chance and attempted to assassinate her? Zhang Ling, who was a step ahead of me, saw the shadow go out the window. When I got there, nothing. Are there really people who can turn invisible like that? I think the purpose of that intrusion was to get Your Highnesses to move her to Yongchun Hall."

Empress Wang smiled coldly. "So moving her for her protection makes it my fault?"

"I wouldn't say that. What I mean is that maybe it may have contributed. Yongchun Hall may have been selected ahead of time as the best place to make Wang Ruo disappear." Huang Zixia took out a sheet of paper from her sleeve pocket and unfolded it. It was the map of Yongchun Hall she had drawn before. She pulled the smaller jade pin out of her hairpin and started sketching on the paper so everyone could see. She showed them the layout of Yongchun Hall and where the guards stood.

Everyone hung on her every word.

Huang Zixia recounted how Wang Ruo intentionally came out of the hall to talk to the Prince. "She made sure we would see her go back inside," Huang Zixia said. She used her hairpin to draw a circle around the east court's inner hall to show the tight watch. "After she disappeared, I kept wondering how she could vanish so quickly after I saw her enter the hall. How did she avoid all those eyes?"

Her audience was silent. Even Li Shubai, who already knew, couldn't help but listen intently.

"It wasn't until I learned a magic trick from a street performer in the West City that I understood. Wang Ruo didn't suddenly disappear from Yongchun Hall; she never went in at all."

"But, according to you," Wang Lin said coldly, "the Prince of Kui and dozens of guards all watched her walk inside. How could they all be under such an illusion?"

"The trick only takes an instant. Under Commander Wang's orders, no guards stood behind the rock garden where Li Shubai and myself were seated. The only guards that could have seen it were told to watch the window. So all of us who supposedly saw her go back inside really only saw her silhouette from behind."

"It's not enough proof to just see her silhouette?"

"Certainly not." Huang Zixia pointed her hairpin to the rockery. "Between the inner and outer halls, the rockery is low with a winding slate path going through it. Here is the tallest part, tall enough to cover the five-foot-seven Wang Ruo. So all that was needed was someone wearing the same clothing, hair, and jewelry as Wang Ruo to hide there in advance. Then, when Wang Ruo reached that highest point, she crouched down and switched clothes with the other woman. Thus, in a moment, the person we saw walk back to the hall wasn't Wang Ruo but someone else entirely!"

"Then who traded places with her?"

"Ran Yun came with Wang Ruo to see the Prince of Kui, so the person hiding in the rockery was the attendant Xian Yun," Huang Zixia said.

"Ridiculous! Xian Yun is shorter than Wang Ruo," Wang Lin said.

"A piece of charred wood was found on the stove. I believe it was from platform shoes," Huang Zixia said. "You did this because you were ordered to."

Wang Lin interrupted. "So what about everyone searching Yongchun Hall for her after?"

"Simple. There would have been clothing for a eunuch or lady hidden in the rocks. She changed into her disguise. Then she joined in the search for the hairpin. She blended in and then left with the Empress's attendants."

Yanji Hall was silent.

The Emperor thought over what she said and looked at the Empress. Her eyes were downcast. "So what is the point of all this? Why would she do this?"

"Think about the man with the birdcage at Xianyou Temple. Who had the power to sneak in and out of the temple? The temple was heavily guarded. The person with the birdcage was someone in this room. It was a slight of hand."

A few whispers filled the hall as those listening tried to put it together.

"This person wanted to get rid of Wang Ruo to preserve the Wang family name. Unfortunately, he didn't know who had really invited Wang Ruo to the palace. He had no way of knowing that his disappearing trick would result in more tragedy.

The anticipation made the room seem small.

Huang Zixia cleared her throat. "You played the disappearing trick, didn't you, Commander Wang Yun?"

Sixteen

Perplexing Situation

Wang Yun looked at her quietly. His facial expression faltered for only a moment. "I'm not sure what you mean by this, Mr. Yang," he said gently.

"I'm saying that you disguised yourself as the mysterious man at Xianyou Temple. And you went to the West City to buy that trick birdcage. When you bought it, you wore an outfit that would stand out in the salesman's memory in order to mislead them. This was pretty cautious, but you overlooked an important detail."

"What detail?" Wang Yun smiled. "Why do you insist it was me at Xianyou Temple?"

"Because you intended to use the spirit of Pang Xun to disrupt this marriage, but by leaving the arrowhead that Li Shubai used to kill Pang Xun on the altar, you exposed yourself!"

Wang Yun now looked slightly rattled. "What would that arrowhead have to do with me?"

"You led troops to defeat bandits in March, yes?"

"Yes, but what does that have to do with anything?"

"Those bandits stole the arrowhead. You took it from them when you defeated them. It was you who planted it. Very few people could have gotten that arrowhead; fewer could have put it in Xianyou Temple. The only person who could have done both is you, Commander Wang Yun!"

Wang Yun frowned slightly, like he was thinking. "You are a great detective," he said to Huang Zixia.

Wang Lin froze like a statue, staring at his son. Wang Yun had no idea what his father had done so many years ago. He didn't know the secret that Wang Lin and the Empress shared. Huang Zixia almost felt sorry for him.

The Emperor looked at the Empress. She stared stiffly at Huang Zixia. He gently touched her hand, then took it in his. "Don't worry. Wang Yun is your cousin, so he's also mine. I'll look after him no matter what."

"Thank you, my Emperor," she said.

"So do you admit to it? Did you spread the rumors about Pang Xun's spirits, and make Wang Ruo disappear?"

Wang Yun stood tall. "Yes. It was all me." Wang Yun spoke slowly but clearly. He glanced at Huang Zixia, then turned to the Emperor and kneeled. "Please punish me, Emperor; this started small and got out of hand. I deserve to die!"

"Oh?" the Emperor said with a frown. "Why did you want to harm Wang Ruo?"

Wang Yun explain how Wang Ruo acted strangely after she found out she was going to be Princess. "I knew that she was brought here by my father. That she wasn't who everyone thought she was. I thought of the unspeakable things Huang Zixia did and felt I should break up the marriage to spare the Prince of Kui the same humility that I faced."

Huang Zixia couldn't help but start at the mention of her name. She saw Wang Yun look back at her out of the corner of her eye and tried her best not to reveal her secret. She clenched her hands in her sleeves and let her nails dig into her palms.

"Wang Ruo was already his Princess-to-be," Wang Yun continued. "I knew she couldn't back out, so I had to move behind the scenes. Since the Prince of Kui put down the Pang Xun rebellion, I thought I could cause a commotion, using his spirits to spread confusion. That's why it was easy to get ladies and eunuchs to help me. The Empress didn't know. Please forgive me, Your Highness."

Huang Zixia frowned. "So what about Jin Nu's death?"

Wang Yun looked at her. He closed his eyes. "Yes, I designed it all." Wang Yun's voice was calm, like he wasn't talking about things he'd done himself. "I never expected the truth to come out. Mr. Yang is truly talented; nothing can escape you."

Huang Zixia knew that Wang Yun played a part in this whole mess. He'd thought that Wang Ruo was an imposter picked out by his father. He was afraid of the shame she would bring the family. He wanted to protect the legacy of his family and also protect Li Shubai. What she didn't yet understand was why he would admit to killing Jin Nu. Wang Yun wasn't the killer. He wasn't the one behind everything; his plan with the birdcage just happened to coincide with everything else. The deaths of Feng Yi and Jin Nu weren't because of him. No, they were because of someone with much more power—the person his father had been helping for years, the person who really requested that Wang Ruo be picked as the Princess of Kui.

Huang Zixia shook her head. "Why are you admitting to more than you did? Who are you protecting?" Huang Zixia said.

The crowd looked around, confused.

"Jin Nu loved that rosin powder. She kept it on her from the moment she received it. The powder was poisoned when she received it," Huang Zixia continued.

Wang Yun frowned and averted his eyes.

"Commander Wang is only responsible for the altered engagement note and trick at Xianyou Temple. As for everything after that, he's just trying to take the blame for someone higher up. The real killer behind all of this." Now Huang Zixia hesitated. She looked at the Emperor, Empress, Minister Wang, his son, and Li Shubai. She knew, of course, that what she was going to say, in addition to being the truth, could be her own death sentence.

Li Shubai nodded at her, encouraging her to continue. His look said, *I can guarantee your life.* His calm expression hid unshakable commitment.

Huang Zixia pressed her hand to her chest. She took a deep breath. "Though you want to protect the real killer, protect the hope of the Wang family ambition, the truth is the truth. No number of scapegoats can clean the blood from her hands!" Huang Zixia stared at Empress Wang.

Everyone followed her gaze.

"Empress Wang, the one behind all this, the person he is protecting is you."

Yanji Hall was silent.

The Emperor slowly let go of her hand and looked at her like she was a stranger.

Xian Run and Ran Yun didn't dare look up from the ground. Wang Lin's expression was steely, apart from a slight tremble of his chin.

Only Li Shubai looked normal as he played with his fan. "Yang Chonggu, what did Her Highness do wrong?"

"A capital offense," Huang Zixia said without hesitation.

"Yang Chonggu," Empress Wang said, slightly hoarse yet dignified, "I would appreciate further details on how you think I'm related to this case. First of all, Ruo was my beloved cousin. Why would I want to make her disappear before her wedding, and leave her whereabouts unknown today?"

"Right, you're very close to Wang Ruo. Everyone who saw it noted your unusual warmth around her, which I also admired."

"So?" she said with a slight sneer.

"Twelve years ago, when you entered the palace, Wang Ruo was only four or five. I wondered how two cousins with such a big age difference and physical distance could act like they grew up together. Why would your love for her be so great?"

"She's an exceptional young woman and is family. The palace naturally cared for her," Empress Wang said stiffly.

Huang Zixia bowed slightly. "That made me wonder why you would want to ruin her marriage and have her go missing."

Empress Wang glared at her.

"I began to have doubts about her identity when I began teaching her the palace law," Huang Zixia continued. "And the music Wang Ruo had studied was not the great music of Langya but common folk music."

"What does lax family discipline have to do with the Empress?" Wang Lin said.

Huang Zixia nodded and held up her finger, indicating she had more to tell. "I also had the fortune of getting a ride with her. In the carriage, I met a woman who didn't enter the palace with her." Huang Zixia turned to Xian Yun and Ran Yun. "I'll ask you first. Who was the woman who came from Langya?"

They looked at each other, too scared to speak.

"Out it with!" Emperor Wang said.

"She . . . ," Xian Yun said. "I think the girl called her Feng Yi."

Huang Zixia took out her copy of the portrait of Chen Nian and Feng Yi from her pocket and held it up.

Xian Yun's and Ran Yun's hands shook as they took it.

"Feng Yi is a musician from Yangzhou's Yunshao Court. Four or five months ago, she escorted Wang Ruo to the capital."

They grimaced.

Huang Zixia told them about Chen Nian's search for Feng Yi.

"Did all of you hear about the migrants who died of poison?" Huang Zixia asked. "Feng Yi was one of the bodies found among them."

Wang Yun's brow furrowed slightly. Xian Yun and Ran Yun moaned.

Huang Zixia ignored them. "Zhou Ziqin and I went to the burial site and found a piece of jade from Chen Nian on one of the bodies. She was poisoned to death and had swallowed that jade to keep it with her, which allowed us to identify the body."

Everyone was horrified. "In your view," Li Shubai said, "what was the cause of Feng Yi's death?"

"She was poisoned because she did that favor for an old friend and escorted the girl to the capital. Her cause of death was knowing too much."

Now even Empress Wang turned pale. "Does this eunuch know the consequences of slander? We're an old and dignified family. You should weigh your words carefully before you speak!"

"Don't worry, my Empress. I was prepared to risk my life to explain the details of this case," Huang Zixia said with a bow. "Shortly after I met Wang Ruo, she asked me worriedly about Emperor Jing of Han's Empress Wang Zhi. She wanted to know if it would've been bad if people found out she was married and had a daughter before entering the palace."

Empress Wang looked at her, and even her petal-like lips were paler now. She glared at Huang Zixia, then said, "That girl didn't know what she was talking about. How could she discuss such a question?"

The Emperor leaned back, his gentle face now ashen. But he didn't stop Huang Zixia or even look at Empress Wang. Huang Zixia finally broke the silence. "I wondered if Wang Ruo had already married and was hiding her past during the selection process. But then I realized she was talking about someone else. Wasn't she, Empress Wang?"

Empress Wang looked at her coldly and slightly lifted her right hand to stop her. She looked at the Emperor. "Your Highness, will you really indulge this person's nonsense?"

The Emperor's gaze slowly turned from Huang Zixia to Empress Wang.

Outside was the verdant shade of early summer, some cicadas here and there in the foliage. Only Yanji Hall was silent.

"Empress, we've listened to this much. Why don't we let the eunuch finish and find out the reasoning before we make a judgment? What do you think?" The Emperor clearly had his suspicions.

Empress Wang looked even paler. She slowly lowered her hand and sat up with impeccable posture, still unmatched in noble arrogance. Wang Lin's eyes showed such annoyance, she was sure he would have gotten rid of her if he could.

Wang Yun stood quietly, his face also pale, watching the eunuch that looked like Huang Zixia and unconsciously pursing his lips.

Li Shubai looked at Huang Zixia. She nodded to say she was all right. "Why did the Empress want Wang Ruo to disappear? Because of the appearance of two people and the death of one."

Everyone leaned forward slightly, in awe of what was unfolding in front of them.

"The first person to appear was Commander Wang Yun. He appeared at Xianyou Temple to scare Wang Ruo into withdrawing, but he ended up scaring you. Commander Wang thought Wang Ruo was just an imposter found by his father. Of course, the fewer people who knew, the better, so the Empress and Minister Wang even kept Commander Wang in the dark about who she really was. But Commander Wang also kept his plans from the Empress and minister. When they heard about the man in the temple, they never imagined it was their own Wang family son."

Wang Lin looked sad, and Wang Yun just stared into nothingness and listened.

"The second person to appear was Jin Nu," Huang Zixia continued. "I'd met her several times, and she always talked about her master, Mei Wanzhi, who passed, long ago. Little did she know Mei Wanzhi was still alive. Alive and living a life of luxury, isn't she, Empress?"

The room buzzed. Everyone wanted to know what this meant. Was the Empress not who they thought she was? Could she really be this Mei Wanzhi character?

Empress Wang's hand trembled slightly, and she raised her chin stubbornly.

"I was with Jin Nu the first time she saw the Empress. She panicked, but I thought it was because she knew Wang Ruo."

Empress Wang sneered. "Mr. Yang, Jin Nu is dead. This so-called evidence can't be verified, so the palace must dismiss it as nonsense. I'd urge His Majesty not to listen any further and punish this eunuch for his disrespect!"

The Emperor looked at his trembling wife. He stroked her back and pondered Huang Zixia.

Wang Lin brushed the sleeve of his robe and kneeled. "Your Highness!" he said, trembling. "Our old, illustrious family has flourished for centuries in Langya. Only the royal house surpasses us. The Empress is our family's greatest daughter. She's been by Your Highness's side for twelve years and is now an example for all women in the empire. I don't know why this little eunuch wants to disgrace us, suggesting that the Empress is an impostor. I beg you not to listen to his nonsense!"

Huang Zixia and Li Shubai could tell by Wang Lin's reaction that Huang Zixia's theory was correct. The Empress was not who everyone thought she was. She knew Ji Nu and Feng Yi. They recognized her for who she really was and died because of it.

"Minister Wang is incorrect," Li Shubai said, calmly playing with his fan as he leaned back comfortably in his chair. "As the Emperor said, if he's wrong, he'll be punished, but so far everything is supported by unambiguous evidence. As I see it, Minister Wang should be more patient."

The Emperor nodded. "That's right. Let him finish. I can determine whether it's true or false." Wang Lin shivered at the firmness in the Emperor's voice and that he spoke without a glance at Empress Wang.

Wang Lin offered a hand to help his father up and the two stood stiffly side by side.

"Jin Nu had to die because she glimpsed the secret. The day after Wang Ruo went missing, the palace gave her a pipa pick, strings, and rosin powder. I thought it was strange since the Empress doesn't like music very much. Jin Nu probably thought it was a reward for keeping the secret."

"This is ridiculous! I just saw that pipa player once and gave her a gift. What about someone in the palace or the academy that had it out for her, or she got involved with some unsavory characters outside? Why couldn't they have poisoned it?" Empress Wang said.

Huang Zixia reminded everyone of the strict process the palace uses to send gifts. In order to prevent mistakes and bribes, the palace has three people inspect all gifts and three more send it. It's inconvenient but prevents tampering.

"I believe that if the Emperor checks, he'll discover the Empress selected that box of rosin powder herself. Also, Jin Nu cared so much for the gift that she carried it close. How could anyone have had the chance to poison it?"

The Empress clenched her teeth.

"These two people appeared," Huang Zixia went on. "And, as I said before, someone died. The person who died is Feng Yi. It is because of her death that I know who Wang Ruo really was. It also revealed who really asked Feng Yi to escort Wang Ruo to the capital."

No one spoke in the gloomy hall. Everyone was slowly figuring it out.

"The person who asked her for the favor was a friend from twelve years ago at Yunshao Court. The second oldest of the Six Women of Yunshao, Jin Nu's teacher, a woman married with a daughter, the pipa master Mei Wanzhi." Huang Zixia spoke quietly and firmly. "Isn't that right, Empress? Or should I call you Mei Wanzhi?"

The Empress glared. She crossed her arms across her chest. "This is all nonsense. You can't believe this little eunuch. He is just seeking attention."

The Emperor didn't say anything. He stared at Huang Zixia.

"And as for Wang Ruo, she is your daughter. But you didn't name her Wang Ruo; you named her Xuese!" Huang Zixia said.

Empress Wang looked deflated as she listened to Huang Zixia. Then she straightened her skirt. "Ha, baseless accusations!"

Huang Zixia nodded. "You can say that if you wish. But I have more. I know what happened twelve years ago. And you may not be able to bear it, but I have to tell you the worst consequences of all your efforts."

Empress Wang glared at her with disregard.

"That woman you beheaded and killed is not who you thought she was. In fact, she is the last person you would want dead," Huang Zixia continued steadily. "Chen Nian told me a story of the six women who founded the musical troupe at Yunshao Court; the second eldest, Mei Wanzhi, disappeared one night, leaving behind a daughter named Xuese." She repeated the story Chen Nian had told her. Everyone listened intently.

Everyone looked back and forth between Huang Zixia and the Empress.

"Another story came from the Prince of Kui." She paused and looked at him, and he nodded slightly. "Four years ago, when putting down the Pang Xun rebellion, the Prince of Kui went to Xuzhou to lead the six governors in a joint military operation. The day Xuzhou fell, he rescued two girls who had been held captive by Pang Xun," she began. "One of them, with the surname Cheng, said she was going to live with her aunt Lan Dai, but she had already moved to Yangzhou because of the chaos. She gave the Prince of Kui a silver leafy hairpin, but he was uninterested so he discarded it. Their faces had been dirty and haggard throughout, so the Prince didn't get a good look at them."

Everyone, even the Empress, quietly pondered her words.

"Those were stories told to me firsthand. It is because of these stories and recent events that I have made my best deduction. Feng Yi received a letter at Yunshao Court, asking to escort a friend's daughter to the capital. That girl was Cheng Xuese. Feng Yi picked her up in Puzhou and took her to Changan. It was only then that she realized the elevated identity her old friend had taken on. The little she knew was too much."

The Empress pursed her lips.

"Meanwhile, Feng Yi's close friend Chen Nian came to the capital to look for her. She looked all over but never found her. She did, however, have a chance encounter with Jin Nu. Jin Nu's connection got her a place in Li Run's palace. Later, I gave Feng Yi's jade tablet to Chen Nian, and she promised to help me get a painting Lan Dai had of the Six Women of Yunshao done by Mei Wanzhi's husband. She asked Cheng Xuese to bring it to the capital.

"The day before yesterday, Cheng Xuese finally arrived from Puzhou with the painting, but she was met with a fatal disaster. The painting was stolen, and she was decapitated and thrown in the channel."

"You just said Xuese came to the capital with Feng Yi months ago," Empress Wang said. "Now she came alone two days ago? Who's the real Xuese?"

"This is the part you aren't going to like," Huang Zixia said with some pity. "The two girls the Prince of Kui saved in Xuzhou were about the same age. They made it to Yangzhou, then moved to Puzhou with Lan Dai. One of them was a Cheng, the other called Little Shi. You thought Wang Ruo was Xuese, but she wasn't. Xuese was actually the woman that was beheaded outside the music school."

The Empress shook. "But how? How can that be? How do you know?"

Huang Zixia mustered a small, compassionate smile. She explained how she had heard Wang Ruo call out Xuese's name in her sleep.

Empress Wang trembled slightly, and her face turned purple. She was still as a statue, expressionless. She looked dead, her soul shredded by the devil, staring into nothingness.

In the quiet of Yanji Hall, everyone could see she'd been defeated by two simple sentences from Huang Zixia.

"Xuese, who the Prince of Kui saved in Xuzhou, was so stubborn, she waited for the Prince of Kui. When the mother she thought was dead asked Feng Yi to take her to the capital to arrange a good life for her, she still didn't want to leave," Huang Zixia said.

The Empress slowly shook her head, realizing what she had done.

Huang Zixia continued. "She and Little Shi agreed that since her mother hadn't seen her in twelve years, she definitely wouldn't know what she looked like and that Little Shi would go in her place. They didn't know her mother was the Empress, or that it would lead them back to the Prince of Kui."

Silence. Silence like death.

Huang Zixia raised her voice to peel off the last layer. "Empress Wang, the woman you ordered murdered in the night and thrown in the channel to look like Jin Nu was your own daughter, Cheng Xuese!"

Empress Wang sat motionless for a long time. Then her dazed eyes filled with tears. When she finally spoke, it was in a faint hiss. "You're lying . . . you're . . . lying."

Huang Zixia felt a mixture of compassion and anger.

Empress Wang kept murmuring, "Lying . . . lying!"

The Emperor was clutching the arm of his chair with such fury, his knuckles turned white.

Wang Lin looked terribly anxious. He gestured for Xian Yun and Ran Yun to go take Empress Wang, while pleading with the Emperor. "Your Majesty, it seems this eunuch Yang Chonggu has terrified the Empress with his nonsense! She's a child of the illustrious Wang family, not some court musician."

"Wang Lin," the Emperor said, turning his eyes coldly from the Empress to him, "tell the truth. Tell the truth about what happened twelve years ago! If one word is proven false, your whole family line will end!"

Wang Lin looked desperately at the Empress, who seemed completely defeated. He kneeled and wailed, "Your Majesty, I deserve the ultimate punishment. I don't ask for forgiveness for myself, but please forgive my family! I was behind all of this. I even manipulated the Empress!"

"Don't make excuses for others," the Emperor said. "Just speak the truth!"

"Yes," he said desperately, pressing his forehead to the ground. "Your Majesty, after the uprising, the Wang family was in bad shape, having lost many heirs. Twelve years ago, we only had four or five male children. The only promising child was a woman, your Wang Fu."

The Emperor thought a moment. "I remember. Bad fate. She died a little over half a year with me in the palace."

"At that time, Your Majesty was still the Prince of Yun, placed in the Sixteen Houses by the Emperor. After Wang Fu died, we were so sad and didn't want to lose our Princess, so we thought you might be interested in one of her sisters. We invited Your Majesty to meet some girls."

The Emperor nodded slightly, then looked at the Empress. She was still as a statue, eyes wide open and tearful, pleading.

"When we brought the girls before you, none of them caught your eye. So someone introduced us to the Empress, saying she was a poor woman, teaching pipa to some girls. I thought her skills were amazing and asked her to come play for you to close out the banquet," Wang Lin said bitterly. "Who knew Your Majesty would fall in love and ask me what family she was from? I had a moment of weakness, and I lied."

"But when she joined the palace, her documents looked real," the Emperor said coolly.

"We switched her identity with a girl who'd died. It wasn't a big deal. So I talked about it with her and she . . . she agreed."

"Not a big deal?" the Emperor said, turning to the Empress with a sneer. "You didn't expect me to really love her so much. Over these twelve years, she joined me in the palace, gave birth to a Prince, and after I ascended the throne, became Empress Wang!"

Wang Yun couldn't hide his shock.

Huang Zixia stood silently behind Li Shubai and watched the Empress.

Wang Lin stood up with tears in his eyes. "I should die! I really never thought it would end up like this! After you took the throne I couldn't sleep. And once she became Empress I was even more restless. Your Highness, I deserve to die, but please, forgive the Empress. I coerced her."

"Stop," the Emperor said, raising his hand. "If you were so conflicted, why did you put on this elaborate show twelve years later? You really thought it'd be so easy to fool everyone?"

Wang Lin straightened up with a shiver and didn't dare to speak.

Empress Wang finally spoke quietly and slowly. "Meeting Your Highness was the luckiest day of this woman's life. For twelve years, I've worried that if Your Highness found out the truth, he'd reject me, but why did I unconsciously rejoice in the deception?" She choked up and looked at the Emperor, sobbing, tears like crystal beads rolling over her cheeks. "Your Highness, I felt so lucky. I wanted to give my estranged daughter what I had."

Huang Zixia and Li Shubai gave each other a look. Her calling her daughter to the capital was her way of reconnecting to her previous life.

But they were just onlookers.

In a flash, the woman who'd killed her own daughter disappeared. Empress Wang "the warrior" was back: cold, calculated, efficient.

The Emperor looked uncomfortable and overwhelmed at the sight of his tearful wife. For years, they'd shared the burden of leading millions of people. He would remember her smile when they first met, her smile when she took the throne, her smile when she first held their son. She was part of his life, and without her, he'd be incomplete.

He stood up and walked heavily toward her. "You lost yourself."

Sadness came over her face. She bowed. "Yes."

"You're a common woman from Shu and have been my Empress for many years. You've always been strong and dignified. After the funeral of your daughter's best friend, you need rest." He was forgiving her.

Empress Wang was stunned. Big tears slowly slid down her face. Her mighty air was gone. She looked weak and helpless as she kneeled and clutched the Emperor's legs, crying.

The Emperor pulled her up sharply. She was pale and trembling, but he finally got her to stand. Despite her tears, she couldn't help but regain some of the haughtiness she'd obtained from ruling over people for so long.

The scene made Huang Zixia feel a touch of tenderness for the cunning schemer—but only for a moment.

The Emperor took her hand stiffly.

He looked from Wang Yun to Wang Lin, Li Shubai, and Huang Zixia. "If anyone speaks of this again, you'll be disobeying imperial orders and disrupting the court!"

No one in the hall dared to speak.

The Emperor tucked a tuft of hair behind the Empress's ear. He tugged on her hand and said, "Go get some rest. Let the doctor have a look at you. You're sick with grief."

"Yes," she whispered. The Emperor led the Empress, who was visibly shaken, away.

Before they reached the exit, the Emperor glanced at Xian Yun and Ran Yun and gestured to Wang Yun.

Huang Zixia felt a sense of melancholy at the resolution of the case.

Li Shubai looked back at her and began to leave. Huang Zixia followed him out of the hall.

As they passed Wang Yun, she heard him speak softly in her ear. "Why?"

Her heart jumped, and she turned and looked at him. The usually warm Wang Yun now stared at her motionlessly.

His voice was soft but clear. "What did our Wang family do to offend you? Why push me again and again?"

Huang Zixia felt a coldness in her chest under his intense gaze.

She clenched her teeth. "I don't know what you mean. All I know is fairness and justice are innate to the human heart. Whether the victim is a musician or a beggar, whether the murderer is the Emperor or a minister, I have to find out the truth to be at peace with myself."

Then she turned away quickly and left.

She suddenly thought of that "again and again."

Was he counting her refusing to marry him and turning him into the city laughingstock?

She broke out in a cold sweat. Then she immediately rejected the idea. She'd embarrassed Wang Yun so much. If he knew she was Huang Zixia, he would've exposed her.

That body, despite being Jin Nu's, was buried with great ceremony, according to the original plan.

Huang Zixia stopped under the tall trees at the gate and gazed back at the black coffin.

Li Shubai turned. "What's wrong?"

She hesitated. "I'm thinking about Jin Nu." She paused. "Does this outcome resolve anything?"

"Why wouldn't it? Telling the killer she murdered her own daughter and forcing her to live with that guilt is the greatest punishment." He shook his head. "Empress Wang is a woman after all, no? No matter how powerful, she can't help but be heartbroken over the loss of her daughter."

"And Chen Nian, though she brought about her own murder, succeeded in getting revenge on Empress Wang, who will have to live with a guilty conscience for the rest of her life," Huang Zixia said softly.

The sun shone intermittently through the trees' green branches. The soft sunlight made Huang Zixia think of the Emperor, who was known for his warmth and goodness. Even if the Empress didn't lose face and no one else found out, the Emperor now knew and would discipline the Empress.

Li Shubai glanced at Huang Zixia. "You're still not satisfied?"

Huang Zixia just looked at him.

"The Empress is tough. She's often abused her powers over these years, having people hung and so on. The Emperor couldn't stop her. You helping the Emperor, punishing the Empress like this, makes you a good servant," Li Shubai said.

"If he believed me, does that mean he'll help with the Huang family matter?"

"It doesn't matter if he believed you or not; when the time comes, I'll personally take you to Shu."

Huang Zixia suddenly felt short of breath listening to his calm voice.

Shu, where her parents were buried.

Now she was about to go back there, break the ironclad case, and seek justice for the murdered.

She felt some mix of bitterness and joy that made her dizzy in the early summer weather.

She didn't know if it was joy or sorrow.

Seventeen

Wind over the Water

News came to the palace that afternoon that due to the sorrow over her cousin's death, Empress Wang had gone to Taiji Palace to recuperate. Lady Zhao and Lady Gao would take care of palace affairs.

The Empress's eunuch Zhang Qing had come. Though he'd been reduced to working at Taiji Palace and looked a little vexed, Zhang Qing hadn't lost his bossy style. He held his chin high and said, "Mr. Yang, the Empress has summoned you to have a chat with someone."

Someone . . . it must be Wang Ruo—no. Little Shi.

Though she hadn't spent much time with Little Shi, they liked each other, and she had some things to ask her, things she still didn't know about the case.

"Hold on a moment, please." Huang Zixia had to go back to her room to change.

When she was halfway there, she stopped to think a moment and decided to speak with Li Shubai first. He had been spending a lot of time in the pavilion by the lake because of the heat. When Huang Zixia got there, he was alone, looking over the lake with his hands behind his back. Lotus leaves broke through the water's surface at various heights.

In the lantern light, a silver layer on the surface made them seem hazy and distant.

He turned and saw her.

She bowed to him from across the lake and he waved her over.

"It's getting late. Where are you going?"

"The Empress sent Zhang Qing. Someone wants to speak with me."

"Oh," he said, motioning for her to go. But as she turned, she felt a foot on the back of her knee. She stumbled and fell headlong into the pond, just like she had the day they'd met.

She pulled herself out and faced Li Shubai. "Why?"

He just looked at her.

Huang Zixia wiped the mud off her face and wrung out her sleeves. "Why, my Prince? Now I have to go bathe before I go to the palace. I'll be late." Her eyes caught movement from the hem of Li Shubai's clothing. She jumped aside to avoid his foot, but his sweeping motion tripped her back into the pond again. Water splashed on the lotus leaves near her, and the drops rolled back onto her body. The surface shimmered in the lamplight, making Huang Zixia's vision blurry. She saw a faint, sinister smile on Li Shubai's face, and the wind gently blew his thin clothing.

She took a few steps forward and looked up at him. "Why?"

Li Shubai leaned forward and smiled. "Why what?"

"Why are you kicking me into the water? Is it fun for you?"

"Yes." He nodded shamelessly. "We finally solved this terrible mystery, so I wanted to celebrate."

Huang Zixia was furious. "So you decided to kick me in the water twice?"

Li Shubai restrained his smile a little. "Of course." He waved her up. Huang Zixia angrily climbed out, but before she had time to speak, a splash hit her ear and she fell back into the water. "Third time's the charm."

Huang Zixia pulled herself up, wiped the mud off her face, and started walking toward the opposite bank. She waded unsteadily through the mud and got back out, then went up the stairs. It wasn't very hot out. She shivered, thinking she'd better get in a hot bath before she got sick. She caught a glimpse of Li Shubai on her way out, but she was too angry to look at him.

She heard his voice call calmly, "Xian Yun and Ran Yun are already dead."

She suddenly stopped, shocked, and turned around.

Li Shubai was behind her, his smile gone. "So if a little eunuch like you disappeared in Taiji Palace tonight, no one would make anything of it."

She stared at the water's surface. She realized Li Shubai was doing her a favor. She could be killed if she went.

"Jing Yu," Li Shubai called.

Jing Yu came through the gate, glanced at Huang Zixia, and said, "My Prince."

"Go tell Zhang Qing that Yang Chonggu fell in the water and it's too late for him to get ready in time to reach the palace without disturbing the Empress."

Jing Yu agreed and left.

Huang Zixia bit her lip. "What about tomorrow?"

"Tomorrow? You fell into the water; won't you catch a cold? Would you go in the palace and risk infecting Empress Wang?" Li Shubai said. "A month or two from now, once you recover, the Emperor and Empress will know you can keep a secret and won't bother you anymore."

Huang Zixia hesitated. "Thank you, my Prince."

Li Shubai seemed embarrassed to see her dripping with water. "You . . ."

She looked up at him, awaiting orders. He paused and turned toward the lotus pond, then indicated for her to leave.

Huang Zixia felt relieved. She quickly bowed and left. Covered in mud, she went to the kitchen and ordered two barrels of hot water. After giving herself a thorough cleaning, she dried off quickly and fell into bed.

Sometime after she fell asleep, she heard a gentle knock on the door.

She got up and threw on clothes, then opened the door and saw Li Shubai standing there with a small lantern in his left hand and a small box of food in his right. The lamplight was a warm orange, which softened his typically stony expression. He put the food box on the table and said, "Good. I don't have to call you."

She gazed up at him and tugged on her tangled hair, then noticed it was dark out. "What time is it?"

"Eleven thirty." He opened the box of food and took a bowl filled with dark-brown liquid out and offered it to her. "Drink it."

She frowned. "My Prince, you came here in the middle of the night just to bring me soup?"

"Of course not," he said as he turned to leave. "Get dressed when you're done. We have guests."

Of course, not just anyone would make the Prince of Kui go wake up Huang Zixia in the middle of the night.

It was a young woman as beautiful as a peach blossom. She wore plain clothing, and unfortunately, the peach blossom had withered from grief and suffering. She looked at them, and the leafy golden hairpin by her temple glimmered in the lamplight. It was Wang Ruo—or Little Shi.

Huang Zixia was stunned. Little Shi quietly knelt and bowed. Her soft skirt silently brushed the ground like a flower petal falling to the ground. "I would like to thank the Prince of Kui for saving my life that year."

Li Shubai nodded.

When she finally spoke, her voice was hoarse. "I've been staying in Taiji Palace. Until today, Empress Wang came and told me if it weren't for me, Xuese wouldn't have died." Little Shi paused and was so quiet, it was as if she wasn't even breathing.

Huang Zixia couldn't bear it. "It was all a terrible accident. You didn't kill her."

Little Shi's face went pale. She looked at her with blank eyes. "But I think Her Highness is right," she whispered. "If it weren't for me, she wouldn't have died."

"And if it weren't for you, Xuese would have been gone three years ago," Huang Zixia said.

Little Shi felt no relief. Her head went lower and lower until it pressed the back of her hand, which was on the ground. "If it weren't for Xuese, I wouldn't be alive. We helped each other through the turmoil and went to Yangzhou together and Puzhou together. Auntie Lan Dai treated us as her own. She taught us music and dance. Those three years were good. If Feng Yi didn't show up, our lives would still be that good now."

Li Shubai looked on coldly.

"The Empress said I was greedy and vain to impersonate Xuese. We didn't know she'd become the Empress. Feng Yi didn't even know." Little Shi gripped her face, trembling and unable to hold back tears. When Feng Yi came to take her to the capital to get married, Xuese told me she wasn't ready. Xuese grabbed my hand and told me I should go instead. That no one would know the difference. She took the ingot the Prince of Kui gave us that day and gave half to me. She told me to use it as proof of my identity and find out what that man was up to.

"I really wanted to tell her that you'd immediately thrown her hairpin away. I kept it from her for three years."

Now Little Shi paused, staring and biting her lower lip. "But when I got to the palace and saw Empress Wang, I realized Xuese and I had made a huge mistake. When I gave Empress Wang that leafy hairpin, she had no doubts about my identity. It was her own engagement present, after all. Because its silver didn't reflect aristocratic wealth, she had an identical gold one made for me. I fantasized about the wealth and status of being a Princess and how its power would allow me to find Xuese's sweetheart. But, then in the rear hall, the person standing before me was the Prince of Kui and . . ."

"That is why you reacted so strangely," Huang Zixia said.

Her lips trembled violently as she choked up. After a time, she covered her face and began sobbing. "I knew heaven had it in for us. Xuese and I were finished. I had nightmares about taking Xuese's sweetheart from her and wanted to die, but I also couldn't help but look forward to the glory of being the Princess of Kui."

Huang Zixia looked at Li Shubai and found him staring expressionlessly at the lanterns rotating over the porch. She thought about what a waste it was to go through so much suffering and longing for a man that felt nothing for you.

"In my trouble sleeping, I let the secret out. I don't know if Feng Yi knew, but she must have been suspicious. And I knew that once it got out, my life in Changan would be ruined. And then Empress Wang had someone ask me privately if Feng Yi was reliable. I don't know why, but I shook my head."

"Then Empress Wang poisoned Feng Yi and disposed of her body?"

Little Shi's body went limp, but she managed to nod her head. Sure enough, it was Empress Wang who killed Feng Yi and put her body among the Youzhou migrants to make it look like she died of disease.

Huang Zixia and Li Shubai glanced at each other. She thought Empress Wang must have long been planning on getting rid of Feng Yi, so why would it matter what Little Shi said?

Huang Zixia sighed and bent down to Little Shi. "Get up," she whispered. "The Empress has spared your life, which is very lucky indeed."

"What did she tell you to do now?" Li Shubai asked.

Little Shi opened a parcel and took out a small jar. Her hand trembling, she held it close to her chest for a time. "These are Xuese's ashes. I'll take her back to Liuzhou and bury her next to her father. From now on, till the end of my life, I'll look after their graves, never leave them."

Huang Zixia stood in front of her, looking at the string of hair hanging loose over her cheek. It wavered in the night breeze like rootless grass—no way back, and no future ahead.

Li Shubai took the two halves of the silver ingot from the drawer and gave them to her. "Take it back."

Little Shi looked at them and spoke quietly. "Xuese knew you might never come back but was determined to wait for the rest of her life. She often said that if she ever saw you again, you'd give her the leafy hairpin, and she'd give you the silver ingot, and these would be your engagement gifts. So I left it there, thinking that there was some small chance it would remind you of us."

Huang Zixia sighed and pointed at one half. "This half came from the woman outside the academy. It was Xuese's proof. Maybe she was ambushed in that room, just before I got there."

"All of this was fate," Little Shi murmured, holding that silver ingot. "My fate, her fate, doomed from twelve years ago."

Huang Zixia sent Little Shi off to her carriage, out into the quiet Changan night toward an uncertain future.

When Huang Zixia got back to the palace, Yong Ji and Zhang Qing waved to her. "Mr. Yang, the Empress said no matter how late it is, however you're doing, whether you got sick from falling in the pond or not, she still wants to see you."

There it was, the indication of her death. Empress Wang knew if Little Shi, who was so important to the case, came for an audience, Huang Zixia would attend and so she waited here!

Huang Zixia made a bitter face and glanced at Li Shubai.

He nodded slightly, indicating for her to go.

Her eyes widened as she looked at him, trying to say, *Empress Wang wants to wipe me off the face of the earth!*

He just looked back at her calmly and quietly, leaving her helpless. How unreliable people were. She'd just helped him solve the difficult case of the Princess's disappearance, and now he was going to forget about all that and let Empress Wang destroy her.

Yong Ji and Zhang Qing were still staring at her. She had no choice but to grit her teeth and go.

"Real person," Li Shubai said quietly.

Huh?

She thought she'd heard wrong and leaned to look at him. He was indifferent, not even looking back. "It gets wet out this time of night. Be careful not to catch a cold."

Real person. What did that mean?

Huang Zixia filed out of the palace with Yong Yi and Zhang Qing. In the carriage on the way to Taiji Palace, she thought hard.

She thought and thought about what Li Shubai could have meant but figured he wanted her to roll over and die. That coldhearted man really wouldn't try to save her life at the crucial moment?

When she was about to pound the wall and scream, Yong Ji spoke. "Mr. Yang, we've arrived at Taiji Palace. Come."

She felt a shiver run down her spine, but she could do nothing but follow. The palace looked completely deserted. It was as if Empress Wang really had been forgotten. Soft, thick grass grew up from the slate path, making her steps feel less sure. The stone hanging lanterns had become smooth and spotty with time. In their light, one could make out the moss marks on their tops. Meanwhile, the succulents drooped, and paint was peeling off the pillars. The once-magnificent palace had long been neglected. The rear hall was dark in the distance. Only the Lizheng Hall had some lights on, which shone on its red walls.

Huang Zixia followed Yong Ji and Zhang Qing toward the Lizheng Hall.

Empress Wang's people were very efficient. She hadn't been there long, but the Lizheng Hall was already set up very comfortably.

Though it was nearly dawn, the Empress clearly hadn't slept. She was sitting on a couch, perhaps in anticipation of Huang Zixia's arrival. Ladies brought out four exquisite small dishes and sorbet. Empress Wang ate slowly and quietly. She looked elegant and comfortable. When she was finally finished, they removed her tray. Empress Wang rinsed her mouth out and took a sip of tea. "Mr. Yang," she said slowly, "do you feel this palace seems deserted at this hour?"

"If you're feeling lively, you can always go downtown," Huang Zixia said. "If you're feeling down, everywhere seems deserted."

Empress Wang looked into her eyes and spoke gently. "Mr. Yang, I was moved here because of you. I'm down because of you. How should I thank you?"

Huang Zixia felt a burning in her chest, and her back began to sweat. She thought desperately about Li Shubai's "real person" and said, "The Empress is fortunate to be living in such a place and should be tolerant of others too."

"Tolerant?" The Empress smiled slightly, but her eyes were cold. "You slandered me in front of the Emperor. Were you tolerant of me?"

Were you? You killed people from your past and your own family and never expected to end up here? Huang Zixia couldn't say what was on her mind. She just stood there and watched a bead of sweat fall from her forehead to the ground.

Empress Wang looked around and said, as if to herself, "How can this be considered fortunate? Emperor Zhang Sun's wife died here. People die in all kinds of palaces."

"She was a virtuous woman whom the Emperor loved very much. You could be like her, endlessly in love."

"Hmm . . . it's a little late for all that, Mr. Yang. If you had been half as clever as you are now, you'd know that whether you decide to say something or not can determine whether you live or die!"

Say something or not . . . live or die. The words resounded in her ears and woke her up. *Real person, real person, that's what that awful Li Shubai meant!* She suddenly understood and kneeled, pressing her head firmly on the ground. "Please allow me to say one thing. Once I've said it, I will gladly die here today!"

Empress Wang smiled coldly. "What?" she said casually. Then she raised her hand, indicating for her attendants to leave, and stared at Huang Zixia.

Huang Zixia pressed her head harder into the ground, then looked up. "Your Highness, I know I deserve to die. Does it matter when and where? I just want to know if you'd like to tell me the charges?"

"Do I need to?" Empress Wang said with a contemptuous sneer. "You know my greatest secret. Isn't that a capital offense?"

"Of course," Huang Zixia said respectfully, "but there's something I want to tell you, which might give you room to change your mind."

"Say it."

Huang Zixia felt her heart pounding in her chest. She knew her life was on the line and hoped Li Shubai's advice would work. "When I was fourteen, and you first summoned me, you said, 'If I had a daughter, she'd be as old and as cute as you.'"

Empress Wang's gaze stiffened and her expression flickered in the lamplight. She was silent for a time. "You? Three years ago?"

Huang Zixia bowed again. "The murderess Huang Zixia is before you."

"You know I hate you and want you dead," she said coldly. "Why further debase yourself?"

"I believe the Emperor has already forgiven you for your secrecy, and you'll be back to your life soon. But my secret really is life or death. I'm telling this so you know that if I ever do anything to hurt you again, all you have to do is say the word and I'll be put to death."

After a period of silence, Empress Wang's steady, gentle voice said, "So you think putting your life in my hands will make you seem useful, and I'll forget what you did to me?"

"Of course not!" she said earnestly. "But I think you know about Emperor Tai and Wei Zheng's past, and how Shangguan Wan'er's fortunes changed after Emperor Wu took power. Things change, even hatred. As long as I can be useful to you, what does the past matter?"

Empress Wang slowly walked toward her. She examined every inch of her prone body. After a long time, the strong woman sighed weakly. "That being the case, I'll keep your life in my hands. If you disobey me in the future, I'll end it."

"Thank you so much for your mercy!" Huang Zixia, still bowing, felt sweat coming from every pore. But she didn't dare wipe it.

"If it weren't for you, people wouldn't know about Xuese's death or that it happened by my hand." She clenched her teeth, then exhaled. "If you hadn't exposed it, I wouldn't have known how horrible I was until I met her in the underworld. I don't know how I could have faced her . . ."

Huang Zixia wondered how she would face Jin Nu and Feng Yi.

"I killed my own daughter. Today, I won't kill anyone." Empress Wang turned and sat on the couch. Leaning on a cushion under the window, she looked up at the dim stars in the dawn sky.

The lanterns were out, and the stars over the palace looked like flowing dust.

"Exile. What's it matter?" Her voice was cold and firm. "If I can get to Daming Palace from the music hall, I can get back to Daming from exile! No one in the Tang Empire, in the whole world, can defeat me!"

Huang Zixia stayed silent on her knees.

In the dim light and the desolate quiet of the ancient palace, the Empress looked at the stars and suddenly covered her mouth as if trying to keep something in.

Huang Zixia pressed her head on the ground and was about to stand when the Empress spoke again. "Huang Zixia, in your life, have you ever thought it'd be better to die?"

"Yes. When my family was killed, and I was accused of the murder. But I didn't want to die with those charges on my head!"

"I really had wanted to die." Her black hair flowed softly over her brilliantly embroidered clothing, her face haggard with fatigue. "Have you seen Xuese? Did we really look alike?"

Huang Zixia shook her head. "No. I just missed her at the academy."

"Oh. I'll never have the chance to see what my daughter looks like." She sighed.

"The last time the I saw Xuese, she had just turned five, and I was twenty-three." She told Huang Zixia the story of her past.

The Yunshao Court had music and dancing, and was full of self-respecting performers. Her husband, Jingxiu, didn't approve of their daughter being raised at court. After arguing with Jingxiu several times, the Empress talked him into moving the family north to the capital, where he might get recognized for his painting.

Jingxiu went out and tried his luck, but without contacts, he had no chance. Before long, he'd tried everywhere and gave up. In Yangzhou, Jingxiu was cheerful and charming. As long as he could paint, he was happy. They were good together. But Changan had broken Jingxiu's spirit. And Xuese got sick. They had to pawn the leafy hairpin Jingxiu got the Empress as an engagement present. They were out of money, hungry and cold. They couldn't afford a doctor, so the Empress had to beg. Jingxiu came and got her. He told her that she was debasing herself.

"All I could do was hold my daughter all night, rub her body, listen to her breath in fear, and watch the sky outside the window slowly brighten. On those nights, it felt like if I closed my eyes, I'd lose control of our desperate situation . . ." Even though it happened twelve years ago, she looked cold and desperate.

"Xuese was lucky to get over that illness, but Jingxiu, because his mood was so low, got sick. We were about to get kicked out for not paying rent. I had no choice but to go to the West City to look for opportunities behind Jingxiu's back."

"I remember very clearly, on a winter day, the leaves of the trees along the West City street were falling. There was a fifty- or sixty-year-old woman dressed in tattered brown linen, sitting there begging. She had a beat-up old pipa and was singing "Forever Together" in a hoarse voice. Her dirty hair was in a messy pile on her shoulders. Her face had dirt in its wrinkles like moss on weathered stones. Her rags couldn't protect her from the cutting wind. Her fingers were frozen; her lips were cracked. The pipa was way out of tune. How could she perform like that?"

Empress Wang's cold eyes filled with tears. She put her hands on her face and choked up. "You wouldn't understand how heartbroken I was. I stood and watched that woman for a long time. I watched her like I was watching myself in thirty years. I didn't want to end up like that." She took a long, trembling breath and continued with difficulty. "That afternoon, I realized that I wanted to live, and I needed to live well. I would never beg like that!"

Huang Zixia looked at her in silence.

"Around that time, I ran into someone I'd studied with. I went with her to the Langya Wangs, said I was her distant relative who'd fallen on hard times after the death of my parents. Everyone admired my pipa skills and I was asked to stay. I went back for some clothes and brought some money my friend gave me to Jingxiu and told him I'd send more when I got my salary," she said faintly. "I hadn't even told him where I was going. Xuese hugged my leg and cried. They stared at me as I left." Her voice trailed off, but her gaze burned frighteningly.

Huang Zixia was quiet for a time, then spoke gently. "It must have been very hard for you to leave Xuese."

"Yes. I couldn't take care of her." Empress Wang looked at her. Her tears had dried and the cold smile returned to her lips. "But I ended up meeting my husband, even though I had to lie to him. I was like a moth being drawn to a flame. Even if I died, it'd be wonderful!" The Empress sounded short of breath, and her extreme emotional shifts unsettled Huang Zixia.

"The world is that absurd. I've spent these twelve years in the palace living in bliss. I somehow beat out Princess Guo Shu to become the Empress, and raised the Emperor's children, who are bound to become Emperors themselves. He loves my children the most—I know the court is where I belong! I've been one of the most loved people in the world. What's it matter if I lost my husband and daughter? I live in the greatest city on earth, the envy of the world!"

Huang Zixia sighed inside and said quietly, "But your daughter wasn't even willing to come to the capital to see you. You gained the world, but doesn't it make you sad or guilty to have the blood of your friends and family on your hands?"

"Sad? Guilty?" Empress Wang's cold eyes flashed briefly with pain. She raised her chin and sneered. "Twelve years ago, I was as innocent and romantic as you, thinking if I had my husband and daughter, even in sickness and poverty, I could be happy. But people change."

Huang Zixia thought a moment. "So you never saw Jingxiu and Xuese again?"

"No. After I decided to enter Yun Palace, I asked my friend in the carriage to buy the hairpin back and tell them I was dead. From that day on, Mei Wanzhi was dead to the world." Her bleak tone couldn't cover up her iron stubbornness.

She waved her hand for Huang Zixia to go. Only when Huang Zixia had gotten up and was about to leave did she hear the Empress speak softly. "What I said three years ago was true."

Huang Zixia looked at the cold woman, stunned.

"When you were fourteen and I saw you in the spring sunlight wearing a bright-red dress like a rose in the breeze. I thought if Xuese were there, she'd definitely be that beautiful."

The Taiji Palace at night was empty and quiet.

Huang Zixia retraced her steps toward the exit.

The stars overhead were dissolving, and the lanterns along her path had been extinguished. Insect songs echoed through the air.

Huang Zixia looked up at the dense, dim stars.

If each star were tied to a person's fate, humanity's luck, at that moment, was running out. Human life was disposable. If all the stars suddenly fell like a wild storm, it would only cause our descendants to sigh thousands of years later.

She walked toward Taiji Palace's gate and slipped through the partially opened door.

Someone was out there, standing tall in the night. He calmly watched her come out, a silhouette against the backdrop of the dawn sky. The moonlight in his eyes seemed to shiver when he saw her.

Huang Zixia stopped, confused.

It was Li Shubai. "What's the matter?" he said coldly. "Let's go."

"Prince . . . ," Huang Zixia said helplessly, looking up at the faint contours of his face. "You were waiting for me the whole time?"

He turned partly away. "I was in the neighborhood."

Huang Zixia couldn't help but smile.

Li Shubai was walking toward the carriage.

Huang Zixia hurried to catch up and couldn't help but ask, "If I hadn't understood what you meant and gotten killed, you'd still be waiting?"

"First, Empress Wang is in semiexile; how could she kill the person who revealed her identity now? How could she explain that to the Emperor?"

She was too inexperienced with the court to know that. *And if there really wasn't anything to worry about, why'd you kick me in the water three times and stay here waiting all night?*

"So . . . second?"

"Second, she let Little Shi go. I think she's exhausted."

"Third?"

"Third," Li Shubai said, finally turning to look at her, a wind flowing between them, "if you didn't understand my hint, then clearly you're not the legendary Huang Zixia."

Huang Zixia smiled.

Disaster had been avoided in the tender night. She and Li Shubai sat in the carriage and headed for Kui Palace. The carriage's golden bells shook gently. Inside, the red fish slept on the bottom of its jar like a flower.

Outside the window, Changan's street lamps slowly passed.

Faint light and deep shadow, time passing slowly.

The two feet of space between them indistinct.

CHARACTER LIST

Yang Chonggu (杨崇古)—eunuch alias of Huang Zixia

Huang Min (官声)—civil governor of Shu, father of Huang Zixia

Huang Yan (黄彦)—son of Huang Min, brother of Huang Zixia

Li Shubai (李舒白)—Prince of Kui, aka Li Zi (夔王): benefactor of Huang Zixia, favorite son of Emperor Xuanzong

Pang Xun (庞勋)—a rebel Li Shubai killed

Jing Yang (景阳)—eunuch who accompanies Li Shubai

Prince Yi (益王爷)—father of Princess Yue Qi

Princess Qi Le (岐乐郡主)—woman who wants to marry Li Shubai

Zhang Xingying (张二哥, 张行英)—solider who helps Huang Zixia

Brother Lu (鲁大哥)—member of royal guard with whom Huang Zixia sneaks into Changan

Li Run (鄂王李润)—Prince of E, brother of Li Shubai

Li Rui (排行第九的昭王李汭)—Prince of Zhao, brother of Li Shubai

Li Wen (康王李汶)—Prince of Kang, brother of Li Shubai

Lady Zhao (赵太妃)—concubine of the late Emperor

Lady Wu Tai (吴太妃)—concubine of the late Emperor, mother of Li Shubai

Wang Yun (王蕴)—nephew of Empress, former fiancé of Huang Zixia, and military commander

Minister Wang Lin (尚书王麟)—Board of Punishments official on Four Directions Case, father of Wang Yun

Cui Chunzhan (崔纯湛)—Minister Cui, minister of Central Court, also helping with Four Directions Case

Yu Xuan (禹宣)—orphan Huang Min adopted after moving to Chengdu

Jing Yu (景毓)—eunich of Li Shubai

Jing Yi (景翌)—eunich of Li Shubai

Su Qi (素绮)—eunich of Li Shubai

Wang Ruo (王若)—wife-to-be of Li Shubai

Chen Nian (陈念娘)—older musician who lost her friend

Feng Yi (冯忆娘)—Yunshao Court musician who mysteriously disappeared, friend of Chen Nian

Zhou Ziqin (周子秦)—undertaker/forensic scientist who wants to be a detective

Minister Zhou Xiang (周侍郎周庠)—father of Zhou Ziqin

Xian Yun (闲云)—female attendant of Wang Ruo

Yan Ling (延龄)—attendant of the Empress

Ran Yun (冉云)—servant of Wang Ruo

Zhang Ling (长龄)—servant of the Wang family

Yong Ji (永济)—eunuch of the Emperor

Prince of Yi (益王)—father of Princess Qi Le

Jin Nu (锦奴)—pipa player, adopted daughter of Mei Wanzhi

Mei Wanzhi (梅挽致)—Empress Wang

Xuese (雪色)—daughter of Mei Wanzhi

Lan Dai (兰黛)—third oldest woman of Yunshao, adoptive mother of Xuese

Little Shi (小施)—rescued with Xuese by Li Shubai

Jingxiu (敬修)—husband of Mei Wanzhi, a painter

Emperor Wang aka The Prince of Yun (郓王)—Emperor, husband of Empress Wang, brother of Li Shubai

Guo Wan (郭纨)—oldest concubine of Prince of Yun

Yongling (永龄)—attendant who waited on Wang Shao when she first joined Yun Palace

Wang Fu (王芙)—first wife of Prince of Yun, died in the palace

Linghui (灵徽)—daughter of Guo Wan

Ying Luo (璎珞)—attendant in Yun Palace

Fang Fei (芳菲)—attendant in Yun Palace

ABOUT THE AUTHOR

Photo © 2016 Guo Yi

Qinghan CeCe is one of China's leading authors. She has been writing for more than ten years and has published eight novels, both in print and online, which reflect her fascination with "one thousand years of history, all for one dream: moving every reader." *The Golden Hairpin*, originally published in her homeland in 2015, is the first of CeCe's work to be translated into English. She lives in Hangzhou, China.

ABOUT THE TRANSLATOR

Photo © 2014 Alex Watson

Alex Woodend is a writer/translator whose fascination with Spanish and Chinese began at Franklin & Marshall College. At Columbia University, he wrote his master's thesis on contemporary Chinese literature. He currently lives in New York and is at work on essays, translations, and original fiction.